One Last Shot

One Last Shot

A Novel

BETTY CAYOUETTE

ST. MARTIN'S GRIFFIN
NEW YORK

First published in the United States by St. Martin's Griffin, an imprint of St. Martin's Publishing Group

ONE LAST SHOT. Copyright © 2024 by Betty Cayouette. All rights reserved. Printed in the United States of America. For information, address St. Martin's Publishing Group, 120 Broadway, New York, NY 10271.

www.stmartins.com

Designed by Gabriel Guma

Library of Congress Cataloging-in-Publication Data is available upon request.

ISBN 978-1-250-29110-3 (trade paperback)
ISBN 978-1-250-29111-0 (ebook)

Our books may be purchased in bulk for promotional, educational, or business use. Please contact your local bookseller or the Macmillan Corporate and Premium Sales Department at 1-800-221-7945, extension 5442, or by email at MacmillanSpecialMarkets@macmillan.com.

First Edition: 2024

10 9 8 7 6 5 4 3 2 1

To my mom, Susan, for always supporting me

AUTHOR'S NOTE

I spent several years struggling through the aftermath of a sexual assault. I couldn't imagine a life where I didn't think about what happened constantly. But then, with the help of therapy and supportive family and friends, I moved forward without even realizing it. It became a part of my past that changed who I've become. But it wasn't a daily reality. Now, I have a happy and fulfilling life full of loving family and friends, an amazing community of readers on social media, and a career writing novels that I care deeply about.

For many, many other women, past sexual violence is their reality. Some surveys show that 97 percent of women experience some form of sexual harassment, and 33 percent of women experience sexual violence. We'll never have an accurate figure because most women never report what happened to them. But in my experience, it's rare to meet a woman who hasn't experienced some sort of sexual harassment or violence. And fortunately, that means that many successful, joyful, amazing women have been able to move forward from surviving sexual trauma.

I wrote *One Last Shot* because I wanted to write a fun, sexy, romantic book where although a sexual assault was something that happened to the protagonist . . . it wasn't the crux of the story. My protagonist, Emerson, has a fantastic life. She's a super-model, she has caring friends, and she's about to reconnect with her first love. Being assaulted as a young woman has influenced the person she's become, but it's an element of her past, not a huge part of her daily life. I let her sexual assault be a messy, life-changing, forever complicating part of her past, as it is for me and *so many* other women. But what *One Last Shot* is *about* is her epic love story.

Sexual violence is not on the page in *One Last Shot*, but what happened to Emerson is a part of the story, because I wanted to ac-knowledge this experience that impacts the lives of so many people around me. Her assault affects not only her, but her relationship with her best friend, Theo, and the course of his life. Sexual vio-lence changes the lives of not only the survivors but their friends and family, and again, I wanted to show that reality while still giving these characters a sexy, romantic love story.

I hope that reading this book and seeing the wonderful lives of characters who have been impacted by sexual assault makes readers who have experienced any type of sexual harassment or violence feel seen and optimistic. Because while sexual violence did change my story, it was ultimately just a chapter.

CHAPTER ONE

Emerson

I always saw myself in the romantic comedies I watched as a child. I was the gawky, awkward girl that hoped I might still *somehow* get the guy. But now I've had the makeover scene, but I still haven't found love. Instead, I'm here trying to disprove a theory about my own boyfriend, the mere act of which basically proves my relationship is doomed. Every one of my relationships has ended in a rather spectacular fashion.

I stand up from the couch, a pure white West Elm leather sectional that Josh bought after watching me save an Instagram photo of it. Romantic, right? Except, I hate pure white furniture, which I told him at the time. I had been saving the photo for my best friend, Georgia. Also, we had only been dating for a week. Kind of presumptuous to already be picking out furniture. I walk over to the bookshelf and pull out one of my favorite titles, *The Object of My Affection* by Stephen McCauley. An older title, but a fantastic read that was turned into a fun movie. Josh swears he's read every single book on this shelf, but lately I've noticed that whenever I ask him about one of them, he finds a way to change the subject.

"Babe? Have you read this one?" I turn the cover of the book toward Josh. He plays for the Red Sox, and when we met I hoped he could be the Real Deal. Marriage material, someone worth the six months I've spent flying from LA to Boston to get to know him.

"Oh yeah, love that one. One of the best." Josh gets up and joins me at the shelf, wrapping an arm around my waist and pulling me close to him.

"I just reread it and can't get over the twist at the end. What did you think?" I turn toward him, still holding the book, and stare intently at him as I wait for his answer.

He pulls me in for a deep kiss, and with one hand takes the book and shoves it carelessly back on the shelf. He doesn't place it in its spot, just throws it on top of others. Then he wraps his now free hand around my jaw—something he *knows* I hate. I can almost feel acne forming where his fingers are touching my face. I pull away slightly. "Babe, the twist. What did you think?"

"Totally shocking," he murmurs into my mouth as he presses back into me. "Best part of the book."

"So you really were surprised when they took that guy hostage?"

"Of course. Great ending." His other hand starts to drop lower. I pull back abruptly. *I knew it.*

"Josh, it's a rom-com, there's no hostages. Something you'd *know* if you'd read it." I stare at him. "Have you read any of these books? Every time I try to talk to you about them, you make an excuse to change the subject, or just kiss me!"

I cross my arms to make clear I actually need a response. He sighs and scans the shelves, probably looking for a book that he's watched the movie of. "Josh, just tell me the truth."

The center wall of his living room houses a floor-to-ceiling bookshelf that is stuffed full of some of my favorite reads. When I walked into his apartment for the first time during a New Year's party, I saw the incredible structure full of books and knew I had to meet the owner. After breaking up with an actor who didn't even read the entirety of his own scripts, I was ready to date someone who shared my passion for reading. I thought I could actually talk to him about the books I devoured, maybe even about the story ideas I dream up at night.

I thought wrong.

I see the moment that he caves, and then re-strategizes. "Baby, I'm sorry I lied to you." He takes my hand and leads me over to the couch. "You were just so excited that we liked the same things, and I figured saying I'd read most of them wasn't exactly a lie, because I would read them and win you over."

"So have you been reading them?" Maybe I can work with this. I squeeze his rough palm with my manicured hand. Gel every two weeks destroys my nails, but they always look flawless once it's on, and according to my agent, that's what counts.

"Not exactly. I've just been so busy with training." Josh eyes his home gym wistfully, like he wishes he could be in there now, bench pressing for the third time today rather than talking to me.

"Have you even read *one*?" Josh winces at my question, but I press onward. I just need to find one redeeming thing here, then maybe I can forget that he lied. Our relationship needs this to survive. "Is this your 'to read' list?"

"Well, my interior designer actually bought them for the party we met at. My mom was over and pointed out that it looked, well she said 'shallow,' but *strange* is a better word; it looked strange with only my own trophies on the shelves. I actually was going to recycle them after, because I wanted to put my stuff back up, but they led to me meeting you, so clearly it's worth it." He smiles at the end of this, as though he said something romantic instead of that he was going to send what must be six thousand dollars' worth of books to their death.

"Recycle them?" It takes everything in me to keep my voice

level. "There's about four hundred hardcovers here. You could at least donate them."

"Who would want this many books?" He looks genuinely flummoxed. Has he never heard of a library?

That's it. I'm out of here.

"Josh, this isn't working for me." His mouth springs open in objection.

"Emerson, I don't understand," Josh pleads. He runs a calloused palm through his curly hair. "Baby, let's just talk about this. We can take a vacation. Go to Cabo, relax, talk it out. I'll buy six grand's worth of more books and you can donate those." He frowns skeptically as he says this, but then wraps my hand in his own calloused one. "This is it for me. You're it for me. This is a silly blip; we can work through it together."

I gently pry my hand out of Josh's grip. "Josh, I don't think we're in love. Not really, and most certainly not the forever kind. I'm so sorry, but you'll find someone that's perfect for you."

I'm ready to go in under a minute. I always have a bag packed so that I can travel at a moment's notice for a shoot. I pause to say goodbye just as Josh stalks away and punches a hole in the wall, knocking a bunch of framed photos to the ground. I'm sure his assistant will have that covered by tomorrow night. And I'm sure I am doing the right thing. The suitcase slides behind me, the silence of its wheels matching my shame as I delicately close the door, nudging a now shattered framed photo of us at the World Series out of the way. I'm sure that photo is one of the many *People* will use in their inevitable "relationship timeline update" on me tomorrow. I can already see the headline: QUICK REFRESHER ON SUPERMODEL AND HEARTBREAKER EMERSON'S COMPLETE DATING HISTORY.

All press might be good press, but for once it would be nice to keep my failures to myself. To be able to walk out of the house with a makeup-free face and not have articles up within an hour saying I'm having a breakdown. I've forgotten what it feels like to be natural. I have to be careful of every bit of myself I show to the world, since once it's out there it's no longer authentically me, it's a part of my public image. I know I shouldn't complain about the downside of the industry. This industry and the way I look gave me fame, and that fame gave me stability. Something I yearned for in my childhood. So I take the bad with the good.

The moment I flop down on the hotel bed I let my posture drop. I relish stooping my shoulders alone in my hotel room once the weight of everyone's eyes is off me. I haven't slouched in front of someone in a decade, not since I became Emerson (no last name) and Emerson became a household name. My career is my life, but looking perfect never ceases to exhaust me. My exes have all loved my "ballerina posture," as do agents and clients, but it means that I never really relax. Which is fine. *Totally fine.* At least that's what I tell myself.

I hunch over my phone and scroll through social media mindlessly, a constant stream of pictures of other models and celebrities flying by. I no longer flinch when I come across my own face in an ad. Images that are me but don't really feel like me. But after a few minutes—or possibly a full hour, it's hard to tell once I'm sucked into the numbing Instagram vortex—I freeze mid-scroll and stare at the notification that has popped up in front of me.

Reminder: if not married by 28 you're marrying Theo!
T-minus one week ;)

Theo.

My stomach drops. I can't believe I completely forgot about this pact.

I haven't spoken to Theo in a decade. Just the thought of

him has several emotions fighting to break free. Regret, longing, shame. He was my first love, and maybe even my last love. I can think I totally love whomever I'm dating and then, after remembering what he and I had, for an instant I doubt that there could be anyone but him, really. I've been chasing the high of how Theo made me feel since high school. The way we connected, how he knew my thoughts before I even voiced them, the way he looked at *me*, not at all the pieces of myself I'm marketed as. To him I was Emerson Grey.

Even senior year, once I had bigger campaigns under my belt, and the whispers around me in the hallway at school were no longer negative, he only cared about whether it actually made me happy. While my mom blindly signed off on every campaign my agent called me in for, it was Theo who realized I was disappointed to miss Halloween in Salem for an Urban Outfitters job. He saw through what I said, to realize what I meant, and offered to pretend to be my dad and call my agent to convince him I had the flu. We then spent a perfect week making matching (and decidedly uncool) skeleton costumes. It was much better than a stuffy shoot.

This reminder must have been in the cloud—I've switched phones a million times, but my Apple ID has remained the same. I had completely forgotten about our pact. I lie back on the bed and clutch the phone to my chest. We made this pact in high school, back when we thought twenty-eight was ancient and a decade after graduation was forever. We both made a big show of setting the reminder for this to go off—first on Theo's birthday, and then again on my birthday a week later. We joked it would give us one week to plan a makeshift wedding. I thought it was so romantic, like the finale to a rom-com where *of course* they ended up together, and their friends and family were secretly rooting for them from the beginning.

I stare at the reminder. It's the first one, which means today is Theo's birthday. I forgot his birthday. In high school it would have been unimaginable that I'd forget his birthday, that I wouldn't be the one he spent the day with. But we aren't those people anymore—so many miles and years between us. It's been *ten* years since we last spoke. The gravity of it pulls me down. This is not how I thought my life would turn out.

If this reminder going off isn't a sign from the universe that it's time to fix my greatest regret, I don't know what is.

I've followed Theo's career avidly from my fake account. I watch every story he posts, but am careful to never like each grid post, and I closely examine his tagged photos. I know he shoots, but he rarely tags the brands. I see more of his nieces and nephews than him. But now I look at his page, click on the most recent post, and am absolutely frantic for more information.

I'm indifferent to most photography, but his shots are incredible. He hasn't tagged the brand, but these images are gorgeous, more artistic than those one might typically see from a big-box retailer. Not only do the inexpensive clothes look great—and he's worked in everything from string lights to space heaters, which I'm sure are also for sale—the models seem to be caught at both their most real and beautiful moments. He's the only person I've seen shoot this well.

I take a screenshot of the page and send it to my assistant, Natalie.

I need to know who he shoots for asap!!! What's his next job?

It only takes her seven minutes to get back to me, but by then I've found a tagged photo from three years ago and am deep into stalking Anthem's page and 99 percent certain I have my answer. Natalie confirms it.

Theo Carson mainly shoots Anthem. They shoot Summer in two days

Two days. I sit up and call my agent. "Emerson?" he says. "Is everything all right?"

I wince at the surprise in his voice. I never call, since I've always been determined to be one of Matt's *easy* girls. Easy for him to book, easy for everyone to work with, never burdening him with my personal problems like some girls mistakenly do. I understand that feelings aren't what help you make it to the top. Which has been my only goal.

I can imagine the possibilities flying through his head. Was it a bad haircut? Overly aggressive chemical peel that would have me out for a week? Food poisoning? He could work with food poisoning. "Hi! So sorry to call." I freeze, unaccustomed to asking him for something. I roll onto my stomach and play with my hair nervously. The strand is brittle, thanks to the highlights my team insists my already blond hair needs to be painted with to make me the perfect all-American girl. Time for a glaze.

"What's wrong? Emerson?"

"Sorry, sorry, nothing's wrong," I stammer. "Um, actually, I was just wondering if you might be able to put me in for a job with a specific brand. It's a bit different from what I typically book."

"What brand?" His voice is laced with apprehension. I'm a high fashion model, and one of his best at that. I consistently book the shoots that front campaigns for Chanel, Gucci, Valentino, Prada. I stopped doing even high fashion ecomm about seven years ago, at his insistence that it cheapened my book, and now limit runway shows to fashion month.

"Anthem? They're way more mass market, which I realize isn't my usual thing. I just really want to work with their team, and they've been running some great spots." I hold my breath. It's a stretch to call Anthem mass market. In reality, they're a Target- or Macy's-esque monolith with a few clothing collections a year, not a fashion brand at all. But what I said about Theo's work for them *is* true. It was gorgeous, more artistic than it had any right to be, rife with beauty shots and storytelling. It completely elevated Anthem and made it look like a place everyone from me to my mom would want to shop.

The disgust is palpable on the other end of the line. "Anthem? That makes no sense. It will tank your career, even if you were the face of it."

"Don't care."

"Why don't I just call Walmart? Or Costco? I'm not booking it." It's clear he thinks I'm losing it.

"Matt, please don't forget that technically you work for me. And I'm pretty sure the AmEx campaign I was the face of last year was enough for you to retire on."

I hold my breath. I've never been this aggressive with him before, in the entire time we've worked together. He's not pleasant, but he's a skilled agent, and he's been with me since the very beginning. I can't argue with his track record. And I know he's kept me safe from the photographers models are always whispering about and steered me clear of campaigns that could get me canceled, which is more than most agents do when faced with a huge payoff. But I need this. "Emerson, I can't cosign this. It reflects on me too."

"I'll book it myself, then. Or have Natalie do it, and let her collect your twenty percent."

"You wouldn't." His words are clipped, enraged at the thought of my twenty-year-old assistant taking his cut. "Why do you care about this? You never give input on your bookings."

"I need to shoot with Theo Carson. He's an old friend."

The pause that follows is loaded. I can't fill it, but I can hear the gears working in Matt's head.

"Don't tell me you broke up with Josh," he finally says. "Every time you were photographed with him it got picked up. You have him to thank for that Nike spot."

"I did. So what's your answer? Will you book me with Anthem?"

He sighs heavily. "Emerson, come on. It's a bad move. Besides, there's actually a silver lining to you breaking up with Josh. You can do the contract with Harry Butler."

"You know I don't want to do that." Harry was the first person I dated after moving to LA and pretending to move on from Theo. It started as a PR relationship with a contract and all, since I had rapidly become the new "it" model, and his music career was taking off. But we actually had fun together, so we tried to keep it going after the contract ended. It didn't last long, but he's still a close friend. Genuinely just a friend. And he's been campaigning for us to do a yearlong PR relationship contract again since the entire world goes wild whenever we're so much as pictured together. It would give each of our careers a huge boost, which is undeniable, and I care for him. But I want the real thing.

"This is a pivotal moment for you. It's one thing to be the biggest model in the world when you're young, but to carry the fame over to your thirties? You need Harry for that. His demographic, his fans. The hype you two get together. Don't you want to be remembered as a true supermodel?"

"Of course I do. But I need to see Theo. And I need the full week with Anthem to spend with him." I know I'm at a tipping point in my career. And in my life, because I just can't seem to find that thing that makes me really happy. But the last time I felt authentic was when I was with Theo, so that's the best place I can think of to start.

Matt actually groans. "Compromise. You get a week on this ridiculous shoot with Theo. And if it doesn't work out this week, you enter into the one-year contract with Harry. And agree to the engagement at nine months."

I take a deep breath as I think it over. If things don't work with Theo, I'm going to be crushed. And I'll have taken a blow to my career for nothing by doing the Anthem shoot. Maybe spending a year focused on my career, which is really what this contract means, since it'll be a year of public appearances, media frenzies, and shooting as many campaigns as possible, isn't the worst thing. "Fine. But no engagement."

"You know his team wants that as part of the deal. You can always call it off."

"Matt, come on. Harry will agree without the engagement."

"He's who's pushing for it. Maybe he's in it for real."

I roll my eyes. "He's not. He just wants to take over the world and knows the absolutely surreal level of press surrounding an engagement between us would elevate him. Exponentially." Which is true. Although he started as a singer, now he's also acting, modeling, working on a clothing line. Our PR relationship was a launching pad for him.

"So go along for the ride. Give the people what they want, because an engagement between you two would be the story of the century, and reap the benefits. I'll get Anthem on the line right after this if you just agree. If you don't make things work with this guy by the end of the shoot, you'll do the full contract with Harry."

I can tell Matt is holding his breath. "Fine," I agree finally. The shoot is in a matter of days, I can't keep haggling. I have one week. To fix my relationship with Theo, figure out what I want the next stage of my life to look like, and maybe recapture the authenticity and passion I once felt.

"Perfect. I'm on it! And if you come to your senses after a day or two there, just say the word and I'll trigger the 'get out of jail free' clause I snuck into your boilerplate. After that it will be challenging, but I will move heaven and earth to get you out of there when you come to your senses."

I know he's right about Anthem. It's a bad move. But for once, I don't feel the anxiety creep in. The pressure to be and stay at the top. I will get to work with Theo. See Theo. I feel calm. He's the one person who's always made me feel like everything will be okay, even when there's literally no evidence of that. I've been pouring everything I have into my career since I was a teenager, so that I don't turn around one day and realize that this was just my fifteen minutes of fame and I'm left with nothing. It still baffles me that I've found this level of success. I wasn't popular enough to stand out in high school, or interesting enough for my own parents to love me, but somehow my team has convinced the world I'm worth something, and it's all I have. Now I need to put my personal life first, because I might not get another chance to make things right with Theo.

I might not get another chance at real love.

CHAPTER TWO

Theo

I'm a fixer. I make the mundane glamorous, create viral campaigns for things like dish soap, elevate brands that want to be for more than the after-work essentials run. I make people actually want those flip-flops so badly they drive to the store for them, instead of going to buy groceries and tossing a pair into the cart because they're on the end of an aisle in the grab-and-go section. It's not flashy, but I do get a certain satisfaction from the challenge, and I've carved out a unique niche in an extremely oversaturated field.

But shooting swim is mind-numbingly boring. Full body hero shot, front, back, top, front, back, bottom, and move the next model into the exact same spot. Ten suits there and we can move to a new spot. The models are so talented, the light and location so beautiful, that they could have either of my assistants shoot this and it would look comparable. Sunset is the highlight of my day. At least then the models can get their hair wet and afford me a tiny bit more variety. This isn't the creative work I'm typically hired for, but I'm happy to be Anthem's go-to photographer because they pay decently and are a chill set.

Campaign shoots are another story. I get to create a vision and execute it, so long as I show the fifteen point five hero outfits and the twenty-five retail items that don't really go with the clothes but have to be sold in the same season. Bonus: the clothes are tailored, unlike the swim, which is pinned and means the girls can't move much without showing it. Anthem doesn't retouch, because they got dinged in the press for it years ago, so they can't erase pins, but they can just hide them and mislead customers about the fit that way. My favorite shoot of the year with them is Holiday, when we truck in massive amounts of fake snow and cover a cabin and plot of woods with it in July and deck it out with holiday lights, and I have nearly unlimited budget to find a way to sell everything from pajamas to vacuum cleaners. But this is swim, so when a new model meanders over from the trailer and is thrust in front of my lens, I smile winningly and turn to the client. "That pique texture is amazing! It looks high-end. I'll be sure to get a detail."

Miranda, the lead stylist, lights up. "It'll be so big this season! And it holds true in the wash, the wear-and-tear tests were amazing. Stacey had to take a call, but we'll definitely need vertis and horis of this. And can you get one with her showing off the pink mug? It was a huge buy."

"Got it!" I focus my attention on the model, who's never worked with me before and thus has likely never shot with Anthem. "Horis are horizontal," I explain. "You can just be super loose and easy for this stuff. We love big smiles, laughs, imperfections. The only thing to remember is not to turn too much because we don't want to see the pins in the back. And we'll find a way to work the mug in, just give me a minute to think." Maybe she can pour sunscreen over herself with it? Or water? That little bit of sexiness always sells.

"Okay, sounds great!" she chirps. I used to worry that telling them not to move too much would stunt the day and make them self-conscious, but after getting complaints about the number of shots lost to pins, I decided to let the girls know. Most of them are pros who won't be scared stiff by my instructions.

When I press the shutter, an alarm rings. I frown down at the camera. I've never heard any camera make a noise like that. I suddenly regret agreeing to use this souped-up version instead of my typical camera. The digi-tech, who rents us the equipment and makes the "best shot of the day" selects as we shoot, sold me on it, but new tech can have hiccups.

"Dude, it's your phone, not the camera," Kevin, my first assist, informs me.

"Oh, right," I say, laughing. I hand Kevin the camera and pull out my phone. Sure enough, a reminder app notification is flashing across my screen.

Reminder: if not married by 28 you're marrying Emerson!
T-minus one week ;)

My cheeks flush instantly. Suddenly, the sand starts swimming before my eyes, and I'm thankful I had the foresight to pass off the equipment. "I need to take five," I mutter.

Everyone splits for either water, bathrooms, or the pure joy of sitting down after standing for four hours straight. I walk out of earshot and pretend to be on a call as I try to get ahold of myself. *Emerson.* How did I forget this pact was going off today? On set I'm so focused I forgot my own *birthday*, but this pact? I never forget anything to do with Emerson.

I sit down and rub my face. I remember exactly where we were when we set this reminder. It feels like yesterday and a million years ago that we were two silly sophomores and agreed that if we were *somehow* still single by the time we turned twenty-eight, we'd have a week to get it together and elope before Emerson's twenty-eighth birthday. I laugh into my hand. I can't believe we thought twenty-eight was *old*.

The last time I saw Emerson I was eighteen. It's been a decade since we were in the same room. On the same beach. I've always been grateful that she doesn't work with the brands I shoot. Or maybe I'm devastated? It's hard to tell when I can barely breathe at the thought of her. I feel the familiar pull of anxiety deep in my chest, tightening across my heart, my lungs, until I feel like I might explode. It was this feeling, a pain that was new to me after the spectacular forty-eight hours that ended us, that kept me from going after her. It's not as extreme now as it was then, but I've still elected to play it safe and respect her space rather than face the panic attack that would come with going after her.

I open my search engine and type in Emerson's name. The last time I googled her she was on the front page of *People* magazine, hand in hand with her MLB-player boyfriend. When I saw the cover, it wasn't a sting. It was a knife to the gut. She never even liked baseball. I try not to look her up too often, but when Emerson is in a campaign, it goes viral. It makes it extremely hard to avoid seeing her, and even harder to avoid remembering the way we were together when the billboard outside your apartment is her face, one manicured hand artfully putting on Dior lipstick. She's so famous now that when she's hired, it's not as a five-foot-nine blonde with perfect bone structure. No, it's as *Emerson*. First name only, like Gisele or Madonna. She's the relatable version of Kendall or Gigi, a Cinderella story of a girl who came from nothing and became a star, without a wealthy parent or a famous aunt. Millions of people all over the world follow her on social, desperately hoping they, too, are destined to be discovered at seventeen and become a household name.

I haven't spoken her name out loud in years. After Allison had to peel me off the bathroom floor of a bar after seeing Emerson in an Instagram ad, I decided it was time to compartmentalize. I set my sights on commercial work that paid decently and could give me a life I enjoyed. I was already halfway in the door at Anthem thanks to a few assisting jobs, and I knew that I could make it with the big-box, mass-market, not-so-glamorous brands, while it might take me years to get noticed by galleries or magazines. I needed to shoot to make it through the day. When I was shooting I wasn't thinking, and that meant I could move forward with my life, make good money, at least look successful to my family and people outside of the industry while I got my bearings for a few years.

But then a few years turned into a decade of shooting five-dollar bikinis and discounted throw pillows. Every kid believes they'll be a superstar, even though for most of them it's a pipe dream. In high school I had much bigger plans. I dreamed I'd headline gallery shows, have work in museums, create great art. But that's all it was for me—a dream. Instead, I grew up and adjusted my dreams accordingly. I'm happy being the guy everyone calls to make the mundane shine—and sell. I'm respected, even if it isn't my dream. Now I'm not even trying to get flashier work, in fashion or editorial, I'm just content to fly out of Boston so I can be near family, coach soccer for my nephews, grill with my brother in the summer, take professional-quality photos of my sister-in-law's cat between shoots. And meanwhile, Emerson is the face of international high fashion. I try not to dwell on what she would think of me now. Her dreams soared higher than we dreamed possible while mine adapted to reality.

With each new phone I buy, I painfully transfer everything over. All the high school photos I have of Emerson, back when I barely understood a camera, when I thought the way she glowed on screen had anything to do with me. And this reminder that had been begging to be deleted. I couldn't bring myself to delete it. To delete the memory of that perfect day. I stand up and take a second to practice the circular breathing Allison had taught me way back on that bar floor—a technique I'd since employed for everything from Emerson to pitching rates to . . . well, mostly I just use it for calming down after I think about Emerson. When I feel halfway normal again, I return to set.

Two models are waiting, their heads bowed, their artfully tousled hair obscuring the phones in their hands. "I literally can't believe it," one says. "They were so perfect together. Well, except he's not Harry. But otherwise he's, like, the guy you marry."

The other model shakes her head woefully. "I know. Their statement was, like, so mature too. That means he's not even some crazy. So sad. But now I hope she'll finally get back with Harry; they were just perfect."

"Have you ever worked with her? She's, like, so good. Kind of seems like a bitch, though. Maneater, you know?"

I frown, already half sure who they're talking about. I couldn't get away from the headlines when Emerson dated Harry Butler. I try to get a look at their screens, but I can't quite make out the words.

"I did a show in Milan with her," the first one says. "She's actually surprisingly nice. And get this, he flew in directly after a game and was literally waiting there for her at the show. I melted."

Wait—*a game*? My heart constricts. They're definitely talking about Emerson. I saw the press when her baseball boyfriend did that. *Harper's Bazaar* broke the story and it spiraled from there, with outlets speculating that he planned a private proposal for her in Milan, that he'd rented the entire Duomo. The night ended with me on Allison's couch, roped into a facemask and drinking way too much wine.

"So, who broke up now?" I ask, trying to keep my tone light. I want to know the details, but I don't trust myself to look it up myself. I'd probably end up back on the nearest bathroom floor.

"Emerson and Josh!" the models say in unison. One of them holds her phone out to show me a shot of Emerson shielding her face while she walks out of a hotel. "Literally so sad."

I nod, but my mind is racing. Her dumping the baseball boyfriend the same day our reminder goes off . . . ? It can't be co-incidence. But then again, she might not even have the reminder on her phone anymore. There's no way she has the same phone. I'm sure someone like her has had a million by now—who knows, she might even have more than one. What are the chances that the pact is still on them?

But even if she didn't keep the reminder and the timing is a total coincidence, something tells me I can't ignore this opportunity. It could be my last shot.

"I have to make a quick call, be right back." Stacey doesn't look up from the phone as I power walk away.

I scroll through my contacts, looking for the number I've held on to for two years, ever since I all but begged Allison on one knee to procure Emerson's modeling agent's number for me through her fancy agent. I had spent several years in denial after Emerson's rejection, but eventually I vowed to take her at her word. But when I looked at old photos of us on our birthdays each year, when I see her star in a particularly exceptional campaign, when I'm buzzed alone at night, it's still hard for me to believe she didn't feel the same way I did. So in a moment of weakness, I asked for the number, just to have it. I never used it . . . until now.

The phone rings, and a peppy voice picks up. "Now, why is Theo Carson calling me? I don't represent any department stores, last I checked."

"He-hello?" I say, stammering. "Hello! This is Theo Carson, a friend of Emerson's. Who is . . . your client. Which you know. Uh . . . I don't think I have her current number, so I was wondering if you could pass along a message for me . . . please?" The line is silent.

"What's your message?" he asks finally, his words now guarded and curt.

"Well, we haven't spoken in a while, and I was wondering if she wanted to meet and catch up." I swallow hard. This isn't enough. She's never going to call me if I pretend we're just old friends and nothing more. "Can you tell her I still mean exactly what I said on the beach back when we were eighteen?" Wait, too much. Back up. "Actually, wait. Just tell her this: I've missed her."

That's the truth. It's not the whole truth—that I was completely in love with her and have never stopped missing her—but it has to be enough. At least for now. I already sound ridiculous, like I've reverted back to being a teenager with a crush instead of a full-on respectable adult with a career.

"Writing it down," her agent says. "Word for word. I'll pass it along."

The line cuts out before I can say another word. I put my phone back in my pocket, and smile. For the first time in forever, thinking about Emerson has left me with an unfamiliar feeling.

Hope.

CHAPTER THREE

—Freshman Year—

Emerson

From the moment I walked into the school gymnasium I knew I was out of my depth. I was one of a graduating class of twenty eighth graders who had all gone to the same school since kindergarten. Most of my classmates had dispersed to private and charter schools and now, with none of my friends by my side, staring at a sea of kids that somehow looked both older and cooler than me, I realized I should have begged my mom to send me anywhere else.

There were more kids in this gym than there had been in my entire school. I foolishly wore track shorts and a tank top, and not one bit of makeup on my face. The upperclassman at the welcome booth eyed me pityingly when she directed me over to my orientation group. The look on her face caused a zing of anxiety to shoot through me.

I eyed the girls in my group. They had long hair that curled at the ends, with no frizz in sight. Did they do that themselves? My hair was in a short, blond bob, not so much because I liked it that way but because it didn't require much more than brushing. That was the only thing I knew how to do, since my mom wasn't exactly *helpful* in the getting-ready department. Mascara lined their eyes and lip gloss shone on their rapidly moving mouths. How could I have missed whatever secret class taught all the girls to look so mature and glamorous? I'd never seen my own mom with makeup, but she never needed it. I'd grown up on scary rumors about what was in the water at the cutthroat mainstream middle school, and for a moment I wondered if everything I'd heard was true.

I looked around the room at the other students, and my eyes landed on a boy a few feet away. He was lanky but muscular, and had beautiful eyes with lashes that would make any girl envious. While the other boys were hulking around like animals, this one just looked . . . nice. And if I was honest . . . *hot*. I raked my eyes back up to his face with effort and was startled to find him staring at me.

My alarmed flush stayed with me for what felt like eternity, all through team-building games and introductions. When we finally moved to go on the school tour, he fell into step beside me. He took a long swig of water and held the bottle out to me. "Want some? You look hot." Now it was his turn to blush, though color barely rose through his tan. "Literally, physically. Like as in: it's hot here." He gestured around us with exasperation.

I could feel other girls staring at us, wondering why someone like *him* was talking to someone like *me*. But I tried to ignore it, instead accepting his water bottle. "Thanks." I took a long drink, suddenly unsure how one is meant to drink water. Did I usually wrap my entire mouth around the small hole? Was that overly sexual? Or should I be dainty and take a tiny sip? I choked on the water, coughing and sputtering as I handed it back to him.

"Loser," a girl muttered to her friend with a giggle. I expected him to leave me and continue on with the group, but he stayed, one of his large hands patting my back while the other grabbed the bottle, leaving my hands free so I could drop both palms to my knees and hack away.

"I swear I wasn't trying to kill you," he laughed. "I'm Theo."

"Emerson," I managed eventually, tears leaking from my eyes. "It's okay, as soon as I got here I knew this day would do me in."

What was I even saying? *Do me in?* I sounded like I was fifty! But his eyes crinkled with laughter. "It is a lot. I don't think I'll remember where any of these rooms are."

"Oh, me either. No way. We've passed four of my classes and I can basically guarantee I'll be completely lost tomorrow. I didn't even have to walk room to room at my old school." I strained to see his schedule, curious if we had a class together. But though I saw familiar courses, there was no overlap.

The tour continued on, the guide droning on about stuff like assembly attendance and off-campus lunch privileges. Eventually we came to a stop outside the cafeteria.

"Want to leave?" Theo whispered. "My brother's a senior, and he told me this is the last stop on the orientation tour. They show you around, then leave you to fend for yourself and mingle in the cafeteria."

I knew I should try to integrate myself, make at least one girl-friend, but the thought made my stomach squirm. It seemed clear I had not dressed to make even tentative alliances, and would do better to minimize the damage and try again the next day, when I could make sure I looked like a girl who belonged at the same lunch table with the coolest-looking fourteen-year-olds I'd ever seen. "Absolutely."

I followed Theo out to the bike rack, glad we were walking fast because I was too shy to look at him. If I had to stare at his eyes, my answers to his most basic questions would have become monosyl-labic, or worse, total nonsense.

"So where did you come from? I've never seen you before." His shoulders were so wide I wanted to trace a V down toward the small of his back. I trailed a step behind him, although my legs were long enough to keep pace, and he immediately slowed to match me.

"I went to Watermark. Yes, the hippie school with no summers, and that I'm just now realizing might be full of nerds. Lovable nerds, but that explains why I have absolutely no friends here."

His laugh was lighter than his voice, and I wondered if he'd been lowering it, playing at being someone for this day of first impressions. "Then I'm a lucky guy. If I'd met you tomorrow, you would have been sucked into a group already."

"Somehow I doubt that."

At the bike rack we paused, both fumbling for the combinations. I took the moment to gather myself. Was I really going to walk out of orientation with some boy I didn't know?

Theo snapped his helmet on. It was blue, beat up, unfashionable, and he had not one iota of self-consciousness about it. "Where's your helmet?" His brow furrowed as he looked around as though it might appear on my handlebar.

"I forgot it," I lied. I'd been too embarrassed to bring it. The older kids I'd seen biking around the high school never had one, and mine was bright pink, a relic of middle school that barely fit but I'd had to hold on to when my mom refused to buy me another since mine was "perfectly good."

Theo unsnapped his helmet and stretched across the rack to thrust it at me. In that split second, his shirt rode up and I saw an inch of tanned abs. My breath caught in my throat and stalled my protests, so that helmet was already in my loose grip by the time I'd gathered words.

"I'm not taking your helmet! You need it. And I'm a fantastic biker. I'll be fine."

"Fantastic, huh? You know, most bike injuries happen close to home, where bikers ride all the time. Because they get overconfident." He pulled his bike off the rack decisively. "I'm not going anywhere with you unless you're wearing a helmet."

"Then I guess I'm leaving alone, because I'm not taking

yours." I tossed the helmet back at him. The space between us was charged, crackling with tension, and I didn't want to be the one to break it. But I also wasn't one to back down.

Theo pulled out a beat-up phone and began to painstakingly type out a message. I stood quietly and rolled my eyes at him while we waited silently for a response from whomever he'd texted. I hoped my eye roll was cute and sassy. When his phone finally beeped, a grin spread over Theo's face. I suddenly knew I would do anything to make him smile like that again. It was like his entire body lit up.

He took two huge steps to unhook a pretty silver helmet from a seemingly random bike a few feet away, and tossed it to me with a bow.

"Stealing now? Whose is this?" A girlfriend? My heart sank. We'd known each other for twenty minutes and already I knew I liked him. A *lot*.

"My brother's girlfriend. She was the orientation leader, at the check-in desk?"

Unfortunately, I knew exactly who he was talking about. She was the girl who first tipped me off that I looked like a loser and was out of my depth. "He'll drive her home, and you can just bring it back tomorrow. On your handlebars, since you'll have your own helmet."

I stuck out my tongue at him, which made him laugh. "So where are we going?"

"Where do you want to go?"

"I thought you had a plan when you coerced me into skipping school."

Suddenly kids started streaming out of the building. I knew I had to get us out of there before he was stolen away by all the other people he must already know. Before he was around more than five girls and realized he'd picked the wrong one to spend the day with. I needed a friend to start high school with, and I wanted it to be him. "Just follow me!" I shouted over my shoulder as I began to pedal away.

We biked in companionable silence as I led us toward the beach. We lived in Salem, but I spent every day of my short three-week summer break at the Marblehead beach, where trash was picked up hourly and the sand was more smooth than rocky. It was a quick bike ride, but with one crucial hill that I often walked my bike up, too lazy to power through. But today I pedaled furiously, unwilling to let him see me walk my bike after I'd bragged so relentlessly earlier. When we got to the hill, he sped ahead of me, his legs stretched long as he stood above his seat. "I know where we're going!" he called back, and I didn't argue.

At the top of the hill he slowed and waited for me to catch up. When we got to the final turn at the firehouse, he signaled, something I never bothered to do, and I laughed aloud. He turned around to grin at the sound. "Look where you're going!" I shrieked, then laughed again when he whipped his head back around. The roads were empty, but teasing him already felt second nature. I had never felt so comfortable with someone after only a few hours, like I could tell him anything and not have to worry about him turning away because of it.

As we locked our bikes, raindrops began to fall, fat and wet on our heads. Theo looked to me, waiting to see if I would run for cover or suggest we turn around and find a new plan. I'd never wanted to swim in the rain before, but now, it suddenly felt like the only thing to do. I stretched my arms wide, closed my eyes, and let the drops hit me, speckling my shirt with sheer splotches. I kicked off my shoes and locked eyes with him. The intensity with which he watched me, his eyes so light but serious, and his face twisting up in a soft smile, was intoxicating. "I'll race you," I whispered.

I ran for the water, not looking back to see if he'd follow me.

My hardened feet pounded effortlessly over the sharp rocks but when I hit the water, the cold knocked the air out of me. The last week of August was the warmest this water would ever be, but on the harsh New England coast the water would never truly be warm. I'd read about beaches in Hawaii and Europe where you could swim without shivering, but they seemed almost fake to me, too impossibly beautiful to be real. I desperately wanted to see them in person one day, but knew how unlikely it was that I would ever be able to afford to go somewhere like that. So I worked hard to convince myself that this beach, my beach, was special.

Suddenly Theo crashed into me, his strong arms sweeping me off my feet as he pulled us underwater. When we rose, we were both laughing and sputtering.

"You can't just do that," I yelled. "What if I didn't know how to swim and had stopped to keep from drowning?"

"No one who can't swim runs into the water like that." As he spoke he gradually moved farther out and I followed, until we were both treading water. His bare chest peeked out of the gray waves. I tried not to stare. "See? I knew you could swim."

"Fine," I agreed. "I love to swim." My leg brushed his under the water and he didn't move away. I turned from him instead and floated on my back. My hair felt silky as it floated around my head, and raindrops washed the salt off my face. The ocean felt warmer than the air.

We stayed in until I could barely bear to raise a shoulder out of the water, until the wind felt so cold I thought it might freeze me, until my stomach became numb; I didn't want to leave and make our day come to an end, but eventually Theo took my hand. "You're shivering. Let's go."

He led me out of the water. I started to shake with the cold, and wrapped my arms around myself, but it barely made a difference against the cold wind. Theo wrapped his arms around me, blanketing me in his body, which somehow still felt warm even though he must have been as cold as I was. "Males have more body heat," he said. "Scientifically."

"Oh, gotcha, makes sense," I agreed. I would have said anything to keep his arms around me for even a moment longer.

We made our way back up the beach to our shoes. Theo picked up his discarded dry T-shirt and handed it to me. "Wear this. Please."

I thought about arguing, but I remembered how I'd lost the helmet argument only an hour earlier. Plus, I knew I'd freeze on the way home if I stayed in my wet clothes. So I pulled it over my head. It smelled like fresh laundry and wind, and something I couldn't place. I knew immediately that it was my new favorite smell.

CHAPTER FOUR

Emerson

Boats have always reminded me of Theo. He spent the summer before we met restoring a tiny old sailboat he'd saved all of his lawn-mowing and snow-shoveling money to buy. We took it to Gloucester countless times, usually mooring there overnight, content to cuddle in sleeping bags on the deck. I always woke up with my face puffy from mosquito bites, but this was pre-modeling so I didn't care. I was buzzing off the thrill of waking up mere inches away from him.

He named the boat *Maple*, after my favorite flavor of donut.

Today, I'm on a gleaming catamaran that I didn't bother to learn the name of. After my breakup hit the tabloids, Georgia extended an invite to her boyfriend-of-the-moment's boat in Greece. He had left her alone on it after being called to some important tech meeting, where the CEOs probably wore sweatpants while asking for multimillion-dollar investments. One red-eye later, and I'm here, drinking green juice and sunning myself on the deck of the boat, my team banished to LA so I can have a minute alone to breathe . . . and to strategize.

"Explain it to me again, just one last time," Georgia prods, adjusting her bathing suit. She's a curve model, and her suit hugs her body perfectly, while mine is a thin layer of fabric that masquerades as coverage even though there's very little to actually cover. Both are from her line of swimsuits, which we wear at every opportunity. We posted a selfie in them earlier today to her branded account, and both suits sold out within the hour. Physically we're polar opposites of each other—from our bodies, to my straight blond hair and her dark curls, my freckled pale skin and her absolutely poreless dark complexion, to our height since I'm pushing six feet with shoes on and she's barely clocking in at five foot six.

Georgia pushes herself up onto her side and stares down her sunglasses at me, sparkling kombucha in hand. We're both hoping to get booked soon—I'm still waiting to hear back about Anthem—so no mimosas or spritzers for us, as much as I'd love to have one. "Josh is nice, athletic, wealthy, romantic. I know you at least like him. So why not give it another chance?" She pauses to rub more sunscreen onto her skin and passes me the tube. I take it with one hand and pop a donut in my mouth to buy some time before I answer. I might be able to say no to alcohol, but I'm helpless in the face of donuts. Maple frosting is addictive.

I slather on another layer of sunscreen to stave off the wrinkles I can already see forming. I could shake fourteen-year-old me for tanning at Nahant instead of hiding under a sun umbrella. "Georgia. He's never read a book start to finish. In his entire life. Plus, we have nothing to talk about. We eat dinner in dead silence."

"We had a great double date last month!"

"Oh, totally. But *we* were the couple." I turn to sunscreen the tops of my feet. Such a neglected area. People need to realize that any part of your body can wrinkle and reveal your age. "We had a blast. And he did too, since he could have spent the next fifteen hours detailing Red Sox training room tips to your boyfriend.

Who was a great sport by the way, since I'm pretty sure he's never set foot inside a weight room."

Georgia throws back her head and cackles. "You're not wrong; he's such a string bean." She sighs happily. "But babe, if you want to find the one, you've got to get serious. I don't want you to keep wasting time with great-on-paper, disappointing IRL guys who waste a few months of your time each go. Let's upgrade your selection process."

"It's not like I'm not trying." I sink down in my chair and put my baseball cap on, content to mope. My publicist blinked back tears when I pressed her to draft a breakup statement last night. Even she had hoped Josh would be *the one*. She tried to caution me about what the headlines would say, as if I don't already know. Ever since I started approaching thirty, they've been extra vicious.

"It does take two to tango, babe. Maybe you could put yourself out there just the tiniest bit more." I refuse to meet Georgia's eyes, although she's staring me down. I'm as open with men as I can be. Which sometimes means *not at all*. But I just need someone to meet me where I am. Go from there. Convince me we can have one tenth of what I had with Theo, and then maybe it'll be worth the hassle . . . and the risk . . . of opening up.

"I just want . . ." I pause as I decide how deep I want to go. Georgia is my only friend who knows about Theo, but she doesn't realize he works in the same industry, and I haven't told her about the marriage pact. All she knows is that I was desperately in love with my childhood best friend, and now I never go home for more than eight hours at a time. Until my mom got worse and things unraveled between the two of us, I didn't go home at all, and would meet her in New York, where we could be on neutral territory and try to make the visit less tense. Georgia knows Theo was the one good thing in my lonely childhood.

"What?" Georgia checks the time on her phone and rotates to

her stomach to ensure she suns evenly. "Because if you have even a faint idea of what you want or need, personality wise, I can get started as matchmaker."

"Well, I'm not sure—"

My phone buzzes, saving me from whatever half-truth I was about to spout. Because the *actual* truth—that I'm terrified of love, that I compare every guy with my fictionalized version of Theo, that I'm afraid no one will love me once they know me—I can't say any of *that*. "Oh, it's Matt. Give me two seconds."

"Emerson!" he barks when I answer. "Tell me you're in Europe right now. I saw your Insta story."

"I'm in Greece! Why?" The green juice is suddenly too heavy for my nervous grip. I set it down on the table, juice sloshing over the side.

"Anthem is shooting in Cinque Terre—that's in Italy."

I grit my teeth and force myself not to tell him I *know* where Cinque Terre is, since I've *been* there before on vacation. I learned a long time ago that Matt is a mansplainer, doesn't matter if you tell him to stop, so there's no point. "That's great," I say instead.

"Sure, if you say so," he grumbles. "Fittings are tomorrow. They jumped at the chance to have you, and I made sure they dropped the other blonde from their roster. She was only twenty but looked sixteen." I roll my eyes at this obvious dig at my age. "And no accessories for you. We don't need your face attached to four ninety-nine water guns. What was most surprising was that they agreed to the outrageous rate I asked for. What island should I book you out of?"

Georgia appears next to me, clearly having been eavesdropping. "Don't shoot with them. Say no!" Georgia hisses. Her disbelief is written all over her face. "If you need bad press, we can be way more creative."

"Santorini, please." I pause, knowing I'm about to give myself away, but unable to resist asking the question. "Did you confirm who's shooting it?"

"Theo Carson. As requested. And while we're on . . . *Vogue* dropped you from their summer cover, and I know you said you're not interested, but I just want you to think about what we talked about, about Botox. It'll set you up well for things with Harry after this shoot, too."

Again with the age shit. "Matt, I did that whole video for that beauty campaign, remember? Saying I would never do Botox or filler? There was a *New York Times* article? Everyone loved it."

"Emerson, it's called *lying*. Everyone does it."

"Not gonna happen. Sorry." I pull the phone away from my face and squeeze my eyes shut until I see stars. It's one thing to take care of myself, but I am *not* putting chemicals in my face. And there's no way I'm lying to all of my fans! "But I'm glad to know Anthem worked out."

He speaks through gritted teeth, as though he can barely choke the concession out. "Yes, well . . . at least the pay is good. We'll talk about all of this when you get back to LA. Just a consult. Anthem isn't Chanel, and Chanel isn't calling every day."

I refuse to take the bait. "Thanks for booking this for me."

He snorts. "A deal's a deal. But think about what I said. At your age, this campaign is a career killer."

"I can leave any time after five tonight." I end the call without my usual pleasantries and place a hand to my chest as I struggle not to hyperventilate. This is happening. I'm going to see Theo. I wonder if I'm too young to have a heart attack, even if I'm over the hill as a model.

Georgia reaches over and takes my sunglasses off, hers already discarded, and looks me in the eye. "Forget what he said. Is. That. Your. Theo. Eye contact and answers, now!"

I nod mutely, then tilt my head to the sky, willing the bright light to help me blink back the tears that are threatening to over-take me. I'm not usually a crier. No one becomes a superstar by showing weakness, and it's crucial as a woman in this business to be able to hold your tears—it's the only way to make it through a fitting as people poke and prod you with needles *and* criticisms.

"Emerson, deep breaths, okay? This is good. Just breathe."

I suck air in through my mouth, hold, exhale, hold, and con-tinue the loop. I push all of my work anxieties out of my head, my fear over stopping for one second and having to sit with myself, because this time tomorrow I'll be looking at Theo, his blue eyes piercing, his hair curly, but stylishly cut instead of falling into his face, his shoulders now even broader, forearms toned from holding the camera. I spent my flight to Greece googling him, dreaming about him, giving myself license to do everything I'd restricted myself from the past ten years.

"I need to tell you something," I say. "When we were teens . . . we made a marriage pact."

Georgia's eyes go wide, but the rest of her body is perfectly still. "A . . . what?"

I explain the pact to her, trying hard not to show how excited I am about it. After all, the likelihood of something like this ac-tually working out is *extremely low*. But by the time I'm finishing my explanation, Georgia is bouncing in her chair, a giant smile on her face. "So the one week prior reminder we set, it went off yesterday. And here I am, no boyfriend, and I requested to shoot with Anthem because that's his main client. And Matt did it be-cause I agreed that if it doesn't work out, I'll do the one-year con-tract with Harry. Engagement and all."

"I can't believe this!" Georgia squeals, reaching over and squeezing my damp, sweaty hand. "This is not like you. Like, at all. I mean, you could just text him, instead of shooting this trash campaign, but whatever, I support a grand gesture. And don't even worry about Harry, because this is so romantic and obviously meant to be and he'll understand."

Color rises up my face. I've never been able to stop myself from blushing, but on set we have so much makeup on that no one can tell. But right now, it's probably totally obvious. I can't help it though—I'm absolutely terrified of the idea of just texting Theo, of giving him a chance to blow me off. At least on a shoot I have four days to try to fix things, and he's stuck with me while I do it.

"I can't believe you're going to rekindle the love of your life," Georgia continues. "I actually thought you'd forgotten about him, since you hadn't mentioned him in a few years."

"Ugh!" I bury my face in my hands. "What will I say? What if he barely remembers me? There's no way he kept the reminder, he'll just think I suddenly became his stalker. And he's right, I low-key *am* his stalker! Also, he probably hates me! Forget everything else, to him I'm just a really shitty ex-friend—"

The thought of Theo making polite small talk with me, treating me like any other model, makes me sick. I could never handle not being the most important person in the room to him. Even if we were talking to his friends, his parents, strangers, I wanted his arm along the back of my chair, his body heat warm next to me, his eyes looking to mine first after he made a joke. My name was synonymous with his in high school, which was exactly how I needed it to be. He was my person. Around him I was the best version of me, the me I wanted to be all the time, and I was constantly looking to him to make sure that I was just as special to him. I have not felt that dynamic since.

Georgia throws her hat at me. "Snap out of it! You are a *supermodel*. He not only remembers you, but he knows you're a badass. Even if he did delete the reminder, you're still the one that got away. This will be okay." She leans forward and takes my hands again. "You walk up to him, tell him what happened when you were eighteen, and then you move forward. I mean, it's been ten years! Just be honest."

My throat constricts, and my minuscule yellow bikini suddenly feels too tight. "You know I can't just jump into . . . all that."

"He's the one person you should jump into that with."

I groan. "I wish I'd gotten my roots touched up, or maybe gone on a juice cleanse or something. Then at least I'd look my best before I remind him of what I was like seeing me at my worst."

"He doesn't need to be your kryptonite! With every other guy, you're so confident. So how come with him you can't just be yourself? You're Emerson, the dream girl!"

"So first off, no. But also, key word, *dream*. The real me is different now. And after how I acted last time I saw him I'm probably in his nightmares." I wince thinking of how harsh I was. And how opposite what I said was to what I actually felt.

Georgia wordlessly rises and offers me a hand. I follow her up the ladder to the roof of the boat. She turns to me, the sunlight shining on her perfect skin. "Let's jump in."

"My suit will come right off."

"Excuse. No one's even here."

"You'll get your hair wet. And it's not even in a protective style!"

"I have a stylist coming tomorrow. I'll live through the night." Georgia gives me a sly grin, then leaps off the roof. She hits the water with a resounding smack. I wince, but can't help but laugh at her shocked expression when she comes up.

"Fine!" I cannonball in after her, glad no one's around to see me do something messy, something actually fun. When we're floating on our backs, shivering and exhilarated, she hammers her point home.

"You just need to break the ice. Do something that reminds him of old times. Trust me, you're still you. Reignite the friendship, see if you still like each other after all this time, and then once you're friends, make him fall back in love with you. Poof, married, done."

"Gee, I hadn't realized true love was only a quick and easy three-step plan away."

"It's a solid plan!" Georgia argues. "And once you're at least friends again, I'm telling you, you have to be honest with him." She splashes me before the protest can leave my lips. "I know honesty and feelings are hard for you! But would you ever have jumped off the boat in front of Josh? Any other guy you've been with? No. But with Theo, you told me you feel like you could do anything, like you could be exactly who you want. Who you actually are. And if that's not romance-novel worthy, nothing is, so you are going after this so it can inspire the story I write when I retire in, like, two campaigns."

I splash a huge wave of water toward her, seaweed catching on her suit. Mine is all but transparent. Another good reason no one is around. "Fine! I'll follow your plan, and when the time feels right, I will explain why the worst day of my life blew up everything for us and we'll find out whether he still hates my guts. Happy?"

"Very!" Georgia yells over her shoulder as she climbs out of the water. "We've got to get back. If you text now I bet Natalie can get some clothes sent to the dock to try on when we land, so you at least have cute clothing options when you arrive. I swear, you packed nothing. And a handheld steamer! You cannot be wrinkled for this. Are you going to bring your team?"

I think of seeing Theo, me flanked by assistants and bodyguards. Suddenly my chills are from embarrassment, not the cold. "No, I'll let them have a break in LA. I haven't gone to a shoot by myself in years, but maybe it'll be refreshing. Plus . . . I don't want him to think I'm a different person now."

"Emerson, you *are* a different person. But that doesn't have to be a bad thing."

6
Days Remaining

CHAPTER FIVE

Theo

I check my phone for the umpteenth time as I walk into the conference room Anthem is calling home base this shoot. Nothing from Emerson's agent. I slide it back into my pocket and take in the setup.

The tables have been pushed to the sides of the room, and racks of clothes are set up against the far wall. Assistants are steaming rapidly, and a tailor has set up shop at a folding table, while the producers are making calls from another. The changing tents are in the center of the room, creating a blockade between the door and what I imagine is the corner Anthem's stylist Miranda is holding court in as she does the fittings.

And then my phone finally buzzes.

Theo, Spoke to Emerson today, she has no interest in reconnecting with you. Please don't contact me again. xo

I'm eighteen again, experiencing my first-ever absolutely soul-crushing disappointment, sure that I'll never be happy again. The shocking realization that I wasn't enough for Emerson and probably never would be. Why did I make that call to Matt? My life is good. I don't need the extra complication of Emerson.

And could he be more of an asshole about it? That "xo" is a slap in the face.

I stop midstride and suck in a rough intake of air. I didn't realize how much I'd let myself believe this pact would be the push we needed to reconnect. To have a second chance. Getting this text is like losing her all over again. I take a deep breath. Maybe this was the push I needed to finally move on.

Another deep breath. I straighten my posture, walk around the changing tents, and I think I might be hallucinating. Her back is to me, and even though she looks different from when we were in high school—her hair is long, she's half as tan, and she's standing with uncharacteristically ramrod posture—it's Emerson.

Then she turns around, and all of the air is knocked out of me.

She has swiveled to let Miranda work on the back of the top, and when her eyes light on mine all the air is sucked out of the room. If you lit a match, the tension would make everything in here combust.

"Emerson." My voice drips with longing, completely unprofessional. I cough, desperate to pull myself together before I tear up or get fired. "Long time no see." I sound like a tool, like the type of photographer every model hates working with. But why is she here? Did she come to reject me in person? Did she decide Matt's text wasn't enough, and she needed to deliver the message herself? Emerson has never been cruel. At least the Emerson I knew wasn't.

Then it hits me. Is she here . . . to work? Anthem is the type of brand she wouldn't be caught dead wearing, let alone shooting. People go there to buy toilet paper, not clothes, which is exactly what I'm supposed to change with this campaign. And yet, here she is, standing right in front of me. Smiling at everyone, a professional look on her face that tells me she's on the clock. I'm clearly so far below her radar that she had no idea I would be shooting this. If I didn't need the income, I'd offer to bow out. That way she wouldn't be stuck working with me, and I wouldn't be forced to ask myself for the thousandth time if I'm the one who ruined our relationship.

"Theo," she says eventually. Her voice quivers, and despite everything I'm feeling, I hate that she's in a situation where she's thrown, where she has to be uncomfortable in front of colleagues. "I can't believe it. It's good to see you."

Knowing how untrue that is, that she actually didn't want to see me at all, makes my stomach twist. Did what happened make her so uncomfortable around me that she had to turn me down through her agent? I know she believed then that we couldn't stay friends, but that was a decade ago. I don't know how to act around her now that she's at *my* shoot.

Emerson makes a move toward me, but is held in place by Miranda's grip on the shirt she's wearing. "Sorry," Miranda says. "Just give me a quick second . . ."

I can't say anything. Every word I could possibly speak is trapped inside me. Sixty seconds ago I was crushed by the disappointment that she wasn't willing to *talk* to me. Now, I'm devastated, because I have to stand face-to-face with the only girl I've ever loved and know she doesn't even want to talk to me.

"How do you two know each other?" Miranda asks through a mouthful of pins. The tailor is watching us avidly from the table behind her, and the styling assists have frozen mid-steam to listen in. "What brand?"

Emerson shakes her head slowly. "No brand. We were from the same town. We are, I mean."

The way she says this, like we just crossed paths once or twice in line at the Dairy Witch, is a punch to the gut. We were inseparable. "We were childhood friends," I add, unable to let it go. "*Close* childhood friends."

"How wild!" Miranda says, mouth finally free of pins. "Emerson, you're good to change." Emerson walks to the makeshift changing room in the hotel conference room, and Miranda turns to me. "What a small world! I can't believe you know her. Our CCO is obsessed with her, so when we got this wild last-minute opportunity to have her be the face of summer, we totally jumped." Miranda lowers her voice to a whisper and leans in conspiratorially. "And I can't believe she's here alone. No handlers? Like, what? She's way too big for that, but it's better for us. Have you ever shot together before?"

The tips of my ears are burning, and the room is suddenly spinning slightly. Or maybe I'm swaying. My phone feels hot in my hand, and I click it off, hide the offending text. Emerson wants nothing to do with me. So why did she *choose* to come on this shoot last minute? My head is spinning in disbelief, and I brace myself on a conference room chair. "Not really. She was discovered senior year, and I didn't really get my start until college."

"He took my first digitals," Emerson interjects, joining us again. "I didn't want to go all the way to New York, so he did them in our high school photography studio."

"Do you still have them?" I can't keep myself from asking. My mom had them framed for me when I got my first adult photography job, memorializing the start of my passion, unable to understand that she was hanging my deepest regret on the wall of our hallway.

"Of course," Emerson acknowledges quietly.

I wonder where she keeps them. They could be in the house where she grew up, but if they are, I doubt she could find them even if she wanted to. For the past six Thanksgivings, I've brought a plate over and eaten with Emerson's mom after our own dinner, and every time there's been more and more *stuff*. The last few years I couldn't even make it in the front door; I had to use the glass slider on the porch. I know Emerson has been paying for an aide to check in weekly, to make sure her mom's still alive under all the junk that's accumulated in there, and she must visit occasionally because her mom always tells me about the last time she saw her. But I've never seen her. Not for the first time, I wonder if she somehow times her own visits for when I won't be home.

"Well, I have to let you two catch up!" Miranda exclaims. "Theo, Stacey went for a coffee, so I'd say just come back in thirty to go over locations."

"Got it," I confirm. Talking about the shoot is the actual last thing I want to do, when I know exactly how it will go already. Last year we shot an Anthem-brand sneaker campaign in Portugal, and this is going to totally mirror that, though I lied through my teeth and told them, of course it'll look different. It looks very similar here, but I'll make it feel different. I promised the best of Italian Riviera celebrity glamour and spring break, shots that would make their budget bikinis and pool floats the talk of Gen Z and Millennials alike. Normally I'd feel confident that I can deliver for them. Excited even, because it's definitely a challenge. But now that I'm standing next to Emerson, after getting a soul-crushing rejection that was so meaningless to her that she did it through her agent, I know I'll have to make sure this is the best thing I have shot in my life. I want her to see that, regardless of my lack of prestige, I have talent. I made my dream work for me.

I turn to leave without saying anything to her. I'm not going to be the one to disrespect her wishes. But she stops me. "Want to get coffee?" Her eyes are bright and hopeful, and to my surprise, she actually grabs my arm to get my attention.

I shouldn't agree, but before I know what's happening, my mouth betrays me. "Sure."

Her face lights up, and for a split second I wonder . . . no. This doesn't mean anything, she's just being nice. *I'm* the one who is going to pay for this later, when I'm even more wrecked than I already am.

I lead the way up to the hotel lobby. The hotel is huge for

Cinque Terre, with views that allow the hotel to charge hundreds of dollars per night. Most of the lodging in this belt of five tiny towns is expensive and minuscule, more private home with a room rented than luxury experience. We're staying in the first town, Monterosso al Mare, which has arguably the least impressive views, but the best hotels and the most expansive beachfront to shoot on. Anthem recently started to spend like crazy on their summer campaign, and as soon as I got in to Cinque Terre I stopped to take in the view. I typically shoot in Florida, Florida, and more Florida, with a shoot in California thrown in for good measure once in a while. I've only left the country for the shoot in Portugal last year; I actually had to get a passport for it. While I'm grateful to be given these opportunities to travel, I always told myself I was saving these breathtaking European trips for when I had someone to experience them with. And now I'm in Italy, and my room is a giant suite, with a balcony that looks directly over the water toward a gorgeous view of the town and water, the hills colored with stacked houses. It's undeniably romantic. There was a bottle of welcome wine, a small lemon pastry, and a travel-size glass vial of pesto—the local specialty, according to the attached note—to welcome me to the area. I immediately stashed the pesto and wine in my bag to bring back to my family. No reason to open it when it would just remind me that I'm alone, and the woman I wish I could take here on a vacation . . . or honeymoon . . . isn't here to be with me.

There have been a lot of days lately where I'm fed up with how repetitive my job can be, where I feel constricted by the tight direction on the inspo sheet for the day. But when I get flown out to somewhere like this, I try to remind myself that I am not just content, but lucky and privileged. I've made it somewhere in this career that most people only fantasize about. So what if every arthouse photographer I know from undergrad has all but called me a sellout as soon as I say what I shoot? Sneering through their teeth and unpaid student loans, because even though I have money and a life I like, they think I don't have any artistic integrity. And maybe I don't. But not everyone can have integrity *and* success.

Not everyone is Emerson.

The coffee bar in the lobby is cute and European, with espresso-based drinks that all crews love, but a variety of milks that shows they recognize that this hotel is for tourists. "I'll have an oat milk cappuccino."

While Emerson looks at the menu, *I* look at Emerson. She's wearing a maxi dress with kitten heels and a sunhat that's worth more than my car. I can identify the type, brand, and cost of every item, my "I work in fashion" party trick. I also have become adept at guessing the sizes of women's clothing, swim, and intimates, but that doesn't typically go over so well, so I keep that information to myself.

Emerson is scanning the menu rapidly, diligently ignoring the people around us, several of whom are openly taking photos of her. "I had a latte earlier," I offer. "Their coffee is great."

"Do you have any matcha?" She looks at me, her face placid under the glare of the people around us, while the bartender begins whisking the matcha. "I actually still don't drink coffee."

I can't believe I forgot that. Everyone in production drinks coffee with the early wake-ups, so I had unthinkingly suggested it. But Emerson always hated the taste in high school, unable to stomach it even when I got her something with countless creamers and flavors. "Right, of course." I fumble with the check and look down to hide my blush.

"It's okay," Emerson assures me softly. I pay for both drinks, assuring her it all goes on the same bill anyway, then guide us toward some chairs. My brain is screaming at me to run the other way and save my heart, but my feet keep on moving.

"Do you mind if we go somewhere slightly more private?"

Emerson says. Her eyes are a golden brown, with a darker rim encasing the shining irises. "I really do want to talk to you, but I don't want pictures of us together. The media is absolutely relentless right now, and I don't want them involved in . . . in us."

I can hear my pulse pounding in my head as I squeeze my thin, eco-friendly coffee cup. I'm such a nobody that being seen with me would create bad press. "Of course," I choke out. I lower my voice and take a slight step away from her. "We could sit on the balcony in my room? It's more . . . private."

Normally, I'd absolutely *never* bring a model back to my room. It's dirty, it's dangerous for my reputation, it's wrong. It's also a fast way to get fired by the client that hired the model in the first place. But in this case, I don't care about the client. All I care about is making Emerson feel comfortable.

"That's—that's fine," she says. "Perfect actually."

She didn't hesitate, but I can see in her eyes that she's anxious. Which makes sense—she didn't even want to reconnect, and here I am asking her back to my room. "We don't have to," I say quickly.

"It's okay. It is." Then she smiles, and even though this is only half of her full-wattage grin, I can't help but return it instinctively, smiling so wide and so hard that my molars ache.

The second we step into the elevator she presses the "close door" button, locking any would-be passengers out before her fans can follow us. We're silent during the elevator ride up, and all I can think of is that time junior year when we got stuck in the elevator. She had dragged me to the local library to hear her favorite author, David Sedaris, speak. She loved his books, this older gay man who on the surface she had nothing in common with, and yet related to so fully. She would laugh so hard that she nearly hyperventilated, her stomach shaking against my sweaty head. We'd gone to the event, but then on the way down, the elevator halted. It was the beginning of summer, and the elevator was muggy with heat, so it only took twenty seconds for a slight panic to set in. I suddenly was parched, claustrophobic, afraid we'd wither away in there. We'd left our cell phones at home, because who would we call? We only called each other, and we were already together.

She knew immediately when I started freaking out, and took over. By the time the firemen got the doors open, I was lying on the ground with my head in her lap, her slender fingers running through my hair, while she read aloud from her newly signed book.

What I wouldn't give to be trapped in an elevator with her again.

"Do you remember?" I chance when the door opens. "At the book reading—"

"Of course." Her eye contact singes me. "I think about it every time I get into an elevator."

We get off the elevator, and I follow her in a daze. *I think about it every time I get into an elevator.*

When we get to my room, her eyes flick to the number. "Oh! Mine is right next door. We're wall neighbors."

I laugh, more out of the irony that I'll be unable to sleep for a week knowing she's only feet away than out of any sense of humor. "I hope you remember morse code."

"I never could get the hang of it."

I press my key to the door, but when it unlocks, I suddenly hesitate. What am I thinking? Catching up with Emerson is one thing, but inviting her into my room is the last thing I should be doing. Matt already made her wishes clear—she doesn't want to be with me. I need to protect myself from getting my hopes up or I'll end up in pieces when she leaves in a few days.

The door lock flashes red, and Emerson shifts awkwardly beside me. "Uh . . . are we going in?"

I shake my head. "I'm sorry. I can't do this."

"Oh, do you have a meeting, or . . . ?"

I glance at Emerson and quickly look away, before the disappointment in her eyes can make me change my mind. "We shouldn't do this. You don't need to worry—I won't be weird or awkward on set."

"But Theo, I—"

Before she can continue, my first assist Kevin pops out of a room down the hall. "Theo! We're debriefing on the scout like *now*. In the conference room. You coming?"

"Yeah, bro, coming!" I shout back. "I've got to go. I'm sorry."

For absolutely everything.

CHAPTER SIX

—Freshman Year—

Theo

When I woke up the morning after meeting Emerson, I had a silly smile on my face. "What the fuck are you smiling in your sleep about?" my brother, Owen, asked after he threw a pillow at my face to wake me up. "You usually look like a zombie in the morning."

"Nothing!" I groaned defensively. I pulled the covers up over my head so I could grin to myself one more time before getting out of bed.

"Is it that girl you took Sara's helmet for? She better bring it back." My brother had given up on a constant stream of first dates to date Sara. He'd said he was going broke from paying for a different date each week, and only got to hook up with half of them, making it a poor investment. Sara was five feet tall, cute, and had lobbied for weeks to be assigned his cheerleader, so he was on the hook for at least football season if he wanted brownies to continually show up in his locker on game day. It seemed like Sara would ruin the life of any girl who tried to intervene, and Owen was already feeling the pressure of needing to call her for at least half an hour every night and to walk into school with her in the morning. To him she was a chore, so I knew there was no way he would understand Emerson.

"I'm just hyped for high school, is all," I deflected. I hadn't gotten Emerson's number, and she split off from me before I could find out her address. My only mission for my first day of high school was to find her and make sure I had some way of contacting her.

Owen ducked his head back into my doorway. "You want a ride? I have to leave to get Sara in fifteen."

"I won't be ready; it's cool. You don't want her mad at you on day one." I planned on biking to school, so worst-case scenario I could stake out the bike rack and wait for Emerson if I saw her bike in the morning.

I already knew a lot of people at school through Owen, playing on the soccer travel league, and from preseason practice. Double days were brutal, and I had thrown up twice during the two weeks we spent running endurance drills all morning and scrimmaging in the afternoon, but it was chill to know someone whenever I walked down the hall. And it didn't hurt that I'd made varsity as a freshman.

But even though I scoured the halls and walked through all three cafeterias, I couldn't find Emerson. It was like she was a mirage. I would be at school until five thirty or so when we got out of practice, but as soon as the bell rang at two I rushed to the bike rack. Sara's helmet was back on her handlebars and Emerson's cute cruiser was locked next to it. Relief flooded through me.

Emerson was the most gorgeous girl that I'd ever seen. Her hair was so blond it was almost white and in this tight cut that emphasized her face. Her face was elegant. High cheekbones, soft brown eyes, a huge grin that made me break into a smile too. The sound of her laugh made my stomach turn. She wasn't made up like the cheerleaders that my brother brought home, or athletic and toned like the girls' soccer team players my friends and I hung out with. She was in a class all her own, dressed in the simplest outfit, tiny black running shorts and a paper-thin white tank that made it hard for me to think of anything smart to say. When she turned away from me yesterday, to peel it off her skin, and put my worn shirt over her delicate shoulders, I forgot how to breathe.

She showed up minutes before I was going to be forced to scrap the mission for practice. Today, she wore denim cutoffs and a T-shirt, and had mascara slicked onto her eyelashes. I'd had plenty of opportunity to stare at her eyes in the water yesterday, and her lashes were blond, almost as light as her hair. The mascara made her eyes pop, and I realized with startling clarity that, even if she hadn't realized it yet, she was way too pretty for me to ever have a chance with her. I was the friend, the guy she would complain to about older, smarter, better-looking guys. But I would be anything if it meant I got to stay by her side.

"What are you doing here?" she asked, eyebrows narrowed.

I couldn't help but smile at her stance. Hip cocked, hand on her waist, so much sassier than the open girl I'd met yesterday. After a second she cracked, and I breathed a sigh of relief, hidden under the sound of her laugh. "I had to find you. But I only have two minutes before practice. Can I get your number?"

Emerson rummaged in her bag's side pocket and pulled out a Sharpie. I had nothing with me—no phone, no paper. I'd left my bag in the locker room. I held out my arm with a winning smile. "Just write it here."

"You're kidding, right?" I was dead serious. I wasn't going anywhere without a way to reach her, not when she was this close, inches away from me.

"I'm not."

She shrugged and scrawled her number on my forearm, her soft hands gripping my arm to her stomach to hold it steady. Her nails were short and unpolished and her fingers were long and thin. I'd never been this close to a girl who was so tall. Most of the girls I knew hovered below my shoulders and tilted their head up to look at me. Emerson was close to eye level, steady with me. My arm felt naked when she let go of it. "There you go."

"Thank you!" I called over my shoulder as I jogged away toward the field. She smiled as she placed a pink helmet onto her head, and I sent up a silent prayer of thanks that she was going to bike safely now. I barely knew her yet and already felt protective.

I was late to practice because I stopped in the locker room to copy down her number. I sweat like crazy during these end-of-summer sessions, and I couldn't risk sweating the number off. When I ran onto the field, coach ordered me to do twenty pushups for being late, but changed it to burpees when he realized it was because I'd been after a girl's number and still wore the evidence on my arm. I would have done two hundred burpees to get her number.

I texted Emerson the moment I got home, but waited until Saturday to call. I bowed out of the post-practice breakfast at Bagel World, a weekly tradition that was replaced with pancakes at Reds on game days, and called her.

"Hello?"

"Emerson? This is Theo."

"I know."

I'd biked to where we split off that day after the beach, so I was as close to her as I could be, freshly showered, with too much of my dad's cologne on. "Want to hang out today?"

The line was silent, and it was excruciating. "Sure. What were you thinking?"

"Let me surprise you. I'm ready to go when you are, though. Just text me your address." I was so enthusiastic that my voice trembled on the line, and I rushed to end the call before I embarrassed myself any further.

I hadn't brought anything to entertain myself, so I biked

aimlessly in circles around her neighborhood, buzzing with anticipation. After thirty minutes of this, I jerked to a stop when I saw Emerson standing outside of a small, tan-colored house, with an unkempt garden and all the window shades drawn.

"You've biked by here at least ten times," she accused me with a laugh and shake of her head.

I shrugged with a grin. "I was early. But I don't want to rush the process." I gestured at her vaguely. My brother was constantly waiting for girls to get ready and had reported to me that it took, on average, two hours for them to prepare for a date. Not that this was a date.

"You could've told me you were waiting on my doorstep. I'm almost ready, so you can sit on the porch." She was in a yellow sundress and had no makeup on, at least none that my relatively untrained eye could recognize. Her hair was tucked neatly behind her ears, and her legs went on forever, leading to bare feet with scarlet nails. In the week since we'd met, she'd painted them, and I must've stared because she snapped her perfect fingers in front of me. "Foot fetish much? I assume we're biking, so I might just throw on shorts."

"You look perfect," I blurted out. Her face turned a flaming red, and I had to imagine that mine mirrored it. "I mean, you look great in whatever you're comfortable in. In anything."

Emerson turned to go back inside, and I dropped my bike and followed her. I grabbed the door as it began to close behind her, and she turned, her tone sharp. "What are you doing?"

I froze. "Coming inside to wait?"

Emerson grimaced slightly and looked inside. "It's messy. You don't need to come in."

"That's fine, no worries," I stammered as I backed away. But just as Emerson was about to close the door, I heard another voice.

"Why don't you want your friend to come in? Invite him in!" a woman ordered. The door was swung open to reveal a woman

who must have been Emerson's mom. She was undeniably beautiful, blond, tall, striking, but tired-looking and with eyes that
looked slightly . . . off. I wasn't sure if she'd been drinking or
had just woken up, but something seemed up.

Emerson looked like she was about to argue, but then she just
wiped all expression off her face and walked away, wordlessly. Her
mom ushered me inside, and then I tried to keep the shock off my
face. The house was full of stuff. Old tables, piles of newspapers,
at least fifty boxes of laundry pods. I followed her mom into the
living room, and she moved piles of toothbrushes off the couch to
make a small area for me to sit on. She sat on a box of plant food,
which I couldn't imagine she used, since their yard was a mess.

"Now, have we met? Are you the neighbor's son?"

I stared at her, unsure if she was joking. "We haven't met. I'm
Emerson's friend from school. Actually, we just met." I tried and
failed to keep from looking around at the room.

"Just straightening up. Did a little shopping." She appeared
to be dead serious.

I nodded. "Right. Can never have too many toothbrushes." I
was surrounded by enough to supply our entire orientation group
for life, but who was counting.

"That's exactly right! And the deal I got, you wouldn't believe
it, they actually paid me twenty—"

"Mom. Stop." Emerson's voice was tense when she reemerged,
navigating around piles in the hallway. "He doesn't want to hear
about coupons. I'll be back later."

My mom would have given me the fifth degree, wanting to
know where I was going, for how long, with whom, what was their
parents' cell, where did they live. But Emerson's mom just waved
us off, barely saying bye.

As soon as we were outside of the house, Emerson turned to
me. "Please don't tell anyone."

"What?"

"Don't tell anyone what my house is like. Trust me, I've tried everything, but she keeps getting worse and there's too much stuff to hide. Please don't tell anyone." I stopped walking and really looked at Emerson, who was still in a yellow sundress, now with bike shorts I could see the outline of underneath, since the dress was so sheer in the sun, and . . . I needed to stop staring. I forced my eyes back up to her face. Her eyebrows were drawn together, and I wanted to wipe the worried expression off her face forever.

"Of course not. Whatever you want."

"Thank you." She breathed a sigh of relief. I followed her around the back to the shed to get her bike. When she opened the door, I saw there were things piled to the roof, and her bicycle was wedged into the tiny sliver of free space.

"I'll get it," I said quickly, afraid boxes would fall on her when she tried to wrench the bike free. I grabbed it and tugged it out carefully, then handed it to her. We walked back toward the front yard. "What about your dad? Does he know about—"

"He's gone," Emerson interrupted. "And I can't wait to get out of here. But we don't have to talk about it."

I fell silent for a moment. We reached my bike and I picked it up. "We can talk, though. If you want to." Owen had told me a million times to ask girls questions because they love to talk.

But Emerson ignored me.

"So where are we going?" she asked once we started riding. On the residential streets we could ride side by side, since there was rarely more than one car going by, and it felt as though an invisible thread connected us, helped us keep pace together.

"Do you want to know, or do you want it to be a surprise?"

Emerson scrunched her face while she contemplated this. She was so beautiful that scrunching her face just served to make her cute, verging on actually approachable. "You can surprise me."

"Good, because we're basically already here." Two turns later, we landed at a small white house that had been converted into a donut shop. "You mentioned you're a bit of a donut fiend . . . so, here we are.".

Emerson's eyes lit up, and she leaned her bike against the wall eagerly. She rested her head on my shoulder for a split second, and my heart split open, slightly wider than it had been the other day. Soon, it would be in pieces and regrowing around her, and being with her would be what made me feel alive. "You may be my favorite person right now," she declared as she reached for the door.

"Wait!" I said. She turned, her thick eyebrows raised. "This is only the first stop of ten. So now I have to ask you—how many donuts can you eat in one day?" I looked her up and down, teasing, but drinking in every second I had an excuse to look at her. "You're pretty small."

"The limit does not exist. I'm twenty percent water and eighty percent donut." When I walked in behind her, I brushed against her and stood close, territorial, wanting everyone in the shop to know: those two, they're a pair.

Ziggy's Donuts made us overly ambitious. They were light and airy, so you could put one down without even thinking. Emerson wanted to try two flavors, but I wanted to make it through the full route, so I compromised. "What's your first and second choice?"

"Maple frosted and glazed," she replied decisively. "How about you?"

"Not sure," I lied. (I always got glazed.) "You order first."

She tilted her head, then leaned over the counter to peer at the donuts. "Glazed please," she finally decided.

"I'll have maple frosted."

I paid for both, a whopping one dollar ninety-seven cents, over Emerson's protests, and when she took the first bite of each donut, she closed her eyes in bliss. Owen and I shoveled down food, unable to ever get enough after hours of practice, and I could watch Emerson eat with this reverence every day and never tire of it. "Which do you like more?" I wanted to know.

A lot of girls would have said the one they got, since I'd paid, and they didn't want to be rude. Not Emerson. "The maple. It's ten times better."

I pushed the plate toward her. "Lucky for you, I'm in a glazed kind of mood today."

She shamelessly took her preferred donut and ate it in about five seconds. Nine donuts and five hours of biking later, she'd slowed down.

"Theo, I don't think I can eat another donut," she lamented, a hand on her stomach. "I can feel them, all mixing in the pit of my stomach. They're like lead."

"We don't have to eat it," I assured her. "Let's just go in and smell it. So we'll have completed the epic donut quest." I knew once she was in Kane's she would want a donut. We'd gone through the same charade at the last two places, though she ate less and less of her donut each time. I'd been picking up the slack, and even I was starting to feel a bit queasy. Although Emerson was tall, I had probably eighty pounds of muscle on her, but this many donuts was tough for even me to stomach.

"Fine," she agreed. Kane's was the final donut shop because it was the most famous one on the North Shore. The donuts were huge, dense, and in all kinds of flavors, like Reese's Supreme or Birthday Cake Bash, and with massive amounts of toppings. If we had gone there first, back when Emerson was still hungry, we would have made it to maybe three other places before we called it quits. "Ughhhh," she moaned as she looked in the case. "I mean, we have to get one. We're so close, it would be wrong not to finish at this point. We may have to sit here for a while though."

Kane's was in the worst location of all the shops. It was set on basically a vacant lot on the side of the road, and as soon as we were en route I regretted having us bike there. Watching cars whiz by Emerson was nerve wracking, and even though we'd dropped our bikes five minutes before, my pulse was still racing.

"We can share one, and just each have one bite. And I asked my brother to pick us up, so we're done biking." I rubbed Emerson's shoulder encouragingly. It was slick with sweat and I was flooded with guilt at how good it felt to touch her. With a teammate it would have been innocent, but with her it was charged. It was probably my imagination, but for a moment it seemed like she moved closer to my touch.

"Okay, no more biking, I can go into a sugar coma on the couch after this. We've got this." Emerson rubbed her hands together, before pumping a fist in some mock game gesture that was clearly the product of never actually watching sports, and she stepped up to the counter. "We'll have one Peanut Butter Cup Delight, please."

As the counter guy turned to get the donut, I moved closer to her, until I could feel the heat of her back against my chest. A thrill shot through me when I heard her call us a "we." We sat outside at the lone picnic table to eat the monstrous donut, and Emerson's eyes flickered shut as she took a bite. "How does this rank?" I asked. We'd kept a running tally of the donuts, but the fuller we got, the harder it was to accurately judge them.

"Oh my god, ten out of ten," she moaned. She pushed the donut toward me. "But I literally can't eat another bite. I desperately want to, but I will explode all over this parking lot." I held eye contact with her while I ate a fourth of the donut in one bite. "You're disgusting," she teased with a shake of her head. Her hair was matted from her bike helmet, and the underside was wet with sweat. Her dress was completely wrinkled and had left red marks on her shoulders where it strained against her as she reached for her bike handle bars all day, and the armpits had half-dried sweat stains. I couldn't imagine anyone looking better.

"You're the one who insisted we eat ten donuts! I might've stopped at six."

"This was your idea!" Emerson came around to my side of the

table and lay down on the bench, the back of her head resting only an inch away from my thigh, her face turned up toward me. "I'm basically dead right now, but this was the best day. Thank you."

I stayed completely still, anxious not to disrupt this delicate moment and cause her to move. I wanted every day to be like this. Suddenly Emerson sat up. "Look!"

An entire wedding party was piling out of a limo in the parking lot of the donut shop. The bride and groom appeared blissfully in love. He couldn't tear his eyes away from her, while she was smiling ear to ear and had a hand on him at all times. Their friends and family piled out after them, and a photographer had hopped out of a car moments after the limo pulled in and was dutifully snapping away. Emerson was entranced.

"That's a great way to kick off a marriage. Almost as good as biking to every donut shop in one day."

Emerson snorted. "That sounds like a great way to ruin your wedding day with sweat, exhaustion, and possibly puking from too many donuts."

Emerson was so close to me I could feel the warmth of her skin, and after knowing her for a week I needed her in my life forever. She was like no one I had ever met. She made the mundane fun, made me laugh until I teared up, knew what I was going to say before I said it, but also said things I would never think of. "I'm really glad we met," I blurted out suddenly.

Emerson leaned forward and rested both hands on my bare thighs, staring deep into my eyes. For an instant, I wondered if she would kiss me right then and there. But instead, she laughed in my face. "Same, weirdo. Now finish the donut so we can go home and I can collapse into my sugar coma."

CHAPTER SEVEN

Emerson

As soon as Theo's footsteps fade down the hall, I let out a sigh of relief—it stung to have him change his mind about talking, but at least he didn't knock on my door and inform me that, *no actually*, we're never talking again *ever*. It's one thing for him to not want to talk *now*. I can work with that. But *ever* would have broken me.

I push the couch from my suite's living room as close to the balcony door as possible. Then I take a seat and get comfortable. I don't know when he'll be back, but my fittings are done, so I fully intend to be here whenever it happens. I lie on the couch and daydream about what would have happened if I'd followed him into his room earlier. He was understandably tense, but I could have broken through that. And after? Would we have sat in stilted silence? Made awkward conversation? Or would he have skipped all that, and instead rubbed a finger over my lips, brought my face to his, and kissed me? I've never had a kiss feel the way ours did when we were eighteen. I've lied to myself over the years—told myself that I must just be remembering it through rose-colored glasses—but after only a few minutes of being near him for the first time in ten years, I know that it would be just as earth-shattering as I remember it. And that's to say *nothing* of what it would be like to sleep with him . . .

I continue to daydream, the minutes turning into an hour, the hour into two. After a while I must drift off, because suddenly there's a loud noise and I bolt upright with a snort. I quickly look around, terrified someone might've heard me, then remember I'm alone. *Phew.*

I look out the window and see that it's gotten dark while I was sleeping. But more importantly, Theo is *finally* outside on the balcony—that must have been the noise that woke me up. It's time to put my daydreams into practice. I quickly check my hair and makeup, then straighten my clothes. I've dressed carefully in athletic shorts and a white tank top, a throwback to the first day we met, except that back then my outfit retailed for maybe seven dollars at Savers, and what I'm wearing now costs . . . a *lot* more. But when I go to step outside, I can't open the door. It's blocked by the couch, because I've pulled it so close my face is practically pressed against the glass when I sit down. *Great job, Emerson.*

I glance out at him. Theo is sitting out with a Negroni, his shirt unbuttoned, revealing firm but not overly sculpted abs, along with a sexy ridge on either of his hips leading down to his waistband. But the best part is: *he's reading a novel.* Or at least trying to. He hasn't turned a page since I started watching him. I pull on the couch and am punished with a tremendous squeak as it drags across the floor. In my rush of energy and scheming earlier, I'd barely noticed the noise I made, but now every sound is excruciating. Theo can't know how carefully I orchestrated this balcony moment.

I bite my lip as I tug the couch a few more inches, then suck in my stomach as I squeeze through the tiny opening that I've made room for. I pull the curtain closed behind me, lest he see the couch and realize that I'm actually trying extremely hard to get a moment with him. "Theo! Fancy seeing you here."

He doesn't look thrilled. I actually think he might have just winced at the sight of me. "Emerson."

That's it. *Emerson.* Nothing comes after it, and I'm left scrambling to fill the gap, to occupy him before he retreats. This is where it would be natural for me to apologize, to clear the air, dive into the gory details of what I did, why, and how much I regret it, but how I also felt like I had no choice. After a decade of on-and-off therapy, I at least recognize *that*, even if I can't do it. Instead, I deflect. "How's your family?"

Theo *definitely* winces this time. He looks around, as though someone else will pop out and answer the question for him, then reluctantly sets the book down on a small glass table. *You Only Call When You're in Trouble* by Stephen McCauley. He *would* be reading that.

"My mom is good," he says. "She's pretty obsessed with Owen's kids, which completely makes sense because they're amazing. I actually coach their soccer team, back home. And he's good. Settled, you know?"

"I can't believe Owen got married before us." I choke on my words in my rush to correct what I said. "Individually, I mean! Not us . . . You know what I mean." I take a breath and watch Theo's jaw clench, which he releases only to take a gulp of his drink. *Get it together, Emerson.* "It's just that he was always such a player. And now he's a dad!"

"When he met Naomi, it was game over. He proposed after six months, said he knew from the moment he met her. She was reaming him out for taking her parking space at the time. And their kids are amazing. Exhausting sometimes, but so incredible." Theo smiles, clearly happy just thinking about his brother and his family. I can't believe I haven't met his nephews.

I suddenly realize I'm leaning off the edge of my balcony toward him, hungry to be closer, and make myself take a step back and sit in the chair. I need to act less desperate. I stay quiet for a minute, in hopes he'll ask me a question. But Theo remains silent, and his eyes dart longingly toward the balcony door. How can I get him to talk to me?

"Let's play the question game," I suggest in a rush to get his eyes back on me. And as I say it, I warm to the idea. I only have a few days with him. We need to get to know the new us as quickly as possible.

"What's the game?" Theo asks apprehensively.

"One question for each day of the shoot week," I say decisively, making up the extremely basic game on the fly. "So today we each get to ask one question. Tomorrow, two. The next, three. And so on."

"I don't know . . ." Theo doesn't look convinced, and my heart starts pounding. I need this. Theo has been giving me an understandably huge radius, but we don't have time for that. I'm on a deadline here, even if he doesn't know it.

"You can go first. Any question you want." I hold my breath, praying he doesn't ask what I'm dreading answering. *Why did you leave?* Or any question that leads to the same loaded answer.

Theo exhales, in what I think might be frustration. But then he looks me in the eye and asks a question. "Why are you here?"

And obviously, I lie. "For the Anthem shoot. They pay well. And I love Cinque Terre." *And I want to see if I fall back in love with you.*

"That's it?" He takes a long sip of his drink.

I swallow nervously. I don't want him to know I'm here for him. It's too much, after all this time. At best it's strange and exposing, at worst it's creepy and upsets him. "Yes. But I'm glad we're both here. And I want to take this time to get to know each other again."

Theo looks away, toward the view of stacked houses that glow in the sunset. When he turns back toward me, his brow is furrowed. "It's your turn."

"Oh! Right, right." My mind is suddenly blank. I don't want to ask too important a question when he's closed off like this. But we need to start this game, because clearly I'll need an excuse to get him to talk to me. At least for now. I used to be able to convince him of just about anything, so I hope that in a day he'll be ready for us to actually start getting to know each other. "If you could change one thing from your past, what would it be?"

Theo flinches. "Let me think."

"I'm pretty sure that face means you know." My gut is leaden. Now I'm the one focusing on the view instead of Theo's face. But I pull my shoulders back, get up, and walk to the edge of the balcony so I'm as close to him as I can be. He doesn't get up. "You can tell me."

He lets out a long breath, and when he looks at me, his eyes are dry but sad. "I wouldn't have kissed you."

My eyes smart and I feel a burn in my nose. Does he regret the actual kiss? Or does he think that's why I left? "Do I get a follow-up?" I choke out.

"Maybe tomorrow," Theo says. He sounds both exhausted and frustrated. "Goodnight, Emerson."

I turn away and try to make sure my tears are the silent kind. Despite how bad his answer hurts, I feel our connection in every cell of my body. I know I am doing the right thing. I need to make things right. This week is for us. To tell the truth. To apologize for leaving like I did, when he's still the best friend I've ever had. "Thank you," I choke out. "Have a good night."

I try to open the door to go back inside, but the way is blocked. "Shoot," I mutter. I forgot about the stupid couch. I slide through the door while Theo watches, pressure building as hot tears gathering behind my eyes. Then I sprint to the bathroom and turn the shower on to cover the sound of what I know is about to be a *massive* breakdown.

I've been called an ice queen more times than I can count. But this time, I let myself cry. I cry for the life I let myself envision with him the past few hours, a life I'll probably never get to have. I cry for the life I lost, and the pain of everything that happened when I was eighteen that led to us shattering, that forced me to let Theo go so he wasn't stuck picking up my pieces, but that clearly still hurt him. I sob so hard, feeling sorry for myself, empty and alone.

I eventually turn off the shower and lie down on the bed. For a moment I imagine that I can hear something on the other side of the wall, something that sounds like crying. And in that moment, I want to go to him, be with him. But instead I close my eyes, and settle for the knowledge that at least in my sadness, I'm not alone.

CHAPTER EIGHT

—Sophomore Year—

Theo

Growing up, the Thanksgiving Day game was just a fun thing to do on Thanksgiving morning. But after two years of Emerson setting me straight about the obviously complex social politics of the bleachers, I knew it was *actually* an unforgiving showcase of *who's who.*

This year, the cold was completely biting, and I could see the frost on the ground. Since it was a home game year, and the Salem field didn't have away stands, the first few yards of bleachers were Beverly students and families, and once we passed the fifty-yard line, it became Salem supporters. Right on the fifty were the parents, and as we got farther down the bleachers, the spectators separated into groups of students and alumni huddled together for warmth.

"See!" Emerson said. "I told you Claire and Tommy broke up. He's with your jock friends, and she's sitting on like the outskirts of the band nerds," Emerson hissed in my ear as we walked the length of the stands.

I glanced at Claire. "But Nessa is over there. Maybe she just wanted to sit with her friend."

This was true. Nessa had her clarinet clutched between fingers, which were red with cold. She was blowing on the reed frantically to warm it up and I could see the Under Armour top poking out the neck of her thin marching band uniform. In contrast, Claire was in a down parka to her ankles, with a Salem High hat, gloves, and winter boots.

Emerson snorted. "Yeah, right."

"Should we sit with her?" I asked. "To be nice?"

"Um, no. We barely know her, and she'll think we're super weird if we just show up. I'm just *observing*."

I shook my head, then led the way up the bleachers. Emerson stuck to my side like glue. She had people she talked to at school, but she didn't play sports or anything, and so more often than not she just came along to my parties, games, whatever.

"We could sit with Owen instead," I said, nodding toward the football alumnus seated at the top of the student section. My brother Owen was clearly top dog up there. He got captain as a sophomore and led them to four consecutive state championships, after a ten-year losing streak. The Thanksgiving Day game was the highlight of his fall, although he drove home from UMass with a few other ex-SHS players for a few regular-season games too. He got up early this morning to pregame with a huge group of alumni at eight a.m.

"Your friends are fine," Emerson said.

"Okay, okay. But if you want to go somewhere else, just say the word."

I led us into the center of the pack of varsity athletes and "generally popular kids," as Emerson deemed my friends. They all liked Emerson fine, so I never understood why she got so nervous around them. While I exchanged high-fives and fist bumps, she just offered a tight smile all around and then nestled close to my side when we sat down.

I personally loved watching any game, since that was how I

spent most weekends with my family before meeting Emerson. But within five minutes of sitting down, Emerson's eyes glazed over.

"Theo," she whispered finally. "We're the only people here who aren't in relationships."

"What are you talking about?" I tore my eyes away from the play to look around us. "Clarissa and Anderson aren't dating, and they're right in front of us."

"They're together. She's wearing his jacket, that's obviously how you tell." Emerson's brow was furrowed in concern, and I followed her stare around us to all the other people. Sure enough, each girl was wearing a guy's varsity jacket. Even the girls who had their varsity jackets from their own women's teams. "Emerson, why do you care so much about this?" I asked.

She shrugged. "My mom always says if no one loves you, then you probably aren't worth loving."

Her words cut. I didn't understand her mother, or how she could say something so awful to her kid. But I knew I couldn't stand Emerson being sad, so I did the one thing I *could* do: I took my jacket off and handed it to her. "Take mine."

"No way! You'll literally freeze out here."

She wasn't wrong. My butt felt numb on the metal bleachers, and I wished I'd accepted the blankets my mom pressed on me on the way out this morning. Or the flask Owen offered me. "I'd rather you have it. Besides, you look good in it."

I loved seeing her in my jacket. It was big on me and huge on her, but she looked perfect in it. Completely worth the cold.

"Thanks," she murmured gratefully as she slid her hands deep into the pockets. Then she pulled out a wrapped condom, her eyes wide, and waved it in front of my face.

My cheeks turned beet red in seconds. "That's not mine. I mean, technically it is, but Owen gave it to me as a joke." I practically choked trying to get the words out fast enough.

"Oh yeah?" Emerson teased. "You don't have a secret girl-friend somewhere who's going to come after me for wearing your jacket?"

The idea of there being *another girl* was laughable. Emerson was the only girl I wanted, in my jacket or otherwise. But I couldn't say that. We were only sophomores; it was too soon to make a move when she was my best friend. When dating her would be *it* for me. "Of course not. You know no one wants to date me."

Emerson shook her head. "Theo, I'm sure you could have your pick. Especially if you hung out with me less and gave other girls a chance." Emerson dropped the condom back in my jacket pocket.

Emerson had it backward—*I* was definitely what was keeping *her* from getting a date. When guys saw her in my jacket, coming to parties in my car, on the bleachers at my games, they thought she was taken. And while I was perfectly happy for it to stay that way, I didn't want her to think something was wrong with her. "Em, trust me, you could ask out any guy here and they'd take you out. You're phenomenal."

"I don't know," she said. "I'm pretty sure I'm going to wake up one day and realize I'm a spinster."

I laugh. "I won't let that happen."

Suddenly Salem made a touchdown and everyone jumped up. The band began playing their victory song and everyone around us cheered. As Emerson clapped politely next to me, she leaned in to my ear. "I'm going to hold you to that, Theo Carson. If you're so sure I'll find someone, then let's make a pact: if we're not married at twenty-eight, we'll get married."

I gaped. "Are you serious? Also, why twenty-eight? That's, like, so old."

"It's a decade after graduation."

A girl with a tray of hot chocolates walked by, and I bought one off her for Emerson to warm her hands up. "Thanks." Emerson wrapped her hands around the cup and offered it to me to sip, to test the temperature for her.

"You should wait." I took another sip. She liked her drinks more lukewarm than hot.

"I'm serious," Emerson said, taking her drink back. "Twenty-eight is *ancient*, so if we're right about each other being *total* catches, we'll be married by then. And if not, problem solved!" Emerson sipped the drink and winced, then went back to using it as a hand warmer.

To our right the wave started. Normally I'd jump up and join them, but I couldn't take my eyes off her. "Are you serious about this?"

Her eyes bored into mine. "Yes."

"Then I'm in. Let's set a reminder."

I pulled out my phone, but my fingers were too cold to open it. Emerson passed me the drink to warm up and set the reminders on both our phones. "Okay, so I'm setting the reminder for your birthday. And then, since mine is a week later, that gives us one week to plan a wedding or remain single forever." She grinned. "Sound good?"

I laughed. A marriage pact was crazy. First of all, she'd never reach twenty-eight without having found someone. But on the off chance I was wrong . . . "Sounds great."

She finished the reminder in my phone, then handed it back. "Well, future's secured, then."

Behind us, someone grumbled about *not even watching the game*, and Emerson cringed.

"You're really playing chicken here, though, since it's, like, *super* likely I'll be single at this rate."

Emerson looked so sweet in that moment, her forehead scrunched, her nose red, swimming in my jacket.

You're perfect, I thought. *What's ten years?*

Then I turned back to the game and said, "I'll take my chances."

5
Days Remaining

CHAPTER NINE

Emerson

Every photoshoot is basically the same. The call time on the first day is always at six a.m. sharp, and shooting is scheduled to go until five, but inevitably ends up wrapping around seven. Coffee is waiting for everyone in the morning, people are assigned to cars on the call sheet, and I always spend an hour in hair and makeup while the crew prepares the set.

The only difference this time is Theo.

I stayed up way too late last night thinking—about his answer, this week, and more than anything, all the time that's passed. Theo has been civil, but he clearly isn't ready to forgive me. He's barely ready to talk to me one-on-one. But I'm not ready to give up on him or us.

I try to stay calm as I run through my morning routine. I shower, dry my hair, do a facemask, and prep my skin with my fifteen-step skincare regimen before heading down to the cars. I want to look fresh, as though I don't need any of the makeup they're painting me with, in case Theo sees me in passing. No one I've dated in the last ten years has seen me without a lash lift and brow lamination—not that they know that. Most people don't recognize all the beauty treatments; they just think it's all *natural*. I'm sure Theo knows all the tricks of the model trade after working on shoots for so long. I almost wish I was completely natural, so it would be less obvious how much I care about my looks, my career, my youth. I want to be the me he remembers. The girl that captured his heart, before she let it go.

The other models are in the lobby when I arrive at six a.m. sharp. They're gathered tightly together, cappuccinos in hand. I can tell they're discussing me from the way they fall silent when I enter the room.

"Hey!" I say, walking over to them. "I'm Emerson. Here for the Anthem shoot?"

The answer is obvious, but I want them to know I'm a normal person, not the celebrity they've read about in magazines and tabloids. At a designer show I'm all business, full glam, no questions, rare smiles, but these girls have likely never stepped over to that world and are less hardened. They probably do lots of well-paying digital work for mass-market brands, but I'm likely the only high fashion model they've ever met.

"As though we don't know who you are!" one of them exclaims. She's pale, short, and curvy, with reddish hair and a smattering of freckles across her nose. "But like . . . what are you doing here, for real? You don't shoot Anthem! I want to know *What. Is. Up.*" She laughs. "Oh, and I'm Rachel."

She goes right for a hug, and a nervous laugh escapes me. Even though I'm constantly being adjusted by stylists and makeup artists, I'm not really a hugger. "Nice to meet you!" I say, directing my words toward the other two girls as well. "I haven't done work like this in a while, so you all will have to show me the ropes."

A tall Black model with braids steps up next. Her arms and legs are super toned—she's built for swimsuit modeling. "I'm Evonique. It's amazing to meet you. I'm only slightly embarrassed to say that I'm a fan."

"And I'm Jillian," announces an Asian model with cropped hair. "And just to address the elephant in the room . . . we saw you on the call sheet, and we were one hundred percent talking about your breakup."

Her honesty is so refreshing that I can't help but laugh aloud. "Wow! I actually appreciate you saying it to my face. Yeah . . . I mean, wasn't meant to be."

"But you *obviously* broke up with him," Evonique says. "Right?"

They all lean in to hear my answer. I usually refuse to speak about my personal life. Some sets are catty, and I know anything I say can and will be sold to the tabloids. But I want these women on my team this week. It'll be hard enough being around Theo without the other models icing me out. Plus, it's been a long time since I could relax on set. It'll be easier if I have some friends to do it with. "I can neither confirm or deny any aspect of Josh and my *conscious uncoupling*," I say with mock sincerity. Then I wink, and they laugh.

"Thought so," Evonique says with a smile.

I'm about to reply when Theo walks out of the elevator. He's wearing what must be his photographer outfit—tan Dickies, Blundstone boots, a wicking top, and a down pullover. I've seen thousands of variations of this outfit on set, but on him it looks weirdly hot. I am *into it.*

He stops in his tracks when he sees me. "Emerson."

I wish that one word was said with longing. But instead his tone is curt. I open my mouth to say something but can't find any words. What do I say? *Good morning, nice to see you again after ten years of ignoring you. Hope my meltdown didn't keep you up through the wall last night. And by the way, you're the only person I've ever actually loved, so you down to get married in a week? Just kidding, it's clear you can barely speak to me, let alone say vows.* I settle for, "Good morning."

"You look great," he says, then cringes.

"You look great," I echo.

I can *feel* the other models watching us. I can only imagine what they're going to say to one another once we walk away. I shouldn't have spoken to him in front of other people. Theo and I were always better alone. I cherished the hours we'd spend in the car, driving nowhere, talking about everything. I always clammed up around his friends. And now, after a decade of becoming amazing at socializing out of necessity, it's like I've reverted to the most awkward version of my high school self.

"You're Theo, right?" Rachel says finally. Bless her for breaking this horrible tension.

"Yes," he says. "Theo here, reporting for duty." He winces again, and his eyes flick to me. I take a breath of sweet relief. I'm not the only one who's awkward. "You must be Rachel?" he asks. "I love your work, can't wait to shoot together. And Evonique, Jillian, it's always my pleasure. This is going to be a great week."

Hearing him use his professional voice is such a turn-on I almost groan. I always knew he was a talented photographer, but seeing him as his adult self, as a grown man, is almost too much for me to take. I can't believe I spent a decade away from him.

"Hey, man, here's the matcha you asked for." The same dark-haired man from the hallway hands Theo a cup. "I'm Kevin, first assist," he says to me. "See you out there."

He leaves, and Theo turns to me, but looks everywhere but into my eyes. He thoroughly examines the construction of the cup, the writing on the side, how firmly the lid is on, anything to avoid actually looking at me. "This is actually for you. I'm sure they'll take orders later today, but I wanted you to have something you liked this morning since you'd be stuck with coffee otherwise."

My heart does a little flip as I take the cup. "It's oat milk," he adds, his voice cold, as though to downplay that he's done something thoughtful. No one in fashion does dairy, but I'm touched that he remembers I like oat more than almond.

"Thank you. That's very . . . very kind of you. Thanks." My voice trembles, and I try to hide it with a sip, only to scald myself on the hot liquid. I cough and Jillian claps me on the back, sending green droplets flying. Theo's immediately prepared, pulling napkins out of his bag and mopping up the mess from the floor.

God, I am a *mess*.

"Theo, don't let us keep you," I say. I need to put myself back together if I'm going to survive this day. And needing to say his name, because I suddenly once again am obligated to remind everyone that he's mine, even though I have no right to this new adult version of him.

He continues off toward the cars, and I turn to find three pairs of wide, captivated eyes staring me down. "Theo," Evonique echoes breathily.

"You don't even have to say anything," remarks Jillian as she shakes her head, a smirk playing on her face. "Just tell us how you know each other and when you fell for him, we're golden."

"Wow, is it that obvious?" I stare at him through the lobby window, watching as he opens the car door and steps in. "We met at fourteen. But it's been ten years since we've seen each other and I'm here to, you know . . . rekindle things. By way of friendship!" I keep the marriage pact to myself.

Rachel nods to herself in satisfaction. "This booking just gets better and better. We'll all be following this like it's *The Bachelor*, just so you know. But we better go; I see our car out there."

I usually like a long drive to location. It gives me more time to wake up, to think about how I want the day to go, how to capture the character they want me to play in the footage. But today I want to get to work as quickly as possible, so I can't spend any more time in my head than I already have. Luckily, today's drive is mercifully short.

Just as we pull up to location, I get a text from Matt.

Just say the word. It's not too late to pull out of this shoot.

I wrap my hand around the phone. I am having doubts. Theo has made his feelings clear; should I be here? Am I being completely selfish? Even though I want to run away and soothe my frazzled nerves, it would be shitty to leave the shoot before it's even started. And I only have this week to make things happen, before seeing me with Harry again makes Theo write me off for good.

I'll think about it, I text back, to placate Matt.

It's still dark when I step out of the SUV and into the makeup trailer. The hair stylist and makeup artist get to work unpacking their suitcases of product, laying out canisters on folding tables, and heating up curling wands in front of two giant LED-lit mirrors. The makeup trailer is always a sanctuary for models. It's air-conditioned, stocked with snacks, has a private bathroom, and is typically a "Talent Only" zone. That last part is why I love it. When I was new to modeling, it didn't bother me that I was surrounded by men. Until one day, it did. Now I put on a happy face, but secretly I dread making small talk with them, feeling their eyes roving over me, or worse, the way they act like I'm not even there the moment I speak.

These days, I typically have my own trailer. Anthem offered it, but I had my team turn it down, much to Matt's chagrin. As silly as it sounds, I figured that if I was in a solo trailer, Theo would see me as *famous* Emerson instead of *love of his life* Emerson, so I decided to sacrifice my privacy. But now that I'm back in a trailer with everyone, I wonder if I've been missing out by having my own space. The trailer buzzes with energy, and it's undeniably more fun to have people to talk to.

It's strange to think about how much I've changed over the years. How different I am today than I was the last time I was this close to Theo. My therapist has helped me realize that I disassociate on set. The useful aspects of my personality are heightened, and I'm on for fourteen hours straight, even when I'm not on camera, constantly striving to be easy to work with and fun to have around and perfectly sleek and professional. I almost black out, unable to call to mind more than a few details of the day when I fall back on my bed at night, weak with exhaustion. But whatever I do works, because I've been consistently booked since I moved to LA at eighteen.

But as unhealthy as that all sounds—even to me—the idea of doing anything else feels impossible. I've been traveling constantly for shoots for most of my adult life, and the thought of it all suddenly stopping makes me sick to my stomach. I don't even need the money anymore, but the hustle gets me through the days and keeps me from having to take a breath, analyze my life, wonder why I both can't be alone and haven't been able to find one truly significant relationship. I'm not a maneater like the press paints me as, but they're not wrong about me always having a partner. I love to be loved. To try to let their feelings convince me I'm not a wreck. But no relationship ever hits right.

"Emerson?" says the makeup artist. "You ready?"

I hitch on my easy-to-work-with smile, and she gets to work. I spend the next hour chatting about skincare secrets and comparing the merits of curling wands while the team gets to work on my hair and makeup. By the time I'm ready, so is the rest of the crew. They usher me outside, eager to take advantage of the early-morning light. A producer guides me to the edge of a cliff that overlooks a gorgeous view of the colorful houses stacked on the cliff in this town, Manarola. Cinque Terre is a belt of five small fishing villages perched in the hills along the Italian Riviera. I've been here once before, but it was on vacation with one of the many handsome but ultimately *not quite right* boyfriends I've had over the years. As distracted as I am by Theo, it's wonderful to be back in such a breathtaking place. Maybe this time I'll even get to eat something good. The region is known for excellent seafood and delicious pesto—neither of which my boyfriend at the time could eat on his preseason nutrition plan, so we mostly ate chicken. *Boring.*

Theo, Stacey, Miranda, and a range of other assistants have scaled up the rocks, and it's clear I'm meant to climb up to the edge about seven feet in front of them. "Is this all right?" calls Stacey, with what I assume is a falsely apologetic tone. As a model, the answer is always "yes," and we both know it.

"Of course!" I call up. Keeping my posture straight, I begin to scale the rocks in my long sundress. The morning wind is biting, and it's a challenge not to feel envious of the jackets the rest of the team has on. When I first started modeling, I got through by reminding myself that I chose this job, it's given me a great life, and I should be grateful to be there at all. And that still helps. But for the most part now I try to be more Zen about it, and just get to a point of flow, focus on the shot. Black out, to not be examined later.

A rock slips under my foot and I slide. I don't make a sound when I slip, but Theo lurches forward, practically running toward me, the camera bouncing on his chest. "I've got you," he says, hands flying to my waist to steady me. I instinctively rope an arm around his shoulder. "Careful, Em." He's breathless, and when I hear my nickname casually slipping out of his mouth, our bodies pressed together with muscle memory, I am too.

"Thank you," I breathe. I let my hand rake across his back, across the muscles that are straining and so new to me.

His PA steps up, thrusting out a forearm for me to grab, which is what crew does nowadays so they can't be accused of grabbing a model inappropriately. I'm meant to grab his forearm, nonsexual and safe on all sides. I let go of Theo and take his arm, but I catch him giving Theo a meaningful look. He doesn't want Theo to get in trouble for touching me. Theo steps away.

"They're childhood friends," Miranda says, who clearly noticed the look, too.

"My knight in shining armor here," I joke, with a rough clap on Theo's shoulder. His shoulder stiffens under my touch, and I start to sweat in embarrassment.

My silly joke works, or maybe it's just the humor-the-talent effect, because everyone laughs, the tension broken, as Theo makes his way back to his own perch. PAs offer arms to each of us, suddenly realizing they'll be the ones in trouble if they let the talent fall to their deaths. But I feel Theo's eyes trained appraisingly on me as I finish climbing up the rocks, reluctant to let someone else help me.

The look passes in a blur, my eyes locked on his lens as I flip my dress, pose, keep moving. The difference between an experienced model and a new model is how they shoot. A newbie poses, moving from one static position to the next, but I just keep moving until the shutter stops or I'm told to do something differently, and I keep my eyes and face focused so that every frame is usable. Up on the rocks it's challenging for hair and makeup to get to me, but I know how to keep my hair picturesque by this point, and no one calls out for a change.

Eventually Theo pulls the camera down. "I need a beauty shot of this," he says, his voice low and rough.

Stacey glances at him, confusion on her face, and I wonder—did they not plan this? If taking an up-close photo of my face isn't part of the plan, then why would he want to do it? I know what I *want* the answer to be, but . . .

Kevin wordlessly hands him a different lens, and he switches it and takes a few steps back to accommodate the new depth of field. I can't pull my gaze from Theo while he works. The way his hands look adjusting the lens, the way his forearm muscles flex in the morning light. How serious his handsome face looks as he considers the shot. He raises the camera and begins snapping away, and I realize I haven't put my beauty shot face on. I have no doubt that when he looks at these photos later, he'll see the way

I'm hungrily taking him in, relishing in every moment I get to
look at him.

"Have you got it?" Stacey asks eventually. "Your folder's going to be huge, and it's only the first shot."

"Sorry," Theo says. "She's just so perfect." He grimaces. "In
this light, I mean. Just look at this."

Perfect. Theo said I'm perfect. I can't help it—I grin. I know
he's talking about how I look, not about *me*, but it's a start.

"Oh, I'm just teasing," Stacey replies, even though we all know
she wasn't. Fashion is fake, until you learn how to speak it. Theo
flicks through the photos, Stacey and Miranda looking at the
screen over his shoulder. At any other time, I'd be worried about
shooting a B-level, okay C-level, fashion brand like this, and not
just because it is a horrible look for my career. The photos could
also totally suck. It sounds mean, but the truth is that lower-tier
brands have lower-tier photographers. Even worse, some sets are
known for selecting bad shots of the models just to generate press.

But with Theo shooting I'm desperate to see how these shots
look. I'm confident they'll be fantastic, but more than anything, I
want to see myself through his lens. I want to see the way he looks
at me, the side of me he captures. Maybe then I'll be able to tell
what's really going on inside his head.

Stacey nods. "I mean, you've got it," she confirms.

Theo turns to me. "Thank you, Emerson."

His sincerity brings a flush to my face, but luckily it's hidden
under makeup. A surprising amount of makeup goes into the "no
makeup natural beauty look."

"Just doing my job." I smile winningly at the crew as I make
my way down the rocks. The first shot of the day is important for
everyone. It sets the vibe and establishes what they'll think of me
for the entire week. And I know I've aced it, despite my literal slip
on the way up the rocks.

Since there are four models to cycle through, I'm only shooting six looks today, which means I have plenty of time to entertain myself in the trailer. But after a few hours, I end up back outside, watching Theo work from the sidelines. He's confident and decisive, clearly skilled. I took a peek at the monitor, and he's making these thin, semi-unflattering swimsuits look like a million bucks. But the longer I watch, the more I start to wonder if he's even trying. Sometimes, while he waits for Miranda to fix a strap, or hair to be sprayed into place, he looks almost bored. It's clear he's done Anthem a million times. And while he was super focused during my shots, he barely directs the other models. They just launch into their repertoire of poses while Stacey nods approvingly. He perks up a bit when he's tasked with a ridiculous request, like working paper straws into a swim shot, but still, I wonder what he'd shoot if he didn't need to check detail shots and crops off a list.

At lunch I make my way over to the craft services table, taking care to get into line behind Theo even though everyone else in the line immediately stepped aside when I approached. A PA took our orders in the morning, which is always my favorite way to do on-set meals. It avoids the worry of whether I'll have to pretend to like something or risk starting a rumor that I don't eat.

"Your food is already in the trailer," a PA informs me cheerfully. "The other models all ordered green juice, so I went ahead and got you one too; just in case." He gestures toward the trailer.

I'd been so tuned in on Theo that I hadn't noticed it was only crew at the table, looking for tins marked with their names. "Thank you so much." I try to force grace into my voice, even as I bite back a sigh of frustration. Theo will never eat in the model trailer with me—even if I invited him; it just isn't done. Looking inappropriate doesn't matter to me, but I'm completely unwilling to do anything that could make Theo look bad.

I leave the line and walk toward the trailer, where the other girls are already eating. I feel the singe of Theo's eyes as he watches me walk away from him. It takes everything in me not to turn around.

"Dude, you look like someone ran over your puppy," Jillian says as I enter the trailer. She takes an oversized bite of salad and crunches loudly. "You've got it bad."

"I don't know what you mean," I say, but from the look the three of them give me, I know denying my feelings to them is pointless. Theo might not see how I really feel, but to these girls it's obvious.

"Do you have, like, any sort of plan here?" Rachel queries between swigs of juice.

The PA was right, I do love the juice. I snap a quick shot of it for social media. "Not really," I admit. "Beyond putting us on the same shoot for a week, I didn't exactly think ahead. I got him to agree to play an icebreaker-type question game with me each day at night, since our balconies are next to each other, which is something. But really this was all a bit spur of the moment. I just hoped—"

My voice cracks, and I'm startled to find my eyes are welling up. I never cry.

And yet here I am doing it for a second day in a row. And even worse, *in front of people*. "Oh my god, this is so embarrassing," I say, wiping the tears away. "I didn't even realize how much I missed him until I got here. And he isn't exactly rushing to reconnect with me. I just want to feel like we're at least friends again, even if it's just for a few days. And then I can work on the rest. But I can barely get him to look at me unless there's a camera in his hands."

Evonique tilts her head thoughtfully. "That's all right. We can work with this. What did you two used to do, back when you were . . . friends, dating, whatever."

"I mean, we'd go biking, swim . . . he had this cute little boat." I stab my lemon shrimp salad with overly zealous attacks. Just this morning I was dreaming of eating the local food, and here I am destroying it. I take a deep breath. "Things were just different when we were kids. We could do nothing all day, and it was perfect. And I was spontaneous back then, but only with him. He probably doesn't even know it, but he would bring it out of me." Whenever I'm driving through LA, sitting on a plane, or falling asleep at night, I think back to everything Theo and I used to do. If I really want to indulge, I pretend he's the boyfriend I'm going home to, rather than whatever unavailable actor or athlete I'm with at the time. Maladaptive daydreaming, as my therapist says.

"You know, your eyes literally light up when you talk about him," Evonique points out. "I can see it now, but I looked at the selects from your looks this morning, and you were on *fire*. I mean, your work is always good, but your eyes were dripping with—"

"With *sex*," Jillian interjects. "Raw, sexy sex. This campaign is going to suddenly be rated R."

I laugh, and it's a huge relief. "Can you imagine?" I said. "My agent would kill me. Matt's a real taskmaster."

Everyone nods—every model can relate to the idea of a scary agent.

"Why do you even still work with him?" Jillian asks. "He was my agent, too, back when I started, but I left that agency after he told me to lose an inch off my waist for like the third time. I had literally nothing to lose."

I freeze. That does sound like Matt. And I don't want to defend his behavior, but he's been with me from the beginning. I haven't let many new people into my inner circle the past decade. I have a slightly hard time trusting people, especially men, so I've stuck with Matt despite his flaws. I'd rather deal with the devil I know than the one I don't. So I choose my words carefully. "I'm so sorry he did that. I wish I could say I can't believe it . . . but I totally can, and it's messed up. And all too common. I wish I had a better reason to give, but I basically am just with him because it's worked for me so far, he gets the bookings."

Jillian frowns and looks at me closely. "Does he say stuff like that to you? Still?" I don't say anything, but she can read the answer all over my face. "You don't need to put up with that. This isn't ten years ago, and you're you. You'll get bookings no matter what."

Each of us has decided what price we're willing to pay for security. All major campaigns look to the same agencies first. And some girls will accept an agent that comments on their weight because he gets the best bookings, while others would rather sacrifice some big jobs or working more to have someone who's actually kind. But she's correct that wherever I go, the big jobs will follow. "You're right, but I mean . . . here we are." I shrug apologetically, uncomfortable.

"To be continued," Evonique teases, lightening the mood. "Now, back to the task at hand?"

Rachel nods enthusiastically. "Okay, here's what you do," she instructs. "We can all tell he still has it bad. Forget about tomorrow, or the rest of the week. We're taking things day by day. It's getting hot out, you have last shot. So at the end of the day suggest walking in the water in your dress. They love that shit. Think it's so real, even though no one I know is going to walk into the ocean fully clothed. But anyway, you get in, get wet. And get him in that water with you, remind him of old times on his boat." She leans back in her seat, clearly pleased with herself. "Then see what happens."

Four excruciating hours later, after brainstorming lines with each girl, I'm in the water up to my knees, dress floating around me, ends of my hair dripping. But not with ocean water, like some people would assume. Instead, my hair is wet with saltwater spray that the stylist painstakingly applied. My heart thuds in my chest during the entire shoot, betraying how nervous I am even as I smile confidently.

After an eternity, Theo finally lowers the camera. "I think

we're good." He glances at Stacey and Miranda, who nod in quiet agreement. "Well, that's a wrap!" he says, smiling at everyone. "Thank you, guys. This has been a great day. Good work."

He hands Kevin his camera and then extends a forearm toward me. I try not to read into the fact that he isn't reaching for my hand or my waist like he did before.

All around us, the crew is dispersing, ready to go back to the hotel and drink, numb away the pain of standing for so many hours. Assists start breaking down the scrims and packing apple boxes and coolers of water onto the cart to drag the gear up the beach. Theo starts to walk back in toward shore after I make no move to take his forearm.

"It's warmer than home," I say, trying to bring his attention back to me. I'm not in a hurry to join everyone else.

Theo turns back to me. The water laps toward him, soaking the hem of his rolled-up pants. "Anywhere is warmer than home."

I move toward him. With only a foot between us, we're the closest we've been since this morning. I feel the hair on my arms prick up, and my entire body leans toward him. When we're together I like to think that our pulse, our heartbeats, synchronize.

He takes a step toward me, water seeping up to his knees. I had goosebumps when we were shooting, but now they're fading as I warm from the thrill of having his attention. His cheeks are flushed from the sun, and his skin is dotted with salt from the ocean spray. I want to lick it off him.

"Will you have to shoot this dress again?" I ask, fighting against the gravitational pull his body has on mine.

"No," he says, his voice barely above a whisper.

I want to reach for him, but it's too soon, and there are still a few people packing up on the beach. Instead, I turn and dive into the water. He pulls his phone from his pocket and throws it up the beach onto the sand. Then he dives in after me.

I move toward him, so that when we rise our shoulders touch, which is suddenly the most sexual feeling I've had in a decade, maybe my entire life. I don't feel the cold, I don't feel anything except those few inches of skin.

All I want is to wrap my legs around him, to press myself against his abs, to wrap my arms around his neck and devour him. I'm braless, and I catch his eyes dropping down to my dark nipples, peaked against the thin white cotton. When I walked onto set in this dress, Theo stopped talking midsentence. I couldn't acknowledge it then, but now I reach out and tuck my fingers under his chin, bring his eyes back to my face. "You're staring," I reprimand, my voice teasing.

As soon as the words are out of my mouth, I feel nervous—I've forgotten what it feels like to not know what a guy will respond to me. It's scary, but it's also exhilarating.

Theo laughs weakly. He takes off his hat and runs his wet hands through his curls before pulling it back on, letting the ocean mix with the sweat that already darkens his brim. "I'm sorry. This dress was made for you."

"I'm keeping it." I decide on the spot that I'll take it home with me, and only ever wear it if I'm going to see him again. "Theo, you're amazing at your job. I love . . . I *loved* today." There's more I want to say—more I almost said—but I stop there.

"You make it easy," he answers. "I could fill every card with pictures of you. Especially in this dress." Theo suddenly steps forward and wraps me in a hug, his strong arms enclosing me. The feeling of safety fills me. Whenever I was with him, I was fearless. Because I knew that as long as he was with me, things would be okay. Even when my mom was consumed with stockpiling toothpaste instead of driving me to school, or a bat got into the house and she just locked herself in her bedroom and left me to deal with it, as soon as Theo arrived I had complete certainty that things would be okay. Because with him by my side it would be impossible for everything not to be. We are different people now, but somehow that feeling remains.

"Hey, you two!" Jillian waves from the beach.

Theo pulls back from the embrace suddenly, as though chastened. His cheeks flush and he takes two giant steps away from me.

"We're leaving!" Jillian yells. "Jeep keys are here for you, but no rush." She drops the keys and scampers back up the beach. I know the other girls are somewhere nearby, waiting for her report.

Theo turns back to me, and the softness that was in his voice less than a minute ago is gone. "We should go back," he says. "Don't want to start rumors."

"Right, of course," I say, trying hard to keep the disappointment out of my voice. If we hadn't been interrupted, if we'd just had another few minutes alone . . .

He nods, and leads the way out of the water. I follow him, knowing that whatever the moment was we were having is passed. But this has gotten us from awkward to . . . something better. I'm not beat yet.

CHAPTER TEN

Theo

Watching Emerson walk away from me is pure torture. Her dress clings to her, and as I watch her stride out of the water I realize with a jolt she might not be wearing underwear. I linger behind her, trying to calm myself down before I lose the shield of the ocean. *Get it together, dude.* I've shot models in the tiniest outfits, topless even, so it's not like I've never seen a girl in a wet dress before. But this is Em. Touching her felt as natural as breathing, and the moment I let go I wanted to do it again. But I can't let her see that. Not after the message I got from Matt last night.

Remember to keep things professional on this shoot. X

The uppercase X felt like a threat.

By then, I had already set up her matcha delivery, because I could hear her crying through the wall. I wanted so badly to comfort her. My answer came out harsher than I meant it. Because it's not the kiss I regret, it's that the kiss ruined our friendship. I'd have rather never kissed and had the last decade as just friends, if those were the options. But I'm also ashamed to admit that it was slightly validating to know she's hurt over everything between us too. I'm just getting whiplash from her back-and-forth. One minute she's coming out to talk to me and saying she wants to reconnect, and the next having a feeling that overwhelms her and she's running away. And having her team tell me off. I made sure to keep my distance today, but just now it felt like I was with the Emerson I used to know, and I want to freeze us in those moments.

Once we're on the rocky sand, I realize she's shivering. I shove my hands in my wet pockets so I can't forget to keep them to myself. Even when we were genuinely just friends we were always touching each other, and I knew it wasn't normal, wasn't like any other friendships around me, but I didn't care. I was hungry for her. "Just wait here," I tell her before running ahead to find something, anything, that will warm her up.

My assists have left my things unceremoniously in a pile on the rock ledge near where our base camp used to be. I grab my pullover and jog back to her. I toss her the jacket from several feet away . . . and instantly regret it. She doesn't see it coming, and so it hits her chest and falls at her feet. *God, what is wrong with me?* She must think I'm such an asshole.

Emerson picks up my jacket and pulls it on. It swallows her. She's tall, and so has never been drowned in my clothes, but I've bulked up a bit since high school. It reaches her upper thigh, and so with a quick eyebrow raise at me, she slinks her arms back into the jacket, and moments later I see the wet dress fall onto the sand.

A strangled sound comes out of my mouth and her laugh is glorious. I rush to say something coherent. "Sorry, they didn't leave much else here."

"This is perfect," she assures me.

I can't stop staring at her. Her legs are smooth and impossibly long, and my sleeves cover all but her fingertips. Her hair is longer than I've ever seen it and dangles across the front, spilling water onto the fabric.

I can't even think about what's under my jacket.

I want to see her in every piece of clothing I own.

Emerson tosses me the keys and we walk up the beach, until we've reached the town. It's quiet now, caught in the early evening hours pre-dinner, which doesn't happen here until nine o'clock at the earliest. An Italian version of siesta, according to our local guide, who was tasked with explaining to everyone on set today why they'd have to wait three hours after wrapping to eat. As we walk, Emerson and I oscillate between being overly close to one another and too far apart, sending us each not so subtly crashing back. I want to reach for her hand or, better yet, to ask her about that text from Matt. But I don't, because I've already stretched the definition of *professional* today, and I don't want Emerson to think I'm pushing it.

When we get to the car, I knock my boots against the pavement, trying to get rid of as much as sand as possible. I've never gotten used to the decadence of a shoot, to not worrying about cost. Every car our team uses this week will lose its deposit to a deep clean, and no one will flinch when they see the bill, which could be upward of five grand in cleaning alone.

Emerson climbs in, not hesitating to cover the beautiful leather interior with wet sand. It's strange how much time can change a person. The Emerson I knew was hyperconscious of money and would have been anxious about being charged for the damage. She saved every penny she made senior year so she could get her own place once she had graduated. But now she just sits in the passenger seat, totally calm, texting with someone I can't even begin to guess at. I shouldn't be surprised—she's famous, and if my online search last night is to be believed, *super* rich. And I'm so happy for her. She deserves that level of success more than anyone I know, and after seeing how she lived growing up . . . knowing she never has to worry about money anymore makes my heart swell. But how could that kind of lifestyle change *not* make you a different person? My only worry is . . . Has the way she sees me changed too?

I start up the car and drive us back to the hotel. I thought it might be strange sitting next to her again, but instead driving with Emerson is the most natural feeling in the world. The summer I got my license we spent five days driving across the country, camping every night and stopping at random attractions along the way. When we drove, talking seemed to be easier for Emerson. Maybe because we weren't making eye contact, or because half her focus was on the road, she was able to tell me things she glossed over when we were sitting across from each other at dinner. How badly she wanted to be the opposite of her chaotic mom, how anxious she sometimes got at school. How much she wanted to be a success once she started modeling, and how scared she was to fail. How much she wanted to leave and have a big life in some way but thought it was an impossible dream.

Back then she was the one full of doubts and dreams, while I was had this absolute confidence things would work out, that I now know was born out of ignorance. Or innocence. I wonder now if she's the one who's content, and I'm the one who will start spilling out everything I'm still striving toward, the doubts I have about my talent, the insecurities over sacrificing the career-focused LA or NYC life for family.

But before I can say anything, my phone buzzes in my pocket. I pull it out and see it's a text from Kevin.

attached Emerson's contract, Stacey sent that last page to all the guys. I know you knew her when but I don't want to see you get screwed. Her agent built in all this stuff about her not being alone with male crew members, only stylist touches her, not the typical deal. Be careful.

My knuckles go white on the wheel. Why is that in her contract? Is Matt going to find out about this and get me fired? But more importantly, *Why is that in her contract?* The thought that something might have happened to her over the course of the last decade when I wasn't in her corner makes uncomfortable pinpricks of emotion smart behind my eyes, my pulse race, my stomach churn.

"Emerson, are you okay? I'm really asking. Because if you're uncomfortable right now, I want you to tell me. Because I want you to be happy. To feel safe." I grip the steering wheel. "And I kept myself from calling all those years by telling myself that you were happy. I don't want having to do this shoot together to upset you, but I need you to know I'm right here with you."

My knuckles are white on the steering wheel as I wait for her response. The silence is excruciating. All I can hear is the engine rumbling as we climb uphill, and her shallow breaths as she decides what to say. I hate that I'm making her nervous, but selfishly I need to hear what she says. After spending a day with her, every feeling I've ever had for her is rushing through my brain. Emerson places a manicured hand on mine, lightly, quickly. My gut twists. "Theo, can you pull over? I will answer, but I don't want us to plummet to our deaths here."

She has a point. The road back to the hotel winds from the beach back up along vineyards and has a tremendous drop-off. We drive in silence for at least a mile, until the road widens enough for me to pull off onto the grassy side. I turn to Emerson, my eyes imploring her to answer me. "Em."

She takes a deep breath and turns to face me in her seat. "Right now? I'm fine. But no one is happy for ten years, Theo." Emerson breaks eye contact with me, but before she does I see the sadness in her gaze, a type of bitterness that was never there when we were kids. "I have a fantastic life. I love my home, I'm good at my job." She brings her gaze back up to me. "I mean, those years with you were . . . absolutely everything to me. But I'm also different now, my life is different. It was a long time ago. I've changed."

Those years *were* everything to her. Past tense. All of the scar tissue I've built up around my heart is ripped out in that moment.

No one I have ever been with has measured up to Emerson. They all eventually dumped me because I was emotionally unavailable. Allison is my closest friend and was my only serious girlfriend, and even she eventually left me. "You were everything to me, too," I finally say.

Emerson wraps her hands around mine, and I lean over from the driver's seat and press my forehead into her wet hair. "To be honest, now that I'm here . . . It's not what I expected," she says, "but I'm glad we have this week."

If she were here, Allison would tell me to protect myself. Steer clear. But I can't lose Em again. I'll prove to her over the next three days that I can be her friend, if she'll let me. Being her friend again can be enough. It'll have to be, because her agent has made it abundantly clear that she doesn't want more than that, and now Emerson has too. "Me too," I say. "I'm glad you're here too."

Emerson tucks her head against my neck, her face nestled into my shoulder, and although I can't see it or prove it, I think her lips are against my head, in a silent, private kiss. I'm not sure if it's a goodbye kiss or something else, but it feels like the end—of an era, of my hopes, of us.

I stay there until I feel her shiver against me. Once Emerson is cold she stays that way until she can submerge in hot water. I used to sit outside her bathroom door while she soaked in her tub, listening to an audiobook, and we shouted at each other through the door.

Emerson pulls back and opens her mouth to say something, the pinch of her eyebrows telling me it's going to be serious, important. And even though I'm dying to hear everything she has to say for the rest of my life, I realize I have to stop her. I'm not ready to hear why she rejected me back then, or why she's going to do it again now. I need at least another day with her before I hear why I'm not enough.

"You can tell me when you're cold," I say in a rush. "You always used to speak up for yourself."

Emerson is quiet for a beat too long, whatever she was about to say swallowed. I feel guilty about just how relieved I am. "Just not a complainer anymore, I guess." She laughs it off but I see her eyebrows pinch slightly. "It kind of gets trained out of you, you know? I always want to be easy for the client, keep my reputation up. Complaining just feels wrong now. Dangerous."

Dangerous. More alarm bells go off in my gut. But she's just talking about complaining, I remind myself. Nothing more. "I get that," I say as I navigate the huge car across the winding road. "I'm always catering to the client. I adhere to their vision, pitch rates that I think they'll support because I know they're not the highest around, but they're also not so low that I look cheap, pretend to not want a break when we're an hour away from overtime and still have five looks and a bucket of skincare and grab-and-go items."

"Exactly," she says, nodding. "I never get to call the shots. Sometimes men say I'm a *creative*, but I might actually have the least creative job in the fashion industry. Bringing other people's dreams to life."

"I get that. I feel like I'm doing the same thing, constantly. I always say I'll shoot my own show, but somehow I never end up doing it."

"You have to do it," Emerson orders me. "You're officially booked. That's your next gig, says me."

I glance at her, struck by how passionate she sounds. It reminds me of when we were kids. "I wish it was that easy," I say.

"Just wait until the end of the week," Emerson warns. "I'm pretty convincing when I want to be."

I laugh. "Trust me, I remember. But doing my own show would mean I'd have to move back to New York. If I made the jump to arthouse, I'd have to blow my savings on my own shoots and space, maybe for nothing. Even to shoot better branded stuff I'd need to rebuild a lot."

"Theo. Please bet on yourself. If you don't, then who will?"

I flush. I have plenty of friends—Allison, Kevin, other photographers—to talk to about this stuff. But while they get what I'm saying, they don't always get *me*. Even after all these years it feels like, in an instant, Emerson can understand everything about how I feel better than they ever could.

Am I still the one who understands her better than anyone? I know I'm pushing this conversation, but I want to know more about who she is now. "What about you? You said you're good at your job, which, I mean, is obviously an understatement. But do you love it?"

Emerson looks out the window, away from me. We've never lied to each other, and I can see her struggling to find a palatable way to tell the truth. "No. But I love everything that it gives me. I never even dreamed I would have all this, and it's what I'm good at."

"Emerson, at this point you've probably made enough money for eternity. If it's not what you love, you should quit and find that thing instead." She doesn't say anything, but I can see her swallow nervously out of the corner of my eye. "What about your writing? You used to love that."

"Theo, I didn't go to college. Yeah I read a lot, but I'm hardly a writer." Her tone is harsh.

"Your writing was amazing! I loved your stories." She used to read the short stories she wrote out loud to me over the phone.

This finally gets her to at least look at me and smile. "Well, you're literally the only one who's ever read them."

"Maybe it's time to change that."

"It would be crazy for me to quit modeling. Being a pretty face is what I'm good at. And my team would flip if I quit to write a novel." Her words are firm, but I can tell that what I've said surprised her. She's thinking about it, and from the way she's trying to tamp down a smile, it seems like she likes the idea.

"Well, all that matters is that you're happy. But I saw you work today, and you should give yourself a lot more credit. For modeling, and everything else." She doesn't answer me, so we ride in silence the rest of the way. Everyone else in her life is probably reliant on her for income, so it's no surprise they'd want her to keep modeling no matter what. I can't help but wonder if she has anyone in her life who's actually looking out for her happiness, not just her success.

I pull the car up to the hotel entrance so she doesn't have to walk in the cold from the garage. "You go, I'll park."

Emerson opens her mouth to argue, but then something dims behind her eyes. "Fine. I'll see you later." She starts to climb out, then turns back. "To confirm the dates for your show, which you are definitely doing."

"Right, right," I play along. "I'll try to sort out the venue on my thirty-second walk inside while you write the first half of the next Pulitzer."

She climbs out, but before she can walk away, I say, "Hey, Emerson?"

"Yeah?" She pauses and ducks her head back into the car while one hand holds down the bottom of my jacket.

"You can always talk to me," I say. "About anything. Even if it's complaining. Or send me your stories. I'll be disappointed if you don't."

I watch through the lobby glass until she's safely inside the elevator, and then pull the car out and back onto the street. I pull into the small Italian convenience store lot and peel my wet clothes off the seat to go in. Emerson was big on snacks, and before any long drive we'd stock up on the essentials. For me, it was Sour Patch Kids, KitKats, and Pringles. For her, it was Reese's Peanut Butter Cup Minis and some form of popcorn.

Today, I only want her snacks, so I grab two of every popcorn snack and every variation of Reese's, plus an Italian peanut butter chocolate cup for good measure. I pay and portion out the snacks into two separate bags. I almost asked her what she wanted when she was getting out of the car, but at the last minute I balked, terrified that her answer would reveal I no longer knew anything about her.

Twenty minutes later I'm walking out onto my balcony to see if Emerson is there. She's sitting at the table, gazing out at the view as she chugs a supersize bottle of water. It's a glass bottle, clearly meant to be poured, but she drinks straight from it in massive gulps. "They'll send more up, you know," I tease as I step through my door.

Emerson swallows with a gulp and laughs. "I don't drink too much during the day. I don't want to bloat in the swim. So now I think I could drink five of these. Although if I knew you were coming, I would have brought out the cups."

"Hold on." I go back inside and get two more bottles of water, then pass a bottle and the bag of snacks across the balcony. She leans across and takes the bag and bottle carefully, so that they don't fall down onto the cliffs or sparkling water. I open the bottle and take a sip directly from it while she looks in the bag. "Don't use cups on my account."

When she looks up, her eyes are sparkling with delight. "Don't go anywhere," she commands. She runs back into her room, and when she returns her hands are full of KitKats and Pringles.

"These are for you. You probably survive on Clif Bars or something now, but I stocked up at the airport just in case." She thrusts the food toward me. "And what's in your other bag?"

I still have one convenience store bag next to me on the table. "I got duplicates of all your snacks," I admit.

She's silent, but a smile plays on her face, and she ducks her head down bashfully. "I won't confirm or deny whether I still have KitKats and chips in my room."

"You hate chips." I hold open my own bag and reach across the balcony, and she drops my snacks into it.

"I missed you." She smiles at me, and it's so bright and real—nothing like her picture-perfect model smile—that it makes my heart stop.

By the time I get over those three words, Emerson has opened one of each of the snack options and is politely waiting for me to become lucid again. "I missed you too," I whisper, but I don't know if she hears me over the water crashing through the rocks and the amount of noise she's making with all of her wrappers.

If she does hear me, she doesn't acknowledge it when she speaks. "So, two questions today?"

"Sure. You start?"

She nods emphatically. "That's only fair." She tilts her head to think as she makes a disgusting sandwich out of Reese's and chips and takes a resounding bite. "What's your favorite thing about your work?"

Not a bad start. "Let's see . . . probably the challenge aspect of it. I'm not doing something as creative or glamorous as editorial work. But I am doing something that requires me to be smart and think on my feet." My cheeks flush slightly. I feel silly speaking highly of what I do when it's so much less impressive than her career. "It's not what I imagined for myself, but I do like it. And I like getting to go to places like this. And get paid for it. A lot of people want to get paid to take pictures, and most people never do, so I'm pretty lucky." I could get more honest, but it feels too soon. I don't want to bare my soul and make myself vulnerable when this is just a game for her. She's going to leave in a week, and I'm setting myself up to get hurt.

"What's your favorite part about your job?" I turn the question back on her.

"This counts as your question," Emerson cautions.

"I know. I want to know." I break into my snacks while she thinks.

"For a while it was the travel. You know how badly I wanted to get out of my house, out of Salem. Just to have my own life. And I've gotten to travel basically everywhere. I even did a shoot for Canada Goose in Antarctica! Now, the travel has gotten a bit tiring, so I'd say it's just that I can have a comfortable life. I don't have to worry about how much a bill will be at a restaurant, I have a home that I love, I have some level of certainty in what my life and future look like. And even if I earned it for something superficial that I'm paid way too much for, I still earned it."

"You did earn it. What does your mom think of it all?"

"It's actually my turn."

I think she's evading my question. But it is her turn. "Fine. Ask away."

She thinks for a moment. "How's your dad?" I hesitate, and she keeps talking for a moment, before I can tell her to stop. "He said he'd walk me down the aisle you know, when we got married. I told him I had no idea what he was talking about. But it was sweet."

My eyes burn. He always knew how much I liked Emerson. And he insisted that when you know you know. He knew my mom was the one from the moment he saw her, and he said I was lucky to meet Emerson so young. That he wished he'd had those years with my mom too. At high school graduation he cheered as loudly for Emerson as he did for me, as though she was already his daughter-in-law. "Emerson . . . my dad died. He had a heart attack."

Emerson gasps and tears fill her eyes. "What? When?"

I sigh and look away. I can see how much this hurts her. But it still hurts me too. "Three years ago this summer. He had his first heart attack a few years before that, which is why I left New York. He didn't want me to, but I didn't need to be there for my 'career' anyway. It was obvious that going home was what I needed to do. After he got out of the hospital, he retired, spent time with his grandkids, with my mom. But he had another one three years ago, and it was just too much for his heart. They couldn't revive him."

Em squeezes her eyes shut, trying to hold back the tears that escape the moment she opens them. She tries to wipe them away, but they're coming too fast. "Theo, I am so sorry. I should have known. And been there."

I'd thought her mom must have told her. But I can see on her face that she genuinely had no idea. I get up and reach a hand across the balcony. My eyes are wet now, too, and when she stands and grasps my palm, her hands are damp. She can barely reach me, and we're both leaning too far out over the few feet of air that separate the ornate railings, but I don't care. I squeeze her hand tightly as a tear escapes my eye. But I don't break my hold on her to wipe it.

"I'm sorry," she says softly. "I shouldn't be the one who's upset right now. You're the one who's grieving." Her light brown eyes are wet and glassy, but trained on me, unflinching in her apology.

"Em, it's okay. I've had time to come to terms with it. I know he was family to you too."

She squeezes my hand tighter. "Theo, if I had known . . . I would have been there."

"It's okay. I know you're busy," I say immediately.

"None of that matters. I would have been there. I'm here now."

I squeeze her hand one more time, then let go, step back, overwhelmed with all the raw emotion coursing around us. I forgot what it's like being around her. I'm alive. I feel everything ten times more. In the best possible way. But when it's related to my dad, it's too much. "I think it's my turn."

"Right," Em agrees.

She's so emotional, I can't ask her about her mom now. I know it's going to be a sore subject. "Is maple still your favorite flavor of donut?" I ask instead.

She laughs in relief at the question, as she continues to wipe away tears. "Are you sure? This is your last question today, and I have to answer anything you ask."

"I'll have more tomorrow."

Her smile is bright and genuine. "Of course it is. But glazed has replaced chocolate frosted as the runner-up slash option that I actually end up getting, since maple isn't a standard flavor."

I throw my hand to my chest in mock shock. "How dare you? Stealing my favorite flavor after all these years?"

She raises both hands in surrender. "What can I say? Fame changes a person."

I laugh and am surprised to realize that it's completely real. That I've forgotten the tension and hurt between us, at least in this moment. "Well it's a good thing I asked. Now I know that if they bring donuts to set, I have to either have them get maple or beat you to the tray."

"Challenge accepted," Emerson says lightly. She picks up her second water bottle and drains the last sip.

"I guess that's our cue," I say quickly. I want to end things on a high note.

Emerson looks like she wants to argue, but instead she puts the empty bottles in the convenience store bag I got her and stands. "Right. Time for room service and beauty sleep. But I'll see you tomorrow."

"Goodnight, Em," I whisper as she walks back inside. I don't mean for her to hear me, but right before the door is fully closed she presses her mouth to the inch it's cracked open.

"Goodnight, Theo."

4
Days Remaining

CHAPTER ELEVEN

Emerson

The next day is exhausting. We shoot swimsuits for hours, barely taking any breaks. I do my best not to show my exhaustion or how cold I am, but when I finally rise out of the ocean after shooting three bikinis in a row entirely underwater, my body betrays me and I'm racked with a dramatic shiver. I'd held it in the past few looks, forcing myself not to run to a towel, to wait patiently while Stacey looks over Theo's shoulders at the shots, even though I know he's got it. But this time I can't help it.

"Can someone get her a towel?" Theo shouts without taking his eyes off me. A PA rushes to offer me one, and I try not to look too relieved.

Temperature aside, I love shooting underwater. I've only done it a few times, but it's always extra engaging. Most sets don't want any bubbles to rise up through the water, so you have to hold your breath entirely, and when you're under you can't hear anything, so you're completely reliant on your instinct and whatever instructions the director gave you before you went under. I hate opening my eyes underwater, especially in the ocean, but I've gotten used to it. Theo clearly hasn't, since he's currently wearing the nerdiest goggles *ever*. They cover half his face. He looks completely ridiculous and utterly charming.

"Emerson, do you mind if we get one more shot?" Theo asks.

There was a time when he never called me by my full name. I want to get back to that. And I think we're on the right path.

"Of course," I say, throwing the towel back to the sand. I wade a few strides deeper into the water. The underwater housing on the camera is surprisingly fragile looking, but Theo palms the camera with confidence. His clothes are slicked to his body and I know he must be almost as cold as I am, since he hasn't been able to run out after each shot and warm up for a minute. I can see the chill through his clenched jaw, but to anyone else he would appear totally relaxed.

"Everything you've been doing is great; we just want to get one from below, of you floating on your back. To show the ruching."

"We should probably get a little deeper, then, since you'll need to be totally below me." I wade out until I can just stand on my tiptoes. Theo follows, his head barely above the water, the waves gently splashing against his chin. Although Kevin initially waded in and was followed shortly by Theo's second assist, hair and makeup lingers by the shoreline, disinclined to get wet. Even Miranda and Stacey haven't gone in past the hem of their shorts. Miranda volunteered her assistant stylist as tribute instead, and has been micromanaging her every adjustment. But Theo and I are the only ones who have gone this deep.

"Hike up the sides!" Miranda yells to me from the shoreline.

I nod to her and yank the side of the bikini bottoms into a position that is completely for show—no one would ever actually wear it this way.

"You ready?" I ask. No one else can hear us now, and from this shorter distance I can see a slight blueish tinge on Theo's lips. I position myself in front of him, ready to lean back while he submerges under me.

"Yup, you lead. Whenever you start, I'll go under."

I turn and grin over my shoulder at him. A real smile, wide and imperfect, now that we're farther away from everyone else. "Tap me when you're up so I don't float all day. It's actually freezing."

"You're telling me."

I lie back and do my best to stay completely still so that I don't make any bubbles and can get this on the first take. I can't hear much with my ears submerged, but I imagine Theo snapping away below me. This bikini bottom is minuscule, something high school Theo would have teased me for wearing. He didn't say anything when he saw me walk out in it this morning, to my frustration. I've forgotten what it's like to feel loved for my brain, to have Theo hanging on to my every word, instead of a boyfriend's eyes wandering while I share a halfway authentic thought. I want to be Em, not Emerson.

Back in high school, before the end of senior year, after my modeling career started to take off, I suddenly started receiving clothes *all the time*. I'd arrive home to a box almost daily, and these weren't small boxes. These were moving-box-size packages of clothes from every brand imaginable, all in my size, with personalized notes. Skimpy, strappy designer swim replaced my trusty sportkinis, handmade rompers replaced my stretched-out cotton dresses from Target and, actually, Anthem. And all the flashy clothes changed how my classmates viewed me. But the way Theo treated me never wavered based on how hot or rich I looked.

We eventually take a break and wade back to the beach. After wrapping myself in an oversized towel, I duck into the changing tent. It's a luxury model, so instead of being a tiny black pop-up held down on the edges with rocks and sand, this is spacious enough for Miranda to come inside with me.

"Can you put this on?" she says, handing me a bright blue mesh coverup. "I want to throw a pin in it."

I pull it on, and Miranda starts tugging on the back of the

coverup, through which my white bikini shines through. It's more Santorini than Cinque Terre, but I love it. "We had these overnighted, because of course the merchants asked for one last change, which delayed everything." She slips the pin in. "But they still want the shot, so the tailor missed them, and now we're stuck repining between fronts and backs . . ."

"Well, don't worry too much, I'm efficient," I reassure her. Miranda shakes her head and keeps muttering under her breath. For all the grief she's giving the merchants right now, I'm sure that in the studio they're her right-hand girls, sending her samples to wear and asking her what trends to lean in to.

Miranda turns me to face her and sets about realigning the coverup. I gaze at the black nylon of the tent above her head and space out, until I hear Theo's voice inches away from us, on the other side of the tent wall.

"Allison, I'm telling you, it's not like that." Theo's throat sounds constricted, and I can imagine his face—flushed, defensive. "We were kids, we're both different people now. There's no reason we can't be friends. There's nothing like that between us at this point."

If I wasn't already standing still beneath Miranda's hands, I am now. He is *definitely* talking about me. I listen hard, desperate to hear what he says next. When he speaks, his voice is softer, maybe even . . . hurt.

"She isn't like that. You don't know her." He sighs. "I know. I care about you, too."

His voice trails off as he paces away. I blink rapidly, desperate to keep my head on straight. I need to distract myself. But I also need information. "Excuse me, Miranda? Who's Allison?"

"Photographer," Miranda barks as she gnaws on the final remaining pin. "Theo's known her since college."

My heart sinks. "Wow, that's a long time."

"Yep. They're sweet together, even if the whole on–off thing seems like a drag."

I suck in a sharp breath. *Oh my god.* Could he have a girlfriend? I close my eyes and try not to start crying again, but I feel like a complete fool. It was ridiculous of me to think he hasn't moved on, when any woman would be more than lucky to date him.

"Her work is good," Miranda continues. "We were going to use her for this shoot, actually."

"I thought you always used Theo?" A note of defensiveness creeps into my voice. He's been shooting Anthem for years. They could at least pretend to have a *little* loyalty.

"Girl, you know how things go. He's great, hasn't upped his rates in years, but sometimes that sends the wrong message to the people up top. Meanwhile, Allison shot a great spot for *Boyfriend* last spring, really made the sex toy bondage collection look PG, and we were willing to pay up for her. But then obviously your agent called and things changed. Budgets shifted, all that."

I can't believe Theo's maybe girlfriend was going to take his job. "Does he know?"

Miranda reaches around me to unzip the tent. "I doubt it. I can't imagine she'd tell him until something was confirmed. Why risk the fight, you know? But she was definitely on hold."

Miranda steps out into the sand. I stay behind, taking a moment to collect myself. A hold is halfway to booked. Brands put models *and* photographers on hold for a shoot so that no one else will book them for those dates. We don't get paid anything for a hold, and in theory could break it for a bigger, better campaign. But if we do, we risk the brand who placed the hold originally not wanting to work with us again. If I were Theo, I'd want to know if anyone was in line to take my most consistent client.

But this isn't my business. He has a career and apparently a *girlfriend*, or at least another woman who he has a lot of history with. He has a life, and I'm not part of it. I need to find out where he stands with Allison, because I'm not going to steal him away from someone else. But if they're not together . . . I need to keep moving forward. Otherwise, when this shoot ends, I'm going to need another decade of therapy to unpack exactly how it came to be that I missed out on being with Theo.

"Emerson, you ready?" Theo's voice instantly cuts through my thoughts.

"One sec!" I grab my phone and quickly fire off a text to Matt. This wasn't in the file Natalie sent me on Theo, but Matt always knows all the industry gossip.

Is Theo dating a photographer named Allison? Please confirm ASAP.

Before I can step out of the changing tent, my phone rings.

"Emerson. Ready to leave this sad excuse for a shoot yet?" Matt's tone is brisk and professional. I'd bet anything his finger is hovering over the Send button on an email, ready to extricate me from this entire situation.

"Are they together?" I ask, keeping my voice low in case Theo is nearby.

"Probably," he says. "I assumed you knew that already. But most men would stray for you, so—"

"Theo would never do that," I say, cutting him off. "And I would never do that to him."

"Fine, whatever," Matt says, clearly bored by this line of discussion. "Emerson, just say the word. There's no need to do this shoot. It's only day two."

The gears are turning rapidly in my brain. If Theo is taken and I leave now, it'll screw up the shoot and, worse, make me look like a total asshole to Theo and the rest of the crew. And if I stay and Theo is with Allison . . . it'll be torture. Pure torture. But Theo means everything to me. The only thing worse than the idea of watching him happy with someone else is the idea of going back to living my life without him. If I want an actual chance at keeping him in my life, I need to make him believe I'm content with being just friends. I need to make *myself* believe it.

"Emerson, you there?" Matt says, his voice sharp. "I have other clients, you know."

"Yes, sorry—I'm staying on the shoot. Have a good day."

I hang up and immediately dial Georgia. "Please tell me you're still in Santorini."

"Babe, what's wrong?"

I take a deep breath. I can't cry. I'm in full makeup and will not look puffy in these photos. "Nothing. Nothing's wrong. Being here is just . . . harder than expected. Can you come here for a night?" It would be less than two hours in her boyfriend's jet, and I'm feeling desperate.

"I'm sorry, babe, I had to pop over to Milan for a big meeting tomorrow morning, so I can't run out just this second."

"No worries," I say immediately.

"But you know, Harry is here with me right now, and he just finished a shoot in Milan." I can hear her whispering to him. "*You have a free two days, right? I think she really needs someone.*"

"Georgia!" I hiss. "No! Put it on speaker! Harry, you can't come, we can't be within ten feet of each other without *Harry and Emerson: Rekindling Their Romance* being the story of the week. I can't have Theo thinking we're together."

"It's always mutually advantageous!" Harry argues. "Let the paps live. Besides, I've never been to Cinque Terre; it'll be fun."

"Just tell Theo it's nothing," Georgia chimes in.

I'm silent on the other end of the line.

She laughs. "COMMUNICATE, BABE. It's not that hard."

I unzip the tent and look out at the water, where Theo is waiting for me patiently, his eyes trained diligently on the tent. He's the only man I care about. The thought him dating Allison for the past ten years is excruciating. Harry coming will complicate things in a way Georgia visiting wouldn't, but I could really use a friendly face. "Let me think on it. I'll text you."

"Too la—Emerson!" Harry has clearly snatched the phone completely away from Georgia. "I'll be there in three hours, we can do a late lunch. I'll have my people tell your people. A little show to make your man jealous wouldn't hurt either, no?"

"Absolutely not!" I whisper yell, but the line has already gone dead. I tuck my phone into my bag, and I walk toward Theo. He smiles, betraying no strain despite the problems me being here is apparently causing him. "This one can be super goofy, happy, splashing. Just go for it."

"Of course." I take a breath and turn my model face on. Then I get to work frolicking, running, and jumping in the water silently for three straight minutes. By the time Theo lowers his camera, I'm out of breath.

"That was great." Theo grins at me, and it feels like a reward, to see his genuine smile, not the tired, pressed one I've seen him using for the other models. "You make my job easy."

I stare into his blue eyes, and memories threaten to overtake me—of all the road trips, late nights, and those perfect kisses in the dark. Then I remember the way he sounded on the phone, talking to the woman he's loved the past ten years. A woman who isn't me.

CHAPTER TWELVE

Emerson

Matt texts me within twenty minutes, clearly having conferred with Harry's team. Now that Matt knows Harry's coming, it's basically guaranteed that paparazzi will be called, and this will become a huge spectacle. My gut churns knowing Theo will see how chaotic my life really is.

Harry Butler is bringing you lunch. I made sure you'll have a full hour break.

I look up from the text and see Stacey, Miranda, and Theo conferring. Stacey and Miranda look ecstatic, and Theo rolls his eyes and stalks off to take five. I pretend to be busy responding to Matt, but in reality am watching Theo's every move. He chugs an entire bottle of water, then fires off a few texts to someone— Allison? And then he turns away, and by the rise and fall of his broad shoulders, I'd guess he's doing some sort of breathing exercise.

Once we've cycled through the other models and it's my turn to shoot again, I place myself in front of him, knee-deep in the water. We've only been going for a minute or so, although it feels longer since he'll only look at me through his viewfinder, and instead of directing me he just tells Kevin how to adjust the bounce. And it's petty, but I'm happy that he feels something, anything, at the thought of me on a date with another guy. It makes me think I do have a shot with him, romantically.

I'm working up to breaking the silence when I see Miranda's and Stacey's eyes light up as they gaze over my shoulder. "Let's break for lunch!" Stacey calls instantly.

"We haven't finished this look yet." Theo and I speak simultaneously, and I laugh awkwardly.

We're still standing in the ocean, and I'm extremely aware of how little clothes I have on. Not that he's making it weird. I just know that while I'd have to mentally remove several layers of clothes to picture him naked, he is about six square inches of fabric away from actually seeing me naked.

"Don't worry about it." Stacey brushes off our concerns. Matt is cutthroat, and I've been easy this shoot, so it's not a total surprise that she's being accommodating. Her eyes are locked on Harry still, and look slightly unfocused, as though she's daydreaming. He has that effect on people.

I turn and wave at Harry, who very enthusiastically waves back. "Emerson! You look incredible!" His voice is suave and deep, and he looks picture-perfect in tan linen suit pants and a button-down. Not dissimilar to what Theo wore the other night, but undoubtedly more expensive. He gestures down the beach. "I've set up some snacks for us."

In the distance I can see a table with a checkered cloth, flowers, wine, and a gourmet-looking meal. There's no way he set that up himself. It's even a stretch to think his team got that together within hours of Georgia sending him to me. One of our agents must have persuaded Anthem to have their local guide arrange it. I understand what Harry's doing with trying to make Theo jealous, but given our history we're way too convincing. "Just give us a few minutes here!" I shout back.

"Of course!" He takes a few steps away and begins signing autographs. Eager fans have been watching from the beach all day, and seeing Harry show up has probably made their vacation.

"Let's finish the look," I say to Theo. He looks pained as he decides what to do. I'm sure Stacey wants him to defer to her. But I want to give him a good shot, something portfolio worthy, something to make up for all that I've done. "I'm sorry," I say softly, just to him. And I am sorry, for so many things, even if I still haven't made it around to my full-on apology. Then I turn to Stacey. "I want to finish it while we're here."

I start posing, and Theo wordlessly begins shooting again. The air between us is thick and silent. It's horrible of me, but I like knowing Theo might be jealous. Or maybe he's just pissed I'm messing up his job.

After a few minutes of shooting, the only sounds are of the slight splash of water as I move and the click of his shutter, Theo stops me. "Got it. Thanks." His words are clipped, and when he walks out of the water, he strolls right by Harry, who he has five inches on, and shakes out his hair.

Harry flinches when the water flecks his shirt. "Watch it," he hisses. "This is silk."

"Sorry, man," Theo shrugs. It sounds genuine. It's not. He shoves his hand in the pocket of his waterlogged pants, his fingers undoubtedly crossed within, his tell from when we were kids. He doesn't look back at me, but I watch until he's out of view, my gut twisting. Why didn't I say anything? I should have whispered to him now, told him that this is nothing. That he's why I'm here. But my stomach is churning and my emotions are so volatile I can't say a word.

When I wade out of the water, Harry bids the fans goodbye and takes the towel from the PA so he can gallantly wrap me in it. And I hear the first click of a professional camera. I wonder if it was my team or his that tipped off the paparazzi, persuaded them to come all this way.

"Let me just change. You look lovely." Photos of him in a suit and me in a bikini eating lunch will break the internet.

"Why don't I just join you?" Harry takes off his shirt and holds it out. An assistant, a small woman with a clipboard and a bottle of coconut water, rushes forward to take it. She puts it on a hanger and holds out a hand. Awkwardly, I hand her my towel, leaving me in the small white bikini. Harry takes a long swig of coconut water while we all wait, then hands the bottle back to her. Next, he turns to the paparazzi. "Thank you all for what you do. Would you mind staying a few yards back from us? Take all the pictures you want. But I just want a bit of privacy while I have lunch with this absolutely breathtaking woman."

"You know that's not how they work—" I begin, but to my surprise, the men back away about ten feet, though they keep snapping away. Harry offers me a hand and leads me across the beach. "How did you do that?"

"It's my natural charisma."

"Bullshit," I whisper as we walk side by side. Every step on sand feels like five. And I might be taller than him.

"Fine. I paid them each ten to listen and make me look good."

I turn toward him, eyes flashing. "That's a hundred grand. What else did you promise?"

He smiles, and it's clear why everyone loves him. He's gorgeous. Perfectly constructed. I would bet money all he's done is Botox too, not even a nose job, though he won't tell even me and Georgia. "That I'd take my shirt off. And that I'd kiss you. And if I don't kiss you, they get double."

"Harry! I told you, I don't want Theo to think I'm into you. We're in stage one, initiate genuine friendship." Everything is fragile.

"This will set the stage for us . . . just in case things don't

work out," Harry argues in a whisper. "And besides, if me showing up here doesn't get you to stage two, which must be what,
make him fall back in love with you? You're done. Jealousy is a
powerful motivator. Seeing you with me should wake him up and
remind him you're a catch and this is his shot."

"You better be right," I mutter. For some reason walking hand
in hand with the most eligible man in the world does nothing to
me, whereas I can barely string a coherent sentence together when
I'm next to Theo. And now I'm thinking of Theo, so of course my
hand is suddenly drenched with sweat.

Harry looks down at our clasped palms, and I can actually see
his gears turning as he works to keep the disgust at my swampy
hands off his face. But thinking of Theo watching this from down
the beach makes me feel sick.

"He's cute, I'll give you that. And I've never seen you act
so . . . so open with someone."

"Yeah, so stop blocking me." I squeeze his hand tighter in my
sweaty one until it makes a disgusting wet noise. I know he won't
drop my hand in front of the paps.

"I'm helping! Current you and future us if the plan fails. And
you *know* I'm right."

"Whatever."

Harry turns his head and pretends to gaze lovingly at me,
only to narrow his eyebrows and glare. "Save putting me in the
doghouse for when we're fake dating, babe."

When Harry pulls out his chair for me, he leans close to my
ear and whispers, "Come on. Just enjoy this lunch. It'll be good
for both of us! After it gets out you're on this shoot, you'll need
the social capital boost. And this is a good reminder of how much
fun we had, back in the day. Because if you can't find real love,
isn't this the next best thing?"

"What about Evie? Or David? You actually liked them. Don't
you want the real deal with them?"

Evie is a stunning, Oscar Award–winning actress, who I know for a fact would get back with Harry in a heartbeat, because she genuinely likes him. And David is an extremely hot ex-NFL player who came out to close friends as gay last year, after dating me and every other model in town, doing all three iterations of *The Bachelor*, and marrying and divorcing an actress.

"Evie is a great actress, but a boring person. And I'm not going into the closet to be with David. My fans love a bisexual short king."

I turn away from the paps, toward the water, and pretend to gag. "You're too old to use that type of lingo. My ears are burning."

Harry sighs heavily, although his face still looks blissful. "I'm trying to stay young and fresh! How else am I going to take over all the industries if you won't date me?"

Harry appraises me, waiting to see how I'll react. I know he really wants this contract between us. And I get it. He's the best boyfriend I've ever had, the only one I actually was myself with, hence our friendship. We'd have a good time together. And to be honest, right now I don't know how things will go with Theo, so maybe it doesn't hurt to set myself up for the future. I glance toward the beach and don't see Theo, so I give Harry a slight nod, and then point toward the water, angling our faces away from the paparazzi, who may as well be professional lip readers.

"No tongue," I whisper. "And I get to pull away first."

"Sold," Harry agrees.

"And then we're done talking about the contract until after the shoot." Harry really doesn't need me as much as he thinks, so I don't want to let him wear down my resolve to go all in on winning over Theo. Harry's the most *it* person in Hollywood right now. He wore a dress on the cover of *Seventeen*, and it only made people love him more. I must remain a woman on a mission.

"Fine. But first I get to say one more thing." I roll my eyes but let him continue. "When we dated before, it was to both of our advantages. And let's be honest, so is our friendship, because it

keeps people guessing. So we *know* this plan is a guaranteed win.
I used all the buzz around us to propel every aspect of my career,
but you haven't. I know Matt's trying to sell you by saying it'll es-
tablish you as *the* modern supermodel. But I say, use this to move
on to the next thing at the same time. Don't retire except for leg-
acy campaigns like supermodels used to do. Start a business. Act
in something with me. Discover the next thing that you actually
love instead of limiting your dreams! This will get you to whatever you decide the next thing is, which, as your friend, I know
will be a completely awesome next chapter that I hope makes you
super fucking happy."

And this is why he and Georgia are my best friends. Because
they believe in me and push me more than I ever push myself.
"That's actually very sweet. And I'll keep it in mind. But that's the
last thing you get to say. Now shall we?" I stare pointedly at his lips.

Harry smiles. Game on. He turns back toward the table and
pours his wine, then rises to pour mine, stretching across the small
table with eyes only for me. Before he can pour it I raise a hand
to his neck and give the slightest tug, guiding him toward me. He
kisses me perfectly, his lips soft, breath minty, no tongue, and
sets down the bottle so he can cradle my face tenderly with one
hand. And then I pull away, and the conflicted expression on
my face is completely real. But I know no one will use that shot.

After Harry sits back down, it takes sixty seconds for the
paparazzi to scatter. Once they're gone I see Theo, who's been
standing behind them the entire time. The look on his face is gut
wrenching. Harry follows my gaze and pours me a healthy glass of
wine. "Everyone thinks we have it all, right?"

"We do have it all." I look away, since I would very much like
to lie to myself without him staring me down, and chase a hearty
sip of wine with a bite of salmon. It's decadent.

"I hope you told yourself that for as long as you could possibly believe it. Because it's clearly too late for you to go back to

how things were. But on the bright side, if you can't, I'll be there at your beck and call comforting you for minimum a year." His words make me feel sick to my stomach. But I don't let myself look over at Theo for the rest of the meal.

CHAPTER THIRTEEN

—Sophomore Year—

Theo

Before Emerson, I had never been self-conscious. I had my first girlfriend, Jenny, in second grade, who I asked out behind the slides and then held hands with for two weeks, until she wanted half of my popsicle, and I wasn't willing to share and broke up with her. Owen had prepped me thoroughly to secure a girlfriend freshman year, and before I even walked into orientation I had good prospects. Owen's girlfriend, Sara, stacked my orientation group with JV cheerleaders, but once Emerson walked over to our little circle, she was all I could see.

Thanks to Owen, I knew the drill. Get the number, text for a week, take them for ice cream (kiss), then dinner (first base in the car), then a movie (make it official). But Emerson clearly didn't play by that rulebook—she didn't even know there *was* one—and suddenly I was hooked.

Owen had told me that since she was low-key not cool at all, and since I was riding the coattails of his popularity while generating my own, it should have been easy. So, clearly, she wasn't interested. But I was determined to work on that and rise from the ashes of the friend zone.

And now, a guy with way worse moves than me was dating her. Jackson was a total idiot. He and Emerson had met in math class. In her date recap, she revealed that when he took her for ice cream, he neglected to pay the parking meter and was genuinely flummoxed when he got a ticket. I knew an opening when I saw it.

"Is this decorative?" I put on my bro-iest voice as I stepped out of the car outside Bagel World. "I've, like, never seen one, dude."

"Oh my god. Shut up, Theo." But I could hear the smile in her voice and see the grin she was fighting to keep down. I took it as a decidedly positive sign.

The line at Bagel World roped outside of the door, per usual on a Saturday morning. The building was completely average looking, more of a house than a business, but their bagels were revered across the North Shore. Two cheerleaders were canning, draped against the rails separating the ramp inside from the parking lot. A killer spot, since if you declined to give them money, you were then forced to stand next to them for at least ten minutes until the line moved enough for you to take shelter inside the building.

Clarissa, the more senior of the cheerleaders, rattled her coffee tin, decorated with a Salem High Cheer bumper sticker, and leaned so close to me that I could count her press-on eyelashes. I'd known her since we were five, and although she was still just as nice, somewhere between Little League and now she became the kind of girl I might not recognize if she didn't do her entire face of makeup. "Want to support varsity cheer, Theo?"

The other cheerleader was giving her a dirty look. But the look Emerson gave them took the cake. If looks could kill, these girls would be eviscerated. And a little jealousy could only help me. "Of course I do." I dropped a dollar in each of their cans.

"I'm cold." Emerson was standing so close to me that our arms were touching. "How long do you think until we're inside?"

"Take my sweater," I offered immediately. I loved seeing her in my clothes. At one point she had every single one of my sweatshirts, and I'd had to wear Owen's football hoodies. Then she returned them. But I was grateful to have them back, because they then smelled like her.

Emerson pulled my hoodie over her and let the hood drape halfway over her face, shielding her from having to see the cheerleaders. She never said anything to me, but sometimes I wondered if people were mean to her when I wasn't around. I knew no one would say anything to her or about her in front of me, but it never made sense to me that she didn't have her own friends. She had people she seemed to chat with in class, share homework with, but so far as I could tell, no one else she'd call at night just to talk to. No one else she really let in.

Once we made it through the doorway, the line was so extensive that Emerson ended up pressed against me by the swell of people. Her back was to my chest, her head against my chin. She let herself linger there for a moment, then moved to pull away. I surprised myself by taking her arm. "Better stay. I wouldn't want you getting crushed by the crowd."

"More like I'd step on them." Emerson was a solid five nine, after a much-lamented growth spurt over the summer that shot her already five-six frame up. Luckily, I had my own growth spurt and now stood at six three. I loved that I was one of only a few guys in school who was actually taller than her. Jackson, for example, claimed he was six feet but was more like five ten.

The line inside Bagel World always felt like it moved faster than the one outside. Though now that we stood so close, I willed there to be a holdup, someone ordering an entire sports teams' worth of complex bagel sandwiches and custom coffees. Halfway up was a cooler case that probably hadn't been replaced since the nineties, to match the signage that I heard was unchanged since 2000. At still only $1.60 for a bagel with cream cheese, it was totally possible the letters were glued to the board. I pulled a chocolate milk for me and a strawberry milk for her from the case.

Drinking an entire bottle of milk sounded gross to the average person. My cousin had pretended to gag when I took him here over the summer. But their milk was straight from Richardson's, a local dairy farm and famous ice cream stand, and these flavored milks were a class part of the Bagel World equation. Everyone knew it was only half an order without one.

When we were finally close enough to the counter to order, I heard a familiar voice behind me. I glanced over my shoulder and saw Jackson sitting at the largest table with five other football players. They each had huge bagel sandwiches laid out in front of them.

"I can already tell she's going to be a total freak in bed," Jackson crowed. His dark mullet was gelled up in an excessive display of vanity, and he wore sweatpants and a T-shirt, bulging biceps straining against the sides of the sleeves. He was probably too short to size up to a large. "Losers like her have to make up for it somewhere. I'm going to fucking break her in."

Emerson inhaled sharply, her cheeks turning scarlet. My shoulders stiffened, and I clenched my jaw. I wanted more than anything to swivel around immediately, but Em would always be my first priority. Making sure she was okay. The woman at the counter was asking what she wanted, but Em just stared mutely ahead. I placed my hand on the small of her back.

"We'll have one toasted veggie bagel, with jalapeño cream cheese and a slice of tomato. And one toasted French toast bagel with strawberry cream cheese and bacon." They moved fast at Bagel World. If I hadn't ordered, she would have just directed her attention behind us and called the next person.

We stood in silence as she prepared the bagels with lightning efficiency. She slid the bag across the peeling counter to us, and I guided Emerson back with me. I tried to meet her eyes, but she wouldn't look at me. "Can you hold these? I'll meet you in the car in a minute." I nodded toward the other exit, back past the line, so she could go out without Jackson seeing her.

As soon as she turned to leave, I was on him. It had been torture even waiting a few minutes after hearing what he said about her. I grabbed him by the collar and slammed him against the wall. "Don't ever go near Emerson again. Don't look at her. Don't speak to her. Don't speak *of* her. To you, she doesn't exist." Jackson didn't say anything, just glared at me. I let him go and started to walk away. But I couldn't let it go. I turned and shocked him with a punch to the face that sent him reeling.

I'd never punched someone before. I'd told Owen it was a waste of time teaching me to throw one, but he insisted on schooling me on both how to throw one and take one until I had to ice my hand and my face. I owed him.

Jackson's friends finally jumped up after I punched him, but I knew they'd think twice before going after their former captain's younger brother. Owen was a legend at Salem High.

"Say you understand." Jackson and I stared each other down. "Say it."

"Fuck off. I never wanted that bitch anyway."

I picked up an iced coffee from their table and dumped it directly in his face. Then I walked away. Adrenaline surged through me. Emerson deserved so much better than a guy like that. I walked out the door to the car, where she was sitting in the passenger seat, waiting for me, wrapped in my hoodie, about to spend a day with me.

I love you.

The thought came into my head, unbidden, as I walked toward her. I'd known I was into her since I met her. I liked her. I had a crush. I wanted her to be my girlfriend. But looking at her now, I realized I wanted so much more than that. I was completely in love with her.

I stared at her as I got into the car. There was no point of hiding the fight from her since news of it would be all over school on Monday. "Em, I—"

"Thank you. For defending my good name and all that. And for the bagel." I swallowed. She never needed to thank me for anything. "Just so you know, it was barely a kiss."

The thought of her kissing Jackson brought me physical pain. "None of my business." I started the car and began driving us toward the Willows. We'd planned to have our bagels by the beach, then drive into Boston to walk around, maybe go to a museum. "That's what friends are for, right? Sorry I went overboard."

"You're a good friend," Emerson murmured. Wisps of hair peeked out of the hoodie, and I wanted to brush them back and look at her. Tell her how I felt. "I'm never going on a date again," she continued. "Guys are such assholes. Except you, obviously. And now I'll never have to make eye contact with any guy on a sports team again."

"Mission accomplished," I joked with a weak fist pump. I pulled us into a parking space in front of the beach. Em opened the bag and without a word began rematching the bagels so we could go halfsies. Like always. "Em, you're better than all the guys at our school. Just forget about it."

"Theo, that's sweet. But I actually thought a guy liked me, and it turns out it was an elaborate ruse to sleep with me. I'm never dating again. Not in high school, anyway. I'll have a take two in my romance heroine era in New York or something when I move."

I hid my dread with a long drag of chocolate milk. "I promise you that he's just an idiot. You're so much more special a person than he is. With him, the first date convo is his peak; he probably used up every intelligent thought. With you, one conversation is the tip of the iceberg."

"Listen, I'm going to get a big head if you keep gassing me up." Emerson took a bite of the veggie bagel and tilted her head thoughtfully. "Surprisingly good combo here."

"Improvising is clearly my time to shine."

She laughed and chased it with a sip of strawberry milk. "Theo, do you mind if I rain check on Boston? I don't think I'm up for it today."

"We don't have to go to Boston. Let's just watch one of your chick flicks. I won't say a word of complaint." The last thing I wanted to do was leave her alone after a day like this.

"Well, you just called them chick flicks, so words have been said." I loved when she teased me.

"Amazing examples of cinema in which the woman is either a baker or a reporter and there's a happily ever after. I'll make popcorn."

"Movie day it is." She smiled, but her eyes looked sad, and before I could stop myself, I leaned across the dash and wrapped her in a strong hug. I pretended not to hear her sniffle and just held her tighter, until she had to be the one to break away.

CHAPTER FOURTEEN

Theo

I know Emerson and I are just starting to be friends again. But it stings to see her with Harry Butler when I know the entire world is rooting for them to get back together. There is nothing more romantic than the most eligible man in the world flying to Italy just to have lunch with you. She's used to a standard I would never be able to give her. The best I could do is take her to the local Italian restaurant in Salem, where the highest-tier entrée is twenty dollars. I am nowhere near the same echelon as Harry Butler. As Emerson. If I were a better friend, I would be rooting for her and Harry, if that's what she wants. Or her and anyone as fabulous as she is. But instead I'm jealous.

After shooting underwater looks for most of the day, I'm exhausted. Years ago, I worried that I was burnt out, and then Anthem booked me for an underwater shoot and I was reinvigorated. We were on a boat in Florida, and I spent two of the days in warm, clear water, completely flowing. For that campaign I shot flared yoga pants and flowing dresses underwater instead of swim, and it made a splash in the press. It was thrilling. Over the years I've gotten so used to shooting their stuff that on land, at least, I could do it without even paying attention, but in the water, I have to be on. I'm holding my breath, straining to see through fogged goggles. We started with the classic method of having someone hold me down by the belt, but I grew up by the water, and I felt constricted by the hands on my waist. Now, I leave a sandbag below me, so if I need an assist, I can tuck a foot under and yank myself down, but generally I just swim and let the weight of the housing guide me.

I push Stacey to do a short lunch and let me start working with the other girls while Emerson continues her date. I need to do something so I don't just sit for an hour and think about how much worse I am than Harry Butler. "Evonique, just give me one more, and really try to splay out your braids when you rise out of the water. I'm switching to a fast shutter and want to capture the droplets. Everyone else, move out a little."

My assists pull the scrim and silver bounce card out so it doesn't risk creeping into the corner of my shot, which happily further blocks my view of Emerson's lunch. The twenty-by-twenty-foot scrim blocks the bright sun from hitting Evonique's skin directly and avoids creating harsh shadows, while the silver bounce card reflects light back up onto her face. This is the last in-water shot that I want, and I know Anthem will love it.

When Evonique eventually rises out of the water and whips her hair at me, I hit the shutter at the sweet spot that I've spent so long finding, and I've got it.

"That's a wrap on water looks!" I shout triumphantly. I'm met with more disgruntled mutters than cheers, but I don't care, because I know that this will be the hero shot for the one sheet. I would say the entire shoot if Emerson wasn't here.

I jog out of the water and hand off the camera, housing and all, so that I can change as fast as humanly possible, yanking sweatpants and a thermal on in the seventy-five-degree weather. Getting back in the water after breaking for lunch should be classified as cruel and unusual punishment. As should watching Emerson go on a date right in front of me. Then I spot my puffer jacket, folded neatly, clearly left behind by Emerson before she went on her date.

Suddenly I'm eighteen again, heartbroken and crying on top of a stack of sweaters Emerson dropped off at my house after we had broken up.

After getting to actually talk last night, I thought maybe her agent had been harsher than she meant him to be. Or if she even knows what he says. I think we could be real friends. I glance around as though she'll see me, even though I know she's busy kissing Harry Butler while the entire world watches through some paparazzi's camera. I bend at the waist and press my nose to the coat, leaving behind only the faintest drops of water, and I inhale.

It's sunscreen, salt, her shampoo, and my own scent that come back to me. It's everything I need to forget, because days ago I was perfectly happy with my life, and now that I've wanted more I'm able to be disappointed.

"I thought you might want it back, after being in the water." Emerson has appeared in front of me, but her face is set in her neutral, public face. I don't see the person I was with last night.

"You could have kept it." Why can't I just say thank you like a normal person?

"That's okay, you need to warm up. I don't want to keep it anyway."

The way we talk to each other has always bordered on flirting. Everything about the way her eyes always lit up when she talked to me, the jabs we'd never dare say to anyone else, the glances that erupted into laugher, were the foundation of us. But Emerson is talking to me now like I'm just another guy on set. I'm facing off with . . . I guess this is *supermodel Emerson*.

"You should really change, before you get sick. Sorry about the delay, with all that." She waves loosely behind her, to where

Harry is posing for selfies with his fans while his team cleans up their meal. "I want you to know . . . we're just friends. I know Harry and I have history, but he's here as a friend. To be clear . . ." Emerson turns on her heel and leaves, walking barefoot down a rocky path toward the beach, clearly too uncomfortable to wait for my response.

Although I tried to hide that yesterday gave me hope I *might* have a shot at something more than friendship with Emerson, a stern reprimand from Allison on not getting my heart broken again, combined with this shitty interaction, makes me doubt myself. Why am I talking to Emerson at all? Once again, I let my heart get ahead of my brain, and now I'm standing here watching her future with someone else unfold right in front of me. Because even if she says it's nothing . . . why wouldn't she go for Harry? They're perfectly matched. I'm sure next thing I know he'll be on a magazine with her and she'll be playing the lead in his new movie or music video. She clearly likes him if they've actually stayed friends all these years since they broke up, something we weren't able to do.

Without stopping to think too hard about it, I pull out my phone and open the Reminders app. I swipe left and delete the reminder of our marriage pact and shove my phone back into my pocket. Done. My hopes are in the past. We're different people now, and it was silly to hold on to the reminder out of nostalgia. I am not hoping for anything more than friendship. Period.

But for the rest of the day, I'm unable to shake off the insecurity that seeing Emerson with someone so much more well suited to her draws out of me. The producers procured four artfully rusty pastel bikes so we can get a big group shot of the girls careening down cobblestone streets, with colorful buildings littering the background. I like to think that I've been focused the past day and a half, but now that I have to balance Emerson, other models in the same shot, and the lead ball in my gut, it's clear I need help. My direction is shaky, and I keep hitting the shutter just a second too late and missing the hero moment. I frame Emerson at the center of every take, her blond hair streaming behind her as she grins over one shoulder or throws her head back, laughing. She's barely looking at me, and although I keep having to drag my eyes away from hers as I look through the viewfinder, I'm avoiding directing her at all costs. I can tell that the flow I had going this morning is gone.

I try to push through, but we're also fielding constant interruptions. A huge crowd has formed around our makeshift set, people who must have taken a train in from other towns in the Cinque Terre belt, or a taxi from Milan, to see the Emerson–Harry show. Since we didn't rent out the street like a movie would, and instead just slipped store owners thousand-dollar checks this morning, the PAs have resorted to shepherding people away and bribing them with Anthem 20-percent-off coupons. Apparently, they ship globally if you're willing to pay extra for it, thus negating your coupon. As soon as the crowd formed, Emerson pasted a soft smile to her face, even when we weren't shooting. A smile that doesn't reach her exhausted eyes.

"Can we take five?" I ask eventually. The crowd is becoming too big to handle, and they're starting to get in the shots.

The second we break, they push toward her, and she immediately looks side to side, like she expects someone to be there to stop them. I know I should just walk away, get water, but I can't leave her to get trampled by these people.

"Are you okay?" I say, pushing my way to her side.

"I usually have a bodyguard nearby. Or at least Natalie, my assistant." She doesn't look at me when she says this, but I can see the clench of her jaw as she tries to keep a smile on. "But I left them in LA. I didn't want to see you for the first time in years through a team of fucking staff."

My mouth drops open. *She knew she was going to see me here.* This shoot wasn't a random coincidence like she said, or a mistake on Matt's part. She wanted to see *me*.

Before I can think through the implications of this, a fan grabs Emerson's arm. "Hey, back off, man." I step between them, holding the camera high above the crowd.

The man eyes me with raised eyebrows, as though he knows I don't have authority here. When Harry told the paparazzi to back off, they listened to him instantly. I can't even get a random fan to back down.

The longer we're there, the closer people press, desperate to get in before time runs out. We need a barricade. "Back off," I bark at an overly aggressive teenager. Both she and Emerson shoot me glares.

"Be. Polite." Emerson hisses at me through clenched teeth. Her shoulders are back, and I can tell she's braced herself for the onslaught of people. Someone else grabs her shoulder to get her attention, and I see her try to hide her recoil. In an instant I have her tucked in front of me, trying to shield her with my body. Her sundress is short, strappy, pink linen, and I can feel her bare shoulders through my thin white T-shirt. Having her against my chest feels like the most natural thing in the world, if I could forget about the mob in front of us.

I have to take charge. "Emerson only has three minutes left of her break," I say, raising my voice firmly. "No time for photos, but if you all take about ten steps back, you can continue to observe the shoot." From where Emerson is tucked against my chest, I feel goosebumps rise along her bare arms.

Stacey shouts above the noise. "This shoot is for Anthem, the number three household brand in the US. We have affordable women's swimwear and your everyday items, from groceries to throw pillows. Have a discount card! You're getting an early look at our summer campaign." Stacey is exuberant, clearly thrilled with the free publicity these articles and fan posts will get the brands. She glances at me. "Theo, why don't we take ten instead. May as well."

I see what Stacey's after, but I can't stand watching Em get exploited like this. "Want to go to the trailer?" I ask her.

Emerson looks at me like I'm crazy. "Of course not!" she says loudly enough for the crowd to hear. She turns a gracious smile toward them. "It's lovely to meet you all. Your support means the world—"

"Emerson! Autograph?" A man thrusts a baseball cap and Sharpie toward her so harshly that she flinches back. I hate every second of this.

I know she said she didn't want me around, but I can't just watch this happen, not when she looks so overwhelmed. "Two minutes of autographs, then we all have to get back to work. I suggest you all watch from the overlook for the best view."

I set a timer on my watch for two minutes and stay glued to her side as she signs shirts and beach bags. I make sure none of the fans touch her, they just take photos and pass her their things. When the timer goes off, I hold my arms up, ready to direct everyone away, but Emerson pulls on my arm. "One more. That little girl." She points through the crowd at a girl who can't be more than ten. "Come over here!" Emerson waves to her, and the girl's face breaks into a huge smile. She skips over, chattering in Italian, and wraps Emerson in a huge hug.

"I'm sorry, I don't speak Italian." Emerson speaks directly to the little girl, getting on her knees on the dirty street to be at eye level.

"Her English is not so good yet," the girl's mother explains. "But she is your biggest fan. The interview you did, with Oprah? About not having friends as a little girl? It meant so much to her." The mom becomes slightly choked up. "She has had friend problems. We live in Naples and it's such a small school. But once she saw your interview and heard that you did, too, and now you're you. It changed everything for her."

Emerson nods, and I can see the tears shining in her eyes. I remember that interview. She talked about being the weird kid in school until high school, having no friends, although she didn't specify that it was because girls made fun of her after she invited them over to play and they saw how her mom lived. When she told me the story in real life, she said was the first time she felt ashamed. On TV she just made it sound like she was an awkward ugly duckling. But the part I replayed again and again is where she says the moment everything changed for her was when she made her first real friend in high school. When she met *me*.

"If it wasn't for him, I'd never have become a model at all. I never would have even made it through high school."

Emerson takes the little girl's hands in hers. "Do you want to know my secret?" she whispers conspiratorially, pausing to let her mom translate. "I doubt myself all the time still. And that's okay, because I know how to put my game face on. I stand up straight." Emerson demonstrates this as she speaks. "Pull my shoulders back, hold my head high, and tell myself that no matter what people say about me, or life throws at me, I've got it. I just have to pretend until it's real. And the thing is, no one ever realizes that I'm pretending sometimes." The girl emulates Emerson's strong stance, and Em nods emphatically. "That's exactly right." She looks to the girl's mother. "Can you wait here a moment?"

She turns and I help her part the crowd so she can run to the model trailer. She returns with a worn copy of *Little Women*, the sides peppered with Post-it notes and the spine cracked, and her phone. "Can I get your address please? I'd like my team to send something." She copies the address down carefully, then crouches again to talk to the girl. "If you ever feel sad, you can read this book. I'm sorry it's in English, not Italian." The mom refuses to translate this, waving off Emerson's apology. "This is what I read when I'm having a hard day. And I write notes to myself, about things I'm grateful for. You can add your own notes."

The mom is crying now too. "We can't accept this." The girl is already clutching the book.

"Believe it or not, I re-annotate this book every year. She'll be doing me a favor by taking it, actually, because then I get to do it twice this year." She stands again, and wipes her eyes. "We have to get back to the shoot, but thank you for coming."

When everyone is finally gone, Emerson takes a gulping breath. "For every hundred assholes, there's a little girl like her. So I can't be rude, let my bad behavior get smeared all over the internet. Because that would ruin everything she's built up in her imagination." She wipes a tear that's broken through off her cheek. "When I was little, I had the characters in books to hold on to when I felt totally alone. I can't write a book like those, even though I wish I could. But I *can* present the best possible version of myself—the character of 'Emerson' people see online. And hope that's enough."

I know I should say something, compliment her, because she's so much more incredible than anyone else I know that it pains me, but what comes out of my mouth surprises even me.

"Em, do you actually want to write a book?" I ask. "Because if you do, do it. You can do anything."

Em's eyes suddenly fill with tears all over again. She squeezes my hand, then darts off to hair and makeup, rather than let us marinate in this vulnerable moment.

I let her.

CHAPTER FIFTEEN

Emerson

Watching Theo direct my fans is undeniably hot. So much hotter than Harry paying people to make it *look* like he has power. I got chills when Theo told them what to do, and when he stuck by my side while I gave autographs . . . so sexy. I have always had complete trust in him . . . except the one time when it counted the most.

He's also *literally* the only person who would encourage my pipe dream of writing a novel, instead of squinting and asking why I wouldn't just stick to modeling, since it pays the bills, or point out that I'm famous for being pretty, not smart.

I need to thank him for his help today. And even though I know it's going overboard, I want to do something special. I pull out my phone and text Natalie.

Can you find a gelato shop and rent it out? I want to go after we wrap today. And can you see if you can find one with a maple flavor? I know it'll be tough here . . .

We return to work, but after all the disruptions this afternoon, we barely get anything else done. Theo calls it quits on the group shot, and we each bang out one more solo look before Stacey calls it. "That's a wrap!"

Theo's shoulders are slumped with exhaustion and defeat at the end of the day. This morning it seemed like he had a great flow, so I suspect my life continually disrupting the shoot is to blame for the change in his mood. I want to reach up and smooth out his shoulders, massage out the knots, and hear him groan in agonizing relief, like he used to when he sat on the living room floor, his shoulders between my knees. I'm so busy reminiscing that I walk directly into his back.

"Oof. So sorry!" I say as Theo stumbles forward.

He catches himself. "Are you okay?"

"Yes! Sorry, just spacey. But, um . . . can I buy you a gelato?"

His face crinkles with confusion. With uncertainty. He's not sure he should say yes, I realize. He thinks I'm with Harry, regardless of what I said. And he might be with Allison. And I was so cold earlier . . . I want to just ask him about Allison point-blank, like I would have in high school. But I can't. I'd rather hang on to a tiny bit of hope before I know for sure that I don't have a shot.

"As a thank you for helping me earlier with the fans," I clarify, desperate to string together the right words that will get him there.

Some of the confusion clears, though for a second I think it's replaced by pain. Disappointment. But I'm sure that's my own imagination. "Sure. Gelato sounds good."

"Awesome!" My tone is far too shrill and enthused for a friendly gelato. How many ice cream cones did we have in four years of friendship? More than I could count. More than I've had in the decade since. But the fear of my simple offer of gelato being rejected makes my heart pound now. "I'll grab my things and meet you by the cars."

I scamper off before he can change his mind. When I step into the trailer, the girls are waiting, eager for details.

"Emerson!" Rachel scolds. "How could you not tell us Harry was coming! I've been obsessed with him since I was like ten. Honestly, with both of you together, but obviously I've pivoted now that I know about Theo."

"I thought him flying in was an idle threat." I look at myself in the mirror. "I think I should change. Do I look okay?"

Not that getting gelato is a date. It is a *friendship meeting*. Or something.

"Is he coming back?" Evonique pauses mid-makeup wipe application, as though she's contemplating redoing half of her face.

"Who? Harry? No, no. I mean, maybe another day. I'm just getting gelato with Theo."

Jillian nods approvingly and begins to undress. "You two have a spark. I can tell. Even if Allison wants to string you up by your neck. Borrow my dress!" She thrusts out the square-necked, white Reformation piece that she had been wearing seconds ago.

I take it, but can feel my eyes bugging out of my head. "She said that? When did you talk to her? You *know* her?"

"Not word for word. She called me today after talking to Theo and asked me to keep an eye out. Don't worry, I told her you're good people. She just said she saw the, uh, aftermath of you two firsthand."

My hands shake as I take my clothes off and redress in the middle of the trailer, sliding wordlessly into Jillian's dress and giving her my Prada. She squeals as she puts it on. "Keep it." Clearly, I need her in my good graces. "What were her exact words?"

"You don't want them."

"Tell me." I start taking deep breaths. It's crazy of me to even get gelato with Theo. He has a girlfriend, and she obviously doesn't like me. "Please."

"Don't do it," Rachel instructs Jillian, giving her a death glare.

Jillian eyes the sweats she's now wearing. "You sure you want to know?"

"Yes." I gasp between my breath cycle, eyes squeezed shut. My heart is racing and I'm about two pieces of bad news away from a panic attack. It's been a long day.

"Don't let that ice cold bitch near him, she'll decimate his heart." She shrugs. "But Allison has a flair for the dramatic. And hasn't met you. And for what it's worth, I totally disagree."

"Are they together? You can tell me if they are. We're just friends. That's all it's going to be." I don't need to open my eyes to know they're all rolling theirs.

"Not at this moment," Jillian declares happily. And relief floods through me, so strong that I don't know what I would have done if she'd said otherwise.

I open my eyes. "Now that is fantastic news."

"Just go get your gelato." Evonique practically has to push me out of the trailer, because suddenly I am doubting everything.

"Em?" Theo asks as I approach. "Are you okay? You look pale."

I force a smile to my face. "Totally. Now, let's get that gelato."

Theo clearly doesn't believe a word I said, but he has the grace to let me lie to myself and him. "We can take this car. The guys will all ride with Kevin. Where are we going?"

"Let me check." Natalie has texted me that she arranged everything. All I have to do is show up. I click the location pin and connect my phone to the car's airplay. "Only ten minutes away."

Theo pulls out and I curl up in the seat next to him. Usually, I put music on, desperate for an excuse not to talk to whoever I'm with. But with Theo I'm content to watch him drive in silence.

Once we've made it onto the main road, Theo glances at me. "How was the date?"

"What?"

"With Harry Butler? Lunch?" Theo's jaw flexes. I want to kiss it.

"Oh! Right." In the haze of watching Theo handle my fans, I actually forgot all about it. "Like I said, it really wasn't a date, but it was good. He's a good friend."

I want to tell him everything. How bizarre it is that, regardless of reality, within hours the entire world will be campaigning for Harry and me to get back together. How it feels like I'm losing my grip on what's real sometimes. How I feel too mature and weary for all of this publicity nonsense.

"Nice?" Theo asks. "That's practically an insult considering all the stops he pulled out."

"I'm sure that was as much for him as for me. He wants the press." I don't want to talk about this with Theo. But I'm also curious to hear more about what he thinks. "But I mean, what more is there? What do you look for beyond *nice*?"

Theo's quiet for a moment as he thinks. "I want someone who believes in me, like the couple in *Legally Blonde*. Who's my best friend, like they are in *When Harry Met Sally*. Who would give me the raft in *Titanic*, except I wouldn't let them. We'd both find a way to fit on that tiny door, because they totally could have. I want my heart to race when I see their message, like in *You've Got Mail*. Basically Em, all your movies ruined me. Because now I need *the spark*."

"You hated those movies."

"Not true. *Obviously*. Do you still watch them?"

"Sometimes." But I almost never do. They remind me of Theo. But now I like that, because he associates what he wants out of a relationship with movies we watched together.

Theo pulls into the parking spot outside Gelato Amore Mio. It's the owner's spot, but Natalie paid them extra to let us use it for a few hours, in addition to the shop. I hop out of the car and walk toward the shop. Natalie chose well. It's a hole-in-the-wall, with signs saying they make their famous basil and lemon flavors with ingredients all from their own garden. And like the stellar assistant she is, Natalie persuaded them to mix maple syrup from a nearby hotel into a small batch of vanilla, so we'd have a maple flavor.

"Where is everyone?" Theo asks. "You'd think it would be crowded given the heat, and that half of Milan came out here to see you." Theo looks up and down the street as I lead the way inside. I lock the door behind me.

"I rented the shop. I didn't want us to be bothered by fans."

"*What*? You rented the shop? How much did that cost?" Theo has stopped walking and is just staring at me.

"Um, I'm not sure. I had Natalie do it." *Lie*. It cost seven grand to rent the shop, plus the three for parking, to make an even ten. "I wanted to thank you."

Theo looks around, examines the laminated price sheet on the wall. "This must have cost a thousand dollars, to make up in lost sales?"

"Sure, that sounds right." An experience like this is the best way I've ever used my money. Something fun and private.

I walk behind the counter. Natalie offered up a staff member to stay and scoop for us, but I declined. I'd rather have time with just Theo, watching his camera-holding toned forearms scoop creamy gelato, drips snaking down the rivulets in his muscles, and—

I pick up a scoop. It's probably better if I don't give him a chance to scoop, since clearly just the thought makes me swoon. "Want to start with basil and lemon? Those seem to be the classics."

Theo grins from across the counter. "We always have to get the classic."

I dig the scoop into the lemon and pile creamy yellow gelato onto a waffle cone. But when I get to the basil, my scoop barely moves, it's frozen so solid. "Need help?" Theo comes around the counter and hovers behind me, the heat of his chest so close to my neck. My hair is becoming slick to my neck with sweat, and it's not entirely due to the exertion of this overzealously frozen flavor.

"Oh no, no, that's okay." It's not like I can admit I have an erotic daydream about watching him scoop ice cream. Or do basically any mundane task. I would pay way more than ten grand to watch him go through his daily routine, to see all the moments I don't have access to anymore.

"Em. Your nails are in serious peril here. Let me help." Theo gently pries the scoop from my manicured hand, but instead of going at it with brute force, he turns and runs the metal under hot water. Now I can add *intelligence and strategic thinking* to the list of things I find unbearably sexy about him. This isn't the puppy love I had as a teen, because he was cute and kind and fun. I'm looking at a man whom I respect, whom I want to spill my problems to, whom I so badly want to collaborate with creatively. I want him as a steady life partner more than I want the thrill of that first kiss.

When he hands it back to me, it does cut into the gelato with more ease, but once I have the scoop in, it's stuck. I tug on it to no avail, and am about to turn and ask him to just do it, when his palm wraps around the scoop above mine. My back is flush to half of his chest, and together . . . well, okay, mainly he does it while my hand is just taking up space on the scoop, but we lift out a perfect ball of basil gelato. "It's easier when you let me help," he whispers.

"I don't need help," I say, my breath catching. "I can do this alone, I can—"

"Em, it's not about needing it." I can't look away from him. I don't answer, because I'm afraid that if I say anything, then absolutely every fear, every need, every joy I've ever had will come tumbling out.

Theo takes over scooping and makes us two perfect cones of

gelato, which he garnishes with a round wafer cookie. I take a taste, and moan. "How is this so incredible?"

Theo's tongue darts out and licks a perfect circle around the rim of the cone. *Fuck*. There's no safe activity we can do that doesn't make me want him.

"How have I lived twenty-eight years without eating this?" Theo devours the top flavor in a few mouthfuls. "I made us small cones. I figure we have a few more flavors to try. Remember when we went to the Scooperbowl?"

"Oh my god, don't remind me. I thought I would never eat ice cream again."

The Scooperbowl is a charity event in Boston where all the local ice cream shops set up tents, and for ten dollars you can try as much ice cream as you want. Naturally, we tried every single flavor, and while Theo was fine, I felt like death after, since I'd eaten half my body weight in ice cream.

"We went for ice cream like two days later."

"Because you're a bad influence!" I say, laughing. "It's not like you can take me to Good Harbor and expect me *not* to get ice cream."

"I will not accept responsibility for your ice cream addiction." Theo eats his cone in three giant bites.

"What are you doing!"

He freezes midchew, eyes wide. "What's wrong?"

"You can't fill up on cones!"

Theo swallows with a gulp and starts cracking up. "Em! I thought you were going to say the cones were ornamental or they'd kick us out if we ate them or something crazy. You sounded panicked!"

"I am panicked! If we don't try them all, we'll be doomed to bad luck or something and eating the cone is the quickest way to fail in our mission." I get up and start scooping tiny samples of each flavor into cups. Theo joins me, setting small spoons in each one, so we have a proper tasting assortment.

"Em! Look at this. They have maple." Theo's face has lit up, like the universe put this flavor here just to remind us of when we were an "us"—of all the maple donuts he surprised me with, of his boat (which I have no idea if he still has), of when everything between us was easier.

"Let's try that next," I say happily.

Theo hands me a cup of maple. "This is perfect. It's nice to be somewhere quiet after all that. I don't know how you live like that, Em."

I take the cup and look at him, the bubbling joy in my chest dimming. He's happy. He's a person who is happy. Without me and all the chaos that's permanently baked into my life. It's selfish of me to try to win him over like this, when I know it would complicate his life beyond belief to be with me. And I love him more than I have ever loved myself. So I cheers his cup and put another two inches of space between us. Because, for today at least, while I figure out what to do, we're just friends.

CHAPTER SIXTEEN

—Summer After Sophomore Year—

Theo

"Theo, we need to find somewhere to sleep tonight." Emerson's eyes were wide, and although her voice should have been panicked, instead she just sounded resigned, because she was looking at me with complete confidence that I would figure out what to do.

We spent weeks convincing my parents that they should let us take a road trip that summer after sophomore year. In Massachusetts you could get your license on your sixteenth birthday, so we were freshly licensed and still getting over the pure terror of driving on the highway for the first time. Emerson's mom had agreed to the road trip without a second thought, and probably wouldn't have noticed if Em had left for a week without mentioning it at all. She'd become less and less "with it" with each passing month, but Em wouldn't talk to me about it. My parents, on the other hand, immediately said no, and it took three months of wearing them down, and agreeing to turn on Find My iPhone, call every night, and text every morning, for them to finally agree. Then they insisted on supplying us with a brand-new tent, a pack of emergency supplies that would keep us going for at least two months if we got stuck on the side of the road, and an emergency radio that could reach the state police even from areas where there was no cell service.

And so we went, and with a car stocked with Gatorade, marshmallows, and trail mix that was now slick with melted chocolate, we were stranded in the middle of the Shenandoah Valley. Our goal was Nashville, and although I hadn't admitted as much to Emerson, I knew we wouldn't make it that far. We were four days deep, and the car had no AC. Yesterday, Em actually teared up at how hot the Gatorade was. The only candy that consistently didn't melt was the marshmallows we'd bought to make s'mores, and if I never ate another marshmallow again, I'd die happy.

We hadn't done much advance planning for the trip, which worked out fine until we got to the Shenandoah Valley. A flashing neon sign greeted us—ALL CAMPSITES FULL. I pulled a U-turn and drove back through the town in search of a hotel, but everything read NO VACANCIES, so now we were pulled over at a decrepit gas station. And I pretended not to panic.

"Should I call my parents and ask what to do?"

Emerson winced. "They'll never let us go anywhere again if we tell them."

I hesitated for a moment. "What about your mom? She's chill. Maybe she'll have an idea. Or she can find somewhere online, since our service is too slow to google things here." Emerson kept her face blank. I wished she would let me in when it came to her and her mom. She didn't have to be embarrassed, and I wanted to be there for her. "We don't have to," I added.

"No, it's fine. I'll call." Emerson pulled out her phone and dialed her mom. It went straight to voicemail. She tried twice more, with the same result. Neither of us said anything, and she looked away when I tried to catch her eye.

"Let me ask at the counter," I offered. We walked into the gas station, and Emerson immediately went over to the drink cooler. She opened the door and leaned in to it, letting the cold wrap around her sweaty body. I glared at the guy who was ogling her, and he rolled his eyes at me. She looked fantastic, even though we'd just spent eight hours baking in her car.

"Hey! How are you?" I asked the gnarled old man cheerfully. He wore jeans and a denim shirt, as though it wasn't almost a hundred outside, and his teeth were yellowed from the cigarettes that jutted out of his shirt pocket. "I'm traveling with my friend here." At this Emerson appeared helpfully by my side, smiling winningly as though a hotel room might appear simply because she looked cute. "And it seems like there are no vacancies anywhere. Do you happen to know anywhere we might be able to stay?"

"You buying anything?"

"Of course!" Emerson set down two 99-cent popsicles on the counter.

"See those two, in the truck out there? They'll know a place you can camp." He pointed through the window, where the ogler and his girlfriend sat in a pickup truck, his hand on the wheel, truck already revved, seconds away from pulling out.

"Thank you!" I exclaimed as I ran out the door. "Hey! Hey— wait!"

He eyed me suspiciously, tattooed arms flexing. "Listen, we really need a place to camp tonight. The guy in there said you'd know a place."

"We will literally suffocate if we have to sleep in the car," Emerson chimed in.

His girlfriend looked us over, then turned to him and rested a hot-pink acrylic nail–adorned hand on his arm. "Babe, they're kids. Come on."

He glared at me as her fingers tightened on his forearm. "Drive straight, past the next three turns on the left. At the first turn on the right, you'll see a white house by the river. He'll let you camp on his land."

"You'll have to pay cash," the woman warned us.

"Thank you so much," I gushed gratefully. "We really appreciate it."

He ignored me and they drove off—in the opposite direction, I was pleased to note. Emerson handed me a now half-melted popsicle, and I let the sticky liquid drip down my palm as I rushed to eat the remainder. "Think it's safe?" she said.

If I had any other alternative, I would tell her no, let's stay far away from some random house. But instead, I shrugged. "It's the only option, so we may as well see."

We counted the turns painstakingly as we drove, but the road continued on for miles, and the sun began to set. "I think we should turn back. We probably missed it." My knuckles were white on the steering wheel as I watched the road with care. It had a one-foot dip on the right-hand side, and in my overtired state I worried I would take us off the edge.

"Theo, I told you, it will be the next turn on the right." Emerson looked peaked next to me, and not for the first time I wished we'd bought a bag of ice at the convenience store.

"There will never be a turn on the right. We're in a fucking horror movie, and this road will never end."

"Theo! There!" Emerson sat up in her seat with renewed vigor and threw her arm out the window. "I see a house. Turn!"

I pulled onto the dirt drive and drove as close as I could to the house. Emerson rummaged through the glovebox, jerking as I drove over outlandishly large divets in the road, and triumphantly pulled out a wad of cash, which she distributed into different pockets. She had a fear of being upcharged if she pulled out too much cash at once, but I thought it was more realistic she'd lose money through sticking fives and tens in different parts of every article of clothing. I stuck to a wallet.

She sprang out of the car before I'd even put it in park and went to knock on the door. I hustled to join her, lest whatever random guy whose property we were camping on thought she would be unaccompanied all night, and we stood in front of the door, breath bated. I hadn't realized how reckless we'd been with our planning until this night. If he turned us down, we'd have to try to pitch a camp on the side of the road somewhere, which wasn't all that different from what we'd be doing here, but somehow felt dangerous.

"If no one's here, I say we camp out anyway and leave money in the mailbox," Emerson suggested. "I can't keep driving around in that car."

"Someone will come out," I assured her, although I felt much less certain. "The light's on."

Emerson rapped her knuckles against the door again, firmly, and it pulled back under her hand and sent her flying forward. I steadied her and kept my hand on her back as we stared at the man in front of us. He looked relatively normal for this area, weather-tanned skin, a collared shirt, jeans, work boots. His face remained blank as he gazed at us, and dread rose in my throat. What if this wasn't the right house? We could've disturbed a serial killer. "What do you want?"

"We heard we might be able to camp here." Emerson flashed her most engaging smile and I did my best to look friendly.

"And we can pay cash."

"Ten for the spot, five more if you want wood. I can bring a bundle over to you in an hour. Go wherever you like, there's no one else here." He gestured vaguely at the expansive property around us. "Wherever."

"Thank you so much," Emerson gushed. Her relief was palpable as she handed over fifteen dollars.

He shut the door on us without fanfare, and we reentered the car new people. I was slaphappy with exhaustion and relief, and based on Emerson's slightly hysterical giggle, she felt the same. I drove to the end of the road, until there was river in front of me and grass to either side. "Do you think I'm meant to drive on the grass?"

"Do it," Emerson urged. "I saw a little ATV thing when we pulled in, and it doesn't seem like he's farming here or anything. Then we can set up camp from the trunk."

I pulled us right and drove until we could barely see the house in the distance and were flush to the Shenandoah River. "Look at this view. This is better than camping in the park."

Emerson laughed as she hopped out and opened the trunk. "Let's not even go to the park. This is our park now. We don't need that stupid park with no campsites."

"Agreed." Although I had no more experience with tents than Emerson did, I still had been taking the lead with our tiny tent. Although it claimed to sleep two, the real question was two of what. Two children might have fit comfortably in this tent, or two Emersons if she shrunk a few inches, but with the two of us together we were undeniably cramped, although neither of us complained.

Ten painfully slow minutes later, the tent was up and Emerson was spreading hot peanut butter and hot jelly on hot bread from the trunk of the hot car while I jumped into the river. After the second day without AC in the car, we'd decided to stop questioning the cleanliness of water when we came across a stream. This water looked muddy, but there were no blatant signs of contamination or dead animals lying around, so I waded in, stripped, and began wiping sweat off of my body.

When I returned we switched places and I tried not to gag on the hot sandwich. I'd never known that some foods are supposed to be eaten only at a specific temperature, until I tried them heated by a steamy car. PB and J was one of the foods that felt unnatural at this place between room temp and grilled, but it beat marshmallows and Gatorade, so I choked it down.

Emerson lay down on a towel when she came back. "At least the water's cold. I'm not drying off, I feel like in two minutes I'll be hot again."

I leaned forward and shook my hair at her, golden retriever style. "Better?"

"Oh my god, don't stop, I love it." She tilted her head up and closed her eyes. "And don't even make a joke about that, I know you could, but seriously it feels amazing. I've never been this hot before." She squinted up at me for a second. "Overheated, that is."

"I know." I lay down on my towel next to her. "Maybe we should plan out were we stay tomorrow, before, like, seven p.m."

"Trust me, I tried. There's no service here, like anywhere. But in the morning we can go somewhere and figure it out." Emerson tilted her head toward me and let it rest on my shoulder, just the slightest half-inch of contact, of my bare skin pressed against her soft, sunburnt cheek. "Thanks for finding us this place."

"Hey, I think it was you batting your eyelashes that was the deciding factor," I teased. The sun was setting, but there was no sunset to speak of. Just a hot cloudy sky, getting darker. I let my hand brush against Emerson's and she didn't move away. I wrapped my fingers through hers and squeezed, ashamed of how good it felt.

"Does batting my eyelashes work on you?" she asked, her fingers tight against mine.

"I mean, obviously. I just drove for eight hours in a car with no AC. That's like living hell."

Hearing her laugh made me forget that only forty minutes before I was trying to remember the signs of heatstroke. With Emerson lying next to me I was utterly content.

"Theo?" The sun was now down, and I was getting eaten alive by mosquitos, but I wouldn't move and break the moment. Emerson smelled of bug spray, so at least she was safe, and I could live with a few bites in order to hear whatever she wanted to say next, to hold her hand for a minute longer. "I love this. Let's do this every year. Even once we're with other people."

I love you. The thought jumped into my brain suddenly, as it did far too many times a day, and I ground my teeth to keep from saying it aloud. I hated that she was planning for our separate futures. That even though I was the one here holding her hand, I still hadn't gotten myself out of the friend zone. "We will," I declared instead. "And even once we have a better car, we'll leave the AC off, just so we can bake and build our character."

"Theo, my character is burnt."

"Fine, we can use the AC. And maybe eat some real food and plan where we stay." I strained to tilt my head down and press it to the top of hers, aching for more contact.

"But we'll do a trip, every year." Emerson stretched her neck to meet me, and we clicked together, a perfect fit like we always were.

"Of course we will."

CHAPTER SEVENTEEN

Emerson

"Georgia?" My voice is a shrill whisper. I've left the bath running slightly while I'm in it, and all of the fans in the suite are on. All in an effort to ensure Theo doesn't hear me through the wall. My room service food is on a tray, untouched, on the side of the tub, and I'm totally submerged, save for my face and the one hand that's extended to hold my phone away from the water. "Can you hear me?"

"Emerson? You didn't warn me this was a naked FaceTime! You're lucky my man isn't here." Georgia and I have no modesty with each other, not after changing in front of one another eight million times. But she's right—usually I give her a warning. Then again, I'm not usually in crisis.

"A bath actually sounds nice, though." Georgia turns on the faucet attached to her bathtub. It's a rose gold, clawfoot tub that sits beside the hotel bed.

"Shhhh!" I hiss, turning down the volume on my phone. "Theo has the room next door. I can't let him hear us."

Her eyeroll is massive. "How is this not in the bag yet? You have neighboring rooms. Lose your key and show up in a towel or something! And where's Harry?"

"In his own room! Now, can you please reality-check me? Am I awful to try to win Theo over like this when he has a perfectly normal, sane life without me?" I let my entire head slide under the water for a minute, then sit up to chug half a glass of wine in one go.

Georgia takes off her dress, steps into her own bath, and sinks down. "Babe, you two have an epic love story. I still remember how you spoke about him the day we met. You have to give this a real shot. You know it's your last chance too, realistically." I groan and take a long sip of wine. "Now tell me, where are you two at?"

"We're friends. Genuinely, finally. And I think seeing me with Harry made him a teeny, tiny bit jealous. And I'm about to go out to the balcony and do the questions, of which we get three today."

"Towel!" Georgia yells, as though she just won the lottery. Or post-Oscars bingo. The prizes at the party Harry hosts are *incredible*. "Go out to the balcony in your towel!"

"That's too much! Right? I mean, I don't want to throw myself at him. But I do want him to start thinking about me in a romantic way. I never second-guess like this, but I just love . . ."

I just love him.

I stop talking, realizing the wine is making me way too forthcoming.

"Just love what?" Georgia's eyes have lit up and she's about an inch away from the phone. I can see every pore.

I swallow the words that had jumped into my head and clamp my jaw shut. "Nothing. Nothing at all."

"Emerson! Come on! Finish the sentence or I'll—"

"I'll wear the towel!" I interrupt. "You win! I'm going out there, wet and naked and in way too small a towel."

Georgia mimes zipping her lips, questions put away for now.
"You two have my blessing. Consider your conscience cleared. Go
out there and make his jaw drop, babe. Phase two commences."
She blows a kiss at the camera and hangs up before I have time to
change my mind and make her talk through outfits.

I drain my glass of wine, which is a remarkably bad idea, and
then get out of the water and use one towel to dry myself off. I
drop it to the ground, take a fresh one, and fasten it around my
chest. At home, I have roughly blanket-size towels. This is a much
smaller situation. It covers all of the important bits, but nothing
else. And I guess that's actually the best I could ask for right now.

I walk out to the balcony and toss a hotel pen at Theo's door to
alert him that it's time to fulfill his contractual obligation to the
question game. He comes to his door so soon after the pen falls
that I wonder if he's been waiting for me.

"Em!" he says. And then falls silent, his eyes widening in
surprise as he takes me in.

I flush. "Sorry. Do you mind?" I gesture to my towel. "They
don't have robes here. But I wanted to do our questions."

"No, no, you're good." Theo looks back toward his room, as
though he's considering changing too. Or maybe he's just trying
not to stare at me. The night air is warm but with a crisp breeze,
and I can feel myself getting nippy through the towel. But after a
moment Theo sits in the chair, and I follow suit, dragging mine
closer to the railing with one hand while I clutch my towel with
the other.

I sit down and arrange the towel carefully. In order to make
absolutely sure my lower half is covered, I let an inch more of
damp cleavage show. When I look up, I see Theo swallow. But he
brings his eyes right back up to my face when he sees I'm looking.
"You start," he chokes out.

"Why did you stop calling?" I blurt out. I sound combative and I should let us warm up, but suddenly I have to know.

"I mean, I know why. But why when you did, specifically. If that makes any sense."

When I first left, Theo called constantly. And then, even after he said he was giving me space, it was a matter of weeks before he tried again. I was almost ready to pick up, two months deep into therapy, when suddenly he stopped.

Theo keeps eye contact with me, but the look on his face is harder than I've ever seen him. "*People* magazine. The September issue had a paparazzi photo of you and Harry holding hands on the cover. Fingers interlaced." He grits his teeth and I see his jaw clench before he continues, his tone biting. "Which is the way you said couples held hands. Friends just grabbed each other. But you said couples interlaced. The photo was the little round one they have in the corner. And you were laughing. You looked happy. So I decided I should let you be happy."

We're both so still, for so long, that the motion-sensor lights on the balconies click off. I wave my arm to turn them on, and my towel slips, leaving me rushing to grab it. Theo doesn't look away for a second, although his gaze stays locked on my face.

His anger stings. And makes me wonder if there's any point to me being out here in a towel, trying to win him over. I wish I could tell him that Harry and I were just in a PR relationship. Because, on paper, there was a contract between us. It hadn't started the day that photo was taken, because I was holding out, sure I would fix things with Theo. That photo was at our preliminary meeting and was probably arranged by Matt to show me just how beneficial the relationship could be. When Theo stopped calling and the photo got me on the cover of *People*, I decided to give the contract with Harry a try. But then it did become real, for a while. So even if I told Theo the technical truth, that it was PR, it wouldn't be honest.

"Theo, Harry isn't you. He's great, but we never had what you and I did. And now, it's just—"

"My question," Theo interrupts. "How are things between you and your mom? Since we're doing hard ones this round."

Now I'm the one clenching my jaw. I pull my towel tighter around me. This isn't the sexy moment I was hoping for when I came out here, after our gelato tasting and navigating fans. "We were much better, until I tried to buy her a house." I wish I could take the bitter tone out of my voice. "We actually got closer after I left. She would come out to visit me, since my therapist suggested neutral territory might be good for us. And it was! We talked, like actually talked, and it helped a lot. I felt like I really had a mom. And now I haven't seen her for more than a few hours at a time in like five years."

"What was it you talked about?" Theo asks.

"That's another question," I caution, since clearly we're not playing nice today. Theo nods, accepting the usage. I wish he hadn't. I choose my words carefully, not willing to get into everything while I'm half naked on a balcony. I feel too exposed. "I wished she'd protected me more. From the industry . . . and everything. I wished she'd been more of a mom. And I was angry, I guess, that I had to grow up so fast. And that she hadn't been a parent and kept me safe, you know?" I can see Theo's about to ask his third question. And I can't answer it yet. I rush to add something that will stop him. "It can just be such an exploitative industry, you know? Even once I was eighteen, I could have used someone looking out for me, making sure everything was fair and whatnot."

Theo nods, his face serious. "And then you bought her a house? So she could move somewhere fresh, without all that junk."

"Right." My eyes are watering, and while I try to blink back the tears that are forming, I have to quickly wipe one away. Usually keeping from crying isn't a problem for me. But since coming on this shoot and being around Theo, it's like a chasm that I've kept stitched shut has ripped wide open, and I feel *everything*. And this is the first time I've talked to someone who actually knows her, knows what it was like with her after she started deteriorating. "I wanted to help her. But she was so upset. Which upset me. And we just haven't been able to fix things."

"Em, it's okay to cry." I shake my head mutely, focused on blinking back the tears. Theo continues, his tone softer than before. "Maybe she felt guilty. Since you were upset she didn't protect you, didn't do much for you. She didn't want to take more from you."

I look at Theo, eyebrows furrowed. I'd never thought of that. Because that would mean assuming she actually cares, which I haven't done in a long time. The few years we were good just seemed like a fluke that she couldn't keep up. "I always just assumed it was because she's kind of sick, you know? That's when I got the aide, to make sure things didn't get worse, since she won't get real help from a professional. The aide I got is secretly a licensed therapist too, though, so I hope it's helping."

Theo winces, and I can tell from his face that what I've done isn't helping my mom as much as I'd like to think. "I can go there with you, if that's something you decide you want," he offers. "You obviously don't owe her anything. But it might make you happier if you two were in a better place. If that's something you want, I'm here."

"Thank you," I whisper. I'm not committing to anything now. This week has my emotions too high. But I know that he means it, that his offer stands no matter what happens after this week. And that sends a chill down my spine.

Which obviously he immediately notices. He pulls his jacket off and tosses it over the balcony. I let it fall, unwilling to drop my towel and risk baring it all. "It looks better on you," he says simply.

"I have to disagree." But I put it on anyway. "Do you want to ask your last question?"

"And leave you to annihilate me with two in a row? I'm good, thanks."

I grin. Usually talking about my mom leaves me in a funk for days. But not with Theo. "Fair point. Let me think of something hard." I raise my index finger to my chin in mock concentration. "Favorite day of the week? And full justification please."

"Thursday. It still feels special thanks to it being our old pizza and movie night. And despite being almost thirty with a rapidly slowing metabolism, I still have pizza on Thursdays when I'm home. I coach soccer for my nephews, then we all make homemade pizza at Owen's place. We actually grill it in the summer, which is surprisingly good. But this year I'm giving them a pizza oven for Christmas, to really cement the tradition in a completely desperate plea to get my nephews to continue it now that they're rapidly getting older and therefore much cooler than me."

"Wow. Fantastic answer. I want in."

"Access granted. So long as you bring your own preferred toppings and at least one unhealthy drink Naomi and Owen won't buy for their kids." Theo's blue eyes . . . they twinkle, even in this dim lighting. I actually am forgetting I'm looking at the most beautiful scenery in the entire world, because I have Theo's perfect face in front of me. Suddenly I'm really feeling that wine.

"Can I go again?" I ask.

"Of course not. Fair is fair; it's my question." I groan, which Theo takes as his cue to continue. "Favorite shoot you've ever done?" I'm about to say this one, when he adds a qualifier. "Excluding this one, since it could still go completely haywire and become the worst shoot in history."

I roll my eyes dramatically. "Fine. If I was being complimentary, I'd say our high school digitals shoot, because that is a core memory. But if I'm being honest . . . I did a shoot for a Super Bowl commercial with Taylor Swift like three years ago, and that would be impossible to beat. She let me go into her green room, where she sang "You Belong With Me" to me, totally alone, and I think I have never been more in awe in my life. I desperately wish I had recorded it. Or made her take a selfie. Anything, really, to prove to myself that it wasn't a fever dream."

"I remember that one!" Theo exclaims. "You two meet in an elevator and everyone thinks you'll, like, duke it out since you're the two most famous blondes in the world. But then you see there's only two coffees left at Dunkin, and you work together to, like, do a crazy obstacle course to the line, and it's a buy one, get one ad. It was ridiculous. And completely perfect." Then Theo blushes, and it's the cutest thing I've ever seen. "I mean, you know all that, though. You were the one in it. It's strange seeing you on TV when I'm just sitting on my couch at home."

"Well, don't you think it's strange for me to see photos you took every time I get an Anthem slushy?" I stay completely serious for at least ten seconds, and then we both start cracking up. "I actually wish I could still just walk into Anthem and get a slushy. Now I have to wait in the tinted SUV while Natalie gets one, like it's a drug deal."

"I'll add slushy maker to my Christmas shopping list," Theo promises. And the thought of still being able to talk to him like this come Christmas makes my eyes start watering again.

"What should I get you for Christmas?" And then I realize I just used my last question. But I forgot for a minute that I was forcing us to talk because of a game. Now it's all us. So I let it go.

"Well, if we're staying in theme, probably some sort of do-nut maker. So then I can make inferior versions of the donuts we actually love, and we can eat them and pretend we wouldn't rather have gone out and spent a dollar on the real deal like a block away."

"Done. I'm on it. Never say I don't pull my weight around here." If there wasn't a cruel two feet of air separating our balconies right now, I would find a way to touch him. Hand on his leg, jostle his shoulder, elbow him even, just to be touching, to progress this moment now that we've made it past the angry beginning to the game. Completely unfashionable, towel, jacket, wet hair, and no makeup combo and all. But instead, I just laugh with him and keep talking.

3
Days Remaining

CHAPTER EIGHTEEN

Emerson

Naturally, actually talking and having fun together was too much for me, and when I get to set the next morning, I act extremely mature, and bounce my eyes off Theo whenever I get caught looking at him. And by caught, I mean either I stare so long I start daydreaming about what I want his strong arms to do to me, how he would hold me, all the places I want to touch him, or he makes eye contact with me and I rush to act normal. Like the type of friend who isn't lusting after her former best friend, who is also still her coworker for two more days, so she must act professional while still trying to make him fall in love. An easy balance!

We started shooting super early today so that we could get in a few shots in the middle of a street. But what production didn't take into account was that in tourist towns like this, that's when all the fresh produce is delivered to restaurants. So as I frolic in the middle of the road, and Theo snaps away, PAs are stationed twenty feet away to yell—

"Car!"

I don't stop posing until Theo moves. The car will be coming from behind me, but I trust him to stop before it gets dangerously close. I won't move until he gets the shot. After a few seconds he runs to the side of the street, and I follow with Kevin, where we wait for the car to pass. It's actually a truck that's so big I'm surprised it fits through the tiny Cinque Terre streets, and it looks as though it solely carries tomatoes.

Miranda runs across from the other side of the street and starts adjusting my clothes. Her AirPods are in and she's on a conference call, instructing her underlings on what to change as she listens in and glances at the photos they're sending her. Her voice is animated while she straightens my top. "I don't care how the ruching looks. We're losing the ruching; by spring it'll be *so* last summer. Just focus on where the back hits, and how wide the crotch is." She moves on to my pants and pulls them down, to make it clear this is a two-piece ensemble, not a romper situation. "And does it look like a V-front? Like, before you hike it up. I want something our girl won't have to hike up."

Theo beckons me back into the street. "Best to keep moving when she has to pause for air." He goes back to shooting me, and I spin and run across the street while Kevin keeps pace with the bounce card. I try to make every movement look effortless, as though I'm a weightless nymph, not an almost-six-foot-tall human woman.

"Car!" I can't see it behind me, but I don't react to the PA. Theo keeps snapping away, so I keep a smile trained to my face and give an even bigger leap.

"This is so good," Theo mutters as he snaps away. He's been flowing all morning, in an undeniably good mood. Until he looks behind me and his smile drops. Before I can react he's roped an arm around my waist and pulls me to the side of the road. A car comes barreling past, driving at least double the speed limit.

"Em, are you okay?" My arm is wrapped around Theo's neck and I'm perilously close to his face. He has stubble. Blond, sexy stubble. And I didn't realize how good he smells in the morning.

Is this the same deodorant from when we were kids? "Emerson?" His grip on me tightens and I straighten up, stop swooning.

"I'm fine!" I declare brightly. "All part of the job. It's not your fault he drove so much faster than all the other cars." I try to extricate myself from his grip, but he stays glued to my side. Doesn't he see how challenging close contact makes it for me to keep it together around him? And the only reason I needed to be saved was because I trust him enough not to move, because I know he would never let anything bad happen to me. It's ridiculous to trust anyone that much. It leaves you vulnerable, and everyone will mess up at some point.

"Let's move on to the next location. It's getting too cluttered here anyway." I assume Stacey's referring to the actual residents of the town, who are now awake and preparing for the day by setting out restaurant signs, hanging laundry, having coffee on the cute little decks. I actually find it picturesque.

Theo looks around, still hovering nearby protectively. "The model car is way up the hill. Why don't you ride with Kevin and me? We're right here."

I do feel slightly shaky after the run-in, though I'm sure that has more to do with Theo's gallant save than any proximity to the car. "That'd be great." I get into the passenger side, and Theo slides into the driver's seat. Kevin packs the bounce card and scrim into the back seat, clocks Theo on the driver's side, then comes around and climbs into the back seat.

Miranda darts over and shoves a bikini on a hanger at him. "Have Emerson change into this. Thank you!"

In the model car we always change on the go, so that when we get to location we can immediately start shooting. It's an SUV with tinted windows, the classic shoot car, so it would be extremely challenging for someone to see in. Though I'm sure I'm much more paranoid about paparazzi stalking me than the other girls are.

This car has similarly tinted windows, but the windshield is clear, so when Kevin hands me the nude bikini, I change out of my shirt with the classic pulling-my-arms-out-of-the-sleeves-and-changing-underneath move. I toss the top in the back. "Can you rehang that so it doesn't wrinkle?" I assume no one else will wear it, because Matt is savvy enough not to let them shoot anything I wear on someone else, so that no one can compare us. But I want to seem polite.

Kevin's face is beet red in the rearview as he tries to wrangle the strappy back of the top onto the hanger. Then he looks up at me to ask how to do it, and it gets worse. The nude bikini is a perfect match to my skin tone, and at first glance I appear naked. "You know, I think I'll ride in the digi-tech car," he mutters and hops out.

"So . . . the one sheet looked really good yesterday," I say as I continue to change.

"Thanks. It was fine, I guess." He glances over at me, presumably to see if I'm being genuine, and now he's the one bouncing his gaze away from my bikini-clad body.

"I mean it. The photos you're taking of me are some of my favorite ever."

Typically, when I'm on a natural makeup, no-retouching shoot, all I see are my flaws. I'd rather let Photoshop work its magic. But he's captured me in a way that makes me look real, happy, and carefree.

"I doubt that. Most of your shoots probably have ten times our budget, and you're the only one there."

"That doesn't matter, because you know how to direct me." I glance at him. "Why aren't you excited about it, though?"

Theo sighs and rolls his shoulders back. "I'm just a bit burnt out on this stuff. Our convo the other day made me realize that I do want to do less commercial facelift work. Or just a more stylized and creative shoot. But right now, I'm able to pay my bills and spend time at home. I shoot Anthem and a few other big-box places, which keeps me booked and busy, and making average collections shine keeps it just interesting enough creatively, and then I go home. I'd have to really believe I have something special that will take me to the next level to make it worth giving up my current situation." He looks at me. "You know, for some people, being *one of the greats* is just a pipe dream. Most of us just do our work, and that's that."

I frown. "Theo, of course you have that *something special*. You have more talent in your thumb than most people I work with have in their entire body."

"Em, you don't have to gas me up like this. It's humiliating, honestly, coming from someone who's actually made it."

I want him to see in my eyes that I'm not lying. But he's driving, so instead I settle for resting a hand on his arm and squeezing it tightly. "Theo, when have I lied to you? You are so incredibly talented. But I also am totally sure that you don't have to choose between your career and your family. You have the talent to make it, to shoot anything you want. It's only a pipe dream if you decide it is. You have to believe me when I say you deserve to be one of the greats, if that's something you want."

Theo pulls into the parking spot a PA is waving him over to, following the end of the caravan. He turns and looks at me, and this time I don't look away from him. "Do you believe that, Emerson?"

"Every word. You are still the most talented photographer I've ever met. And I mean, making this stuff look as good as designer swim, without retouching? Everyone who knows anything recognizes that you're doing something special." I tug on my suit, which, to save on costs, is cut to look okay on a huge size range, rather than adjusting the design to look great on an XS and an XXXL, like a more expensive brand would. The fabric is thin, the stitching is mass produced, and I know in the photos, Theo will make it look like a million bucks. Which I kind of love, because a million girls who are just like me only have the option of a swimsuit in this price point, and after his images go live they'll actually be excited about buying this one. They'll get to feel like they're buying something cool, not just something that fits their budget.

Theo closes his eyes and leans his head back on the seat. "That means a lot more coming from you than Owen or my mom. They think any photo I take of his kids should be in a museum."

I laugh, but don't let his joke distract me. "I mean it," I whisper. I squeeze his hand, wrap his calloused palm with both of my smooth ones. "You're the whole orange, remember?"

Theo chuckles. "Of course I remember. Spanish one, the only class we ever had together."

Which is because after I barely passed, and he aced the class, I was stuck in normal Spanish two while he jumped to AP Spanish three. But in that sophomore-year Spanish class, the teacher had taught us that in Seville, Spain, people say *mi media naranja* to express *I love you.* It literally translates to "my half orange," or "your perfect other half," the other half of your orange. So one day, when I was down, Theo told me that I was the whole orange, I was everything I needed. Which crushed me at the time because I wanted to be the other half of his. But I said it right back, and over time it became something I loved. Because I don't need to be half of anyone else, I am the whole fucking orange, and so is Theo. And I mean, isn't two awesome oranges better anyway?

"Exactly. It's my mantra now, at the end of a yoga class, or when I'm up for a job I think is out of my league, or when I want to do something that's outside of my *pretty face* lane. So, I'll tell you: You're the whole orange."

Theo opens his mouth, and from the look in his eyes I know it's something important. I lean toward him, desperate to hear what he'll say.

But then Kevin raps roughly on the window, and the moment

is gone. "Theo. Next shot. Jillian's already out there. Emerson, you're next, head over in five."

Theo leaves the car with one last squeeze of my hand, and I'm left there, my head swirling.

A complaint I've gotten from several men I've dated is that I tune out while I listen to them talk. Or I don't ask enough questions. I don't seem genuinely interested or supportive. I always dismissed this, since everyone knows all A-listers are raging ego hounds, but now that I've sat here, desperate to hear Theo's every thought, because I think anything he says is the most interesting thing in the world, I feel guilty. Because they're totally right. I never felt the same way about listening to them talk, never encouraged them in the same way. Was never honest like this. But I would feel lucky to listen to Theo talk all night long.

And I want him to have everything he wants, and know exactly how I can get him instant career buzz. I pull out my phone and text Harry.

If Theo can shoot it I'll do a social post with you

CHAPTER NINETEEN

Theo

"Theo, change of plans for after lunch." Stacey's tone is brisk and her eyes are wide when she walks over to where I'm sitting with Kevin. "You're going to shoot Emerson and Harry for the digital cover of *GQ*. You'll have one hour."

"Sorry, what?" I must have misheard her. A cover of *GQ* doesn't just land in your lap like this; it's unheard of. I put my pesto focaccia down slowly.

"Check your phone."

"There's no service here. I mean, there must be some mistake." I look around, but Emerson is nowhere in sight. I was just talking to her about my aspirations; does she really have the power to ask for a cover and have it happen in a matter of hours?

"You can connect to the trailer Wi-Fi. Password is Anthem123." Although I'm sure the Wi-Fi could handle our entire twenty-person crew being on it, Stacey enjoys rationing out the Wi-Fi in order to create a distinct hierarchy. She's loath to let me on, but I guess this is considered extenuating circumstances.

I connect and immediately have a rush of texts from Owen's wife, Naomi. I don't actually have an agent because I never found I needed one. I've curated client relationships myself, and am known for the very specific type of service I provide, making an average collection sparkle like it's couture, and so I get more than enough bookings through word of mouth. But I don't exactly want the clients to know that, so occasionally I ask Naomi to pose as my agent, just to keep the peace during negotiations and sticky situations.

Her texts start out baffled, then become increasingly overwhelmed.

Theo. Some guy named Matt got my contact off your website (who knew anyone could find that lol!) and said he wants you to shoot GQ for Harry Butler and Emerson??? Seems like a scam

Maybe not a scam. Someone from GQ called. How much $$$should I say?

OMG Owen told me this is THE Emerson

Their first offer was 10k for the hour should I take it?

SOS I'm not a real agent please help

Google said to go higher . . . I said 50k and they accepted? You're welcome, I want a new grill for Christmas

"I see," I choke out. "You want to do this right now?"

"You have ten minutes to prep, and one hour to shoot. They're covering the hour of overtime costs for us, and Emerson must wear Anthem in it." Stacey sounds positively gleeful. Anthem being worn on a magazine cover is unheard of. She walks away and I see Miranda dumping out an entire wardrobe suitcase behind her, rifling through, probably to find a way to outfit Em in both swim as a top and pique in one go.

To say I'm stunned by this turn of events would be an understatement. If I was a better guy, I'd just feel grateful, but I can't help but feel slightly . . . pathetic. I know when we were kids I helped Emerson out more times than I can count, coaching her through her math homework question by question, making sure people invited her to parties, taking photos of her senior year in the clothes from brands she wanted to shoot with so they'd notice her. But when she hands me *GQ* on a silver platter, I just feel embarrassed, because there's no way in hell they'd ever think to hire me themselves.

Not to mention it'll be hard to make this look *GQ*-worthy in ten minutes. And while it's relatively simple for me to take stunning photos of Em, taking photos of her with Harry is a nauseating thought.

I shoot off a text to Allison. I'm shooting Emerson for GQ with Harry Butler . . . SOS, losing it

I get no response, then remember it's four a.m. where she is. I'm on my own.

I'm broken out of my anxiety spiral by a rough clap on the back from Kevin. "Lit, dude. Where you thinking? I'll get the boys and grab some scrims, it's really fucking bright."

I look around. It's two o'clock, the worst time of day I could possibly shoot this. The light is harsh rather than dreamy, and it's so windy I know hair and makeup will be running in every other shot. My best bet is to try to get Emerson and Harry in action, so that people will forgive slight imperfections.

"Do you want me to stand in while you frame up?" Emerson has materialized next to me, skin radiant and hair blowing majestically in the breeze, while the rest of us mere mortals have to settle for sweaty and rumpled. "I'm not dressed yet, but I can step in."

"You don't have to do that." Emerson is so far above stepping in. Typically, I'm sure they pre-light for an entire day everywhere she'll shoot, and she's in and out as quickly as possible. She must think our operation is totally unprofessional. I do a more "run and gun" style, because I know exactly what I'm doing with my typical clients, but for *GQ*, even I would prefer to pre-light. "And you didn't have to do this for me."

"Theo, I want you to have everything you've ever wanted. But I actually didn't do this, exactly. I asked Harry if he wanted you to shoot a pic of us for social, since it'll blow up overnight and would have your name attached. But apparently he had this offer from *GQ*, and they went wild when he suggested we do it together." Here Em rolls her eyes slightly, but my gut still twists. The whole world wants them together. How long until they actually are? "At least like this it'll actually be fun. And you're more talented than anyone they would have found."

"It is short notice," I acknowledge, my anxiety slightly quelled by her words.

"With any amount of notice. Now let me stand in for you. We're a good team."

Rather than have Emerson and Harry stand in front of a classic Cinque Terre overlook, I pose her on a corner where three streets intersect. The warm tones of the colorful houses frame her, and it looks likes she could be basically anywhere in Europe. Most importantly, she's subtly backlit, instead of in direct sun or full shade, and a stream of light shines between the houses onto her back, creating a halo around her head and a great lens flare on camera.

Since she was just on lunch she's in jean shorts and a white tank top, which is all too reminiscent of the Emerson I used to know. After seeing her be vulnerable yesterday, laughing together over gelato, feeling how intensely she supports me, it's harder to keep my feelings in check. And when I snap the shutter, the image is incredible. It's the kind of shot I wanted to take of her when we were eighteen, but I didn't yet have the tools or the skills to. It might be my favorite shot I've ever taken.

And then Harry ambles into frame and plants a huge kiss on her cheek. I recoil from my viewfinder.

Harry's voice is flippant and completely overconfident. And the way his hand casually dropped to Emerson's back was far too territorial for my taste. "Marissa? Mandy? Maria? That crazed woman with the clothes has your outfit. I can stand in for . . ."

"Theo," I mutter.

"This is Theo," Emerson fills in. She's shooting daggers at him, and her jaw is clenched. What is the deal here?

"Right. Thanks for doing this, man, hope it builds your book or whatever. My right side is my good one." Then he turns to Emerson. My Emerson. "And every side is your good one, babe. You look stunning. Doesn't she?"

That might have been directed at me, but I pointedly ignore him, and Emerson runs off to change. I'm left staring at Harry, who looks all too amused by my obvious annoyance. But who is he to call Emerson "babe"? "Hello? Did you get that?" He waves a hand at me and overexaggerates turning his right cheek toward me. *Pompous prick.*

"Right side, got it," I confirm. "Anything else?"

"Can you make me look taller than her?" Harry looks around and his eyes light up when he spots the apple box Kevin is carrying over. "Won't look right to the fans if we're the same height."

"But you are the same height." I keep my tone even, professional. But inside I'm gloating, because I both am genuinely taller than Emerson, and man enough not to be emasculated when she's stood next to me in heels and we're the same height.

Harry looks at me like he's concerned I might be a bit slow, then directs his attention toward Kevin. "Let's put that here."

Kevin hides a smirk and drops the apple box at Harry's feet. We stand in a tense silence, the only sound the chatter of fans and a few stray paparazzi who are watching from the wings, until Emerson rushes back over and we all come back to life. She eyes the apple box skeptically, but ultimately ignores it as Harry steps onto it and gains a solid six inches.

I adjust my frame to hide the box and start snapping away without saying anything to them. If I was shooting any other celebrity couple, real or not, I would be directing them to lean in close, stare into each other's eyes, be romantic. But I just can't make myself ask them to do those things, even for *GQ*. Because watching them, I can't help but admit to myself that I wish I was in Harry's place, fitting into Em's world so effortlessly that everyone with a pulse is rooting for them to make it official.

Fortunately for the cover, they're both pros and need no direction. They wordlessly launch into a series of poses. He places a hand on her lower back and brings his forehead to hers, and my stomach churns. She stands on tiptoes and nestles her head into his neck, and my pulse races. He wraps a hand around her neck and she pushes through a flinch, and I stop shooting, my blood pounding.

"Emerson, are you okay?" For a moment she looked uncomfortable, I'm sure of it. Although I'm automatically adjusting my stance, aperture, framing, my focus is trained on her.

"Yes. Great." Her words are obviously clipped, but no one else seems to notice. I'm reluctant to raise the camera until I know that she wants to keep going. "Theo. We only have an hour."

Message received. I continue snapping photos of them, getting a range of shots. I can't help but notice that when Emerson stares into Harry's eyes, she looks almost bored. Nothing compared with what I captured of her on the rocks our first day.

I position myself slightly behind Harry, to his right, as requested, and line up a tighter shot of Emerson with her hands wrapped around the back of his neck. I have a three-quarter shot of him and his frustratingly strong jaw and classic profile, and Emerson almost in full. If she could just look the tiniest bit toward me, and get an ounce of passion into her gaze, this will be the shot.

"Em," I say, my voice low. "You look incredible."

When she looks toward me, her face having broken from her on-camera mask to reveal a soft smile and wistful eyes, I snap the shot and immediately pull back to look in the viewfinder. "This is it," I declare. Since she looked at me, not at the lens, you can't tell that she's looking at me rather than Harry in the shot, and she looks both gorgeous and expressive.

I turn the camera toward them and catch Harry watching Emerson's expression fall as she realizes I complimented her to get a shot. He looks surprised that she cares. I hope she isn't hurt by it, but I love the shot and secretly like that my compliments are what gets her to feel something real.

Emerson texts a photo of the shot to her agent, and after a moment she nods in approval. I hand off the card to Kevin so he can run it to the digi-tech to be retouched and send out the images. "When will this come out?"

Emerson freezes midtext, and then looks up at me and grins. "In twelve hours."

I whistle and gesture toward Harry, who walked away the second the shot was approved, after giving Emerson a brief hug. "This is moving fast."

Emerson rolls her eyes. "I told you, that's show business. And the original cover got axed because the starlet posted a video she shouldn't have and is basically canceled. Harry and I are a sure-fire viral moment. Who knows, maybe they'll even print it, and you can get your mom one."

I wonder if Emerson has to worry about getting canceled. If she's afraid all of this will be taken away. But I don't ask. "Well, thanks for thinking of me."

"Of course you're who I thought of."

We walk in silence toward the trailer. I don't know if she's annoyed by how I got the shot, concerned over Harry practically blowing her off, or just not looking forward to shooting more looks. But whatever has her down, I want to bring her back up.

When we split, her to change and touch up, and me to shoot Jillian, I call after her. "Hey, Em?" She turns back toward me, pauses. "You do look incredible. Just so you know."

The smile she gives me makes my knees go wobbly.

CHAPTER TWENTY

—Junior Year—

Emerson

At promptly five thirty, after leading the team in a rousing chant and sweating for two hours straight, Theo jogged directly off the field and over to me, ignoring the shouts of guys on the team, or any halfhearted calls from girls in the bleachers. Everyone knew that when I was in front of him, I had his full attention. I lay on the turf and daydreamed, read, wrote stories, generally occupied myself with solitary activities since the girlfriends who watched the weekly scrimmage from the bleachers wanted nothing to do with me. I couldn't hack it in the honors classes, where the girls might actually have appreciated my book recommendations and dry humor, and I didn't have the encyclopedic knowledge of mascara brands and clothes necessary to have a successful chat with the girls in my classes. They just thought I was weird, so when a few months after that dismal day at orientation my friendship prospects didn't become more promising, I gave up on girlfriends and convinced myself that all I needed was Theo.

A good example of humor that was clearly only funny to me was how, while the popular girls typically yelled things like, "You've got it, Chad!" and "Kill him, Josh!" and "Go, Tommy!" I offered up more *creative* praise. "Theo, if you get that goal, I'll flash the team!" This, I learned, was too rousing, so today I went with, "If you get a point, we can watch *Legally Blonde* for the twentieth time! I know it's your favorite!" Theo responded well when he was slightly embarrassed, his irritation propelling the ball into the net with more force than he'd demonstrated five minutes earlier.

"Em, you know, you really don't need to keep cheering for me." Theo lugged his tremendous gear bag over one shoulder, and like the gentleman he was, hoisted my backpack over his other shoulder, where it dangled, laughably small in comparison. "Your cheers aren't especially motivational."

"Theo, I have to entertain myself for two hours straight. I've got to keep things lively." I slid my hand through the crook of his arm, which was slick with sweat and had small black pieces of turf plastered to it.

"You don't have to come! I could get dropped off at your house after." He subtly flexed his bicep under my hand, which I refused to acknowledge, although a thrill traced its way down my spine.

"Maybe I like watching you sweat." I got into my passenger seat and threw the keys on the driver's seat. Theo had his license but had another few months until he inherited Owen's car.

Theo slid into the car, as comfortable as if it were his own, and headed toward my house. Thursday evenings were our long-standing movie night. Back when my dad was around, he handled Thursdays while my mom went out with friends. He would pick up pizza on his way home from work, and we'd eat it in bed, without my mom there to scold us, and I'd stay up too late, then rush to pretend to be asleep when she came home. It only lasted until I was ten, when he went to work one morning and never returned, and our house began accumulating things as though my mom might one day be able to trade fifty shoeboxes of random crap for her husband.

When I'd told Theo Thursday was my favorite weekday, due

to a now-defunct tradition, he took it upon himself to reinvigo-
rate the magic of Thursday nights. I typically kept him as far away
from my chaotic household as possible, but on Thursdays I made
an exception, and we holed ourselves away in my room, watching
movies and eating junk. After doing this for two years, he'd run
into my mom fewer than five times.

This was his week to pick the movie, but first I had agreed to
let him read my short story, after months of him asking to and me
insisting it wasn't good enough to be read. I opened the file on
my computer and curled up in the corner of my headboard and
the wall while he sat a charged two inches away from me and read
it. It was the first time someone besides the Salem High creative
writing teacher had read my work, and it was terrifying. Theo's
opinion mattered more to me than anyone else's.

Suddenly he chuckled quietly. I strained to look at the page. I
tried to remain silent and let him keep reading, but I couldn't do
it. "What's so funny? What part are you reading?"

Theo glanced up. "Em, you said not to say anything until I
finish it."

"I know, I know. But just tell me what part."

"She's dressing down the guy at the end of their first date. It's
hilarious."

I exhaled a sigh of relief and smiled. "I'm glad you think it's
funny."

"Of course I do." Theo jostled my knee with his own. "Why
don't you go fill your water or something? It's hard to read with
you watching over my shoulder like this."

I was watching every tiny movement of his face, desperate to
hear that he liked what he was reading. He wasn't even a reader,
so I shouldn't have judged based on his opinion anyway, but I was
greedy for feedback. "Come on," he added. "I'll tell you everything
afterwards, I swear."

"Fine," I relented. I spent ten minutes on my phone in the

kitchen, watching the minutes tick away, and then Theo called my name and I raced back up the stairs. "So what did you think?"

He looked up at me from the bed while I tapped my foot impatiently and picked at my cuticles, too nervous to meet his gaze in case he hated it. "You can tell me if you hate it." There was silence for all of two seconds before I changed my mind. "Actually don't. I don't want to know. Don't say anything." I climbed over Theo, back onto my place on the bed. "Let's just watch the movie."

"Are you serious?"

"Yes! Don't tell me. I don't need to know. I know it needs work."

"Em, I loved it. I know it's an early draft, but it's funny, and smart, and I think it's really good. The characters felt real, and I liked the Salem details. And I don't know how you came up with the flashback stuff, and then made it jump back to the present and all that . . . impressive, honestly." Theo moved closer to me, so that our shoulders were touching. "It's good, Emerson. I swear. I want to read everything you write."

I swallowed the lump in my throat and forced myself to look at Theo. To confirm he was genuine, even though I knew he wouldn't lie to me. "You're biased, though."

"It's good. Take a compliment for once."

"Thank you."

"I'll read it again tomorrow and leave notes in the margin for you."

"Thank you," I repeated. "Really. I'm glad you don't hate it."

"Don't be silly."

I pressed my shoulder into Theo's slightly, then leaned forward to grab the computer he'd set down. "Movie time?" When I leaned back, he grabbed the pizza box from the floor and moved back to his original position, and the two inches of space was separating us again. Like every other night we sat in bed. It's amazing how small a few inches feel when you're hyperconscious of it for several hours straight every week for a year.

"How about *The Departed*? I know you love a guy with a Boston accent." Theo folded a slice of pizza in half and took a gulping bite, causing half of it to disappear in one go. He always insisted on getting an extra-large pie, even though I only ate two slices, and the amount he put down nauseated me.

I eyed the laptop apprehensively. I hated gory movies. "Fine, but only if you'll talk in a Boston accent to me."

"Will ya watch *The Depahted* with me?" I could feel the hot air of his pizza-laden breath on my face.

"Fine," I agreed. We spent the first half hour of the movie talking over it, imitating their accents, and finishing our food. At the first truly violent scene I jumped, and instead of laughing at me like he might have any other week, Theo raised his arm from where it was pressed tight to his side, preserving the crucial two inches, and wrapped it around me. I was so shocked that I forgot to breathe for a moment, and my exhale sounded ragged and violent when I finally let it out and leaned in to him.

The heat of his palm on my arm was sensual. We'd probably watched over a hundred movies together and had never cuddled. Not once. I didn't want to move. I never wanted to stop, his broad chest holding me close, my heart pounding in my chest, so loud I couldn't stop to listen and try to decipher how fast his own was beating.

Theo didn't say a word, so I didn't either.

"So, what did you think?" Theo asked at the end of the movie. His voice rumbled against my back and I felt the baritone in my chest. His finger absentmindedly stroked my arm.

"I have to admit, it was good." I didn't move. Could we really not mention how momentous this was?

After sitting silently for a moment, wrapped up in each other while I tried to memorize every inch of him that was touching me in case I never had another moment like this again, he extricated himself and began to gather up his things and the trash we'd left on the floor. He always cleaned up for me on Thursdays and let himself out, saying it was so I didn't have to get up out of bed, even though as soon as he left, I would get up anyway to brush my teeth.

He was acting the same as any other week. The only thing that betrayed him was a slight flush that was stuck on his cheeks. Otherwise, I might have thought I imagined the past two hours. "Call me when you get home?" I said, the same words I said every week.

He flushed even deeper as he ducked out. "Of course."

Twenty minutes later his disembodied voice was back in my bed. "Em, I'm sorry if I made things weird. You're, uh . . . my best friend."

"You didn't," I assured him. I squeezed my eyes shut, grateful that he couldn't see me, because I couldn't keep pinpricks of tears from overflowing out of them. Letting him read my story was the most vulnerable I'd been in years. I thought his arm around me might actually have meant something after that.

"Okay, good," he replied finally.

I put my line on mute and tried desperately to get my voice back under control. I had been completely fine for two years, but now that I had let hope break through for one night, I was racked with disappointment. We were just friends. I knew that. And couldn't let myself think otherwise.

"Goodnight, Em."

"Goodnight, Theo." I hung up the line without waiting to hear if he might say anything else.

CHAPTER TWENTY-ONE

Emerson

I'm never more shocked than when an early wrap time actually
happens as scheduled. The call sheet had us arriving at four a.m.
for hair and makeup, but wrapping at three p.m., which sounded
way too good to be true, especially considering we took a late
lunch and had to squeeze in *GQ*. But the sun is still high in the
sky at three fifteen when Stacey calls it. "That's a wrap!"

It takes a lot for me to keep things remotely professional with
Theo. I need more time with him off set when we can act like
friends, not coworkers. I think I made it clear that the shoot with
Harry is just press, so hopefully it's not too much of a wrench in
my "Win Theo Over" plan.

"Should we go shopping or something?" Rachel asks as we sit
in the trailer, wiping makeup off our faces.

"The hotel has a great hot tub," Evonique offers. "I went in
for like five minutes last night because all the underwater work
left me so cold."

"Let's do that. I've kept too many clothes this week already,
and my carry-on won't close if I buy literally one more thing."
Even now, Jillian is dressed entirely in yet-to-be-released Anthem

clothes that Miranda has relinquished to her. Some sets don't let you take anything, and I was always told it was unprofessional to ask, especially on designer jobs. But Jillian shoots Anthem a lot and reassured me that they actually liked it, and with my follower count it would basically be free advertising if I kept a few things. So my sundress from the first day hangs in my closet at the hotel.

"Emerson, you could take a scenic walk with your guy. I hear the path along the water to the hotel only takes like twenty minutes." Rachel pulls her hair into a messy bun while she speaks, but her eyes catch mine in the mirror and are full of mischief. "I may have suggested the walk to him too."

"He's not *my guy*," I choke out. Jillian snorts and I double down. "Seriously. Not yet." But I do like to hear that they think of Theo and me that way. As an "us" again.

Evonique comes up behind me and begins massaging my shoulders, which I absolutely hate but pretend to appreciate. "Don't think we didn't notice you two running off last night. It seemed like things got pretty friendly today. And the shoot's almost over . . . it's time for things to go to the next level."

"Okay, I'll just mention the walk, and see if he's up for it. Sunset is gorgeous here. A bit romantic, even. And if not, I'll go in the hot tub." I sound like a teenager being coached along by her sister for a first hang with an unrequited crush.

In Cinque Terre, there's a train that runs directly between the five towns all day. It's the quickest and easiest way to get around, although of course for the shoot we're caravanning up and down the mountainside in luxury SUVs that are each carrying suitcases of clothes and lights. I have no idea how the trailer makes it up the steep hills, but every morning it's waiting at our destination without fail. I hear the hike between the first four towns is pretty grueling, a steep ascent and descent, but it's what most people travel here to do. The only exception is this last leg of the hike, which is twenty mainly flat minutes all along the water, no steep winding staircases involved. It's the reward after doing all the more treacherous trails that connect the first four towns.

We traipse out of the trailer, and I see that while Theo isn't waiting at the door like yesterday, he is hovering nearby on a FaceTime call. Maybe he's just close by to use the RV Wi-Fi . . . but I'd rather tell myself that he's waiting to catch me on my way out. He's been standing for the last ten hours straight, so it's hard to imagine he actually wants to go on a walk, no matter how leisurely, but I don't have any other ideas.

I walk over to him and loiter a few feet away, clearly eavesdropping but trying to look nonchalant. "Wow, that looks great, bud! Seems like your dad's really holding down the fort." Theo glances up and sees me waiting for him. *Owen. Want to say hi?* he mouths. *It's okay!* I mouth back. Theo looks back at the phone. "Now, team, I want you to know that if you don't win today . . . it's okay, I know it's because Owen's the only one coaching. But I'm rooting for you and can't wait to be back at practice next week! Witches on three, right? I have a special guest who's going to count down with us."

Theo turns around and gets me in frame. "This is my friend Em. She's going to lead our chant. You all ready?"

He glances at me. This took me by surprise; usually everyone tiptoes around asking me to do things, since typically a guest appearance or social share comes with a fee attached. And I love that Theo doesn't even think of that. And that these five-year-old soccer players don't care who I am. Like at all. "Ready!" I exclaim. Completely in sync, Theo and I count down. "Three, two, one . . . WITCHES!"

The children shriek and laugh, their hands flying up from the circle before they run off. I expect Theo to hang up, but instead Owen's face fills the screen, and my gut twists. It's one thing to see Theo. But Owen . . . he should hate me for abandoning Theo. So why is he smiling?

"Emerson! It's so great to see you. When Theo told me he was shooting you, I couldn't believe it." Owen's tone is lighthearted through the tinny iPhone speakers.

"It's great to see you too!" And it is. I miss Theo's whole family, and want to see Owen's kids, his wife, to be the one on the sidelines with lemonade for the soccer team. "And yeah, this shoot has been amazing. The most fun I've had on set in years."

And the most anxiety. But I haven't done a decade of therapy for nothing. I can do this, I can handle seeing the family I abandoned, unexpectedly on FaceTime, and watching the life Theo has without me play out right in front of me. "Well, it's great to see you two back together."

Theo snatches the phone away. "Owen!" he says sharply. "We've got to go," he mutters over his brother's reply.

"See you soon I hope!" I shout out as he hangs up.

"Sorry about that," Theo says quietly, his discomfort obvious. "You know Owen. Always . . . meddling."

Theo blushes, and it's the most adorable thing I've ever seen. "Want to walk back together?"

He puts his phone away immediately, and his face lights up with a huge smile that's so genuine it makes my eyes water. The kind of smile I felt spread over my face at the end of my shoot with Harry, the one that's reserved only for him. And it's selfish, but I hope this smile is the edition he only breaks into with me. "Great idea. I hear it's only like twenty minutes between Riomaggiore and Manarola, all along the water." I eye Rachel over his shoulder, who winks and waves goodbye. "Want to combine bags?"

This is a trick he'd sometimes pull when I was making a valiant effort to carry my own things and save his back, when he knew I didn't actually want to. He was always more of a hiker than me and would save me a few pounds by folding my bag into his own, or just slinging my purse over his own shoulder, because he was always trying to make my life easier. I didn't realize how thoughtful it was at the time, until I started dating and my boyfriends didn't want to hold my things and risk looking *emasculated*, as if holding something for someone you care about is somehow the opposite of manliness. Still, I decide I won't let him carry my stuff this time. I want him to know that I'm my own person, and that we can actually be just friends. If that's all he wants. "No, thanks."

"So, tell me more about your life," I command as I walk alongside him, trusting he knows where he's going. "I feel like you already know everything about me."

"I know the SparkNotes of the last decade or so," he corrects me. "I'm still waiting on your actual life story."

"Fine," I agree, breathing slightly heavier as we walk up the hill to the start of the path. Shoots always leave me more tired than I realize once the adrenaline wears off. "But I want more than your SparkNotes. So start talking."

He laughs. "Well, you can imagine what my life in Salem is like. Between shoots I spend a lot of time with family, but I also try to go to as many art shows and museum exhibits in Boston and the North Shore as I can. Keep myself fresh. And I go into New York so much I should probably have kept my apartment there. But I can't afford it on top of the mortgage."

"What? You bought a house in Salem?" This shouldn't shock me, but it does. Not that he can afford a house in New England—which *is* impressive—but how established his life is.

"You'll laugh, but I actually bought my childhood home. Mom decided to sell it after Dad died, and I just didn't want to see someone else living in it."

"I love your house." I dreamt of living in a house like his as a teenager. It was the perfect family home.

"You'll love it even more in about a year because Owen's helping me put a pool in this summer. We're digging it ourselves, then outsourcing the rest."

A daydream overtakes me. I'm bringing him lemonade and

watching him work. When he's done, we head off to do chores, then make dinner together. I can see what my life could've been so vividly that I can almost taste it.

And it doesn't slip my attention that he mentioned the future, a future that includes me.

"That's amazing. Truly. I want to see it."

At this point we've reached the entrance to the trail, but it's blocked off with a makeshift UNDER CONSTRUCTION sign, its lettering bold and red in both Italian and English. A red arrow points to an alternative path, which looks blissfully deserted. "Should we try it?"

"Why not?" Theo shrugs and we continue up this slightly steeper path. "Normally I'd say *no way* to hills on a shoot, but I hear this is one of the best views in the world. Shoots are the only time I'll get to travel like this, so I should make use of it."

"You should charge more, work less. You don't want to burn out and not be able to work on your gallery show." It's unnecessarily blunt, more like the old me than who I am now, but Theo's unperturbed.

"Em, the gallery show stuff is all talk. It would be nice, but it's not a priority. I enjoy my work now just fine." The path has gotten progressively steeper, and even Theo's getting out of breath, but I won't be the first to call uncle and ask for a break.

"Theo, you should have it all. Not just fine. You deserve to have everything you've ever wanted and to wake up every day and be so excited for what you're going to do that it hurts." I'm audibly gasping at this point, and the path has evolved to just be a steep staircase made of stone. Theo doesn't say anything. "Sorry," I manage after I catch my breath.

"I have no ideas for a show anyway, so what's the point?" Theo stops to fish a water bottle out of his bag, and I gratefully rest beside him. I don't acknowledge his side step of my impassioned advice.

"You had so many ideas senior year."

"They all revolved around you." He offers the bottle to me, and I take a long sip to avoid responding. He does the same, not bothering to pour it like most people do on set, and I watch his lips wrap around the bottle where I've left a ring of lip gloss.

"I'll be in it."

"Then I'll really have to up my rates, because you know I can't afford yours." Theo trudges up the stairs again and I follow reluctantly.

"Theo. Come on, you know I'd do it."

"Well, we haven't talked in ten years, so actually I was pretty convinced that if I called you up, you'd say no. You did change your number." His tone is biting. I deserve that.

"I'm saying yes now. And I've had like five serious stalkers. I had to change it."

"You could've told me. But you didn't want to reconnect."

"I should have acted differently. I'm sorry. Really sorry." I can barely talk at this point, due to the exertion of this scenic walk turned vertical climb, and my words hang there, but I'm grateful for the silence. I want him to hear my apology, because even I know it's not enough, but I do mean it. Although it would be more dramatic to let it sit until we reach the top, only a few minutes go by before I have to tap Theo's shoulder in front of me.

"I need a break. This path is brutal."

We chug more water and Theo shields his eyes to look around toward where the peak presumably is. "I can't see where it levels out."

I peer upward. We're about a third of the way up a rather large mountain, littered with tiny vineyards that seem mostly abandoned. The path is overgrown, but there are markers here and there. "You don't think we have to go all the way up, do you? Because I don't think I'll make it."

"I mean, I'd like to think the sign would have warned us if we were going from a twenty-minute walk to a level red two-hour hike. Let me look." Theo pulls out his phone and attempts to zoom in on the map, with no success. There's absolutely no service. "We could go back down?"

"Everyone will be gone at this point. We might as well just keep going; we'll have to get to the other side eventually."

We trudge onward, and it hurts more and more with each step. My Apple Watch alerts me that my blood oxygen is low. Apparently barre classes and yoga don't leave me in hiking shape. "Do you miss home?" Theo asks suddenly. Even his words sound strained at this point.

"I miss you," I say immediately. Then I hesitate. But it's easier to be honest from three steps behind Theo, without his gaze trained on me. "And I do miss Salem. It's so much better than LA or New York. Or at least I remember it that way. The food, the ocean . . . but I don't miss my home. My mom . . . It always made things a mixed bag."

Theo pauses for a moment and lets me catch up to him. "I think you'd like being home again if it was with me. My family. I know it's not as flashy as your life now, but it's nice. Comfortable. And you know what I said last night is a standing offer."

"I think I'd like being home with you too," I whisper, so quietly that I'm not sure he even hears. And I think with him, facing my mom wouldn't be so hard. In fact, it sounds like something I might actually want to do.

Three breaks later we're still hiking up a path that's completely vertical. I'm drenched in sweat and wheezing and I'm calling up ahead to Theo's now bare back. "Theo, I'm not going to make it. It's never going to peak, we'll just eventually be in a cloud or something."

"Emerson! Em! There's a trail marker. It says only .1K to peak left!"

His words propel me up the next twenty steps to him, where I catch my breath and look at the sign myself. "How is that possible?"

He hands me water, which I drink gratefully. "Em, wait—"

I chug the last sip and put the empty bottle back in his bag. "What?"

"That was the last of the water. But don't worry, I'm sure we're close."

"Okay, we've got this. Once the path peaks it won't even be so bad." I march forward with new resolve and Theo falls into step behind me. There's a brief moment when the path looks like it's leveled out, but after one enthusiastic whoop I rein it back in, because we're now just on a slightly less steep staircase. "I take it back," I correct myself finally. "We could probably die here. We can't call for help, there's no way down besides walking forever. What if someone broke their ankle up here? We haven't even seen any other hikers."

"I would carry you down, Em, don't worry. You don't even weigh much more than the camera."

"Don't make me laugh, I don't have enough moisture left for that." I drop to the ground and lie down in the dirt, not caring how disgusting it is or what bugs crawl on me. He plops down next to me but stays upright. "You don't think there are animals here, right?"

The extreme hike must be getting to me because I never let myself unravel like this anymore. Josh used to say that the least put together he ever saw me was when I helped him repaint the condo, but the thing is, I still had makeup on. There were just a few flecks of paint on my designer jeans. He had no idea what not put together could look like. Theo's the only person I don't mind seeing me like this.

"I think we're in the clear. Come on, do you want a lift up a few steps? I really will carry you, because that's how convinced I am that the peak is right beyond that tree." His hair is plastered to his face with sweat, and I can tell his nose will peel tomorrow from the sunburn he's getting. He gave me his hat so I wouldn't burn, since it's my face that will be in the campaign.

"I can't let you carry me; your legs must be dead from standing all day," I protest halfheartedly as I rise onto one elbow and push my hair out of my face with dirty hands. I hadn't brought a hair tie with me, and I have never regretted anything more.

Theo just rolls his eyes at my protests, and I climb on and wrap my arms around his neck, which is broader than I remember and deliciously slick with sweat. Theo bounds up the steps as though I weigh nothing, and when we get to the tree I see it. The peak.

There is nothing beautiful about this peak, beyond the hike now behind downhill. Since this is the alternative path, trees block the view and the dirt is dry and parched. But it's flat, and I can see the downward staircase, which is one of the most glorious things I've ever seen at this point. I hop off Theo's back and wrap him in a giant hug, giddy with relief, momentarily forgetting all of the awkwardness of the last decade, and any boundaries I planned on maintaining.

Theo remains frozen, arms held slightly out, as though afraid to touch me even though my legs were just snaked around his sides, my entire body pressed flush to his back. He's clearly reluctant, but at this point I'm already hugging him, and it just feels so good. We can hug. It doesn't have to mean anything. And if it does, maybe that's okay. The more time I spend with him, the more I admit to myself that I don't just love how authentic I feel with him, I love who he is now too. And there's only one day left on this shoot, so we need to start progressing, and fast. "I thought we'd never make it," I exclaim into his neck when he finally wraps his arms around me.

"I was doubtful for a second too." Theo pulls back and peers up at the sky, holding his sun tracker app toward it. Every photographer I've ever met has had one of these apps, which tells them where the sun will be at any point in the day. "This is actually one of the tougher hikes I've done lately."

"This is the toughest hike I've done in years. I hate hiking." I eye the trailhead down apprehensively.

"You admit it! You always claimed you didn't mind it." Theo's eyes light up, and his eyebrows shoot up his forehead. We're both a bit delirious at this point.

"If I admitted it, you wouldn't have hiked anywhere with me!"

"I won't confirm or deny," Theo argues.

"I actually haven't hiked since I was like twenty. I posted my hike to my story one time, and some really intense fans showed up and didn't respect my personal space; it freaked me out. Learned a lesson." I've made this story into a fun anecdote before, but saying it now, to Theo, it just sounds sad. And I never share sad things with anyone. It's not on-brand, and I always know to stay on it, since after I break up with someone, who knows what they'll say.

But this is Theo, and every instinct I've built up to protect me over the last ten years has been turned upside down by seeing him again. "Are you serious?"

"Yup, can't live post. That was the lesson, I mean." I pretend to be overly interested in retying my shoelaces.

"Em, you know that's terrifying to me, right? I didn't realize how extreme everything was for you. I kind of thought you were kidding about the stalkers." Theo's eyes are so earnest, it tugs at me, especially after seeing how well he handled the mob of fans yesterday on no notice.

"I'm much more careful now. But at the end of the day, it is part of the job, and I'm really grateful for my life. It's just how it is for me, and there's no going back at this point. It's accept it or become a recluse, basically."

Theo jostles his shoulder into my own. "Well, I'll be a recluse with you, if you want."

"I'll take it under advisement."

"So, Harry. Why don't you want to date him? He seems like a catch." Theo's voice wavers as he asks, and it's clear he's been holding in the question.

"We're just friends, I told you. For years now. Actually just friends." Not like we were *just friends*. "We tried dating and just didn't work as a couple. We don't have chemistry."

"You definitely have chemistry."

"Trust me, when the cameras are off? We don't. And it's not something you can force. It will never happen between us again for real." Harry texted me YOU'RE WELCOME after the *GQ* shots, as though I wanted to make Theo more jealous. I don't! His reaction after the lunch was the perfect balance. But the bit of jealousy I hear in his voice now . . . isn't hurting anyone.

I can see Theo's brain working. He digs his shoe into the dirt absentmindedly. "Was it real before? Or press? Like you're letting happen now."

I nod slowly. Cautiously. Because it's a yes to all of the above. "It started fake, and became real. And now we're friends. For real."

Theo stops moving completely and looks up at me, his face shocked. "Em. Are you serious? When that first photo came out, I thought . . ."

"That photo was taken the first time we met. Which was arranged. But it doesn't matter; all that matters is what's real now. And my friendship with him is what's genuine. And it's nothing like the friendship you and I have." History is being rewritten in Theo's head, right before my eyes. If only he knew everything. I open my mouth to tell him what actually happened, but then he stands up.

"Should we keep going?" Theo sounds casual, but he's not looking at me.

"Ugh, I guess so. We should get water." I'm already parched, but complaining won't make me any less thirsty.

We start down the steps, which are incredibly steep. I go in front of Theo, since I'm walking at a snail's pace, terrified of slipping, my hands gripping the rocks that are built up on either side of us. "So, do you hike a lot? There's not much hiking in Salem, or New York."

Theo's breath is on the back of my neck as he hovers behind me, prepared to grab me if I slip. "Allison and I do one hiking trip each spring. Like big hikes, the Grand Canyon, Yosemite, places like that. This is honestly steeper than the main trail at the Grand Canyon."

"Allison?" I ask, my voice as level as possible while walking down a mountain.

"Yeah, she's a photographer too. I've known her since college, she's great." We continue on in silence for a few beats. It's excruciating. I've never been jealous of any boyfriend I've had, but with this, with Theo, the jealousy risks burning a hole in my stomach lining.

I miss a step and slide forward, my hands grasping for a nook on the wall to cling to. Theo reaches forward and effortlessly catches me, pulling me up by the waist with strong hands. "Thanks." I'm breathless, both from the scare and from trying to act nonchalant when everything in me is screaming that I should tell him how I feel. That I don't want someone else holding the top place in his heart. But I've been as forthcoming as I can be, so instead I stop leaning on him for now, and keep moving forward.

CHAPTER TWENTY-TWO

Theo

Painstakingly plodding down the mountain with Emerson on the scenic walk from hell, I actually feel fully at ease with her for the first time since she arrived. The stress and discomfort of the unnaturally steep path and the lack of water has forced us to push through all of the lingering tension.

Going down is less physically taxing but slower, since we don't want to slip and fall. I can see the sun creeping lower as we continue. While I tried to motivate Emerson with promises of sunset, I really just don't want us to be stuck here after dark. The path is treacherously steep and will be a death trap without visibility. There are barely any trail markers, so there's no way anyone's put guiding lights here.

"Do you think we're almost there?" Emerson asks without looking back at me, her focus entirely on the steps in front of her. "The kilometer marker said point one like twenty minutes ago."

I snort. "Maybe if you jump. These kilometer markers are completely ridiculous. But I think we're almost there, those rooftops look kind of close." The elevation is so steep here that houses are basically built into the mountain.

"Okay, I might need to beg one of those houses for water," Emerson mutters. She's slowed down significantly since we started descending, once the initial burst of hope we were almost there wore off. I've put on ChapStick three times to try to ward off cracked lips as my mouth dries out, and the thought of water makes my salivary glands go into overdrive. "Oh my god!" she suddenly shrieks. "Look!"

She speeds up and I almost trip over myself to keep up with her. Just below us is the roof of a house to our left and a small garden to the right. And exactly level with the roof, the path changes from ragged and uneven, to stone steps. A golden light shines onto the houses below, through cracks between buildings, as though we're descending into heaven. Which is what it will feel like when we finally drink water again. "A staircase has never looked so appealing."

"I could actually kiss the steps," Emerson adds with a glance back at me. I meet her on the step and she lets her head fall back against my chest in exhausted relief. I've kept some space between us today, but having her next to me settles something inside me, like we're two magnets that have been trying to get back to each other for years. And seeing her wear my hat makes my stomach twist.

"Do you think we can still make the sunset?"

I eye the already deep golden light with apprehension. "We can try."

The pace Emerson takes off at is completely reckless, but I follow her without question. We both know the goal is the lookout point. It's a quarter of a mile from the hotel, and from it you gaze out at the postcard view, tiny rainbow-colored buildings stacked on top of one another. I trail her down staircases until we reach a flat street, and she whoops in delight.

Pink buildings are to our left, with flowered vines protruding from windowsills, and on the right the path drops sharply, revealing how high up we still are, and from there we can look out at the golden glow that's lowering itself onto the town like a blanket. It's so warm it looks almost fake. Emerson absolutely glows everywhere the light hits her.

"Theo, selfie, quick!" I pull out my own phone and she snatches it. We push our faces together and grin and she snaps the photo. "I'm sure we look disgusting," she laments. "But this light is stunning."

I know I'll look at this photo every day for weeks, if not for the rest of my life. I wish our sweaty faces could be my lock screen. "Come on, I think we can make it." We sprint down the sloped streets as the light creeps closer.

I shout apologies to tourists, or maybe they're locals, that we brush past, dropping hands only long enough to get by before coming back together. Emerson's hair looks darker in the deep glow of the light, streaming behind her as we run. We come up to the edge of a drop-off, where we have to decide whether to take an up or a down path to the right. Emerson tugs me to the downhill, but I hesitate. "I feel like we won't get to the overlook. If we make a mistake we'll miss it."

"I have no idea which way. I think I just don't want to go up." She's gasping for air as she talks, but her smile stretches across her entire face and I wish I had my real camera to freeze this moment.

"I think we have to go up." Running uphill is the last thing that I want to do either, but I can already imagine how crestfallen she'll be if we miss this.

Without another word, Emerson turns and we head up the path. My calves burn and I know I'll be exhausted tomorrow. We race up the path with energy that is coming from some unknown reserve, energy that I can only access when I'm within yards of Emerson, until we reach the path leading to the overlook.

The way the path is set up, you climb up it with your back

facing the town, then once you reach the top, you turn around and can look out. But the light is fading so fast that I stop and turn, halfway up. "Let's just look for a sec."

I raise my arm without dropping Emerson's hand and she laughs as she spins, landing against my chest.

After we gaze for a minute, Emerson pulls away from me and begins to actually walk backward up the path. "This might be too slow. But I don't know if I can run anymore."

"I think we made it," I assure her. "This is ninety-five percent of what you see from the top, with about half as many people." From where we stand no one is directly in our line of sight, but I know if we walked another hundred yards there would be at least fifty people jostling for a spot. And fifty people jostling for a photo of Emerson.

"Want to sit?" Emerson drops to the nearest remotely flat rock without waiting for my response, and I join her. She glances up at me. "Can I lean?"

"Of course." I brace myself against the cliff and she leans back onto me, her weight warm against me.

I slowly wrap my arm around Emerson, so I'm holding her close, almost holding my breath, as we sit there. But she doesn't move away, and I think I hear her give a little sigh as she rests more of her weight on me.

"I'm sorry I was harsh," Emerson whispers eventually, when the sun is almost gone. "Things are just different now. A lot has happened, and I thought I needed to protect my heart, and you."

I suck in a breath of air. She's acknowledging her agent's rejection. "Em, it's okay. It's us. You can be honest with me." My words are barely audible. In this dusky light, between the harsh light of day and the secrets of night, the capacity for truth seems greater, and I don't want loud words to ward it off.

"Not anymore. Not since we were eighteen. Things changed."

"Because of . . . me?"

She tenses, and I can tell that even though I only said three words, they were the wrong ones. "No, Theo," she says. "Please don't think that. It's . . . complicated . . . and we don't need to get into it. But I've missed being close to you."

I'm completely lost, but want her to know I'm here for her, for whatever this is. Even though less than twenty-four hours ago I swore to myself I'd stay away after this shoot. I know that in the space of a few hours, the wall between us has broken down. I'll never be able to stay away again. I need to find a way to reach her, to convince her she and I . . . that there's still an "us" here.

I deleted that pact off my phone, but it doesn't mean I've forgotten what it said. I want the deadline in three days to mark the start of a future for us, even if it's different from the one we had envisioned.

"Em, you can tell me anything. Whenever you want to, I'm here. Or a few feet through the wall at the hotel." I pull her a bit closer to me, and she sighs, her head nestling into the crook of my arm. But she seems almost sad. "Whatever you need."

"Can this be enough? At least for now?" Her voice is barely audible, but I hear her.

"Of course."

CHAPTER TWENTY-THREE

—Senior Year—

Theo

"Look straight at me and do, like, a half-smile? Like when you want to laugh at someone but you're holding it in." I directed Emerson with more confidence than I felt. She stood against a giant, plain white piece of paper that I'd taped to the wall in the photography room at school, and although she looked incredible, it was my first time taking a picture of something that actually moved.

I started Intro to Photography three weeks earlier, and we spent the first week learning how not to break the camera, and the next two weeks photographing fruit on a platter. Which was much easier than photographing Emerson, who seemed incapable of standing still.

"Theo, there's no point to doing this. That guy in Boston was a scammer."

I lowered the camera for a moment, but kept a hand on it, not yet comfortable enough to let it dangle off my neck. For all I knew, I tied the strap wrong and it would go crashing to the floor. "Em, he's legit. I looked him up. I don't know why you think he's fake!"

The week before, while we were walking through the Institute of Contemporary Art in Seaport, giddy with sugar and being together, a man had stopped us in our tracks and looked Emerson up and down. Just when I was getting ready to tell him off right in the middle of the gallery of portraits made from found objects, he procured a card from his pocket and told Emerson she should think about modeling. That he would be able to get her work, and he would love to represent her.

And she laughed in his face.

I snatched the card and thanked him profusely, then basically forced Emerson to call him the next day. Still convinced it was a scam, she refused to go to New York to get digitals done, so I offered to shoot them myself. But I underestimated how challenging the jump from pears to humans was.

Emerson sighed heavily and sat down on the paper, wrinkling it so much I knew I'd have to put a new sheet down when she got up. She leaned her head back against the wall and held out a hand, beckoning me to sit with her. Instead, I started snapping away. These wouldn't work for digitals, since according to Google those are a pretty simple front, back, side, other side compilation, but the look on her face was just too good to not shoot. I had to see if I could capture her face in one frame. Her expression was weary, as though she was beaten down and waiting for the other shoe to drop, but also had the tiniest bit of hope peeking through in the slight curve of her almost smile, and her eyes twinkled despite her furrowed brow.

"Theo. Just sit. There's no point in taking these."

I snapped one more quick photo, then joined her, sitting so close that our thighs were touching. She twisted onto her side and leaned in to me, and I took the camera off and set it on the floor, then wrapped my arm around her. "Em, I really think this could be big. He's from a huge agency, and his other clients shoot for big places. Worst-case scenario, we get to hang out and you help me practice my photography skills, right?"

I squeezed Em to me slightly, and she leaned in more. And I

wished I could just relax and enjoy this, but I felt guilty because I enjoyed having her pressed up against me way too much. "I guess you're right. It doesn't hurt."

I knew that if it turned out to be a bust, it would hurt. For her it was a ticket out of here that I knew she wanted so badly she couldn't admit this could be a real big break. But that was too much to say. "Exactly. So let's make it fun!"

I stood up and pulled her with me, then ripped down the wrinkled sheet of paper, letting it tear right down the middle. And then, instead of rolling out a new white sheet to tape up, I turned to Em. "You pick the color."

She frowned skeptically. "I thought you said that the background for these is always white."

"So what? You don't have to be the same as everybody else. So let's do this your way."

Em broke into a huge grin and walked over to the rolls of paper and started looking through them. After a minute she pulled out a roll and turned back to me. "Then I choose this."

It was a hot pink paper. Barbie pink. Completely in your face, and almost ironic since she was dressed hyper-casually in blue jeans and a white tank top with minimal makeup. She looked like an all-American girl next door who got dropped into a beauty pageant backdrop. I loved it.

"Let's do it." I took the roll from her and climbed up the ladder, then let the paper unroll to the floor. Emerson passed me pieces of tape and I secured the paper, then climbed down and rolled it all the way to the next wall, so she could stand on it and I could shoot her whole body on the pink.

Em tapped her phone and turned the volume all the way up, then started blasting Taylor Swift. And I started shooting while she danced around, laughing, pulling funny faces, both of us screaming the lyrics we knew until she was breathless with laughter.

I tried to capture as much as I possibly could, and it was like time stood still. I couldn't tell if it was two minutes or an hour, it was like the feeling I got when I was playing really well during a soccer game. Complete focus on the goal, every sense heightened. But instead of the satisfaction of winning or of pushing my body to the limit, this was pure joy. It was like nothing else.

I felt like I could keep going on forever, but eventually Emerson tired out and dropped to the ground. This time when I sat next to her, I kept the camera. "I don't need to see. You can just pick a few and we'll send them," Em said immediately.

"Just look at them," I pleaded. I knew there was something special here. It didn't feel possible that these photos weren't good, when taking them felt so perfect. Emerson reluctantly looked over my shoulder as I flipped through all of the images, until I made it all the way back to the stiffer-looking ones on the white backdrop.

She didn't say a word, so once I finished I moved to put the camera away. Her hand shot out and gripped my arm. "Wait. Go through the pink ones again."

We clicked through all of them again, and when she broke into a smile, relief flooded through me. Because I loved these photos. But I needed her to love them too.

"These are amazing, Theo. I think you must be a genius or something, because you made me look . . . better than I ever have."

"That's not true. This is how you always look to me."

Em stared into my eyes, and we were so close, our mouths only inches apart, and I felt on top of the world. I not only made Emerson happy with the photos, but I might have just found the thing I would love to do for the rest of my life.

I let out a breath I hadn't realized I was holding, and rested my chin on top of her head. "Thank you," I whispered. She couldn't hear me. But I knew that this day was the start of something big for me, hopefully for both of us.

CHAPTER TWENTY-FOUR

Emerson

As soon as Theo and I step into the hotel and are within the vicinity of Wi-Fi, both of our phones start buzzing frantically. I start to pull mine out of my bag, but before I can, I hear a familiar voice shouting my name.

"Emerson! Emerson!" Georgia is standing in the waiting area of the hotel restaurant, waving at me.

"Georgia! What are you doing here?" Theo and I walk toward her, and even though I'm in shock, I notice Theo is reading his phone and his face is growing paler by the second. When we round the corner and have a full view of the bench Georgia is sitting on, I see why.

She's with Allison.

I recognize her instantly, because I obviously looked at every single photo she's ever posted to the internet, all the way back to when she was in middle school. (In fact, I think the CIA-level dossier I had Natalie make on her included tweets that were deleted fifteen years prior. I *might* have gone a little overboard.) But the pictures didn't do her justice. In person, she's gorgeous. Tiny and blond, with a tight bob—exactly how I'd want my hair if I didn't have to keep it long. She's wearing a pink linen shorts suit with only a bralette under the jacket. Incredibly stylish.

"Allison," Theo chokes out. "You should have told me you were coming."

"I did actually," she says. "I called. And texted." She sounds angry but hides it behind a smile that's either naturally perfect or the result of expensive orthodontia. I'm hoping it's the latter.

"We were on a hike," I explain. Which is why I now look disheveled and decidedly unglamorous. In the showdown with Allison that I had imagined, I was wearing stunning couture and in full hair and makeup, effortlessly beautiful.

"We should all have dinner together!" Georgia interjects. The three of us stare at her in abject horror. She stands and signals the host. "Table is for four now," she commands. He goes to argue, then sees me and promptly closes his mouth and starts scanning for an available table.

I make eye contact with Theo and try to signal to him to walk away from this dinner. But I'm too late.

Allison places a hand lightly on my arm. "Actually, I'd love to get to know you better. *Em.*"

My eyes bug out of my head when she uses Theo's nickname for me. But I recover quickly, and we head toward the table the host has found for us. Prime view, direct waterfront, resulting in an angry group at the entrance who's enraged that we took it out from under them. I smile apologetically at them—what else can I do?—and then shoot daggers at Theo. What is he *thinking*?

Theo grimaces. I can see fresh beads of sweat forming at his temple. *Good.* He should be sweating. Not only is Allison evidently pissed enough to fly here from the US, he's letting us get dragged into some kind of dinner from hell.

At the table, the host tries to seat Theo and me next to each other, but Allison deftly maneuvers to his side and pulls out her own chair to sit next to him. I smile calmly and wait for the host to pull out my chair directly across from him, and slide in as gracefully as possible.

Once I sit, Georgia pulls me into a quick hug to disguise her hiss in my ear. "You don't look happy to see me. And you smell."

"We were hiking! You're the one who rushed us to dinner the second we walked in."

"It was clearly an emergency."

I ignore her and turn my attention toward Theo and Allison, who are having their own conversation with glares and tense smiles, as the waiter lists out the specials. None of us are listening.

"So what would you like?" the waiter asks eventually, after he's given the world's longest specials and wine list monologue. He directs the question toward Theo, as the only man at the table, and probably the only person with prices listed on their menu since this is an old-school Italian restaurant.

Theo looks flummoxed, clearly not paying attention since he's busy watching his love life go up in flames on all sides. I jump in. "You pick," I tell the waiter. "Whatever the chef recommends, please, for all of us."

"Theo doesn't eat meat," Allison interjects with a tight frown in my direction.

I wilt. Theo doesn't eat meat? Since when? It's not like it matters, but how could I have not known that? "Seafood, then, please. And wine, lots of wine." The waiter practically runs away, clearly aware this isn't the typical celebratory vacation dinner most guests come for.

"Since Dad's heart attack, I've cut back," Theo explains softly, his gaze on me.

"Of course," I murmur. I look out over the glittering cliffside. I'd rather be hiking down that alone in the dark than be at this table. The truth is, there's probably a lot I don't know about Theo.

Whereas Allison has supported him through his dad's death, the heart attack, starting his career. She's actually been around for double the time we were friends. The thought makes me feel sick.

The waiter returns to pour the wine. As soon as he's done, Theo and Georgia take gigantic sips, while Allison and I lock eyes.

"So how did you two meet?" I chase that unpleasant question with a gulp of my own wine, which is a fantastic white.

Theo starts to answer and is stopped by Allison gripping his arm so hard that he jumps.

"We met at a party first semester of college," she says. "He was there, completely drunk over . . . over a girl, wasn't it? Some silly high school girl?" She looks at him, but her words are obviously directed at me.

Theo chokes on his wine and starts coughing violently into his napkin. She ignores him. "Anyway, he was wasted, and I was taking photos of discarded cups for NYU's student exhibition. We hit it off immediately and the rest is history. Isn't that right?"

Theo can barely talk, but manages a nod. He's sweating profusely now, and uses his napkin to dab at his forehead. A waiter wordlessly comes by and replaces it.

"You picked him up while he was drunk?" Georgia asks innocently. "And aren't you a few years older than him? You were saying you just turned thirty."

Allison's smile grows marginally tighter. "We connected."

"Right, right. Theo, do you even remember it?" Georgia's smile is positively gleeful as she turns her gaze on him. "I mean, what was she wearing?"

Theo shakes his head. "I don't remember."

Allison rolls her eyes. "Men don't remember clothes."

Georgia leans forward. "Theo, what was Emerson wearing the day you met?"

"Athletic shorts and a white tank top," Theo answers instantly, his piercing blue eyes trained on me. I can feel my blush creeping over my face. "That's what Em wore to freshman orientation."

Allison shoots daggers at me. I try not to sink into my seat. Beside me, Georgia takes a happy sip of wine.

The waiter sets down our first course. Lightly grilled octopus with fresh-squeezed lemon and miniature pesto and ricotta tarts.

Georgia tilts her head as she cuts into her octopus. "You know, my swim line is expanding to athleisure. Very colorful athleisure. Very flattering on short people." She points at Allison with her knife, which from me would constitute a threat with a deadly weapon, but in Georgia's hand is innocuous. "You would love it."

"How kind," Allison remarks dryly.

"I'm going to run to the restroom," Theo mutters as he pushes out his chair. When he turns, I can see the sweat through the back of his shirt.

Georgia looks between Allison and me as he walks away. "It wouldn't hurt me to freshen up." She walks after him with remarkably efficient strides, considering the height of her stilettos.

Allison and I eat our octopus in silence, until finally I can't take it anymore. "Do you love him?"

My words hang there, in the air. We stare at each other, unblinking. "I'm willing to fly across the world for him," Allison says finally. "So, in short, yes, totally. And I know he's always got my back too. Even though we're not dating right now, it really doesn't matter." And then she drops what must be her ace, although her face actually looks strangely sympathetic as she speaks. "Listen, Em, I don't know if I should be telling you this . . . but you're the reason things didn't work with him and me. He just never got over you, and now you're here . . . and I just want to keep him in one piece. If you love him, more than your career, more than anything, then please, go for it. He's been waiting to be with you his entire life. He holds every other woman up to you, which is a hell of a bar. But if you can't give him absolutely everything, just leave and let me clean up the pieces. Let him move on."

It kills me that she's nice. That she gives my hand a reassuring squeeze after she says that, and her tone is gentle, not combative. I can't breathe. I break eye contact, unable to sustain it after this punch to the gut. I ruined his relationship, without even being there. But also . . . he never got over us either. It feels like we sit there, her eating, me blinking back tears and staring out the window, forever. When I finally spot Theo and Georgia coming back to the table, I lock eyes with her for just a moment.

"I do love him. And I'm going for it," I whisper. But Allison's whispering in Theo's ear, her brow furrowed, and doesn't hear a word.

CHAPTER TWENTY-FIVE

Theo

I can barely breathe as I walk to the bathroom. And I didn't think I had enough water in me to sweat this much. But watching Allison and Emerson go toe to toe like this is a nightmare.

I pull my phone out and look at all of the unread messages I have from Allison.

Theo are you okay?

It's messed up of her to have him on set in front of you, even if you get to shoot the GQ cover

Also you don't need her to do GQ, you're great

You're not answering is everything okay? This isn't a bar floor situation is it?

Cuz you really can't fuck up things with Anthem they're like all your money

I'm in London for a job, there's a flight to you for like twenty euro

Taking it

I'm at the hotel

Where are you???

I can't believe you're hiking with her. You need to stay away and get your head on straight

I'm dealing with this just let me talk to her

Allison has a tough shell, but is extremely loyal. But right now she's choosing the wrong fight. I understand why she thinks the worst of Emerson, but she doesn't get that even though Emerson walked away . . . I also let her. I let the month of space Owen said I should give her turn into a decade of silence, because my feelings were hurt. And this chance to make things right between us is a once-in-a-lifetime opportunity.

I put my phone back in my pocket, and just as I'm about to step into the restroom I feel a hand on my shoulder. "Theo?" Emerson's friend Georgia is standing behind me. "Hi! Sorry to intercept you on the way to the bathroom, but can we talk?"

I step out of the bathroom doorway. Emerson didn't have a lot of girlfriends in high school. I'm glad that's changed. "Of course. It's great to meet you."

"And you!" She gives me a quick hug and then looks quickly over her shoulder to where we can see Emerson and Allison staring each other down. "Let's go in here."

She drags me into the men's room, ignoring the flustered remarks in Italian from the men using the facilities, and shoves me directly into a stall with her. "I didn't want them to see us talking."

I can hear men arguing in Italian outside of the stall. Someone bangs on the door angrily, but I have no idea what he's saying. "Um, okay. What's up?" Emerson's friend is clearly losing it, but I'm not going to question her.

"Emerson is in love with you. I know there's a million reasons for it not to work. I'm sure Allison could name a few big ones."

I wince, but Georgia squeezes my arm reassuringly. "Clearly, she's unhappy Emerson is here. But I'm telling you, if you still love Emerson, you need to shoot your shot. This is it. You have tomorrow and then you both will leave, and your opportunity is gone."

I rub the bridge of my nose. "The thing is . . . Emerson *isn't* in love with me. She just wanted to reconnect as friends. I mean, after the past few days I've hoped . . ." I trail off. Georgia's words have lit a spark of hope within me. "Do you seriously think I have a shot?"

"Theo, you have way more than a shot. Just trust me. Let's wrap up this dinner. Then tomorrow, get out there and win her back."

Suddenly this cramped bathroom stall feels like the best place in the world, because I'm finally getting good news. My damp back is pressed against the door, Georgia's heel is digging into my toe, and we're so close together it's hard to breathe over the smell of women's perfume mixed with men's restroom. It's the best moment.

"I can do that."

Georgia releases my arm and unlocks the stall door, swinging it open and directly into a crowd of men that have formed around it. They clap when we leave, and I'm not sure if it's because they think we got it on in the stall, or if they're just happy we're out of their way. Doesn't matter. Because all I need to do is run damage control on the Allison situation, and then tomorrow is my moment.

I hold the door for Georgia as we exit the bathroom. "Thank you," I say, gratitude pulsing through my entire body.

"You're the one holding it."

I laugh. "No, for being there for Em. And for telling me this." We walk back to the table slowly, both of us watching Emerson's and Allison's heated whispers from across the room.

"I already knew how she felt. But when I saw you two walk in from the hike . . . I mean, Emerson doesn't hike. She doesn't go in public looking less than perfect. And she doesn't let anyone call her by a nickname. She really deserves to finally be happy, and

based on what I've seen . . . it seems like you're what happy looks
like for her."

"She's everything to me," I whisper as we near the table.

Georgia laughs, looking like a carefree, glamorous model on
vacation, not the crazy woman who shoved me into a bathroom
stall minutes ago. "Well, babe, try not to fuck it up."

CHAPTER TWENTY-SIX

—Senior Year—

Emerson

Theo and I stepped off the rank bus and into the land where dreams were made—New York City. The past six hours had been grim, the bus seats were stiff with gum and dried sweat, the passengers broke the unspoken rules and used the tiny bathroom, and just when I had thought we were almost there, we sat in gridlock for two hours straight. But from the moment we walked down the street I felt that we'd made it somewhere important.

"Where do you want to go first?" Theo asked, our shared oversized backpack heavy on his shoulders. "My aunt said we could leave our stuff there at five, so we have like two hours to kill."

As we stood in the middle of the sidewalk, people streamed around us, screaming into phones, pushing strollers, generally ignoring us. Boston was a big city, but compared with the hustle and bustle around us within seconds of arriving in New York, it felt almost quaint. "Let's see the Times Square board, I think my Target ad could be there."

I had yet to see one of my ads in person, but I was making thousands of dollars a day on shoots, and bookings were going so well that my agent had begun a campaign to get me to obtain my GED and start modeling full-time immediately. I hadn't mentioned modeling full-time to Theo, because nothing would persuade me to skip out on even one day of high school with him, and since my ads weren't exactly plastered over the front of the *Teen Vogue* magazines at the grocery store checkout line, no one we knew was even aware I modeled. I kept the miraculous images from the shoots as private proof that with enough elbow grease I could clean up well. But I already knew I wouldn't be going to college with him in the fall. School had never been my strong suit. The only class I'd enjoyed was the creative writing class my guidance counselor shoved me into, an easy A course, flush with half-baked jocks and burnouts, designed to boost our floundering GPAs since grades were based solely on fulfilled assignments, not quality of work. I hoped Theo would choose a program in New York so we could live together in some horrible studio efficiency.

I stayed close to Theo's side while we walked the fifteen minutes from Penn Station to Times Square. (Since we'd taken an off-brand bus, we were dropped outside Penn Station on a random street corner.) Theo watched the faces and storefronts around him, and I watched Theo. Over the past few months he'd started to look more like an adult, his face had gotten leaner, his muscles thicker, so his broad frame suddenly made me look small next to him, despite my height. He'd always been cute, but now he was stunningly handsome, the slight imperfection of his nose and his one crooked tooth somehow making him even more good-looking. Since he took my digitals and discovered his hand was meant to be wrapped around a camera, he only ever wanted to photograph me, had said it was our makeshift shoots that got him accepted to NYU, USC, Emerson, and RISD.

"Em! Emerson! Look, your face is huge!" Theo pointed excitedly to a giant electronic billboard that was wrapped around the corner of a building.

I looked over just in time to see the ad change to a Spotify banner. "We'll have to let it come around again. It must be on a cycle."

Theo wrapped an arm around me from behind and pulled me close to his chest. I leaned against him, relaxed into him. We'd become touchy without explanation since that first day he put his arm around me, and neither of us questioned it, both seemingly at home with this constant contact, although we never took it the final few inches to a romantic level. I stopped letting myself admit that I wanted more, and so I remained content.

After seeing the same Spotify ad cycle through five more times, I was convinced that Theo'd been tricked by some other blond girl and my face was never going to come onto the screen. "Maybe we should keep going. It could be a different board."

"Just wait five more minutes," Theo countered. "I'd recognize you anywhere, even if it's only up for a second."

This I knew was true. I could see Theo from behind, fifty yards away, for a split second, and I would know it was him by the angle of his shoulders, the way he moved. He had a certain lope about his gait. "Five. Five minutes."

I only had thirty-six hours to sell him on New York. I didn't want to waste too long vainly searching for my own face. Just as I moved to pull away, he gripped my shoulder tightly. "Look. There you are."

And there I was. My face was blown up to the size of a car for a beauty shot, and then I spun around a set, laughed with other models. There was one moment where my top and bottom half were rudely bisected by a break in the screens, but otherwise it looked amazing. "I actually can't believe it," I breathed. I'd seen so few of my ads in real life that all the shoots felt like a fever dream that left thousands in my bank account.

"That's your face."

"That's my face," I echoed.

I looked good on the screen. *Really* good. I'd never thought of myself as a knockout, or anything close to it, especially compared with the snub-nosed, skinny-jean-clad girls at school. I was too tall, too strong featured, too awkward. I thought I was being punked when the scout came up to me in Boston, and Theo was the one who actually accepted the card and persuaded me to call him back, and who took the first photos I sent him. I still thought that if you looked too closely at me, the illusion was broken, but somehow when hair and makeup and wardrobe all came together, I actually did look pretty.

"We need to wait one more time through. You'll hate me later if I don't get a picture of you in front of it right now." Theo had let go of me, and my skin felt cold where I'd lost his touch. He reached into the side of the backpack and pulled out my phone, a brand-new iPhone that I had bought with my first modeling check, because my agent said the camera on my ancient phone wouldn't cut it for the Instagram account they wanted me to start posting on. "Okay, I'm ready."

"We're going to have to wait another ten minutes I bet."

"Doesn't matter. This is a once-in-a-lifetime moment." Theo began framing up his shot, directing me on where to move to for the optimal angle.

"What should I do?" This was the question I'd been told never to ask on set, but that I loved asking Theo, because he always had an answer. He was a natural director.

"So for the beauty shot, try to make the same smitzy face you did in the picture. Then, I'll tell you when the board changes, so you can turn halfway toward it and I'll get a candid of you looking at it for the next photo. For the group shot you can look right at me and do your fake laugh."

I nodded as I tried to cement his instructions into my memory. "Got it." I pulled my hair out of my stunted ponytail and tried to fluff up the short strands. I'd always had it at or above my shoulders, since my mom gave up on giving me braids or any styles after my dad left, but I'd started growing it out at the bequest of my agency. Theo promised me he'd learn all of the braids.

"Em, quick! It cycled early." Theo pointed at the sign wildly. "Keep a clear path here! Photoshoot!" he barked at the confused tourists who tried to walk between us.

I bit back a laugh and jumped into action. "Switch!" he yelled, and I moved onto the next pose.

"Whew, that was more high pressure than the actual shoot," I teased. As soon as we had the images, we moved on, walking aimlessly away from the crowds.

"Well, I bet they have more than thirty seconds to get their shot." Theo bumped his shoulder into mine and grinned.

"Fair point. You know, we have an hour until we can meet your aunt. Is it crazy to walk all the way there?" We'd made it to Central Park and were spiraling aimlessly down the paths, sampling shared overpriced pretzels and slushes. "I know you're the one with the heavy backpack."

I'd long ago stopped offering to carry our bag, because I knew Theo would shoot me down instantly. It's good cross training, he'd insist. "I can't think of anything I'd rather do."

We spent the next hour meandering toward the Upper East Side apartment and people-watching intently. "What's their backstory?" Theo gestured toward a group of twentysomethings who sat in a circle on the grass passing a blunt across upturned books.

"Art students," I said decisively. "Probably NYU. Only she made it into Tisch, but the rest of them pretend they're content with screenwriting or whatever, to save face. Oh, except him, with the Docs, he's clearly serious like you, a photographer-director type."

"How can you tell?" Theo said, stealing a backward glance at them as we continued by.

"Well, his is the only book that's face up, like he's actually reading it. And he's sitting an extra foot back, so he can see everyone and observe. Lately, you stare at me like you're lining me up for a shot."

Theo flushed and swiveled to walk backward for a moment and openly stare. He made awkward eye contact with the boy then jumped back around. "Fine, maybe I do that. On occasion!"

"It's not a bad thing! I like that you're observant." And I did. He'd noticed that I wore a new tank top that morning, when my mood was off, if I did my hair differently. He observed everything that my mom had stopped noticing years before, even though we'd spent almost every day of the past three and a half years together.

"I just like observing you." The way Theo looked at me was charged. His light eyes were unwavering, and he always had this slight smile.

"You like observing everyone. Luckily, there are about a million people here for you to be inspired by." I waved my arms in a grandiose gesture and narrowly avoided taking out a middle-aged woman who was glued to her cell phone. I was laying it on thick, but I didn't care; I was willing to do everything short of asking Theo to choose New York.

"I can't argue with that. I think this is my aunt's place. She said number seventy-five."

The building in front of us was tall and narrow, made of crumbling brick, and shielded by a black iron fence. I followed Theo up the front steps and he pressed the small plastic button next to the second-highest unit, 7A. Nothing. After a moment he pressed it again, his short, clean nail digging into weathered plastic. "Theo?"

We turned and were met by the sight of a tiny, somewhat round woman, whose arms were laden down with at least five Trader Joe's bags. "Aunt Marge!" Theo bounded down the steps and began to take bags off her arms. "Let me take these."

"Please, you two are my guests. But look how big you are!" She craned her head up toward him dramatically. "I have no idea how my tiny sister made such large boys. Even as a baby you weighed nine pounds."

"Nine?" I teased as I rushed to take the remaining two bags from Marge. "Theo, you never told me you were the Hulk of babies."

"And you must be Emerson! I've heard it's you who keeps my nephew in check." Marge unlocked the door and led us to a staircase. "I hate to break it to you two now that you're the ones carrying all my groceries, but I live in a walk-up. It's worth it for the space, but it's seven flights."

"We love walking," I assured her. "We actually walked here from Times Square."

"That's ridiculous." Marge shook her head in horror as we trailed her up the dimly lit staircase. "The subway exists for a reason."

"Emerson was on a billboard there," Theo bragged on my behalf. I shot him a look. It wasn't that I was ashamed of modeling, but this was the first time I'd actually seen it look impressive, and I could tell by the way our teachers at school shook their heads when I gave them an absence slip with my mom's signature on it that they thought I was wasting my time on a pipe dream. But it wasn't even my dream. It fell onto me, and for the first time I had possibilities beyond my absolutely average academic record and sitting at home deluding myself with romance novels.

"Now that is worth going to Times Square to see," Marge remarked. We'd made it up three flights, and although Theo seemed fine under the weight of three bags of groceries and our backpack, Marge and I were both a bit short of breath. "I told myself when I bought this place that the stairs would keep me young. But now I think they're just going to give me a heart attack by sixty."

"Cardio's good for you," Theo reminded her. But when Marge

finally opened the door to her place, it became clear why a seventh-floor walk-up was worth it. The apartment was soaked with after-noon light. Plants lined the windowsills, and it was surprisingly spacious for New York. The kitchen had an island, and I could see into both a bedroom and a work room that I assumed had the pullout couch we'd be sleeping on.

I could instantly imagine Theo's and my future in New York. He'd go to college while I modeled for a few years, and we'd come home to an apartment like this, or a smaller one if we couldn't afford anything, if he wouldn't split rent unevenly, but he'd come home with groceries and I'd cook us something. Omelets, home-made pasta, something elaborate, since I'd have the time when I wasn't on set. After his graduation we'd both be going to shoots, but we'd have our oasis together, where we could stay up all night talking or collapse in after going out. I let myself gloss over the bedroom, the fact that we'd need two. We'd go to the overpriced New York farmers market on the weekend, but go to Chinatown for dumplings afterward, even though we'd just bought groceries. The walls of our place would be lined with photos Theo took. My closet would be bursting with clothes from sets.

Marge's friendly voice cut through my reverie. "This is it! Rent stabilized since '96, and in the 2008 crash, they let me buy the place. Feel free to take a look around, and I'll give you the full backstory of each and every item in a minute. Don't tell your mother, Theo, but since I'm your cool aunt, I'll let you two share the bed in the study."

Theo's head whipped back toward Marge, his cheeks flushed red. "Emerson and I aren't together like that."

Now it was my turn to blush. I ducked into the study, under the guise of examining it.

"Whatever, Theo." Marge didn't look up at him as she put almond milk away. "You know, your mom and I do talk. Take the couch if you want."

"I can always take the couch," I offered. It was tiny, and I doubted Theo could even extend his full body on it.

"I mean, if you're comfortable, the bed is pretty big," Theo hedged. It pulled out into a comfortable full, which was enough room for a reasonable night's sleep for both of us. It was bigger than the tent we'd camped in the past summer. And like always, I knew nothing would happen. He never made a move.

"Yeah, that works for me."

I splashed water on my face in the bathroom and repeated a mantra back to myself. A mantra I'd been saying since Theo started putting his arm around me when we watched movies, but never leaned in for the kiss. A line I thought I might be able to not feel disappointed by if I said it enough. *Just friends. You are just friends. Just friends. You are just friends.*

CHAPTER TWENTY-SEVEN

Emerson

When I get to my room after dinner, I collapse. Georgia rushes off to a spa appointment she's booked for an hour with Harry, and I'm left alone to dwell on every detail of dinner until I can rehash it with them. And then I hear something hitting my balcony door. Over and over.

I walk over to the door and pull it open. Theo is throwing pebbles onto mine because we still haven't exchanged phone numbers. Because things are not progressing as fast as they need to. "Where's Allison?" is the first thing I ask.

"She went to the gym," Theo says. "Question time?"

"There's no gym here." But this is the first time Theo's brought up the questions first. That he's sought me out.

He shrugs. "I told her we needed time to talk."

I nod and let loose a small smile. "Georgia's at the spa with Harry for another forty-five minutes. And we each get four questions today, so we'd better get moving."

Instead of sitting, Theo walks over to the edge of his balcony, and I walk to the edge of mine, so only two feet of air separates us. I'm still in my dirt-crusted hiking clothes, and Theo's hair is matted to his head with dried sweat, but I couldn't care less. I need to make this time count. "I get to start today. Did you break up with Allison? Or did she break up with you?"

"It was mutual," Theo says instantly.

"Don't give me the party line! It's me."

Theo grimaces slightly. "Fine. She broke up with me. The first time. And I broke up with her the next two. What about you and Harry?"

"I broke up with him. But just because he was too nice to break up with me." He was worried I was too fragile, is more accurate. Once we got big, being his girlfriend kept me protected from the more powerful creeps in Hollywood, and Harry knew how much that mattered to me. But eventually I had to cut him loose, because we weren't in love, and I knew he wanted to explore his sexuality more. But he's been campaigning for us to get back together ever since we hit twenty-five.

But Theo accepts the short version of the story. "Sorry. His loss." But he doesn't sound sorry at all.

"What's your most controversial opinion?" I ask next.

Theo's eyes widen, and his eyebrows shoot up. "Do you have these prewritten or something? I'm throwing that back at you for my question too; so if you have your answer already, you go first."

I lean farther out across the balcony, so we're just the tiniest bit closer. It's just far enough between us that I don't think I could step or jump across. And the tension in the space . . . it's making me sweat even in the cool air. "Fine, I'll start. But yours better be good! I think that we were all better off before smartphones and social media. Which is so hypocritical since I'm basically making my living off it. But they're like playing the slots, like your brain lights up the same way. I know I'm addicted to it too. And I just think back to when we were kids, and how much fun we had before all this, and I don't think kids now are getting the same experience. I think it's the worst part of our society. But of course I'd never say that publicly, because I'm reliant on it."

"I mean, you're right. I'm way happier when I'm with family, phones off. Naomi is really good about it, she has a cell phone collection basket at the front door, and if you need to use it you have to stand there in shame." Theo laughs to himself as he thinks about it.

"Sounds like a smart woman. But okay, your turn. Most controversial opinion, three, two, one, go!"

"Ahhhh, I don't know!" Theo looks around as though the answer might come to him. "There's nothing controversial about me. That New York is overrated? The best era of photography is in the past? Half of what's in galleries is business, not art? When I say something controversial later, just take that as my answer."

I should argue, make him come up with something better. But I like the thought of us talking so much more that eventually a new answer comes up. I'm about to ask another question when I hear a rap on my door. Georgia's face is pressed up against the glass door, her eyes wide. *Five minutes*, I mouth to her, and pray she doesn't burst out onto the balcony with Harry in tow.

Then I turn back to Theo. "Time for lightning rounds. Georgia's back early."

Theo nods seriously, takes a deep breath, and pulls his shoulders back, in a rough approximation of the power pose I modeled for the girl earlier. "My game face is on. I'm ready."

"Favorite food to cook?" I start.

"Maple soy salmon with brussels. Best vacation you're ever taken?"

"Santorini, at this incredible hotel with private pools on each room's balcony. We should go there. Any near-death experiences?"

"Hmm, I got lightly tapped by a car while biking. Mild concussion, no worse for wear now. Best date you've been on?"

I hope he wants to know for research purposes. "Your boat, to Provincetown. If that counts."

Theo's intake of breath is rough, and his knuckles are turning white where he grips the railing. "It absolutely does."

2
Days Remaining

CHAPTER TWENTY-EIGHT

Theo

I stayed up half the night thinking about what Georgia said. And Emerson's answer to my last question. At four thirty in the morning my alarm goes off, and I jump off the couch to try to turn it off before Allison kills me.

Just as I locate my phone a pillow pelts me in the head. "Turn it off!" Allison moans from the bed. "What time is it?"

"Go back to sleep, your train isn't for three hours." I start getting dressed in the dark, as quietly as possible. Which isn't that quietly, because since it's pitch-black in here, I immediately knock over a lamp. "Fuck! Sorry," I whisper.

Allison pulls the covers over her head. "Why are you up so early?"

"I want to take Emerson to watch the sunrise," I explain as I pull my sweatshirt on, and grab another one for her. "Today's the last day, and I need more time with her."

"You're going to wake her up?" Allison's words are muffled by the comforter, but I can tell her tone is incredulous. "Sounds like you want to scare her off forever."

I freeze for a moment. "Wait, really? We used to watch the sunrise all the time as kids, when we were in P-Town, sometimes even in Salem." Allison doesn't respond. "It's romantic!"

"Well now you're older and she might want to sleep before working a fifteen-hour day. At least bring coffee or something. Now get out and let me sleep."

I exit the room quietly and take the elevator down to the lobby to get a coffee, a matcha, and an assortment of breakfast pastries to take with us. Then I head back up to our floor and pray Emerson is as nostalgic as I am.

When she opens the door, all she's wearing is a T-shirt. "Theo?" she says sleepily. "What are you doing here?"

I hold up the bag and smile, hoping I don't appear completely desperate. "Want to watch the sunrise in Riomaggiore? I have breakfast."

Emerson blinks, still waking up. "Right now?"

"If you want to. It's our last morning here, since we fly out tomorrow. So I just thought . . . why not?" It's too earnest for six thirty in the morning, but I don't have much time left. I have to start putting my chips on the table.

And so when Emerson smiles, my heart soars. "Just give me a minute to change. And brush my hair so it doesn't look like a total mess."

"I'd be honored to see your tangled hair." She shuts the door with a giggle and I blush and blow out an exasperated puff of air. *What am I saying? Honored to see her tangled hair? I sound ridiculous.*

But when she walks out of her room, she's just in a tank top, and what she says makes me so happy it should be illegal. "The other sweatshirt's for me, right?"

"Of course."

When we walk out of the hotel to head to the train, it's so early that no one is up yet. We quietly walk along the sidewalk overlooking the beach, toward the train that connects the towns. "I'm glad we're finally riding the train," I say at last. "Experiencing Cinque Terre like everyone else does for a minute, you know?"

Emerson nods and sips her matcha. "This is the only time we could do it. Or that I could anyway, before the crowds set in."

I hadn't even considered that. That I'm taking Em on public transit without a security team. Fortunately, when we get to the train station, we're the only people there. In the crisp morning air I can smell the ocean and hear the waves, and it reminds me of so many mornings with Em when we had nothing bigger to worry about than which beach to bike to.

When the train pulls up, we board it and have the car to ourselves. But still sit right next to each other. My knee brushes against hers, and when we start moving, I don't know whether it's the jostle that presses her knee right up against mine or it's her choice. But neither of us move.

The silence should feel strange, since there's so much we could be talking about. Meeting Georgia and Allison, since the dinner was insanely tense. What we'll do tomorrow when we fly to homes across the country from each other. But sitting together, not saying anything, feels perfect. Like for a moment I can be completely content and not worry about the future or stress about the past. When I'm with Emerson, it's like my entire body knows I'm exactly where I'm meant to be.

It only takes a few minutes to reach Riomaggiore. I stand reluctantly and follow Emerson out of the train. There are signs directing us into a long, damp, dark tunnel. We both stare down it apprehensively. "Are you sure this is the right way?" Emerson asks finally.

"Oh yeah. One hundred percent. My Spidey senses are tingling." I take a confident step forward into the tunnel, and she follows me without another word. The walls are damp with condensation, and it smells decidedly murky, like a boat that hasn't been cleaned, possibly ever.

But I hear her take a deep inhale next to me. "It kind of smells like home," Emerson explains when I look at her. And I'm glad she can't fully see my face in the dark because it makes me way too happy to hear her call Salem home.

"It does," I say softly.

When we exit the tunnel the sky around us is just starting to brighten, and in a few minutes I'm sure the sun will start peeking out. We follow the signs directing us toward the lookout point and walk downhill through the town, only to have to trudge back up a rocky path to get to the overlook. There's a few other couples there, probably on honeymoon, who are so wrapped up in each other they don't look twice at us.

We stand among them, leaning against the railing, and I touch Emerson's arm lightly. When she looks back at me, I catch a glimpse of hope on her face. Hope that I'll do something? That I'll make a move? If what Georgia said is true, today is the day.

"I think we could make it down these rocks, if you want."

Emerson grins wider than I've seen her smile all week. "Hope Anthem has a good insurance policy on talent."

"I would never let you fall," I scoff. I duck under the guardrail first, then offer a hand to Em and take us down the path that's been created by all the other people who have decided they wanted to feel like they were a part of the scenery, not on an overlook. We walk down to a flat area first, that's so close to the water that we can touch it, and both immediately reach down to test the temperature.

With our free hands. Because Emerson is still clutching mine, and there's no way I'll be the first to let go.

"Think we should go swimming?" I ask playfully. "It's not bad." And I would jump in, in an instant, fully clothed, cell phone in pocket, if Emerson said yes.

But she shakes her head firmly. "Not unless you want hair and makeup to last two hours this morning. It is pretty warm, though."

We make our way across the rocks and climb down to a flat rock that was hidden from view until we were actually down here. It's almost at water level, and directly in front of us we have a perfect view of the bright stacked houses. To our left there are three small row boats anchored and bobbing, and to our right we can see the rocky beach, and the town just starting to wake up. Emerson sits next to me, and I pull out the array of pastries I got, flatten the bag, then lay them on top of it, with our now half-empty drinks securing the corners.

"Not a moment too soon," Emerson whispers, and I follow her gaze. The sky has been brightening ever since we stepped off the train, but now the stacked houses are being overtaken by a rich golden glow. The colors look more vivid, and this entire setting, from the water and boats to our left to the houses and tiny town, might be the most beautiful place I've ever seen. The color is incredible, and for the second time in twelve hours I wish I had my camera.

On instinct, I wrap an arm around Emerson and pull her to me. She leans into my chest with a slight exhale of relief, which I feel in my bones.

I want to kiss her, to say how I feel, but not before we work together shooting underwear for the entire day. I don't want her to feel uncomfortable if her response isn't what I hope. I don't want us to have to rush back to set after what could be the biggest moment of our lives.

So I just hold her to me while we watch the sun rise, all too quickly. "I want everyone to be able to experience this," Emerson whispers. "I mean, fifteen-year-old me never thought I would go to Italy. Ever. I just want to help all the girls who grew up like me dream big. I didn't dream big enough."

I respond in a whisper too. It's such a fleeting moment that it feels like speaking at full volume could break it, even though in reality the sunrise will power through every day no matter whether Em and I are watching, shouting, or across the world. "Are you dreaming big enough now?"

Emerson's exhale is heavy. "I still don't know. But now I'm trying to. How about you?"

"I dreamt bigger when we were kids. But I think I could use some scaling up now." I squeeze her tightly to me. "You inspire me like that."

Emerson burrows her head deeper into my shoulder. "Your work is stunning, Theo. You make me look better than anyone else, and when we do this together it's actually fun. Promise me we'll shoot together again?"

"I promise." And it's the easiest promise I've ever made.

CHAPTER TWENTY-NINE

Emerson

"Emerson, why don't you try by the fireplace?"

I can hear the frustration in Theo's voice as we try to find a good shot in yet *another* area in the living room. Each model has shot at least two looks in this room and Stacey's no longer happy with anywhere in the house. I try to position myself in a different way, but indoor days (i.e., undergarment days) are tough when it's a tight space.

On indoor days everything moves slower, because the assists have to move the artificial lighting around between shots and there's limited space to work with. We also have what feels like a million and one household items to work in, from throw pillows to lamps to cutlery, since Anthem sells it all, even if this shoot is swim focused. There's not as much depth to the images, and there's much less movement to be had when you have to stay within the three-foot radius of living room that's lit. On the other hand, the benefit of an indoor day is that it's completely private, and we finally have some peace from the crowds of people that have gathered each morning since TMZ revealed I was here.

Theo snaps a test shot and it's immediately clear that Stacey is displeased. She picked the locations and which looks would be in each spot, but it's obvious she expected Theo to make something out of . . . not much.

Theo clears his throat. "Emerson, why don't you take five and we'll look around."

I'd rather stay and rearrange myself until Stacey likes his shot, but Theo looks super uncomfortable. "Sounds good." I jump up and head into the kitchen to get myself a juice from the fridge. It's a gorgeous kitchen. The appliances are high-end but with a retro look, and the cabinets and island are made of a stunning white marble. The side of the room opens onto a terrace that overlooks the coastline, and I hope that whoever owns this place spends every morning out there with their coffee. But since they're renting it by the hour on Peerspace, they probably spend about a month out of the year here.

I hear the click of the shutter as I close the fridge door, and when I look over my shoulder the camera clicks again and the flash goes off in the other room. "Stacey!" Theo calls. "This is it."

I freeze with my juice half uncapped, waiting for their determination. Stacey nods in agreement. "Let's clear this room." Immediately, PAs and producers begin moving craft services, the impressive layout of charcuterie and snacks, off the island. Lighting assists carry the flash into that room and Theo begins taking test shots of me.

"You can just keep doing what you're doing. Drink your juice."

I laugh. "Usually I only fake eat when it's on camera." I'm wary of having food stuck in my teeth, juice marring my lipstick. I can't see Theo, his camera's blocking his face, but I like to imagine his eyes are dark and sultry.

"Em, I've always liked watching you eat. You shut your eyes and it's practically org—" He stops himself and takes a photo as I break into laughter, his entire face going red.

Orgasmic. That's how much he likes watching me enjoy myself. I'm glad the crew can't tell my real blush from the fake one that's painted onto my cheeks. "I think that's been trained out of me. An ex of mine thought it was weird." I still shut my eyes for my first bite when I'm alone, but I've long since stopped doing it in public, no matter how decadent the meal. My first real boyfriend, a football player who shoveled his own tasteless health food in mindlessly, had made fun of me over it, and even though when Theo teased me I loved it, when it came from this near stranger it stung.

"Well, we hate him," Theo declares quietly. In high school he'd sometimes ask me to remind him why I didn't like someone. *"Why do we hate him again?"* he'd ask, and I'd explain my rationale. I was pettier then, but Theo was always steadfastly by my side.

"Emerson, can you fry an egg? Just do it however you normally would." Theo stares at me expectantly, camera halfway to his eye.

"I'm not much of a cook." I have a chef that prepares my meals and leaves them in the fridge when I'm home, something I'll never admit to Theo.

"It's okay if you burn it," Stacey assures me.

"Burnt eggs in lace underwear. I love it!" Miranda darts in and pulls down my boy shorts, tweaks my bra strap.

"Fine, I'll do my best." I open the fridge and look for eggs.

"They're on the counter; room temp is better," Theo interjects.

"Hey! No backseat cooking. You said to do it how I normally would."

"Comment withdrawn." The shutter snaps.

I turn back to the counter and put the eggs in the fridge, then start again. I preheat the pan on the stove with exaggerated movements, keeping my face on the entire time so the shots are usable. No frowns for this cook. Then I break the egg with one hand, a smile aimed at Theo through the camera. We spent one day in the

summer cracking egg after egg, until we could each do it flaw-
lessly. We had to bake hearty omelets and three different cakes
afterward to use them up, after my mom chastised us for wasting
eggs. She was never going to use the forty-eight eggs she bought
because they were on sale, but she hated to see them wasted. Much
better to waste flour and sugar too, to bake them into things we
wouldn't finish. But Theo always made whatever problems I had
with her feel less severe, almost comedic.

I hop up on the counter while the egg cooks, and Theo moves
toward me, snapping away. I stretch and lounge, swinging my legs
and doing all sorts of things that would look good in the images,
but no one else would ever do on their counter. After a minute I
hop off to get the egg and flip it perfectly. "Anyone?" I offer.

When we're shooting indoors, the sets stay small. In the kitchen
it's only me, Theo, Stacey, Miranda, and hair and makeup, but I
know that in the living room everyone else is watching the images
live on a monitor. Theo is tethered, so everything he shoots shows
up there. But with such a small set it almost feels like I really am
cooking for friends in my kitchen, while Theo takes a few photos.

Theo offers Stacey a look at the photos, and she nods her approval as they go through. "This is great. I want to do a group
shot here after lunch. I'll have production get ingredients for
waffles." She eyes the kitchen. "And a waffle maker. Try to get a
few color options. Early lunch, everyone!"

It's only noon, earlier than we've broken for lunch any other
day. Everyone leaves to eat in the garden out front, but Theo lingers, so I kill time washing my hands, eager for a moment alone
together. "Any idea what lunch is today?" It's the most superficial
of small talk, but I want to tear his eyes away from his camera and
onto the live version of me.

"I would place bets on something involving pesto." Theo sets
the camera down on the table, only to have Kevin instantly whisk
it away, to dump cards and put batteries on charge.

"Where are they hiding these massive basil gardens? One tablespoon of pesto has a massive amount of basil, but I haven't seen any gardens. I'm starting to think we've been duped."

"You think this is"—he whispers the next words dramatically, hands cupped around his mouth—"imported pesto?"

"I don't think we can rule it out." I hop back up on the counter and he makes his way around the island to me, leaning against it, pulled by some invisible tether. I offer him the plate with the egg, and I pull my legs up onto the counter while he pulls a fork out the drawer under me.

"This is a pretty mean fried egg." He eats it in three bites. "I didn't realize you were such a cook."

"Is there a word for the type of cook that only makes egg-related dishes?"

"An egg-cellent chef?"

I whack him with an oven mitt and my heart races. The clock is ticking, and I only have two days left to tell him how I feel before the marriage pact, and my self-imposed deadline expires. "I'm withdrawing the offer I was about to make to cook you my signature scramble. That pun doesn't deserve my cooking."

Theo's laugh is smoky and rough. I'm suddenly conscious of still being in my underwear, just a thin boy brief and a lacy balconette bra, both white. My nipples are now hard through the fabric. He's only inches away, clad in his rough-and-tumble on-set clothes, and I want him to close the gap and press me to him, let his skin and shirt be rough on my smooth skin, rip the lace of the bra—

"I'm more of cereal guy anyway," Theo says, interrupting my inappropriate thoughts. "Do you still eat the peanut butter Kashi one? I think Anthem actually sells that."

I only bought that cereal so he would have it at my house, but I still keep it stocked in each of my places, out of habit. But admitting that seems grossly inappropriate, way too intimate, and also a little embarrassing. I jump off the counter and grab the robe Miranda left out for me and wrap myself in it. It's thin, but I'm less exposed with it. "Oh, occasionally . . ." I mutter, trailing off as I knot the robe's sash aggressively.

"It's still my favorite. Want me to bring both of our lunches out here?" He nods toward the terrace, which I've been admiring all morning, but I can't tear my eyes away from his face. Theo's eyes are earnest as he braces an arm on the counter next to me, so close I want to sink into him. The muscles in his arms that flex lightly with each movement, begging me to press my own lean torso into him. There's been so many times when we were young that I did exactly that, leaned into his side with an audible sigh of relief and let him wrap me up in safety and comfort.

"I'd like that. I'll meet you out there after I change." I dart around him, taking care to let our skin brush the tiniest bit when I slide by. Sliding by, instead of going around him through the totally open path on the other side of the counter.

"Em!" I freeze when he calls after me. Every hair on my arms stands up while I wait to hear what he says. "Want a dessert? They're going fast these days."

Catering has been bringing three trays of miniature Italian desserts in addition to our specific lunches each day. Absolutely decadent looking. All of the models split one miniature tiramisu yesterday, and it was outrageously good. "Oh, I shouldn't. The tiramisu is fantastic, but we have more intimates this afternoon. But . . . maybe one thing? You know what I like."

I change into a sweatsuit and wait for him on the balcony. When he comes out, his arms are stacked high with the tiny take-out containers from catering.

"I hate to break it to you," I say, "but you may have taken a few other people's lunches."

"Just wait." Theo sets everything down on a chaise and then drags a small table over and begins unboxing the containers. He has our meals, pesto chicken and pesto gnocchi, but also grabbed one of every dessert and is laying them out in a tasting line. "I can't rent an ice cream shop. But I wanted to make sure you have something you like. I'll take one for the team and eat what you don't."

"Theo. This is so sweet of you." There have to be ten different desserts lined up for me to try.

"Now you're the one with cheesy one-liners."

I crouch down so I can go eye to eye with the desserts. The last one is a miniature donut. "Catering got donuts? So American. They must have made them just for us."

"I found a donut shop in Monterosso the other day, after I realized we were still on the . . . same snack wavelength. Priorities, you know? I thought you might need some extra sustenance after that hike last night."

My stomach twists as I look at Theo's gorgeous, thoughtful face. I want to kiss him, between bites of donut. "Let's split it."

"It's all for you!"

I pick it up and sit next to him on the chaise. "It'll taste better if we eat it that same time. Remember how we went halfsies that day? The great donut expedition of freshman year."

"I designed that day to cement our friendship through plying you with sugar. Worked like a charm." Theo jostles my shoulder lightly with his own and my entire body heats up.

"So share it."

"I'm only willing to because I know where you can get more." Theo has a twinkle in his eyes, but he accepts the donut. We bite into it at the same time, and though it's not Ziggy's or Coffee Time or Kane's from where we grew up, it's pretty phenomenal.

"Ranking out of ten?" I ask, just like I did back when we were fourteen.

"At one time, I would have given it a solid seven. But I'm a connoisseur now, so I have a harsher scale." Theo licks his fingers one by one, and I can feel the blush creeping up my cheeks as I will my eyes to stay away from his mouth. "Six and a half."

"Wow, harsh. I give it an eight. I haven't had a donut in days, so I'm sugar starved." I'm starved for more than sugar.

"How much do you want your lunch? Because I have a proposal."

I choke on the sip of water. It's silly, but hope soars through my chest. "A proposal?"

Theo looks at me steadily. "Yeah, a proposal. Let's forget our food, save it for later, and sample every dessert. I think that's a much better use of the final catering meal."

"Of course. Let's do it."

We start to eat our way through the desserts, but my mind is still on the word *proposal*. It's completely ridiculous, totally illogical to think he was about to suggest we get married, but the crushed feeling in my gut now is definitely real.

CHAPTER THIRTY

—Senior Year—

Theo

It took me three months to plan a promposal. Senior prom was supposed to be fun, but after spending more time agonizing over the perfect, rom-com-worthy promposal than I did on sports and classes combined, it was feeling uncomfortably high-stakes.

Emerson made sure at least 70 percent of what we watched were rom-coms, so I had the good fortune of learning everything that she did and didn't like. Flowers after a fight or before a date—*like*. Casual, spur-of-the-moment proposals—*dislike*. Guys stepping out of their comfort zone for the grand gesture—*like*. Weddings that were planned in under a year—*dislike*. I knew we were just friends, and that now that she was modeling she had to be meeting guys who were hotter and cooler than me every day. But when Owen came home for Thanksgiving and saw me and Emerson talking by the half-eaten dessert table, he pulled me into my room.

"Bro, you're clearly completely in love with her. And although she is out of your league, out of even my league—" At this my scowl transformed into an eyebrow raise, since Owen had never, ever, admitted someone was out of his league. "Hey! I can admit the obvious, on occasion. But anyway, somehow you've tricked her into spending all of her time with you, and if you don't make a move now, she will move on."

"I-I don't—I don't want to ruin our friendship," I stammered. "She doesn't think of me like that."

"And she never will if you keep being the guy who drives her to the train and buys her tampons."

"She uses a cup. It's sustainable."

"The fact that you know that but haven't slept together?" Owen shook his head in disgust. "Look, she has no prom date, right? So this is your chance. Get a haircut, step it up, and make a move." He cuffed me on the side of the head, and I tackled him to the ground. He had me pinned in a headlock in seconds, since although I'd learned to be scrappy, he had fifty pounds of muscle on me. "Hitting the weight room wouldn't hurt either."

Owen rolled off me with a grunt, and I hauled myself onto the bed. A three-hour meal of every food imaginable threatened to come up at the thought of asking Emerson on a date. "And if she says no?"

"She won't," Owen smirked.

For my promposal, I would combine the three romantic things Emerson loved most: a guy making himself look silly for a girl, flowers, and the grand gesture. I'd gotten myself five minutes at intermission of the school talent show through promising the drama teacher that I would put her glee club signs up in the locker room. Initially, she was under a fantastical delusion that I would join glee club, but after stopping me three bars into an off-key rendition of "Happy Birthday," I was off the hook.

While Emerson flew to LA to model for Free People the weekend before the show, I enlisted my mom's help to make an oversized sign covered in glitter and readable from the last seat in the auditorium. "You Belong With Me" was our song, but I worried it would be ruined if Emerson rejected me, so instead I practiced the lyrics to "Love Story," which would be much more embarrassing and thus fulfill the goal.

As I sat in the auditorium next to Emerson, I began to feel physically ill. I was sweating, possibly more than when I played soccer, and I felt feverish. Emerson whispered snarky comments to me throughout the show, but by the time we were five acts from intermission, she looked concerned. "Do you have food poisoning or something? You look horrible."

The fear of rejection, of ruining our friendship, gripped me with a claw-like vise. It was squeezing the life out of me. "I'm fine," I muttered as sweat dripped down my temple. "I'll just get some air. Meet at intermission?"

"Want me to go with you?" Emerson's brow furrowed with concern for me.

"No!" I practically shouted as people began clapping for the act that had just ended. "You stay here. Fill me in later."

I booked it out of the auditorium and rushed to the bathroom. If this went south, I'd gone too hard to claim I was just asking Emerson as a friend. She would know I'd pulled out all the stops, and the thought of altering our dynamic was absolutely paralyzing.

My family thought Emerson was interested in me by virtue of how much time we spent together. I saw how that was the obvious assumption and was only mildly surprised when I caught my dad awkwardly placing a box of condoms on my dresser the summer after freshman year. He'd turned to me with a guilty expression. "Mom made me do this."

"It's not like that," I assured him, but I was met with a skeptical wince and a swift exit.

Owen ducked into the bathroom and began banging on stall doors until he knocked mine open, smacking me in the back. "Get up. You have like three minutes, and then it's showtime. I didn't come home from school for nothing." He hauled me up by my shirt and propelled me toward the sink, where I was greeted by my absolutely dismal reflection.

"He's in here," Owen shouted out the door while I splashed water on my face.

My mom walked into the men's room, change of clothes in hand. I had ironed my suit that morning before school, so I could dress up for Emerson.

I braced myself against the sink and one sweaty palm slipped off entirely. "I can't do it."

"You have to," Owen said firmly. "You've been inseparable for three years. Man up and get out there."

"This will ruin everything." I was unrecognizable in the mirror, my eyes wide with terror and my face pallid.

"Dude, you told me yourself that she's a romantic. She's not going to walk up to you one day and be like, *Hey, bestie, I'm madly in love with you, let's bang.* Not gonna happen."

"Owen, language," my mom said.

Owen rolled his eyes. "Theo, just get out there and shoot your shot. Man up."

"I can't," I choked out. I suddenly began to hyperventilate, gasping for air, hunched over at the counter. Someone tried to open the bathroom door, and my brother slammed it shut. "She's everything to me. I can't risk messing things up between us."

My mom put her hands on either side of my face. "Honey, you don't have to. I do think she'll say yes, but you don't have to do this. There will be more opportunities."

"Yeah, why not just try again at college graduation?" Owen asked, his voice dripping with sarcasm. "Or would her wedding be more convenient?"

"Owen, lay off," my mom barked. "Listen, honey, we won't make you go out there. But in a few minutes people will break for intermission and then this window is closed for today. So it's time to decide: Do you want to go out there, or do you want Owen to go tell that theater teacher you're sick and can't go on? We're here, whatever you decide."

"I'll do it."

"That's my man!" Owen clapped me on the chest and shoved the bag of clothes at me. I changed quickly, already late for the five minutes I'd spent months meticulously planning.

I was barely conscious of walking out of the bathroom, but in what felt like seconds later, I was on stage, giant sign propped next to me, and flowers and mic in hand. The lights were blinding, and I couldn't see anyone beyond the front row. Emerson was three rows from the back and as the song began to play, Taylor Swift's voice still on the track because I was too musically challenged to sing alone, I shielded my eyes and tried to find her in the audience.

But then suddenly I realized I'd been looking for too long—I missed the first few bars of the song. In a panic, I locked eye's with Clarissa, a girl I'd known since we were in the same kindergarten class, a perky cheerleader whom even Emerson had admitted was pretty nice. She began to sing along with the song. Her aisle of cheer teammates joined in, and soon the entire auditorium was belting out this Taylor Swift song. This was exactly the kind of gesture Emerson went crazy for, and I wished more than anything that I could see her face. My eyes stayed trained on Clarissa as the momentum of the sing-along she started dragged me through the rendition, and when I got to the end I turned and picked up the sign.

I held the sign above my head for a moment, like the guy in one of Emerson's favorite eighties movie, *Say Anything*, and prayed that from the back of the room Emerson was smiling. But I couldn't see her. I had a speech planned. But I was paralyzed, and just mutely stood there holding the sign.

I knew I was making a fool out of myself, but I couldn't say a word. Emerson had to know she was the only person I would ever do this for.

"Ask her!" Clarissa had her hands cupped around her mouth, shouting up at me. She yelled it out again. "Ask her already!"

A few of her teammates picked up the chant. "Ask her. Ask her. Ask her!"

I still couldn't see Emerson. And I had forgotten every word of my speech. But I took a deep breath.

"Emerson. Prom?"

Every second felt like an eternity once those words left my mouth. The audience was silent, and I felt a bead of sweat trickle from my brow. But then I saw her. Emerson walked briskly up the center aisle of the auditorium, and relief coursed through my veins. Because she was smiling.

She ran up the steps and I dropped the sign to the floor and split the difference of the stage, stopping a foot in front of her. I stared at her, my heart in my throat. "Yes," she said, with a huge grin.

A smile spread over my face and I sprang forward and wrapped her in a huge hug. The audience started clapping, and she wrapped her arms around me tightly. I hadn't admitted my feelings yet. But this was *definitely* a good start.

CHAPTER THIRTY-ONE

Emerson

All afternoon I've practically begged Theo to try a few more an-
gles and locations because I'm desperate for anything that will
extend my time with him. I only have tonight or I need to finally
put an end to this and move on. But it's the final shot, and after
Theo humors my fifth location suggestion and takes us dangerously close to overtime, Stacey intervenes.

"Let me see what you have." Theo turns the camera toward her
and clicks through the shots. She smiles triumphantly. "You've got
it. That's a wrap, everyone! Let's break this down fast. Thanks for
a great shoot."

Everyone sets about breaking down without fanfare. Lights
that were being kept partially built out all week are taken apart,
and wardrobe is packed back haphazardly into suitcases. The
other models left one by one when they wrapped their final shots,
and Theo is whisked away by the digi-tech to look at the one sheet.
The second we're done working, I'm alone.

But I have one more chance to see Theo before I go. It's a
tradition after most shoots that there's some sort of wrap night
festivity—a dinner, drinks, a party—followed by everyone flying

out the following morning. I haven't gone to a wrap night party in years. I typically take a red-eye home because I hate pretending to let loose. I would rather sit alone in my apartment. But this time I had Natalie change my flight to a leisurely ten a.m. departure tomorrow, so I can stay out all night if I want to. If Theo wants to.

I can hear his shower turn on through our shared wall when I step out of mine, so I take my time getting ready. All week long I've been in natural makeup, but tonight I go all out, pulling out the sparkly eye shadow and dramatic lipstick that Georgia pressed on me last night. After I assured her I was okay, and confirmed Harry was staying another night just in case things with Theo completely blow up in my face, she went back to Greece to see her boyfriend. And, happily, she reported that she got Allison booked for a test shoot for her swim line, so I could have this day alone with Theo to say goodbye.

My dress is short and slinky, form fitting without being skintight. In this look I am the Emerson on the magazine covers, the confident supermodel that can do anything she puts her mind to without even a moment of self-doubt.

I wait until I hear Theo's door close behind him to leave my room, so that I can walk with him to the club. Tonight is it.

I step out of my room and spot him stepping into the elevator. "Wait!"

Theo's hand slides out and stops the elevator doors in their tracks. They creep back apart and reveal Theo. It's my first time seeing him in street clothes, rather than set clothes, and he looks amazing. He's wearing a pale blue shirt tucked into broken-in jeans, the kind that once were stiff cotton and now have been worn in to fit him perfectly. The shirt makes his eyes pop, and the way he's rolled it up to reveal his tanned forearms is dizzying. But I can barely take him in because of the way he's looking at me.

It's as if he's devouring me with his eyes. I feel spread wide, vulnerable. "Emerson. You look incredible." His voice is a ragged whisper that sends shivers down my spine.

I step into the elevator with him and stand entirely too close. "You clean up pretty well yourself."

The elevator doors open too soon, and we're forced into the harsh light of the lobby. Most of the crew is there, in various levels of attire. When I step out, clearly dressed to go out, I see the glances and whispers start to pass between crew members. Miranda looks around, as though someone might miraculously appear to take me on a date, or just explain what's happening. She seems surprised that I'm here, or maybe that I'm this dressed up to hang out with the crew.

But my girls are ready for the last night. I walk over to meet them and Theo trails behind me.

"You two look so good!" Rachel squeezes my hand encouragingly.

"Let me take a photo. I can't believe you're coming out with us!"

I hand over my phone. Theo wraps his arm around me, pulling me close, and it only takes a second for me to sink into his side.

Theo takes a quick photo of all us girls together, and I share it in a group chat with all of them. I appreciate their support this week, so I extended a standing invitation to each of them to come over next time they shoot in LA.

"You guys ready?" Jillian asks. "I have three hours before I have to be back here in my bed. My flight's at five a.m."

Evonique winces at the thought of the early wakeup. "Oh, girl, you're better off staying up all night."

"I can't, I'd fall asleep at three a.m. and ruin everything. I was on the ten a.m., but my agent had me change it because there was a weather alert."

We step out the door and into the night, the air crisp and cool on my bare shoulders. Theo and I trail the group, and it's the first time I can remember him being the one to tag along with *my* friends. Walking next to Theo feels deliciously normal, and for a moment, just a second really, I wish my life was normal, so that this is something we could have every day.

I wobble for the briefest moment, my heels pinprick on the cobblestone, and Theo's hand steadies me. The heat of his palm on my back is scalding. I jump into the conversation, desperate to deflect, to hide how much he affects me. "I'm on the ten a.m. flight too. Connection in Milan, then direct to LA."

"I leave on the same flight to Milan at ten," he adds. "Think we should change them? Don't want to get caught in a storm."

My eyes slide up to his. I love that we're a *we*. "I think it'll be fine." I already know I'm going to spend the rest of tonight wishing on stray eyelashes that our flight is delayed and I can get a few more precious hours with Theo.

"I'm changing mine as we speak," Rachel announces, pulling out her cell phone. "Why risk it?"

"We all changed ours!" Miranda calls up to us, from the second group of crew that lingers ten feet back.

I let my hand brush Theo's ever so slightly, pulling his attention to me. I shake my head just the slightest bit and a smile creeps up from the corners of his cheeks. We'll keep our flight, take our chances together. Have one more morning together.

When we step into the club, it's practically empty. A few tourists linger at the bar, and one couple stands on the balcony that overlooks the town. It's only eight p.m., so we have a good three hours before the locals come out. Stacey puts down her corporate card for drinks and I take two shots in quick succession with the girls, throwing back the liquid courage with a cough.

By my third drink I'm properly drunk, which is rare for me. I throw my head back and dance, no longer worried about whether I look cool or awkward. I shake my hips, moving my body to the music. I'm relaxed in a way I haven't been in a long while. Maybe ever.

When Theo appears beside me, I wrap my arms around him and give him a sweaty hug.

We've drifted away from the other people, toward the balcony, and I let myself move closer to Theo, until we're pressed together. I vaguely remember that this was the reason I never let myself get drunk around him in high school—I was worried I'd throw myself at him. But for every inch I close between us he does the same.

"I'm so glad we had this shoot together," I say. "I orchestrated it, you know!"

"Em, what are you talking about?" His voice is hot in my ear, his hand cupping my head.

"The pact went off on your birthday, so I told my agent to get me on the next Anthem shoot. So I could see you." I let my hand rest on his waist as we sway. "He was pissed, but did it." I laugh, and it's loud even to my own ears. I am *drunk*. "Obviously."

The song changes to something too slow, too romantic to be what the club usually plays.

"A request from the Americans," the DJ mutters into the mic apologetically.

Theo's hands reach for my hips and I interlace my hands around the back of his neck.

Theo hitches me closer to him, and I rest my head on his chest. He's the perfect gentleman, hands never slipping, but the intensity of his palms burn through my dress.

"Em, you rejected me the day you got here."

I pull back so I can look him in the face. "What are you talking about?"

He looks completely shell-shocked, his hands still glued to my sides. We're not moving, just intertwined. "I reached out to your agent, asking to reconnect."

Now I'm the one who can't move. "What?" We stand, staring at each other while couples dance around us.

"You rejected me. Through Matt. Five days ago."

"Theo, I would *never* do that."

Theo pulls his phone out of his pocket, cursing as it's slow to load while he pulls up the text. He turns the screen toward me and my stomach drops. "I never even knew you reached out."

"Why would your agent do that?" I can see Theo's mind working, his brow furrowing. "He doesn't want you to be with someone like me. A hermit who's behind the camera when you could be with Harry Butler."

I grab Theo's hands and squeeze them tightly, bringing them up in front of my chest. "Yes, my agent wants me to be with him for publicity, a showmance. And you're right that this shoot is bad for my brand, but I don't care about that. All I cared about was getting another chance to see you. When I got here it was clear you're still hurt, and I understand. I deserve that. I don't deserve another chance with you. But I want one."

Theo takes a step back, releasing me, and the cool air from the balcony fills the space between us. "Emerson . . ."

The gap between us hurts. I sense a "but" coming. I've always known it couldn't just be easy with him. "But what? You love Allison? You're torn?"

Theo reaches for my face and stares deep into my eyes. "Allison and I are just friends. And not like you and me. She and I are, genuinely, *just* friends. For years now. We never made sense as a couple; you're the only one I've ever made sense with."

"But Matt said . . ." My voice trails off as I realize just how much he's been manipulating us. Manipulating *me*. "Fuck," I mutter. "I can't believe this."

"Em, forget about him. This is so much bigger than that guy. Do you seriously mean what you just said?" Theo stares into my eyes. "About wanting another chance?"

I look up at him. "Of course I mean it," I whisper. There's so much more to say. But the space between us is electric, and his mouth is so close. I tilt my head up and he wraps a hand around my jaw gently and guides me toward him. When our mouths connect, there's nothing else. Every kiss I've had since I was eighteen has felt horribly wrong, because it wasn't with him.

But I want to do this *right*. When we break away, I look around me, at all the other people inches away from us. "Can we go outside? On the balcony?" I hold out a hand, and Theo takes it and follows me out.

We step onto the balcony, and the music quiets just enough so I can hear myself think. I still feel the alcohol coursing through me, but the cool air is sobering.

It's time. I'm ready to do it. To stake my heart on the one percent. To say my piece, even though there are still a million reasons it might not work. My crazy job. My impossible schedule. And the lie I told him all those years ago.

I sit on a bench overlooking the gorgeous lights of Manarola and face Theo, so close our knees touch. "I lied. Ten years ago. I lied when I said I didn't love you." Theo starts to say something, but I squeeze his leg, stop him. "Let me tell you. Please. I lied. I loved you more than anything. But I—There was—I'm so, so sorry—" I'm crying now, tears streaming down my face, and my words have to be forced out in heaving gasps.

I let Theo wrap his strong arms around me and hold me while I cry. "Em. It's okay. We were eighteen then, we were so young." His forehead is pressed to my own, and even though I look horrific, covered with runny snot and streams of mascara, he doesn't even ask why I lied. All he cares about is that it wasn't true. That I loved him.

"You are way too good for me." Just saying it makes me cry harder. "But Theo, being with me will ruin your life. You've seen the tiniest example of what my day-to-day is like; it would make your life impossible."

Theo wraps his arms around me more tightly, pulls me into his lap, and presses me against his chest. I feel something wet hit my face and realize that he's crying too. "Em, I don't know why you've never been able to see this. The only life I've ever wanted is the one where I'm with you."

"You just think that now." I'm still encased in his arms, and for the first time I can remember in ten years, I feel totally safe and secure. Giving this up will destroy me, but I need him to be happy. I need him to know what he's getting into, and still want it. "You'll never have privacy again. You'll have to stop coaching your nephews. And we'd end up spending a lot of time in LA. And your house! Fans would track down the address and come gawk at us there. We'd have to move, or get security. And the paparazzi would track our every move. You might hate me after all that."

Theo turns me around in one fluid motion, so that I'm staring into his eyes. "Emerson. Do you really think that I care more about coaching a youth soccer team, or living in a particular house, than being with you? Please, you have to let us at least try." Theo cups my face in his hands. "Can you try for me?"

I stare at him, at the man I have loved since we were teenagers. The feelings of fear and nervousness I've learned to fight off over the years come roaring back, but as I look into his eyes, I know there's only one answer to his question.

"Yes."

Theo crushes his mouth to mine and kisses me. And this time, Theo takes his time. He cradles my cheek with one hand, threads the other through my now tangled hair. My entire body reacts to him. Every hair is standing up, my pulse is racing, heart throbbing. "Theo," I murmur.

He moans. His mouth is hot and hungry on my own, desperate after a decade of want. Of need. I meet him without reserve, unable to control myself now that I can finally give in.

How I feel for him is so primal it scares me, but I lean in to it and wrap myself around him. He leans me against the wall of the tiny club, my face lit by the city lights, his arm to the wall, his entire weight against me. I try to meld myself to him as we devour each other, completely desperate.

I don't know how long has passed when we finally come up for air. Theo presses his head against mine, temple to temple. "I love you," he murmurs, so softly I don't know that I'm even meant to hear. "Stay in my room tonight?"

"I want to spend every night with you."

CHAPTER THIRTY-TWO

Theo

I can't stop touching Emerson on the walk back to the hotel. I keep rubbing her arm, putting a hand on her back, anything to convince myself that this is real. I've spent so many years dreaming of her saying that she didn't mean what she wrote in that note. When we step into the elevator, I stare at us in the mirror. Emerson wiped her face clean with a makeup wipe Jillian procured from her purse when we passed her on the way out the door, so she looks younger. Less like a supermodel, more like herself. And she can't keep herself from smiling, And although my eyes are red from tearing up at the club, I'm clearly elated.

"Look at us," she whispers. "This is what getting everything you've ever wanted looks like."

I kiss her, lightly, quickly, on her cheek. I could feel in my gut when I met her that first day that she was who I needed to be with. Now, after ten years of trying to believe otherwise, I can let myself believe it again. I feel completely calm, like everything has clicked into place.

The elevator door opens and I lead us out, toward her room. I thought my suite was nice, but hers is incredible. It's basically a full apartment, with a living room and a bathroom the size of my old apartment in New York.

Once we're in the room we immediately start making up for lost time. I crush Em to me and kiss her, let my hands run up and down her body. She starts playing with the buttons on my shirt so I pull it off and discard it on the ground. She reaches behind her for the zipper to her dress but I stop her. "Can I?" I want to cherish every moment of this night.

"Please." The need in her voice makes me somehow harder than I already was. She turns around and I pull down the zipper, slide the strap off her shoulder, and watch the dress fall to the floor. She's braless.

"Fuck," I moan. I've seen her half-dressed almost every day this week, but this is different. This is just for me. "Can I touch you?"

"Yes, Theo, please." Hearing her say my name is too much. I take a deep breath, try to regain control of myself before I let my hands explore her every curve. I press myself against her from behind and my erection, straining against my belt buckle, is flush against her tiny thong. I trace my hands up and down her body, let my fingers play over her breasts, tug her nipples, and let one hand trace her until she's gasping in front of me and I'm practically holding her up.

I turn her around and lay her back on the bed. She tries to pull me toward her but I hold back. "Wait, wait. I just want to look at you. I can't believe that I'm this lucky."

She snakes her legs around my waist and pulls me toward her, so that I'm flush against her. "Theo. I'm the lucky one."

I swallow her words with a kiss.

CHAPTER THIRTY-THREE

Emerson

Theo kisses his way down to my center, and it's like everything I thought I knew about sex, about what sex is for me after everything, has come undone. I am absolutely desperate for his mouth to be on me, to feel him, to have him in every possible way.

"Is this okay?" he asks again, pausing, his mouth an agonizing inch away from my clit.

"Yes. Theo. Please keep going."

My first time, when we were so young still, was magical, but halting and unsure. And with all of my boyfriends since, it was an exercise in avoidance, in willing myself to get wet for them, in smiling and bearing it because wasn't that normal? And then, as soon as I was alone, I'd whip out the alarmingly effective vibrator that Georgia bought for me when she realized I'd only orgasmed with Theo.

Theo dips his tongue inside me briefly before circling my clit, artfully, getting faster and faster until I'm straining against him. He reaches up to my breasts and toys with my nipples while he buries his face deeper in me, and I want it to go on, so much longer, but suddenly I'm exploding around him. Crying out.

"I've learned a thing or two since we were eighteen," Theo jokes lightly as he kisses his way up to me. I pull him down toward me, on top of me, and kiss him deeply.

I grind myself up into him and moan. I want more of him. I want to completely meld us together. But he's still half-clothed, a cruel layer between us.

"Em. You feel so good. But we don't have to—I'm happy just making you feel good. Thrilled, actually."

I run my nails down his hips, stroke the forearms that I've been looking at all week. Kiss the curve of his jaw. He groans. Seeing him like this, with the ten-year gap, makes me so aware of how much he's grown. I hate that I missed the moments that he changed, that he filled out, got broader, grew up.

But they also may have passed by in a blur if we were together every day, and for the first time, I feel a prick of gratitude for the time we had apart, because the space has done what it intended. It allowed me to grow, to recover from my trauma, so that I could experience how incredible he is without being distracted by memories of what happened. "Theo. Theo." I pocket his name between kisses. "I want you. All of you."

He pulls away and I let out a soft growl of disappointment, which turns to relief when he undoes his belt buckle, lets his pants drop to the floor, his underwear following shortly. I'd forgotten how huge he is. "Em, I don't have anything."

"I have the arm implant. I'm clean. I trust you. I want you so badly, Theo."

"Me too," he whispers, and I guide him toward me.

I want him in me, now. He's at my entrance, touching me, and I strain, try to move enough that his tip pushes into me. Theo pushes into me slowly and I cry out.

"Should I stop?"

"God no," I say.

He keeps pushing, slowly, until he's in me to the hilt, and I'm so full I feel like I can barely move. "Is this okay?"

He traces my clit softly, so sensitive from all the work he just did with his highly skilled mouth, and I buck against him. "Yes, yes."

He moves slowly, but I'm shaking already. "I can't wait to feel you come all over me," he whispers, one hand still toying with me, the other in my hair, as he joins us together with blissful strokes. He's so sure of himself, large enough that the stretch of him almost borders on pain. But I crave it, crave him. I do everything I can to draw him deeper into me. I can feel the ten years between us fall away with every thrust, every kiss.

I nip his ear and he stops, suddenly. "Emerson, you feel too good. I need to stop for a sec." He goes still, but keeps stroking me. "Don't move, Em, I don't want to be done with you yet and you feel so good."

I stay still for as long as I can, but eventually I can't take it. "Theo, I need you. I need to feel you." I start moving around him, his huge fullness and the weight of him keeping me pinned mostly in place as I desperately try to press us closer together, get more, feel more, until suddenly I'm coming again, crying out. The second I start to come he can't hold himself back any longer and he starts moving, faster, rougher than before. I keep coming, spurred on and on into waves of orgasm by his frantic movements, until he's come and we're completely joined, tired and blissful on the bed.

And suddenly I know exactly what sex with someone you actually, truly love is meant to feel like.

1
Day Remaining

CHAPTER THIRTY-FOUR

Emerson

"I can't believe I get to be this happy." I'm sitting on the bed, wrapped in a fluffy white robe, my hair wet from the shower, croissant and matcha in hand that the concierge sent up. We woke up to find our flights were delayed until the evening, and to say we were happy is an understatement. We celebrated with more time in bed.

Theo puts down his croissant, and I want to lick the stray flake of pastry that's landed on his bare chest. "Em, you deserve this. You should always get to be this happy. It's a high bar, but I'll always try to make you as happy as I can. Because all of my best days are with you."

I rest a hand on his jaw and guide his face toward me, leaning in to a deep kiss, while I let my hand trace his chest until I feel him shiver against me. I can't believe I just get to touch him. No pretending I don't like him, that it's just friendly, meaningless. We're together. "I love you," I whisper into his lips.

"I love you too." The smile on Theo's face right now is worth more to me than anything. But despite how perfect this moment feels, the reality of what being in my life really means is looming over me.

"Theo, I just want to warn you, it might be intense when we get to LA. My team will meet us at the airport, so we really just have to make it out of the terminal, and then we'll have privacy again at my place." I'm getting worried about how this will go.

Theo slides closer to me and wraps an arm around my shoulder, pulling me into him. "I don't care if we're photographed, or what people say. I've been waiting to be with you my entire life and nothing will change how I feel about you."

I nestle my head closer to his side and try to let the sweet sentiment of that statement sink in. I want to believe that. But I know I haven't been totally honest about how jarring the media storm my everyday reality is to people who aren't in the industry. And if I'm being honest, despite being a talented commercial photographer, Theo is more like industry adjacent since he does lifestyle photography, not high fashion or celebrity editorial.

"Are you sure? Things can get a little vicious." I kiss his jawbone as he nods decisively. "Sorry to sound pessimistic. I'm so glad you were able to switch your flight." I didn't ask him to come to LA with me. But to say my heart soared when he offered would be an understatement. I know there's still so much more to figure out, but having even a few more days like this before he has to leave for a job back in Boston feels so lucky.

Theo takes my hand and rubs his fingers over my knuckles gently, but over, and over, and over. It calms me. "You don't need to worry about me, Em."

I sink in closer to him, until we're spooning, and wrap his arms around me. I can't get close enough. His touch is like a drug that I've been craving for years. "Okay."

After a few minutes Theo breaks our comfortable silence. "Should we finish your question game before we go? We skipped last night."

I sigh happily. "I mean, we have to, right? It kind of brought us back together. Forced us to actually talk again."

Theo picks me up and carries me to the balcony, and I shriek with surprise and laugher. He sits in the chair and I sit on his lap, our faces so close our foreheads or nose or lips touch whenever one of us moves.

"Five questions, right?" he asks.

"Right. Favorite breakfast pastry?"

"Wasted question. Donut. Jump into a pool, or wade in?"

"In private, jump. In public, sit and dip my toes in." Five days ago I would have been embarrassed to qualify my answer. But I want Theo to know everything about me. "How many kids?"

"I want that one too. Countdown?" I nod. "Three, two, one— three!" We both say it at the same time and he kisses me gently. Before we can get carried away, I launch into the next question.

"Sledding or swimming?"

Theo hesitates and starts kissing me all over my face while he thinks. "If I'm with you or Owen's kids, sledding. If I'm alone, swimming."

"Do you still have the boat?" I ask, jumping into my next one.

"First answer mine," Theo chastises teasingly. "When outside, would you rather read in sand or grass?"

"Sand, because there's no ants. Now answer on the boat."

Theo kisses me so deeply, I almost forget the question. "It's been in storage in the garage for a decade. But yes, I still have it. We can take it out this summer." He rests his forehead against mine. "Have you been in love before?"

"Only with you," I whisper. "But it's better the second time."

"Why?"

"It's my turn." But when I pull back and stare into his blue eyes, which just make everything feel so *clear*, I decide to answer anyway. "Because when we were apart we each grew up. I loved you when we were kids, don't get me wrong. But I didn't know anything then; I was a baby. I didn't know who I was, what I wanted. Now I could have anything I want, but you are all that I want, be-

cause I love you and how I feel with you and who I am with you."
I kiss him, lingering. "And I'm using my last one to ask you the
same question. As a two-parter."

"That's breaking the rules."

"It's my game."

Theo pulls away slightly so he can see me completely. "You're
the only person I've been in love with. And I tried to fall in love
after you left. It wasn't possible. When I saw you again here, I also
tried so hard not to fall back in love with you, but I couldn't help
it. I really believe you're my other half." We kiss again and Theo
holds me so tightly I don't think anything could ever hurt us.

But things immediately start to unravel when we get to the airport.
Harry is there, waiting on the curb when Theo and I step out of the
car. "Emerson!" He steps over and plants a kiss on my cheek, taking
the chance to whisper in my ear. "Matt said we're on. Try to look
happy, not panicked, will you?"

I can't believe this. Matt is well aware that Theo is coming
home with me and the contract with Harry is not happening; I sent
an email to my full team to prep them for our arrival and any press.
He should have already called things off with Harry. I had thought
that with a firm meeting I could move past his manipulation of
Theo, since I have known Matt for eleven years, and I believed he
has my best interests at heart. But if Harry being here is any indi-
cation, his heart may be too firmly tied to his bank account.

I paste a smile on my face. The paparazzi is taking photo after
photo, and what else can I really do? I let Harry take my bag from
Theo and turn to head inside, trying to ignore the shell-shocked
look on Theo's face. The second we get through security, paparazzi
can't follow, and I'll be able to set everything straight.

Then Harry stops me. "Emerson. Baby. There's no need for
TSA today. Let me fly you to LA. My plane's already here."

"Harry! That's too much, you shouldn't have." I pull him into a tight hug so that now I can whisper in his ear. "Theo comes too. Or I can't." I feel his slight nod of assent, release my hold on his neck, and take his hand, turning the full wattage of my paparazzi grin toward him.

"Anything for you. And your friend must come too, I insist." Harry nods at Theo, seizing every opportunity to appear the gentleman. Though, I imagine Theo will be cropped completely out of all the photos that are sold.

"That's so sweet." The three of us pile into his car and start driving.

Theo's jaw is clenched, and when I try to link a finger with his, he's completely still. My heart is pounding in my chest, and I can't do my breathing routine now, when Harry is right next to me in the back seat, so I force myself to appear placid. But I *can* try to explain to Harry what's changed since we last talked.

"Harry, I—"

He cuts me off. "Baby. This is a random car service. Let's save the lovey-dovey stuff for when we're on my plane, shall we?"

I grimace. He's right.

We spend the twenty-minute drive in silence. Harry plays on his phone, while both Theo and I are clearly trying not to have panic attacks. I can't believe how royally screwed up this is.

When we get out of the car, Theo moves to get the bags, but is stopped immediately by an attendant. Harry's ten-seater plane is on a private tarmac. The steps are already down, so I walk directly on and sink into the plush leather seats. Although he owns the plane, the only thing he's done to customize it is replace the standard couch fabric with what's hopefully fake snakeskin. I swivel my seat around, as well as the one next to me for Theo, so that we'll all be facing each other for this conversation.

Theo walks onto the plane, eyes wide as he takes everything in. I don't fly private on my own because I think it's a waste of money and horrible for the environment, although I always accept a ride when offered. But it's clearly Theo's first time.

"Take a picture, mate. Any friend of Emerson's is a friend of mine." We start taxiing, launching into the jerky takeoff all small planes have, and I try not to fall out of my unbuckled seat. The seats are more like luxury movie theater recliners or armchairs than plane seats, and farther back the couch opens into a queen-size bed, in case of overnight flights.

I can tell Theo is itching to take a photo of the plane, probably to send to Owen, but instead he plays it cool. "I'm good, man."

"Can I make you each a drink?" Harry offers as he walks over to the bar.

"Just San Pellegrino for me," I say. "Can we talk openly?"

"Yes. I thought we'd want extra privacy, so there's no flight attendant today, and my team stayed back to fly commercial. My pilot is completely discreet, and also probably can't hear us at this point." Harry hands me the water and pours whiskey for Theo and himself. I try not to get too nervous when Theo drains it in one long gulp. Harry refills his glass without a word. Theo probably isn't aware, but it's a two-thousand-dollar bottle of whiskey.

I waste no time turning to Theo and taking his hand in both of mine. "I am so sorry. I had no idea this was going to happen. I told Matt that we were together and to expect your arrival, and he set this up anyway. I had to act back there because I didn't want to ruin this for Harry."

Harry sits down in the chair opposite Theo and me. "So he knows this is nothing. Good. Does he know . . . anything else?"

I shake my head. "No."

Theo narrows his eyes. "What else is there to know?"

I look back and forth between them. Harry looks between Theo and me, then shrugs, giving me the okay to spill whatever I see fit. "Harry and I have had a contract in the works to fake date for a year. It's not happening now, obviously."

Now it's Harry who drains his glass. "We really are just friends," he declares matter-of-factly to Theo. "It would've been great business for both of us. But now that I've seen you two together . . . Emerson, I'm sorry I gave such a hard sell. I should've been encouraging you to make things happen with Theo, if I was a less selfish friend." He tilts his head in thought. "But I'm only a little sorry. Because you don't get to the total world domination level without being selfish. But I really am happy for you two! I will throw you the best fucking engagement party, just wait. There will be a balloon tree. A sushi cake. Donut cake. Cake cake. All the cakes! And—"

"Harry! Too far. Too far." My face is beet red with embarrassment. I don't want Theo to think I'm totally jumping the gun here. We can date like normal people.

But tension visibly drops from Theo's shoulders. Harry grins, then goes back over to the bar, leaving me to stare at Theo. "I think we all need another round." This time Harry gives me a glass too, and I take a sip and choke on it, but the warmth rushes through me.

Harry holds out a hand to Theo and they shake. "Probably should have led with this, but I know this isn't the best of circumstances. Anyway, it's a pleasure to meet you. As soon as I saw her look at you the other day, I knew she was head over heels for you. I'm going to put my noise-canceling headphones in now, go to the back of the plane, turn the seat to the wall, and let you two talk. But take it from me, you are so lucky to have found your person, instead of just the next best thing. So it wouldn't hurt to have a little grace, because life gets complicated, especially in our world."

True to his word, Harry makes a swift exit. Theo still hasn't said anything since the airport, and I'm panicking. My heart is beating so loudly I think he must be able to hear it over the sound of the plane, and I'm drenched in sweat. I immediately turn to Theo. "Theo. I am so sorry."

Theo sighs deeply, and when he takes my hand relief flushes through me, warming me more than any drink could. "Em. I love you. It's wild that we're here on a plane with Harry Butler. I may have underestimated how much getting used to this all will take. But you're what matters to me. If this is your life, it's mine now too."

I take Theo's face between my hands and pull him into a deep kiss. "Thank you."

It's all I can manage, but I mean it so much. Once we break away, Theo lifts up the arm rest between the seats and puts his arm around me. "As for the whole Harry thing . . . What do you want to do? I know it's for work, and if it's what you need to do . . . it's okay." He's giving me a choice, but his blue eyes, his face, have always been honest, and the hurt of the last hour is still evident in them.

I look over at Harry, thinking for a moment. I want this to have a good outcome for everyone. And though I know Theo would let the Harry façade go on a bit longer out of respect for my work, I will not do that to him. "Why don't we let him say he played match-maker? Helped us seize a second chance at love. He looks good, so at least he gets something, and we have his blessing so I don't get hate articles for the next five years for moving on with someone else and disappointing literally the entire world."

A small smile creeps onto Theo's face and I can sense his relief in the squeeze of his hand on my arm, the crinkle around his eyes, the slower rate of his breathing. "Sounds like a plan to me. You know my mom is going to freak, right?"

"Let's call her once it's a reasonable time in Mass. The Wi-Fi should be good up here."

"You're telling me these private jets actually have functional plane Wi-Fi? Is there anything money can't buy?" Theo plants a kiss on the side of my face.

"Clearly, money can't buy any of the *important* things." I lean in to him, letting his scent and touch envelop me.

"You lovebirds make up?" Harry calls over his shoulder without turning around.

I let Theo take the lead. "Better believe it. Want to talk strategy? Em has a pretty great idea for how to make the best out of the situation for everyone."

Harry's eyes light up when I explain the plan. "You're brilliant. I'll have my people get some paparazzi to the landing strip to get all three of us. And maybe you two can step out for something else this week?"

"Exactly. Then you can jump in with an exclusive." It occurs to me that I've gotten pretty good at this kind of scheming. I don't need Matt as much as I thought.

"You sure you don't want the exclusive? I'm going to look better than you here. The poor rejected heartthrob who put your love above his own heart. I can already see the headlines. This will be the story that sells a million papers. Print papers even!"

I laugh and squeeze Theo's thigh. "I have everything I need. You take it."

I spend the next few hours watching *New Girl* with Theo until he falls asleep, then retreat to the other side of the plane and put my headphones in to call Matt. He picks up on the first ring.

"Emerson. How's the jet treating you? The photos of you and Harry at the airport have over a million likes on *People* magazine's Insta."

"You're fired."

He's silent for a moment. Then he laughs, but it's strained. "You can't *fire* me. Just take a minute and get over yourself. Have your fun with your boy toy from back home, and then we'll get back to business and, you know, your *real* life."

"He *is* my real life. I know you've been lying to him, and manipulating me. So believe me when I say this: You. Are. Fired." My voice is stony but calm, and I'm proud of myself for standing so firm.

Matt changes tactics quickly. "Emerson, I was just trying to protect you and everything we've built. You understand that. Your career comes first."

Listening to him now, I hear just how manipulative he is. I've looked the other way over and over again because he's good at what he does. But he's not the only agent out there, and I *am* the only Emerson. "Fuck you, Matt. You're fired, end of story."

I hear a bang, and I'm pretty sure he just hit his desk. "You will regret this, Emerson. You are absolutely nothing without me. A small-town girl without enough brains to go to college. You're just a pretty face. And you're not even that special; blondes like you are a dime a dozen. The only reason you have all this is because of me. You—"

"Goodbye, Matt."

I hang up the phone and text Natalie. Just fired Matt. Please change all my account passwords and send me the new ones. Better safe than sorry.

Natalie texts back a moment later, a string of champagne emojis. Did everyone else secretly hate Matt? He's been around me for so long that I never stopped to think about whether he was good for me, since it was obvious he was getting results for my career.

I look over at Theo, who is blissfully asleep, sprawled out in the fully reclined seat. I would be terrified to fire my agent if I didn't have Theo by my side. But with him here, I know I can handle anything.

CHAPTER THIRTY-FIVE

—Summer After Senior Year—

Emerson

"I'm sorry I couldn't make it to prom."

I had skipped prom to be the lead model in a Prada campaign. It was my first high fashion shoot, but I had asked my agent to turn it down anyway. Nothing was worth missing prom with Theo. Not when I hoped that would be *the moment*, the night we finally became something more than friends. But when Theo found out, he basically forced me to go, claiming he'd have a fine time with teammates and that he would never be able to get over the guilt of me missing the opportunity for prom with him. So I went. But I could tell he was disappointed.

"Em, I told you. It's totally cool. This is better than prom anyway."

The day I got back we'd sailed all the way from Salem to Provincetown, which was no small feat in a boat that tiny, as a sort of replacement celebration. I brought the dress I'd bought for prom and he brought his tux and we had big plans to wear them to Sal's, a fancy restaurant on the beach that added tables in the last few inches of water as the tide went out.

But first, we were lounging on the beach, enjoying the sunset. We were on a tiny inlet of beach, banked on one side by a dock and tiny shack-like houses that were barely big enough for two people to move around inside; on the other side were huge, colorful, six-million-dollar beach houses with sprawling decks and artificially weathered shingles. If I were a millionaire, I'd want one of each.

The water had turned a deep pink hue, mirroring the lush colors of the sky. I stood and walked to the edge of the water, the cold froth licking my toes as I watched the sky turn. Theo came up behind me and wrapped his arms around me, his skin warm and sticky with dried sweat and sunscreen. I relaxed into him completely, letting us balance against each other as the sand shifted under our feet and the wind whipped my hair, now longer than it'd ever been, into both of our faces.

"I can't wait until we're in New York together," I murmured. I could already see our lives there so clearly. In three days we'd start looking for an apartment together, exactly two weeks before moving, which felt crazy, but everyone I'd worked with said was the way to do things. I didn't let myself worry about us living together, if it would be weird, because I knew that with Theo next to me everything would be okay. Even if I'd tell any friend to run the other way if she was planning on living with a guy she was in love with, who *might* just love her as a friend.

"Me too," Theo whispered.

"Why did you ask me to prom?" I whispered. I wanted to know if it meant everything that I hoped it did.

I felt Theo's rough inhale. "Em . . . There's actually something I was hoping to tell you at prom. I was going to tell you at dinner—"

I turned to face Theo and my movement startled him into silence. He was so close to me, his face only inches away, and everything in that moment felt perfect. I knew in my gut what he was going to say. And our faces were just so close.

I opened my mouth to say something, anything, but my lips just hung there, slightly apart, and I saw his eyes drop to them. His gaze flicked back up to mine, and I let myself stare at every inch of his completely perfect face. We were so close together that it was impossible to say who moved first, but our faces were suddenly touching, his forehead pressed into mine, lips only an inch apart, and I couldn't take it. I closed the last inch and let my mouth meet his.

His kiss was gentle and tentative, but it was there. He pressed his mouth to mine, then pressed his entire body to mine, and I returned the touch. I could have spent all night kissing him there, preserving a moment I was terrified to let end, but then I shivered, and he broke away. He wordlessly handed me his sweatshirt, which I knew he'd brought for me. I pulled it over my head.

But then he just stared at me, unmoving, and my stomach sank. Was he regretting the kiss already? Was he realizing he just thought of me as a friend? Was he going to say something different from what I'd assumed a minute ago?

"Em, that was . . ."

"You don't have to say anything," I whispered. If he was going to reject me, I didn't want to hear it yet. I wanted one night to savor the feeling of his lips on mine. I could still feel the ghost of his kiss.

"Emerson, I love you relentlessly." He let out a sigh of release after he said it and wrapped me so tightly in his arms that I could barely breathe, before pulling back to look at me. "I have loved you since the day I met you and you persuaded me to go in that freezing water. Every day. I've thought about you every day. And I was planning to make prom this huge perfect night, where I told you everything, and it would have been so much more romantic . . . but anyway, I love you, Em."

I reached up and touched his face, ran my hands down the curve of his cheek, as though by touching him I could feel if it was truth in his pale blue eyes. If I was dreaming. "I love you too. So much I can barely stand it. But Theo . . . are we crazy to do this?"

"We'd be crazier not to. There is nothing that could make me stop loving you."

Theo's eyes were wide and his voice was earnest, his gaze intently on me. I pressed myself into him again and he wrapped his arms around me. I never wanted it to end. That night, we had sex. It was my first time, and the best day of my life.

CHAPTER THIRTY-SIX

Theo

By the time we finally pull up to Emerson's house, I feel dead. My heart has gone from bursting with joy, to pulverized, to cautiously reformed, all in the space of twenty-four hours. When Emerson stepped out of the car and into Harry's arms, it was like all my worst fears come to life. Even if it was for publicity. There is so much about her world that I can't process.

When we step out of the car, I go for the bags, just to be stopped again, and am left staring up at a building no one in their right mind would call a house. It's *huge*. When we went through the gate, I thought we were entering a gated community, but this entire property is hers. We drove by tennis courts and at least two pools, and now are staring down the barrel of the largest mansion I've ever seen.

"This is my main LA property," Emerson explains. "But I also bought my first apartment, because I totally love it. It's the place where I learned how to actually be me, where I grew into, you know, the adult version of myself. Maybe after our photo op tomorrow we can stop by." Emerson is walking into the house, casually narrating, but frowns at her own words. "Actually, I don't want paparazzi to follow. Better that we wait for that one."

"That one?" Her foyer may be the size of my entire home.

"I have a New York brownstone too, for when I'm there. It's way smaller, though." I've lingered, trying to take in the decadence of this home through tired eyes. Emerson walks back over to me and wraps herself in my arm. "Do you like it? I know it's . . . big."

"Emerson, from what I've seen, this is a beautiful place." And it truly is. I've watched enough *Architectural Digest* videos with my mom and Naomi to know what's tasteful. And this place is not just huge, it's well done.

"I'm glad you like it." She glows at my words. Which is mystifying, because what does it matter what I think? I'll never afford anything remotely as nice as this, and I'm sure she's had actual artists and designers over who have gushed over it. "Georgia's place was done by the same architect, and I gave him complete free reign over mine. I stayed at my other places for an entire year and came back to this. The only thing I did was fill the bookshelf."

She leads me into what I suppose is the living room. Or maybe a library? Three walls are lined with bookshelves, with one wall still empty, and there's rolling library ladders on every side. Back in high school, we were banned from Brookline Booksmith after I pushed her on the ladder so fast that we sent entire shelves of books cascading to the floor. "They offered to have a book stylist select books for me, but I wanted to fill the room with every book I've ever read."

I walk around the room slowly. "There have to be thousands of books in here. You read all of these?"

Emerson nods, trying to keep a proud smile off her face. I want her to be comfortable enough that she doesn't think to limit her emotions around me. I want all of her. "I spend a lot of time on planes."

I tug her toward the ladder, and she leans back on it while I brace my arms around her. "This is a bit more than plane reading."

"It's my only hobby." Emerson's breath has become rapid and she's flushed. She grabs my hip and tugs me toward her. I pick her up and she wraps her legs around my waist, back pressed to the ladder. "Theo," she breathes. "Remember—"

"I remember everything." I kiss her, so hard our teeth clink together, and when she presses against me we both moan. "Em, you should write a book."

"I want to." Emerson's words come out in a rush, as though she's been thinking about this forever. We've spent so much time talking about my career, but I suddenly realize she hasn't been quite as forthcoming. "But I never even went to college. I'm a model. I'd be better off starting a clothing line, like Georgia."

"Better off for who?" I pick her up and carry her over to the couch, so we can sit for a minute and actually talk. "Em, the only thing that matters is that you're happy. That you're doing what you want. Forget about the money, success, all of it."

Em buries her head in my shoulder. Her words come out muffled. "I can't fail. This is what I'm good at."

"I'm calling bullshit. You've been telling me to follow my dreams. So let me tell you. You're the whole orange. *Todo de naranja.*"

She looks away. "I'll think about it." Then she drops a hand to my belt and brings her lips to mine.

It's not until a half hour later, after we've slept together in the library, that I realize she was deflecting. She wouldn't actually talk to me. I thought we could be completely honest, tell each other everything like we used to. She's who I want to turn to first, to brainstorm ideas with, to photograph, to tell my hopes and fears to. But what if, despite everything she's said, she's still not ready to fully be herself with me?

I feel my old doubts slipping in. Am I really good enough for her?

The Day of
the Pact

CHAPTER THIRTY-SEVEN

Emerson

"Are you sure it's not too much so soon? We don't have to actually go."

We're in my main pool, which is a lazy oval, and always warm because I have a solar cover for it. Theo lays on a rainbow-maned unicorn, and I'm on a pink flamingo. It's crazy seeing him here, in my pool, at my house. Theo got me bagels for breakfast, since we always used to kick off our birthdays with Bagel World, and we've been spending the day doing not much of anything. It's already the best birthday I've had in ten years.

When Georgia invited us to the launch event for her new swim line, I immediately wanted to go—first, to support her, but also because it aligns perfectly with our plan to be photographed together one more time before Harry's exclusive. He's giving it to *People* today, for release tomorrow. But from his pool float, Theo is conspicuously quiet. "Theo?"

"We should go," he says. "I want to spend more time with Georgia. And it's the plan."

I nod, but Theo sounds weird. He's been distant since we got to my place. I paddle over to him.

"Are you sure?" I squeeze his hand one more time, so he knows I'm here.

"Em. I mean, twist my arm a bit more, but going to my first big Hollywood party doesn't sound all bad. There'll be snacks right?" His grin is rakish.

"Of course. But we may want to eat first; the snacks are probably bite-size so no one gets food in their teeth." Theo starts to respond, but before he can, I roll off my flamingo, my grip on his hand firm, and pull him into the water with me.

He rises, sputtering. "That's cold! I thought you wanted your house to be a safe space? Now I have to live in fear."

I wrap my arms around his neck and droplets of water fall from his hair to my still mostly dry face. "Whoops. I needed you closer to me. I missed you."

"Em, we were holding hands," Theo argues, but he can't wipe the smile off his face.

"I need to maintain at least fifty percent skin-to-skin contact at all times. And you can't deny me on my birthday." I press myself against him, and he picks me up, weightless in the water. My bikini is a thong, something I only wear in the privacy of my home. He feels me up shamelessly and my pulse starts racing.

"Or what?" He kisses me quickly.

"I melt. I *am* from Salem after all." I kiss his neck, then trail my way up to his jaw, then his mouth. I feel him get hard and grind into him.

"Em, you know what they say about witches . . ."

In an instant he throws me toward the deep end. I submerge completely and shriek when I come up. "Theo! How could you?"

He swims over and wraps me back up in his arms. "If you're gonna dish it, you've got to take it. Besides, you're cute when you're all wet."

I probably look like a drowned rat now that my hair is wet. But I let him kiss me again anyway. "I love you." I'll never get tired of saying it. "But, now I have to go shower and blow dry before we leave. See you in an hour." I slide out of his arms and swim over to the pool steps, walking out slowly since I know he's watching.

"All my future plans to dunk you are hereby canceled," Theo calls after me.

Right as I step into the house, Theo calls after me. "Em!"

I turn back toward him. He's leaning on the side of the pool, and in that instant, with his hair wet and unabashed smile, looks so much like eighteen-year-old Theo that my heart skips a beat. His eyes shine when he looks at me, and I can feel how ridiculously huge my grin is.

"Em, I love you too. And I'm really glad we're together today." My heart soars. "Me too."

I get ready in record time. I curl my hair so quickly I almost burn my forehead on the wand, and do my makeup in fifteen minutes flat. Finally, I slide into the gown Natalie sent over for me. It's a nude Valentino gown that perfectly matches my skin tone. Crystals litter the bottom, but become scarcer as they climb my body, until it's just sheer fabric hugging my chest. I could zip it myself. I have a zipper helper tool, like every other woman without a partner, but instead I call Theo in.

He stops in his tracks when he sees me. "You look stunning."

"Can you zip me up?" I turn to give him access to my back. My face is split open with the biggest grin. I usually don't smile this big. Not since a photographer on one of my very first shoots said it made me "look gummy." But with Theo, I don't have to care about things like that.

"Do I have to?" Theo runs his finger down my spine, caressing me, and I shiver.

"Unfortunately, yes. I can't be late for Georgia. There's a tux Natalie sent for you in my closet too."

Theo kneels and kisses my lower back. He traces kisses up my spine, and chases the path with a slow tug on the zipper. I shiver.

When he reaches my neck, he sucks on it gently, before taking my hips and turning me toward him so he can plant a light kiss on the corner of my mouth. "I wouldn't want to mess up your lipstick."

"I don't care about the lipstick." I pull him toward me and kiss him deeply. I'll never be able to get enough of him now that I have him.

Theo breaks away first, which is good, because in a few more seconds I might have unzipped my dress myself. "I better get dressed. I don't want to get on Georgia's bad side."

"I think that would be impossible. If she wasn't traveling until this morning, I'm sure she would have shown up here already."

Theo peeks his head out the door of my closet, shirtless. "I forgot that you call this full-on New York apartment a closet."

I throw a pillow at his head and he ducks, laughing. "Let me live a life of luxury. The more space I have the easier it is for it to look empty." He's the only one who would understand what I mean by that. I can't stand clutter after living with my mom; it makes my skin crawl. My house is almost completely white and very sparse.

Theo comes out and pulls me up. "Emerson. You are nothing like your mother. You only have her good qualities, like these cheekbones." He kisses my cheek. "Your sense of humor. Because you have to admit, she can be funny." He kisses my dimple. "But I know how much you wanted all this. And I'm so proud of you."

"You're going to make me cry, and we don't have time to redo my makeup." I tilt my head back and blink back tears. I forgot what it's like to have someone actually see me.

"Don't worry," he says, turning his attention back to getting dressed. "I'll tell you again later."

"Theo?" He looks back toward me. "Tomorrow, let's pick a time to visit my mom together."

His smile is knowing and kind. "Sounds like a plan."

In the car ride to the launch party, I recline my seat all the way back and basically lie down to avoid wrinkles. Theo teases me mercilessly about my strategy, but I love it. I used to drive separately from boyfriends, then get into their car a block away, so they wouldn't see me like this. They'd think it was stupid or, even worse, might tell someone. But with Theo I actually laugh, because it is totally ridiculous, and it's nice to be able to have a sense of humor about my work. Someone to laugh with.

I can see the chaos from outside of the car window when we pull up. He moves toward the door, but I stop him with a hand on his arm. I want another minute, just for us. "Hey, Theo?"

"What?" He plants a gentle kiss on my head.

"I don't want to go out there yet."

"We can stay." He leans back comfortably, his palm resting on my thigh, engulfing it.

My phone buzzes, and when I look down, I see the final reminder flashing across my screen. *Time to marry Theo!* I hold up the phone and show him, smiling ear to ear.

He takes my phone from me and gazes at it, a smile playing across his cheeks. "Em?"

"Yeah?" I wonder if I'll always have this jump of anticipation when he says my name. All I want is to hear whatever he has to say next, no matter what it is.

"Can you believe it's this marriage pact that got us back together?" He's grinning, impish, as though he's completely joking around, but I sense the serious undercurrent.

"I mean, technically, we haven't fulfilled it." I can't help but smile as I wiggle my ring less finger to tease him. "It is a bit cringey."

"It's not. Since it's us, it's cute. Since we've always been endgame." I could listen to him say that over and over, forever.

"It was my only hope."

"It was *my* only hope," he corrects me with a kiss to my temple. "Ask Owen. Or my mom. I told everyone I knew that we were destined to get married one day. Each separately in confidence, of course, so it wouldn't get back to you."

"We'll have to agree to disagree on who was more invested. But I'm happy it brought us back together."

Someone raps on the window. "Let's keep it moving!"

Theo hops out of the car. Even though someone is there to open my door, he runs around and takes over, helps me out.

But something is nagging at me. Something feels . . . off.

The reminder.

His didn't go off.

Maybe he doesn't have notifications on. Maybe it's on silent, so he's not distracted tonight. Maybe he forgot his phone altogether.

Or maybe he deleted it, and the ironclad certainty in us he expressed moments ago was an exaggeration. I take a deep breath and try to bury the doubt in the back of my mind. For some reason I'd thought that when I was with the right person, I wouldn't have any doubts. Isn't that how it's supposed to be? But I've got a job to do, so I save that worry for later.

Cameras start flashing as soon we step onto the red carpet. My smile feels glued to my face. Harry has waited for us, so that they can get a candid of the three of us talking, and we walk over to him with Theo's arm snaked tightly across my waist.

"You two look good together," he remarks immediately. "I don't think the world has ever seen Emerson look like this."

I instinctively clamp my grin down a notch, but then I see how Theo's looking at me and I can't hold it back. My smile is clearly contagious, because I see the glances we're getting from photographers and other partygoers, people typically totally in the zone. "Well, someone told me I was lying when I said I had it all before. And I realized they were right." I can't help myself, and I kiss Theo quickly on the lips, photographers and lip liner be damned.

"Emerson! Harry! Photo?" Photographers are yelling at us, and an usher is trying to move us along. I pull Theo with me onto the red carpet prime spot, and he wraps an arm around me. He feels hot, and I can actually see his pulse jumping in the vein on the side of his neck.

"Theo. It's just us." I look up at him and lock eyes. "Just think of it as the prom we never had."

This breaks through his anxiety and he smiles—a real one.

"Emerson!" calls a photographer. "Who is your date tonight? What happened between you and Harry?"

I turn my head toward Theo, so that the photographers don't take a million pictures of me mid-words. "Theo, ignore their questions, okay?"

He gives a curt nod. "Got it."

"I need to do a solo picture. If you head over through that door, you'll be in the party, and I'll follow in a minute. I'm sure Georgia will make a beeline for you."

"I wish I was the one taking your photo in this outfit. You look stunning." Theo kisses me softly on the lips, causing a collective stir from our audience, and walks inside. I hit my poses quickly, so there will be something for any press Georgia needs tomorrow, and then start to glide off, ignoring the questions that are still being yelled at me. Until one makes me stop in my tracks.

"Emerson! What's your response to former agent Matt Bauer's claims that he dropped you because you had work done?"

"Emerson! What is your response to Bauer's allegations that you've relied on quarterly Botox since age twenty-two? That your all-natural beauty campaign was a complete lie?"

I feel like all the air has been pulled out of my chest. I can't believe Matt would say that. Or . . . maybe I can. He's always had a "kill or be killed" mentality. But this is so cruel. The photographers continue to shout questions at me, but I just stand there, alone, frozen. My fans are going to *hate* me. The whole world will think I'm a fraud. A liar. All the girls that looked up to me . . . they'll be crushed.

"Emerson, is it true that you've had a nose job?"

Suddenly Harry takes me by the arm and ushers me toward the door. "Just keep moving," he whispers. "Don't let them see they've gotten to you."

I struggle to fix my face as we leave the red carpet and head inside. "In here it's only friendly photographers," Harry says. "At least in theory. But if I were you, I wouldn't trust that, not after what just happened outside." He looks around. "Let's go to the bathroom."

We blow right past Theo, who's having an animated conversation with Georgia, but he immediately follows us into the bathroom when he sees my face. Harry pulls me into the men's room. "Everyone out! CEO says," Georgia calls as she walks in, and one scared-looking TikTok wunderkind scrambles away from the mirror where he was painstakingly redoing his eyeliner. I collapse onto the couch and start my circular breathing, head held high, posture perfect, trying to keep it together. *I am ice. I am untouchable. I have built something great and I will not let anyone destroy it.* I repeat this to myself silently as Theo drops to his knees in front of me and takes my hands in his.

"Em, what happened? Talk to me." I know if I look into his eyes, at his sweet, sweet face, I'll break down. So I ignore him and just try to pull myself together silently.

"Apparently Matt released a statement saying he dropped her because she lied about getting work done in that big campaign last year, and he couldn't stand by the lies anymore." Harry leans against the counter nonchalantly, as though he's not in a men's bathroom gathered around a combusting, over-the-hill supermodel.

"That Botox-loving son of a bitch," Georgia curses. "Racist prick. We will burn him to the fucking ground."

"Wait, what do you mean?" I knew Georgia didn't love Matt, but she'd never mentioned him being racist before. If he said something inappropriate to her . . . "What do you mean?"

Georgia blushes slightly. "Sorry, I didn't mean to make this about me."

"No, no, tell me. What did he do?" The sad thing is, I don't doubt for a second that Matt did something. I'm just sad Georgia didn't tell me.

"I mean, you've seen his roster, babe. White, white, white. And even after I blew up, became genuinely popular for me, my curves, my skin, my natural hair . . . when I was looking for a new agent and asked him if he was interested, he made it very clear it was never going to happen."

"Georgia, why wouldn't you tell me? I never would have kept working with him if I knew that."

Georgia smiles wanly. "Babe, you were a bit fragile back then. You trusted him because he was from . . . before. And I didn't want to take away one of the only people you trusted."

Theo is looking between us, confused by what's happening, while Harry is extremely absorbed in his phone, but takes care to give a wan smile and a quick thumbs-up. I get up and wrap Georgia in a huge hug. "I hope you know that I would always choose you over any stupid agent, manager, job, anything. You're my best friend. The best friend I could ever have."

Georgia hugs me back, tightly. "I know. But no crying. We have makeup on." We pull apart and she claps her hands together once. "Now, problem at hand. We'll fix this."

My gut sinks and I drop back into the chair. Matt is horrible. The things he said to Georgia, to Jillian . . . clearly he has no qualms about destroying me now that I've dropped him. "I have no proof that he was actually pushing me to do it and lie about it. He always brought it up over the phone. I can't believe people think I could have lied about this." I know that's how it goes. People want to believe the worst, most scandalous headlines. But after how hard I've worked to be a good example for young girls, it stings that more people aren't jumping to my defense.

Theo squeezes my hands. "I'm sure no one cares what he says. How long can a story even last? Tomorrow it will be something new." Theo's tactic is sweet, but unrealistic. This is a tantalizing story about me, and I'm sure everyone will run with it, regardless of whether it's true.

Harry holds up his phone. "It's already everywhere. Not gonna lie to you, it's not pretty. They've obviously pulled all your worst photos to accompany it. And quotes from that campaign and all the press you did about it. Some people are defending you . . . but the big outlets aren't. I'd sic your PR team on it and hope for the best. And hate to say it, but you should get back out there before it looks true." What Harry has said sends the breathing I was gaining control of in a much worse direction. I squeeze my eyes shut. But not too tight. A tiny voice in the back of my mind reminds me not to ruin my mascara.

"Way to help," Theo shoots at Harry darkly. "Em, let's go home. We can watch a movie, I'll make popcorn. Pick up some donuts."

But Harry is the only one in here who understands how much I have to lose. Georgia has already effectively retired and has her own self-sustaining business. I take a deep, wavering breath. "No, Harry's right. I'm fine. This will be handled. I should go back out there. Georgia, you go now before people wonder where you are. I'll follow in a minute." Georgia looks like she wants to try to change my mind, but I can also see that she does need to get back. This company is her baby. "Really, Georgia. We're fine here, go."

She eyes Theo, then nods. "But you don't have to stay for me. If I don't see you out there, I'll call tonight. Love you." She walks to the door. Right before she exits, I see her pull her shoulders back, paste on a bright, easy smile, and open her eyes wide. Transformation complete, she rejoins the party.

"I think that's my cue to leave too," Harry states blandly. It's less of a transformation for him, but I see his slightly concerned look fall away, and it's replaced with a life-of-the-party smile. "Don't let them see you flinch. They're vultures, every last one of them. Love you, though." His words are jarring, since he's now saying them with his face on, but I just nod.

Theo waits until the door has shut behind Harry before he speaks. "Screw what he said. You don't need to do anything you don't want to. A few articles will not make you lose your entire career. Just let me take care of you."

"No, Theo. He's completely right. I need to keep up appearances." I let my head rest in my hands for a minute, but brush Theo off when he sits on the bench next to me and tries to rub my back. "Don't." I should say why, say that if I let him comfort me for a second, I will break down and be unable to do this. Instead I sit up, pull my shoulders back, take a breath, and paste a smile to my face.

I offer Theo my hand when I stand. "Ready?" I am so grateful to have him next to me. Because even though I look composed, anxiety is shooting through me. I feel like I might crack at any moment.

But Theo doesn't take my hand. "I need a minute to wrap my head around this. Is that okay?"

"I need to keep moving." I'm shocked. But if I stop for even a moment longer, I will break down. Especially now. Because it never occurred to me that I might have to walk out there without him.

"I'll be there in one minute," Theo tells me. He squeezes my hand. And then he lets go.

I know this is my fault. If I tell him I need him, that I don't feel as put together as I look, he would sacrifice his needs in a heartbeat. But the words feel too big, too complicated. And I've already started the process of shutting my feelings away, of becoming *supermodel Emerson*. So instead, I walk away.

CHAPTER THIRTY-EIGHT

Theo

I'm reeling when Em leaves. I want to wrap her up and bring her home with me so she can actually feel her feelings. I've never seen her put herself back together like she just did. It didn't look healthy. But Georgia's her best friend, and she was okay with letting her go back out there, so maybe I should relax? Even if, to my untrained eye, it looks a bit like Emerson would rather self-destruct than take a minute to breathe? I also hate that Harry was able to give her the right advice when I couldn't. I know that's petty. But I wish I knew what to say, how to advise her in this world that is so far out of my league. This whole situation is making me doubt my instincts.

For the first time tonight, I wonder if I belong here at all. I don't know how to just put my face on and keep moving like everyone else seems to.

I splash water on my cheeks and grip the side of the sink. This is Emerson's life, her choices, and I will support her. Even if it burns to watch her fake it when I know she's hurting.

I leave the restroom and scan the crowd. She's talking to a group of people—actors, models, musicians, creative directors, producers—all people I recognize from watching the MET gala and awards shows.

When I join their circle, Emerson pulls me close and immediately introduces me. "This is my boyfriend, Theo. Not yet announced, so—" She puts her finger to her lips in a cheesy *shhh, don't tell* gesture and everyone laughs with her. "He's a photographer, and he's so talented. Like insane. He was just shooting me, and it's my favorite photos anyone has ever taken of me."

"And she's not just saying that because they're in love," Harry jokes. "I've basically had to beg to get him to shoot my next movie poster."

I balk. Somehow, I don't remember that conversation. Emerson smiles at Harry, clearly grateful for the new addition to the public narrative of our relationship. I know it's business, it's their life's work, but somehow it feels cheap. Transactional.

A woman introduced to me as the editor of Condé Nast is appraising me, top to bottom. "He'll have to do *US Vogue*. Or maybe you two should be on the cover together. Exclusive, of course." Emerson squeezes my hand tightly. Clearly, this is big, even though I have at least six copies of *Vogue* editions that she's been on at my house in Salem. I always buy a magazine when I see she's the cover, something I take great care to hide from everyone that I know. The editor hands me a sleek business card. "This has my direct line. Call Monday. Nine o'clock sharp."

"I'll do that." I can barely get the words out of my mouth. Shooting the cover of any Condé Nast magazine is as high prestige as photography gets. I can't believe how quickly this is happening. And being on the cover of *Vogue*? It's unthinkable. Impossible.

I barely hear what anyone says for the rest of the conversation. Blood is pounding through my head as I try to wrap my brain around everything that's happening. Suddenly, the lights dim and Georgia takes the stage.

"Before we start, I just wanted to invite a few special guests out for a song. Because I don't know how many of you know this, but today just so happens to be my best friend's birthday!" Georgia raises her glass of champagne, gesturing toward Emerson, who plants a serene smile on her face. She squeezes my hand so tightly I feel my knuckle pop and I shift ever so slightly closer to her.

"Without further ado . . ." Georgia steps to the side, and Irizia comes out on stage. The biggest pop star in the world. But instead of breaking into any of her own songs, she jumps into a rendition of "Happy Birthday."

My jaw drops. I can't believe the biggest singer in the world is singing an original arrangement of "Happy Birthday" to Emerson. It's like asking Mozart to play "Hot Cross Buns," or Michelangelo to make a mug for your mom's morning coffee. And yet no one else is batting an eye.

As she finishes singing, a waiter brings a cupcake on a tray over to Emerson. It has one candle, which she daintily blows out. Then Irizia is dismissed, Georgia announces the runway show, and girls start strutting down the runway in bikinis.

I'm racking my brain for ways to elevate the birthday celebration I set up. I scheduled a delivery of pizza and cupcakes for when we get home, and while Emerson showered I put some string lights and a picnic blanket out by the pool. It's pathetic compared with this.

Emerson takes my hand and steers me deeper into the crowd so we're slightly more secluded against a wall. "Sorry, this is a lot. That was honestly so embarrassing. And I didn't mean to throw you to the wolves there with *Vogue*. I know you might be more interested in arthouse stuff. Or what you're doing now!"

"You're kidding, right? *Vogue* would be amazing." It's been less than a day since we arrived home, and my career has been completely catapulted. It should be amazing. But I feel anxiety deep in my chest because this is all just falling in my lap because of

Emerson. I don't deserve it. It's not based on my own work, it's just proximity to her.

Em smiles and nuzzles her head against my neck as we watch a runway show of models of all sizes strut down the runway in bikinis. "Good. I'd love to do *Vogue* with you too. And Harry wasn't kidding. He's been on me since I showed him the one sheet on the plane while you napped, but I told him to give you a week to get used to all this."

"Is that part of the scheme? Like a tie-in for the story?"

Emerson pulls back, her brow furrowed. "What are you talking about? He wants you because you're talented, Theo."

When she told me that a few days ago, before seeing her home, how she lives, how charmed being on her arm is, it was a lot easier to believe that.

But I shouldn't have let my worries creep in here. My only job tonight is to support her, especially after what happened earlier. Just because she's acting totally fine doesn't mean I can forget how upset she was. She couldn't even talk. I wrap my arm around her and pull her to my chest, so we're as close as possible. "Forget what I said. How are you?"

"I'm fine," she insists. "I just overreacted for a minute. Too many lights, not enough sleep. I'm fine now."

Her face is totally placid, and I don't know why she'd say that if it wasn't true, because I'm the one person she doesn't need to put on a show for. She should know that. And yet . . .

"Well, then let me get you a glass of champagne, so we can celebrate you."

"There's waiters for that," Emerson points out.

"But I want to get it for you." I kiss the side of her head and stroll off as worries fly through my head. I walk just out of view and take two glasses off a tray, then pause to collect my thoughts. I don't want to ruin things with Em. I need to stop worrying about work tonight, about what I am to her. In the car things were great.

I have to remember that. Believe what she says, that she's happy, this is what she wants.

Once I've slowed my brain down sufficiently, I head back toward her. Georgia and she have their heads pressed close together, so it's not until I'm right behind them that I hear what Emerson is whispering to her.

"Maybe things have just run their course, maybe this is all it was mean to be. But I'm not going to talk to Theo about it until tomorrow. I don't want to ruin the night."

I stop in my tracks. I thought we were being completely honest now, and an insecure part of me wonders if she's keeping things from me because I'm not enough for her, not someone she views as truly on her team. She never explained why she lied a decade ago, and now she's already keeping more secrets. This can't work if we don't communicate, but this conversation isn't going to happen at her best friend's event, and I can't stay here without having an anxiety attack over where this all is going.

I set the glasses on a waiter's tray, and leave.

CHAPTER THIRTY-NINE

—Summer After Senior Year—

Theo

I couldn't believe I got to be with Emerson. I kept waking up next to her in her sleeping bag and pinching myself. I hadn't been waiting for her, exactly . . . I wasn't sure it would ever happen. But I was *so* glad we lost our virginities to each other.

I was so gone for her.

She left for a shoot in the Hamptons when we got back, and I slipped up to my room and spent the night sitting around with a dopey grin plastered to my face. I kept staring at the selfie we'd taken on the beach, a commemoration of sorts to our first kiss.

The next morning, my family knew something was up as soon as I walked into the living room.

"What happened to you?" Owen asked. I let my grin spread even wider, unable to hold it in. "Bro, is it Emerson? You two?"

I nodded. "I can't believe it."

"Mom, get in here!" Our mom came rushing in, afraid someone was grievously injured. "Theo has something to announce."

I could feel my blush from my toes to my forehead. "Emerson and I are together."

My mom actually clapped. "I've been waiting for this! Wait until I tell your father. And invite her for dinner!"

While Emerson was occupied on set, I took the Boston Fast Ferry directly back to Provincetown. When we had been walking down Commercial Street, she had stopped in her tracks outside a jewelry shop, gazing at a ring. It was understated and elegant, and it cost a cool four thousand dollars. Exactly as much as the camera I'd been saving up for. But I didn't care—I knew I had to get that ring. Emerson was my future, and I needed her to know how much she meant to me. That the only future I could see was the one with her in it. I knew it was a lot at eighteen, but seeing that ring—not an engagement ring, but a promise of our future together—would be well worth spending another year saving for my own equipment.

I pulled out my phone. We'd been texting nonstop the night before as a car service drove her from Salem to the Hamptons. This morning we'd FaceTimed for all of five minutes before she had to peel off her sheet mask and go to set, but since then it'd been radio silence. Suddenly I worried that my five unanswered messages were too many. But I knew she'd tell me I was being ridiculous, so I went ahead and sent another, inviting her for dinner.

Five hours later she still hadn't answered my messages. I tried calling her but the calls went straight to voicemail. I made Owen try, and my mom, convinced something had to be wrong with my phone. When five hours turned to eight, I told my mom I wanted to call the police, but she talked me down, assuring me it was a long drive back, her phone just must be dead, give it time. But I knew something was wrong.

At ten p.m. I went to her house. When no one answered my knock, I opened the door with the key I'd been given years prior. "Em? Are you home?"

Her mom appeared, hair wild. "Theo. Emerson isn't well. She got back from the shoot and went straight to bed."

I moved to go up to her room to check on her, but she blocked me. "I just want to check on her," I said. "I won't wake her up."

I tried to move around her again, but this time she gripped my arm with a surprisingly firm grasp. "She'll reach out when she wants to see you. She needs to rest now."

I struggled to maintain respect for Emerson's mom after watching how she treated her daughter over the past few years. This was the woman who sent Emerson to school with a 104-degree fever at eight years old. She might be right that Emerson just needed rest, but I was unable to take her word for it.

I gently removed her mom's hand and continued on up the stairs, but when I got to Emerson's door, it was locked. I tried the door again anyway. "Em, I'm so sorry to wake you up," I said through the door. "I know your mom said you're sick. But do you need anything? Want me to take you to the doctor? I just want to know you're okay."

Her room had no key, only a deadbolt on the inside. But then I heard the bolt snap, the handle turn.

"Theo?" Emerson did look pale, dwarfed by my sweater, hair limp.

"Are you okay? Your mom said you're sick?"

"You shouldn't come any closer. I've been throwing up."

"Oh no, was it something from the shoot? Catering probably sits out too—"

Emerson suddenly gagged and pushed past me to the bathroom, where she began to dry heave violently into the toilet. Hardly anything came up. I stepped behind her, grabbed a hair tie from the counter, and pulled her hair into a bun.

"Theo, you have to go." She waved a weak hand at me.

"Listen, if it's food poisoning, I really won't get sick, it's okay. I'll stay the night with you." I sat down on the lip of the tub. "I don't mind."

"I'm okay. It's okay. But this is disgusting, please."

Her voice was so beseeching that I had to relent. "Fine, just let me get you some water. And crackers; it looks like there's not even anything left." I reached over her and flushed the toilet after she waved me off aggressively when I tried to help her stand.

By the time I returned with crackers and water, she was already back in bed. I left the plate I'd made up on her bedside table, but when I reached out to stroke her hair she flinched away. "I'm just gross right now," she muttered fretfully.

"Don't go getting all awkward on me now," I admonished her playfully. But panic had started to snake its way through me. I'd seen Emerson throw up before. She'd never pulled away like this.

She wouldn't meet my gaze as I let myself out.

I gripped the wheel with iron fists the entire drive home. I knew Emerson, and it was clear something was wrong, something more than just food poisoning. Something wasn't right.

The next day I showed up at her house, but she was already gone. According to her mom, she'd flown to LA, without a word. But I'd missed her by minutes. Because when I got home there was a note, on top of a pile of my sweaters.

Theo. I can't be with you. I don't love you. I just wanted to see what it would be like to try to. I'm so sorry.

It felt like I had been punched. But as hurt as I was, I also didn't believe her. I knew her better than anyone in the world. There had to be something else going on.

I called her a hundred times in a row, left a voicemail every time, until her mailbox was full. I called her landline, begged her mom to tell me where she'd be staying, so I could go to her. She wouldn't budge. "Emerson told me not to tell you where she is," she said. "She doesn't want to see you, Theo. She said she wants you to stay away. Please . . . just let it go."

Suddenly, all the stories I'd been telling myself about this not being real, about something else going on, about Emerson being happy . . . it all crumbled away. Because as much as I didn't trust her mom to do what was best for Emerson, I'd never known her to be a liar. Which meant the only person lying was me—to myself.

She might not have had food poisoning, but it turned out whatever was going on with her was contagious in its own way, because I spent the next twenty-four hours getting sick on the floor of my bathroom, until I had absolutely nothing left.

CHAPTER FORTY

—Summer After Senior Year—

Emerson

"Hey!" The other model who had been in the studio getting digitals taken ran after me as I left the building. "Wait up!"

I paused and held the door open for her. "Oh, sorry." Since moving to LA the week before, I'd ignored hundreds of calls and messages from Theo, and I didn't have the energy to muster enthusiasm for a stranger. She was with the same agency as me, but we might never work together, and I could barely put one foot in front of the other.

"I'm Georgia," she declared brightly as she fell into step beside me. "I heard you just moved here too?"

I nodded and launched into the story I'd been telling people. The one more palatable than wanting to run as far away from a certain photographer as possible, of not being able to look my best friend in the eye anymore. "Yeah, it just seems so beautiful out here. And easier to work all the time, which is what I want." I was booked solid for the next month, and would make more money than I'd ever dreamt of, so that wasn't a total lie. Other girls had told me to work as much as I could while my look was in, because you never knew when things would dry up.

"Girl, same, if I can get it."

I smiled politely, unsure how to respond to her. Georgia was a curve model, which made getting booked much harder. Most brands would book one curve for every three straight sizes, which was messed up, but I didn't know yet how much was rude to say. "Listen, I moved here a few months back, and it was so hard. If you need a hand, let me know."

I was so used to Theo always being there that I hadn't realized how challenging it would be to move alone. I'd had a bed frame and couch shipped to my new apartment, but they were unassembled on the floor and I'd been sleeping on a mattress. My instinct was to say no. But I really did need the help. "Actually . . . that would be great. I'm literally sleeping on a mattress because I can't put anything together alone. Not that you have to help put stuff together, I mean, I know that's lame. You probably meant get lunch or something. Or juice?" Every single model I'd met out here was infinitely healthier than I was and was obsessed with green juice.

But Georgia just laughed at me, so open and gregarious that I couldn't help but smile too. The muscles of my face felt stiff from disuse. "Fuck the juice. I need another six months before I actually like living on juice and sushi. Let's get a pizza and make your bed."

A few hours later we were collapsed on the fully assembled couch, the bed frame in pieces around us. The first hour we'd been giddy with food and the first glass of wine and gossip, convinced we'd assemble everything in one go. But once we moved on to the bed frame our momentum slowed, and with each Ikea-induced roadblock we devolved deeper into talking instead of building. We'd split a bottle of rosé Georgia brought, and as I drank I became less and less able to ignore the events of the past week.

"I just can't face him. I can't have him looking at me, knowing what happened. I just feel so dirty. Like, I feel like I'm ruined, and I'll never be able to be with a guy again. I'm having nightmares, I'm afraid to go anywhere. Every time the photographer adjusted me today, I just felt . . ." I shuddered violently. This was too much for a first hangout. But I was destroyed and didn't know what to do, so I just kept talking. "Theo is who I would usually call after something, and now I just . . . I don't know, I'm alone." I was crying by now, but lightly, because I'd spent the first two days in LA sobbing, and I didn't have that much left anymore. But this was worse. My voice sounded dead, totally off, and I was sure Georgia would be making her excuses to leave soon. Our foundation was three hours of building furniture and I was already spilling my guts, clearly a mess.

"Babe, I'm sure he's great. I'm sure he is, but you don't need any man, and if after you make it through this you decide you want him, trust me, you can get him back. But now, we focus on you." This made me cry harder, and Georgia passed me her glass of water. "You have a beautiful place. It's actually a miracle you're renting this and aren't stuck in some shithole model apartment, so there's that. Theo clearly does love you, and so I'm going to say what I'm sure he would. Your relationship doesn't matter right now; all that matters is you getting through this. Because he's not fucking here. You're on the brink of being huge or completely fading away if you show up to a real set like you did today. Because girl, you looked like shit. So, we're going to get it together: today, then tomorrow, then the next day, and once you've put yourself back together you can worry about a guy. And you're going to therapy. No arguing. I'm sending you my girl's number."

"Why are you being so nice to me?"

"You're not the first model to have things go wrong on a shoot, babe. I get it, and I don't know for sure, but your guy probably doesn't. You need friends that do. And do you know how some of the other girls are? I can tell you're a good one."

She reached out and squeezed my hand, which was wet with snot and tears. But she didn't even flinch. I couldn't remember the last time I'd confided my hardest secrets to a girlfriend. Probably before I met Theo, when he replaced everyone else. I pushed away my pounding anxiety, because he already had stopped calling, because his last message just said, *This is on you now, Em, you know where to find me,* and squeezed her hand back. "Thank you. Really. Do you want to stay over on my floor mattress?"

She laughed now, the seriousness of our conversation dropping from her face with an ease I couldn't imagine it dropping from Theo's. "No! We're finishing the bed. Chug some water and let's go."

For the first time, I wondered if it actually had been a bad thing that Theo and I had been so close. If we were codependent, not best friends. Because if he'd been here with me, I would have brushed Georgia off to go home to him, his friends, his family, his life. And for the first time, I was just me, no *and Theo* attached. Being without Theo was what I had been afraid of basically since we met. But now that I was on my own, I was realizing for the first time that he might not be the only one who thought I was special. Someone worth being friends with. Someone with potential. I might actually be all of that all on my own.

CHAPTER FORTY-ONE

Emerson

"What do you mean he left?"

Harry, Georgia, and I have reconvened, this time in the now-empty models' dressing area. I'm hunched over on a folding chair in front of a dirty mirror, dress completely wrinkled, while Harry perches carefully in his pristine tux, and Georgia stares me down in the mirror while she reapplies her white waterline liner.

Harry blows an exasperated puff of air out of his mouth. "He left. Walked out the door, didn't say a word to me. That's all I have to report."

"What did his state of mind look like?" asks Georgia, moving on to re-lining and setting her lips.

"What kind of question is that? I don't know, bad? He didn't look thrilled." Harry picks an imaginary piece of lint off his suit sleeve so he can avoid looking at me.

"Where was he going?" I ask. "Did he get in a car? Why didn't you ask what was wrong?" I can't believe Theo left me. Tonight, of all nights. It was ridiculous of me to think this would work. I knew my life would be too much, that he'd be miserable. Now I've ruined my career *and* I might have just lost the love of my life. I drop my head into my hand with a groan, makeup be damned.

"Maybe there was an emergency," Georgia offers.

"Great idea!" Harry chirps. "Work emergency." He sees our doubtful faces. "Family emergency?"

"It's okay, guys. Let's just . . . leave it." I drag myself out of the chair and turn on the handheld steamer so I can get ready to go back out there.

Harry takes the steamer from me gently and gets to work on my dress, steaming from a foot away so he doesn't burn my skin. I pull the folds taut as he works, and he dutifully ignores the tears I can't keep from falling.

Georgia stalks over and takes the steamer from him. "Stop steaming that fucking dress. It's not like we're going back out to the party." She re-holsters the steamer as though it's a lethal weapon. "Emerson, you love that man. And we will not let you write him off for being overwhelmed tonight when it is an undeniably over-whelming situation for a normal person."

"Georgia, he's not here, okay? He left. We're not meant to be." I can't breathe, and no matter how much I blink I can't stop the tears from spilling over and rolling down my cheeks. "The pact went off on my phone when we were in the car, and . . . it wasn't on his. He'd deleted it. Either way, the moment is over."

"The pact!" Georgia says. "It's still the night of the pact—"

"It's over—"

"No! It's not midnight yet on the West Coast and you live here now. I say you have until midnight to tell him everything, which I *know* you haven't done. It's not over till it's over."

Even my sniffle sounds guilty. "But I have no idea where he is. He hasn't showed up on the security cameras at my place, and he's not answering any of my messages."

"I guess it's time to go find him, then." Harry calmly grabs each of our purses and hands them to us, along with a makeup wipe for me. "I'll have my driver bring the car around. I'm not letting you date me on contract when you could be with your person, as much as it pains me to say it."

Harry's car is a massive limousine, and as soon as we're inside, Georgia pours glasses of champagne for each of us, even though I'm going to need something harder to get me through this. "So, where do we start?" she asks.

I drain my glass in one long gulp. "I have no idea. He's East Coast, so I don't know that he really has any go-to places here."

"Perfect. Griffith Park, please," Harry instructs the driver.

"Why there?" I ask as I pluck off fake eyelashes one by one.

"I figure we go to tourist traps. They're probably the only places he knows offhand to tell a cab driver. And they autofill on rideshare apps."

Georgia has kicked off her shoes and plops her feet in Harry's lap. He starts massaging them absentmindedly. "That's smart," she declares. "I know you stole it from the detective movie you did last year, but respect."

"I'll pretend I didn't hear that," Harry admonishes.

I can't make myself join in on their banter. For them, this is the next episode of a big night out. But I just lost my future.

When we pull up to Griffith Park Observatory, all three of us pile out of the car in our formal wear. The park surrounding it is semi-empty, but everyone there immediately turns to look at us, and then continues to stare as we traipse around, shouting Theo's name.

"Theo!" I yell, as I pull my Louboutin heel out of the mud it's sunk into. Georgia's having the same issue. After exchanging a glance and shrugging, we each step entirely out of the shoes and go barefoot in the soggy grass. "Theo! Where are you?"

By now, everyone, from the couples taking an evening stroll to the teens drinking not so covertly under a tree, are filming us. I walk by a group of kids, toward the building, and hear them talking amongst themselves.

"This is, like, unreal."

"One of them must be having a psychotic break. And who the fuck is Theo?"

"I'm obsessed with Harry Butler. This is going to go like so viral."

If Matt's smear campaign doesn't ding my career, tonight definitely will. I'm beyond grateful to Georgia and Harry for coming with me. I never would have done this alone, and I wouldn't have asked it of them. I understand just how much it means that they're here, because we're all going to be torn apart in the gossip rags tomorrow, and they have just as much to lose as I do.

Once we've covered the park thoroughly, the three of us slide back into the limousine, leaving mud caked all over the interior.

"I hope this is a rental," Georgia mutters.

"It's my personal . . ." Harry eyes the state of the interior. "*Was* anyway."

"Santa Monica Pier, please," Georgia instructs the driver, and we set off.

"Thank you for coming with me, guys, it means a lot." I choke up on the words, and they each take one of my hands. "I know this isn't an ideal look, and I understand if you want to leave before we get paparazzi'd."

Harry leans his head back on the seat and squeezes my hand. "This is the most fun I've had in a long time. And I want to see you get your love story." He starts singing "You Belong With Me" quietly, and now I'm fully crying.

"That's our song. How did you know?"

Georgia drops my hand and rolls her eyes dramatically. "Anyone, in the literal world, could guess that's your and Theo's song. It's not rocket science."

Before I can launch into why, no, this song is actually incredibly meaningful specifically to Theo and me, the driver pulls up to the pier. "Want me to wait?"

"Yes, please," Harry shouts over his shoulder as we run off.

"You're going to get a ticket," I warn him.

"You know, someone said to me once, when you're rich, tickets are just the cost of parking."

I shake my head at him. "Don't ever let anyone hear you say that."

We've only just made it from the pavement to the boardwalk, but my feet are already full of splinters. The flashing lights from the rides and games feel garish and menacing as I scan the crowd for Theo. This feels like a long shot. On our senior week trip to Six Flags, I had been incredibly excited and rushed us to the line for the biggest ride. Theo dutifully waited alongside me, but when we made it to the top, he told me he'd see me at the bottom, because he didn't like rides. And then he did that for every single ride there. He's the only person I could imagine paying a hundred dollars to wait in line next to me while I had fun, and genuinely enjoy the day.

But since he actually hates rides, I think it's unlikely he'll be here. Even if he came here, I bet he would have left for somewhere calmer. Georgia, Harry, and I do a cursory run-through. We stick together now, so the story won't be about any one of us running around and looking crazed. Much better for it to be all three of us. Paparazzi have clearly been tipped off by the TikToks from Griffith Park and are snapping away as we scan the crowd.

Teens are posting TikToks and Insta stories of us live, and at least one couple seems to have followed us from the park. But the one person I want to see isn't here.

"Where to next?" the driver asks when we're safely in the car, fans and photographers pounding on the tinted windows.

The champagne-fueled enthusiasm we had initially has waned. "Hollywood Boulevard?" I offer wearily.

"By way of In-N-Out, please," Harry adds. "At this point may as well refuel."

At the In-N-Out drive-through we place a massive order of burgers, fries, and shakes. When the driver has finally maneuvered the limo past the order kiosk and to the drive-up window, via twenty-point turn, the teenager at the counter leans his entire torso out the window to look into our car.

In Salem, a teenager working at a fast-food joint would be totally average, acne ridden, seventeen but looks fourteen, horrible haircut and clothes. But since we're in LA, this kid is basically a male model. His jaw drops when he sees the three of us through the window.

As Harry presses the button and the divider starts rolling up, obscuring us, the kid shamelessly pulls out his phone and takes a video. I wave, deadpan, Georgia flips him off, and Harry flashes his gorgeous grin. "Thousand-dollar tip if you delete that in front of us."

The teen scoffs, pockets his phone, and only then does he hand the food over to the driver. Once his tinted window is rolled up, he hands it back to us and we dig in. My dress is so tight when I'm sitting that I've barely had half a burger before I can feel it cutting into me. Georgia notices my discomfort, wipes ketchup and grease off of one hand with a plasticky napkin, and unzips me.

I take a huge breath. "Ah, for a minute there, I forgot what it felt like to breathe."

Harry snorts and takes a long sip of his shake. "The shit we do for this life." He opens his mouth to elaborate but stops mid-word when he catches sight of the crowd outside the window. We've just pulled up to Hollywood Boulevard, and clearly someone overheard us saying we were going to each iconic LA place, or they figured it out, because the street is completely swarmed.

Despite its fame, Hollywood Boulevard looks distinctly seedy when you're actually there. Yes, the TCL Chinese Theater is there from all the red carpets, and, yes, the stars on the ground are intact, but otherwise it's an area that's covered in litter and gum that will likely never decompose, and filled with tourists who are pretending not to be disappointed.

The driver pulls over, and the three of us just stare at the window. "I don't think we can go out there," I acknowledge finally. Harry and Georgia breathe twin sighs of relief. They clearly didn't want to be the ones to say so, but if Theo was here he'd be long gone, and the crowds out there would tear us apart without security.

We pull away without ever leaving the car, and I bury my head in my hands. Georgia and Harry have the grace not to try to console me with false platitudes, and instead Harry just grabs the aux and puts on Taylor Swift to match my emotions and hide the sound of them continuing to eat.

First, the driver drops Harry off at David's house, since he's who pays the bill. Right before he shuts the door, Harry stops and ducks his head back in. "Emerson, that man loves you, and I just want you to know that I think your love story is one worth fighting for."

He slams the door and strides off before I can respond, and Georgia chuckles to herself.

"What?" I say defensively. "I thought it was sweet."

"Babe, you need to watch more movies. He's borrowing pretty liberally from old scripts."

"Ah well, it's the thought that counts."

Georgia bids me goodbye minutes later with a long hug and pledges to check on me tomorrow. "I'll text you if I find him," I promise.

This night has been an emotional gauntlet. With each street closer we get to my own, the ball in the pit of my stomach grows. When we go to make the final turn, I suddenly have a thought. "Wait!" I call out. "Can we go one more place?"

It's a long shot, but Devereux Beach was the site of our first moment, and Provincetown Beach was our first kiss. We've only ever talked about one beach in LA, the strip of ocean across the highway from Malibu Seafood. I went there the first time I shot in LA and entertained Theo with stories of the other models and me dashing across the highway with greasy bags of food to sit in the sand. It's probably a waste of driving time, but it's the only other place I can think of that Theo might know in LA, that he might associate with me.

When we pull up to the beach, I instantly know the man hunched in the sand is him. I could see Theo from any distance and recognize him by the slope of his shoulders, the lope in his gait, the slight mannerisms that are completely him.

My heart is in my chest as I walk across the sand. "How could you run away like that?" I shout across the sand at him.

When he turns to look at me, still dashing in his suit, I can see he's been crying. "Em, I'm so sorry I left. I just couldn't be there anymore."

"But why?"

"I heard what you said to Georgia. *'Things have just run their course. I'm not going to talk to Theo about it.'* I thought we were being totally honest now?"

I rack my brain, trying to figure out what the hell he's talking about. I never said that things with Theo had run their course. I said that about—

"Theo, I was talking about my modeling career."

"It's not about that. It's about being a team! Being honest with each other. You lied back then, and so I need to trust we're being totally honest now, especially if you're not going to explain what happened." Theo's face crumples. "I just needed a minute . . . that was all a lot."

I reach for him. "Theo, I would never just end things with

you like that again. But we also need to cut it with the miscom-munication! You should have just walked up and asked me what I was talking about!"

He shakes his head, jaw clenched. "I know! You're right. But I was feeling anxious and didn't want to have an anxiety attack at your event. I needed some time to breathe. When you hide things from me, it makes me worry I'm not enough for you, just like back then. I don't have advice like Harry or epic surprises like Georgia. Tonight just rubbed in my face what I've spent a decade agonizing over—I was never enough."

Now I'm the one who's crying. "Theo, that is not why I left." Tears are streaming down my face, and I'm starting to shake. "Can we just talk about this somewhere private? Please come with me. We can talk this out."

He stares at me, and for a moment I'm afraid he's not going to come. But then he relents.

The car ride home is silent, even though I have the divider up so the driver can't hear us. Theo takes in the state of the car with-out a word, but he sits right next to me even though there's plenty of space not to. Still, when I hold out my hand, he doesn't take it.

When we pull up to my door, I move to put my heels back on my dirty feet and Theo stops me. "Just wait there." He rushes around to open my door, and scoops me right out of my seat. I wrap my arms around his neck and nestle into him. "Thank you," I murmur.

"You deserve a break after tonight." Theo carries me all the way up to my bedroom and collapses us both onto the bed. I get up and strip off the tight dress, wrap myself in a robe, and wind myself around him tightly.

Theo's intake of breath is sharp when I touch him, but word-lessly he wraps his arms around me and just holds me. He under-stands how tired I am and just holds me together for a minute.

I'm tense, alert, and my heart skips a beat when he finally asks. "So what happened then, Em? Why did you leave, and write me that note?" I can hear how quickly his heart is starting to beat.

I let go of him and sit with my back against the headboard. He moves to sit cross-legged in front of me. "I do owe you an explanation." And that's the most I can say while making eye contact. I look down, but my posture is perfectly straight, my face devoid of emotion. I never talk about this. I've done my best to distance myself from what happened, but it is time to put it all out there.

"Remember that shoot I had, in the Hamptons? The day after P-Town." Theo nods, and I keep plowing through. I suddenly do want to dump it all out there. It will be a relief to no longer have this secret between us. "The photographer hurt me. And when I came back, I don't know if you remember, but I was a mess. I just had to process."

"What do you mean he hurt you?"

I can't look at him. I hate that he'll know this about me. It feels so dirty, even after ten years, like it cheapened me. I got one night, one time, of sex being something miraculous. Joyous. And then a lifetime of . . . this.

I look at the ceiling. "He raped me." I try to let me words stand firm, but they come out as a barely audible whisper. "I don't want to get into the details."

I'm tense when Theo reaches for me, but once his arms are around me, I relax into him, and he holds me tightly. He's crying when he speaks. "Emerson. I am so, so sorry that happened to you."

Suddenly I'm sobbing. Because this is a conversation I've imagined having a million times, and somehow it never ended like this. Some days it ended with him mad at me for lying, others he was disgusted with me and never looked at me the same. Unrealistic, I know, but that anxious part of my brain didn't care. I imagined all of the ugliest outcomes. But never this.

Theo holds me more tightly and rocks me back and forth. I'm

crying for what happened, for the decade I missed with Theo, for letting what happened rob me of him. Of so much.

"Em, you didn't deserve what happened to you. You never should have had to go through that. I love you so much," Theo murmurs as he rubs my hair. We lay there until I fall asleep, and he never lets go.

CHAPTER FORTY-TWO

Emerson

Theo is still holding me when I wake up in the morning. I sneak out of his arms so I can assess the damage to my face. My makeup is caked on, my hair is matted, and I have never seen my eyes look this puffy. I look atrocious. And my heart is thudding in my chest because I'm afraid of how Theo will look at me when he wakes up.

Theo told me he loved me, told me I didn't deserve what happened to me. But now that he knows the truth, a voice in the back of my head still asks, *Does he think I'm damaged now?* I've had ten years of processing, and spent a solid chunk of those in therapy, so I like to think I've moved past what happened. I can enjoy sex again, especially when it's with him. I don't think about that night every waking minute. I've always had the mentality of "if working a lot is what gets me through it, that's great." And it's hard to argue with the results I get. Who's going to tell you you're acting crazy when you're one of the biggest supermodels in the world?

I step into the shower and let the water wash away how gross I feel. Despite using my amethyst roller on my face for three times as long as usual, I'm not able to hide that my eyes are puffy, but I do dab a bit of concealer on to try to hide the redness and make me look more alive. When step out of the bathroom, I see that Theo's suit is folded carefully on the bed, but he's gone. A jolt of anxiety hits me.

I make my way downstairs to the kitchen and am filled with relief when I see Theo at the counter, with my never-before-used waffle maker out. I walk up behind him and wrap my arms around him, hold him close. "Thank you."

Theo puts down the spoon he's holding and turns around, kisses my forehead tenderly. "You don't need to thank me for anything. Thank you for sharing that with me." Behind us the waffle maker dings. "Now sit. I made waffles. This is an extremely nice waffle maker, and it was gathering dust."

In my fridge there's pre-portioned containers for every meal of the day, prepared by my chef, who collaborates with my nutritionist, to make me optimal meals. I rarely deviate when I'm home, and never for something like waffles. I'm surprised Theo was able to find the ingredients. He puts an enormous waffle on my plate, and piles it high with berries and whipped cream.

"My nephews call this the happy breakfast. If they win a soccer game, I come over and make this for them." Theo hands me a fork, then sets about putting more batter in the waffle maker.

"So it'll make me happy?" I smile, and can feel just how swollen my face is from last night. I need a little happy.

"Exactly right. Now don't wait for me, eat it while it's hot. I compensated for your egregious lack of real maple syrup with extra whipped cream."

"I'll be sure to rectify that situation immediately." I stuff my mouth with a big bite of waffle.

It's only once we've both finished our waffles and I'm sitting there, content, anxiety mollified, that Theo brings it up. "Em. Do you mind if I ask you a question about what you told me last night?"

"As long as it's not about the details, you can ask."

"Of course not. I was just wondering why you left the note. Why not tell me? I would have been there for you, we could have dealt with it all together. Why leave like that?" Theo's eyes are earnest, and I can tell he genuinely does want to know. So I'm honest.

"I was afraid to tell you. I didn't know what you'd say, and after finally getting to be with you I didn't want you to look at me like damaged goods. And I couldn't let you put me back together when you were about to go off and be great. I left that note so you could move on. That's also why I dated Harry, to be honest. Because I knew you were better off without me, since at the time when you stopped calling I assumed you'd moved on." I let out a huge sigh of relief when I finally say this. It feels good to be honest, completely open, after holding it in for so long. Georgia would be proud of me.

But Theo is silent for a long time. Too long. "Theo?" His jaw is clenched, and it looks like he's trying to hold back tears. I take his hand and he clutches mine tightly. "Are you okay?"

"Em, I just hate that I didn't realize what happened. That I didn't know something was wrong and chase after you." Theo is taking gulping breaths and trying to blink back tears. I'm frozen. Everything related to that night is like an open wound for me, and I don't know what to say that won't unravel me. "I should have been there to help you. I was your person."

"I didn't tell you because you're my person too, Theo. I couldn't let you throw away college to watch me cry myself to sleep at night and have nightmares that left me screaming. I did not want you to see me like that. I would have had to keep it together so it didn't ruin you too, and I just couldn't. And I didn't know what I needed, and I loved you so much I couldn't have taken it if your response disappointed me, even if you tried."

Theo drags his sleeve across his face. "I wish you would have let me try, because I would have given everything to have helped you through that, to have made it just a tiny bit easier for you. You can always count on me."

Theo reaches for my hand, and for just the tiniest moment, I stiffen. I'm not sure why it happens, and it's so quick most men wouldn't notice it. But I know that he does, and it's like something collapses inside of him.

"I know, Theo, I know." I squeeze his hand because I want to show him how much I love him. That my response was just a result of this stressful moment. But I can see the pain in his face, and suddenly this all just feels like too much. I need a minute. I need to breathe, to figure out how I'm really feeling, how I want to move forward. "I love you too. This has just been a lot." I take a breath. "I think I just need a little space right now. Is that okay?"

"Em, anything you want and need is exactly what I want right now. If that's what you want, that's what we'll do."

I wish he hadn't agreed so fast. I know he's just doing what I asked, but I can't help but overcorrect. "Great. Why don't you see your family in Salem before your shoot? I'll just take the weekend to decompress."

Theo looks shocked. "Em, no. I meant I could hang out in the living room or go for a run while you take a bath. Not leave. I'm not going to the shoot. This is a big deal and I'm not leaving you."

I take a deep breath. I can't have all of these feelings in front of him. We only *just* got back together. It's too much. "Theo, I need space. You should go to the shoot." I can tell he's not convinced. "Change your flight afterwards to come back here. You'll see your family and I'll decompress here. I'm used to having a lot of alone time, and I need that right now. And I promise you, this is what I want." At least, I *think* it is. I can't tell if the anxiety I feel is over worry about him staying and seeing me upset or over whether he'll actually leave.

Theo takes a gulping breath and reaches for my hand, pausing just short of taking it, in case that's not what I want. I take his and squeeze reassuringly. Only then does he nod hesitantly. "Whatever you want."

When he leaves, and I'm all alone in my giant house, it's hard to remember why him leaving was what I thought I wanted.

CHAPTER FORTY-THREE

Theo

It feels like my heart has been ripped out of my chest. If I hadn't been so wrapped up in my fear that she was rejecting me all those years ago, I wouldn't have ignored my gut telling me something was seriously wrong. Instead, Emerson dealt with horrific trauma by herself. I've heard too many stories of incidents like this one happening in our industry, and I resolve to find some way to help stop it from happening. It makes me so fucking angry to think of this happening to Em. And yet here I am, letting her deal with everything by herself. Because it's what she said she wanted. I want to respect that. She *told* me to go to Salem. But at the same time I want to find out who the guy was, make sure he never works again, beat him up, get him arrested, and then hold Em so she knows I would never *ever* blame her or think less of her because she's gone through an assault.

I've texted her already, just saying that I love her and am here for her, and she at least liked my message. But I'm still afraid— what if she doesn't want me to come back? What if I've screwed this up in a way I don't even know? Men are universally idiots when it comes to women, and I'm no exception. I tried to say the right things last night and this morning, but I'm not an expert on assault. I know I can't fully understand what she went through. All I can do is listen to her, and what she told me to do is to leave.

So why does being here without her feel so wrong?

Once I've made it through TSA, I drop to the most secluded bench I can find and call Owen. At this point it's midafternoon his time, so he's probably just getting home from the kids' soccer practice, the one I skipped in favor of being with Emerson. If I had gone home and continued my routine, I would be fine right now, but instead I'm alone in the airport, wishing I was with Emerson, and watching my world crumble.

"Bro. What's up? I saw you on TMZ this morning with Emerson. Mom's freaking out, she's practically planning your wedding."

"Maybe she should hold off on that." Tears are pinpricks in my eyes. I take a heaving breath and slouch backward on the airport bench.

"Babe," Owen whispers to Naomi, phone held away from his ear. "Can you watch the kids for a sec? Something's wrong with Theo." He clears his throat. "Theo, what happened? What's wrong?"

I can't talk through my heaving breaths, a decade of insecurity catching up to me in one fell swoop. "Em and I talked about everything. You know, about what happened. Back then. Turns out she lied in the note."

"No shit," Owen mutters.

"But the reason she lied is because, she was, she—" I can't speak through my gasps. Everyone who was sitting on airport benches in my vicinity has cleared out. Owen's only seen me like this once, back at eighteen, and since then I've reserved my meltdowns for Allison, who handles them better. But she doesn't remember what it was like back when this all went down.

"Just breathe. Breathe." I hear a chair scraping as he sits down. "Deep breaths."

I try to steady my breathing, until it's even enough for me to talk. "Something happened, and she didn't trust me enough to tell me. She didn't trust me to decide whether I wanted to be there with her, whether I could. She was convinced I would react badly. But how—how could she not let me try? She didn't even trust me enough to tell me the truth." I devolve into tears again, wiping my snot all over my sleeve, which is now streaked with dark blue marks.

"Theo, I know. But I saw her the day she left. She was destroyed. I have never seen anyone look as wrecked as she was. She just said someone hurt her, and she needed space."

It feels like my heart has stopped beating. "You knew? When?"

"I saw her when she was dropping off that box of your stuff. All the sweaters?"

"Except one." That she kept one sweater has haunted me. Did she sleep in it? Was it just lost, and that's why it wasn't in the box? "How could you not tell me?"

"She made me promise not to tell you, said she needed space, you needed to do your thing. All true, but she also just seemed sick at the thought of telling you. I mean, she actually did literally throw up on our lawn at the thought. I hosed it down. She made me promise not to say a word, at least for a while, until you calmed down, and she just needed space. I mean, if you'd seen her . . . I knew her for four years too, man. I wasn't going to hang her to out dry for you in that moment."

I rush to a garbage can and throw up, bracing my hands on the cold metal ridge of the side. When I come back, I can hear Owen calling after me, his voice small and tinny through the speakers. "How could you not tell me? I'm your fucking brother." I feel too dead to yell.

Owen sighs deeply. "I'm sorry, but it wasn't my secret to tell. Then you left for school, and by winter break you seemed good. You were talking about your work, you'd met Allison. And so I thought, why not wait until summer. Didn't want to disrupt your first year. But by then she'd moved on with a singer or actor or whoever, and I could tell it hurt you, so I figured no need to dig the knife deeper. I knew you two had something . . . but, I mean, most women would choose a real celebrity over you, no offense. I figured you were better off not knowing so you could move on."

"You can't seriously believe I'd ever do that. You knew how I felt about her."

"I didn't. Not until I met Naomi. And I've talked it through with her a million times. She's a woman, and she felt this was Emerson's story to tell. It's her trauma. However hurt you are, she was dealing with something a million times harder."

I wipe my eyes. "That's true."

Over the intercom, they announce my flight to Boston. "Wait, are you at the airport?" Owen asks.

"Yeah. Em told me to go back to Salem for the weekend; she said she needed space."

I hear the mute button click on and wait, knowing he's conferring with Naomi. "I don't know about that, man. I don't think you should leave her right now."

I sigh deeply and pick up my duffel bag, walk over to the line. "I know. But she told me to, and I have to trust that she knows what she wants. And this is what she said she wanted."

The line is silent. "I'll see you at home."

Eight hours later, when I walk into my house, Owen is already there. "Dude, what are you doing here?" I ask.

He has Naomi's apron wrapped around his chest and is at the counter. The shock of seeing him do domestic things like this should have worn off by now, two kids in, but I always still have a jolt of surprise when I see him in the kitchen. Naomi completely reformed him.

"Um, cleaning your house, for starters, so Emerson doesn't dump your sorry ass when she sees it. She's used to seeing this place Mom-level clean. And now that you're here, you can help me make those oatmeal chocolate chip cookies that she likes. Mom dropped off all the ingredients." Owen opens the fridge and pulls out butter and milk, throws them down on the counter.

I drop my duffel bag to the floor and sit at the table. Then I let my head sink into my hands and just groan, loud and long. "Get over yourself," Owen retorts. He throws a wooden spoon at me, which catches me in the side of the head, then falls to the floor with a thud. "Mix the fucking batter while I measure shit out."

"She's not here to eat these cookies. What's the point?"

"Theo. You know she doesn't want anyone but you." Owen picks up the spoon, rinses it, then places it on the table in front of me with the bowl that he's haphazardly adding rashly measured ingredients into.

"I just feel like we've done this whole thing before. Now is when, without me actively next to her, she realizes she's way too good for me." In the absence of anything else to do, I reluctantly start mixing the ingredients so these cookies don't turn out completely botched. "And you forgot to preheat the oven."

Owen reaches over and sets it to 350. He's acting delusional. Emerson will never eat these cookies. But before Owen can add the eggs, I measure a cup of chocolate chips and add them into the dry ingredients. The secret to the perfect cookie is mixing the chocolate chips in with the dry ingredients, to coat each one and help them distribute into the batter evenly. Mom taught me and Emerson this one summer day when it was too hot to use the oven, but we insisted on baking anyway. She said if we were going to heat up the whole house, we might as well do it right.

"What if Emerson and I were better as friends? Every time we try to make things between us work, they combust. Look at you and Naomi: you never fight."

Owen cracks an egg into the bowl, with two hands. "Well, these are some extenuating circumstances with Emerson. And that's also not true. Naomi and I had a lot of problems when we first got married. We're completely different. I thought if I just went to work, provided for her and our future family, that she would know how much I loved her. But she wanted me to just be there, to cook dinner with her, talk to her, be spontaneous. We both loved each other so much, but we showed it differently and it led to fights. And when we fought, I shut down, and she needed to talk it out, which at first made things even worse."

"How did you solve that? I had no idea." I take over whisking duty, combining dry with wet ingredients as he gets out a baking sheet and lines it with parchment paper.

"Well, Naomi is a genius and I'm an idiot, so once she recognized the problem and explained it to me, it was easier. We would both do anything to make each other happy, so after we knew where we were going wrong, it wasn't so hard to try to do a little extra to make each other feel loved." He gets out a cookie scoop and starts dropping balls of dough on the tray.

"You and Emerson grew up differently. You were a kid, too, when you met her, but we could all see how fragile she was underneath all that positive energy. Her dad abandoned them. And her mom was never there for her, too wrapped up in her hoarder shit. Emerson raised herself, and you were the first person she met who was even capable of loving her through anything and everything. But she doesn't know what that is like. You've had that your entire life. Mom, me, Naomi, Dad when he was around, we would all do anything for you, just like I know you would for us. But Emerson doesn't know what that's like, and you shouldn't stand there blaming her for that. Just show her. Talk it through."

I silently take the cookie scoop from Owen and start scooping, so that I have something to do with myself. "And she's not blameless. What happened to her—not her fault. Not even a little bit. But cutting you out entirely, out of nowhere? However well-intentioned her motivations were, it was wrong. But don't sit here and act like she hasn't been showing how much she cares. She flew to freaking Italy to be with you. Clearly she loves you."

I think back to Emerson getting me to play her question game so we'd talk, introducing me to everyone, even when she must have been itching to network for herself after the rumor Matt spread. Having her team get me the right clothes for the party, so I looked the part. Sitting on set with me and telling me how much she believes in me. Meaning it. "You're right."

"No shit." We've finished with the cookies, and after I put the pan in the oven, Owen sits down at the table with me, bowl between us, and we start to scrape the sides clean. We're an eat-cookie-dough type of family. Em had asked what I was doing the first time I took a bowl to the living room while cookies baked. Her mom had never made cookies, and she didn't know you were obviously meant to lick the bowl clean.

"I don't know what to do; she said she wanted space."

"Dude, come on. You have everything you've wanted at your fingertips. I know you've been happy with what keeps coming to you, but this is something worth putting yourself on the line for."

"Fuck you, man. I go after things! You're looking at the youngest all-star soccer player in Salem's history."

"Allison told us at Thanksgiving last year that you haven't reached out to a new client yourself in five years. You just take incoming."

"I have good clients. I like my routine, I'm here with you all, what more could I need?" But now that I've had Harry's album, *Vogue*, and better shoots dangled in front of me, I'm itching to do more. I don't know how Emerson persuades me to believe I can do things I'm convinced are out of my league. I could hear the exact words from friends, but when they come out of Emerson's mouth I'm able to believe them. She makes me greater.

"You're afraid of failing, of losing something you want, like you lost Emerson. But if you don't fix this now, you will regret it for the rest of your life." Owen takes the spoon and snags the last scrape of cookie dough, eating it with a flourish. Then he gets up and pulls a small, rumpled brown bag out of his pocket. He places it on the table in front of me.

"You still have this?" I pick up the bag carefully. It's precious.

"I think you're going to need it."

CHAPTER FORTY-FOUR

Emerson

"Are we almost there?" I'm in complete agony, and the Hollywood sign is nowhere in sight. Georgia dragged me out of the house and onto this hike, convinced that doing something touristy with physical exertion would be the ultimate cure for my broken heart. We drove by Harry's house and she tried to rally him, too, but he politely laughed in our faces and said he'd buy lunch afterward. Neither of us have ever done this hike, despite all the years we've lived in LA, and it seems we've chosen the wrong path. Service was weak and maps were vague up the hill, so she pulled over into a spot on the side of the road once she saw a trailhead, and we've haphazardly made our way up. The path is treacherous, and we've yet to see another person, which does nothing to reassure me that we'll ever actually make it to the sign, although it is nice to have privacy. I put on a full face of makeup in an attempt to hide my puffy face, dark circles, and stress-induced splotches, but with each passing step I look less photo ready. "I think we should turn back."

"Babe, I swear this is the way. It's like right over that hill. Besides, it's good for you to get outside, you look pale." Georgia looks effortless in a coordinated hot pink set, but I can see the sheen of sweat on her own forehead.

"I'm always pale. I wear too much sunscreen to tan, like, ever. If that's the goal, let's go back, please." I stop, in hopes she'll join me, but she just signals me to keep going, and I end up rushing after her. "C'mon, let's fix things with rosé and sushi. I'd much rather eat my feelings."

"Been there, done that. Literally last night." Her words come in short puffs.

I do feel like I'm sweating out several bottles of wine, but I relent and follow her listlessly for the next twenty minutes, until we reach the crest of the hill we're on. I grab her arm and squeeze. "Look!" The sign is in the distance. It's not close, but being able to see it at all is progress. A few tiny flecks move along the path, other people stupid enough to embark on this hike.

Georgia sprays herself with her water bottle, and I take a huge gulp of mine. I brought three, unwilling to dehydrate like I did with Theo, knowing Georgia isn't going to carry me. She turns to me, eyes fierce. "Okay, now decide. Do you want to run away back to the car, or do you want to finish this and make it to the sign, see things through, and have an amazing experience?"

"Georgia, we're like one mile away now. Obviously I'll go the last bit to the sign." She arches one eyebrow at me. "What?" I say. "Don't try to tell me this is a metaphor. Sending Theo home was the right thing to do. I needed space. I *wanted* space."

Even as I say it I know it's a lie.

Georgia continues walking. "Emerson, babe, I know this is a sensitive area for you. But he had a pretty great response, all things considered. The experience was traumatic to him too— obviously in a totally different way." She rushes to add this, but doesn't need to. I know she's right. Leaving him the way I did was hard on him. Not as hard as what I went through, but still hard. He had to build up walls to protect himself. Just like I did. But now the walls are down, and I feel vulnerable. If Theo decides what I told him was too much, or if he starts seeing me as damaged . . . I'll fall apart. And that scares me.

"I'm lucky, Georgia. I have my work, a life that I love. I'm better off just focusing on that. He can be an extra. I'll go see him in a few weeks, after the next campaign or something. We don't have to make this . . . serious. Maybe it's better if it's not."

"Emerson, you're a great model. You've built something amazing for yourself. But if you try to tell me you're completely happy, I will have to call you out. That man is what happy looks like for you. And you just spent a week going for it with him. You can't give up now!"

I kick at the grass. "Fine. Maybe I *was* happier with Theo in my life. But I need to take a step back." My breath is now ragged not just from the exertion of the hike, but from the thought of actually doing what I'm saying—of pulling even further away from Theo before he can pull away from me.

"Look, I get it. You've never been with someone who you love just as much as they love you, and it's fucking terrifying. But I saw you with him and you need to take a chance." We start trudging uphill, Georgia's strong legs striding up the hill at twice the speed of my own. I trail behind her, like she's a pink North Star. "I know it's a sensitive subject for you, but you barely opened up to him. And then you sent him away! Imagine how that felt for him. Yeah, you have the history, but let him get to know you. Tell him what you need. Fight for this! As hard as you've fought for your career, because at the end of the day when you are completely done with modeling and this industry, *he* is who you'll still have." She smiles. "And me and Harry, obviously."

We start on another downhill, the sign looming larger, and I breathe a sigh of relief. It's the one thing about Hollywood that actually is better in real life. While the stars and the red carpet are on a trash-filled street and are completely underwhelming, this sign is gigantic, bigger than I'd ever imagined. I've done a few drive-bys, but this is already the closest I've been to it. "But he *did* leave. If I matter so much to him, why leave?"

"You told him to! You're afraid of letting yourself have something good, of letting someone in who you can stop and smell the roses with." She looks around us. "Or the cacti, whatever." She pulls me into an entirely too sweaty hug, leaving makeup and dirt streaked across her bra. "Babe, stop punishing yourself for what happened back then. You deserve to get the guy. And get a life!"

I collapse into her embrace. And I let her hold me for way longer than is an appropriate-length hug, even for us. I can't believe I didn't see that I was putting Theo in the same position as when we were eighteen. I want him to act perfectly in the face of my biggest trauma, but somehow have been oblivious to putting him through his again. Obviously this triggered him. I can't believe I didn't see this. And I can't admit it out loud, but she's right about the reason too. My parents were never there for me so I got used to only relying on myself, and at least from the outside it's worked really well. I could not be more successful. But it hasn't made me happy, and I know exactly what would.

Theo.

I give Georgia one last squeeze. "You're an angel. Now let's finish this. I want a picture with you in front of the sign."

Her words run through my head as we continue forward with renewed purpose. I'm still afraid Theo will realize I'm not worth all the trauma and leave me. But I know deep down, that's not who he is. When we were growing up, no matter what the other did, we'd get through it together. He could have murdered someone, and I'd have been at his door with a shovel. I should have listened, should have worked through what happened to me with his help instead of running. I don't blame my teen self—she did the best she could. But I'm an adult now. It's time to stop running.

Georgia shakes me out of my thoughts. "This is it."

I crane my neck to ogle the sign. It's larger than life, so great up close—at this point only accessed by a lengthy hike made lengthier by our random start point—that it seems unreal. "Thank you." I squeeze Georgia's hand tightly. And then I turn us around, because it's time for me to change my life.

CHAPTER FORTY-FIVE

Emerson

I step off the plane for my layover in Dallas and make a beeline for Peace, Love and Little Donuts. It's a quasi-chain, one from which I've gotten tiny, two-inch–diameter donuts with an addicting array of flavors countless times over the years, so instead of taking a direct flight I routed myself through here. Simply by virtue of countless layovers here they've become my favorite donuts, and I'm committed to getting them for Theo. Because what apology isn't softened with sugar?

This shop is all the way in terminal D, which I'm convinced is a sham since I've never had a flight out of it. I speedwalk past Starbucks, Hudson News, countless anonymous airport bars, and wave politely to anyone who's eyes widen in recognition when they see me. But today, I don't stop, because I only have one thing on my mind, and it's winning Theo back.

He's sent me so many sweet texts since he left LA, and I've barely responded. I pushed him away just like I did before, and even though I had my reasons both times, I know he's likely hurting. But the only thing scarier than spending the rest of my life without Theo in it is knowing I didn't even try.

I arrive at the donut shop out of breath, and to my dismay I see there's a lengthy line. "What is this?" I mutter to myself.

The teenager in front of me turns around, the words slipping out and trailing off as her eyes settle on me. "This is the shop from the BuzzFeed list. 'Best Airport Food in the World.'"

"There's just never been a line here before." I smile apologetically before glancing at my watch. I have exactly ten minutes until boarding starts. So twenty-five minutes until final boarding. This is my typical layover here, a smooth forty-five minutes, just long enough for a jog to the donut shop and back to my terminal, where I can walk right on since I'm in first.

"Wait, aren't you . . . Do you actually *eat* donuts?" The girl's eyebrows are narrowed in skepticism.

"I do!" I confirm enthusiastically. "I'm going to propose with donuts that say 'Marry me.'"

Her jaw drops, and to be honest, so does mine. I didn't know that was my plan until I said it, but now that it's out of my mouth, I realize it's perfect. I'm going to make a grand gesture, like in the movies Theo and I used to watch.

"To who?" the girl asks.

At this point, a few more people from the line have turned around, curious about why this girl is staring at me like I'm famous.

"My best friend," I say. The line scoots forward a fraction, and I groan. "Except I won't be able to if my flight takes off before I can make it to the front of this stupid line."

"On it," she says, a look of pure deviousness on her face. Then she pulls out her phone and starts to livestream. "Oh my god, EMERSON?" she says, her voice loud. "The SUPERMODEL? I can't believe you're here, you're like, SO FAMOUS. And you're going to PROPOSE with THESE DONUTS???"

I laugh, but play along. "If I make it! My flight boards in eight minutes!"

"Please, go ahead of me!" She gestures gallantly, still filming.

"Thank you so much!" I normally hate spectacle and try to keep a low profile, but desperate times call for desperate measures.

"And me!" says the woman in front of her. "This is so romantic!"

"Me, too!" says a guy in his twenties, before muttering, "Man, you are so hot . . ."

More and more people in the line begin letting me pass. "Thank you so much, thank you, thank you," I say, moving forward. Eventually I'm at the counter, trailed by my teenage camerawoman, a crowd behind me.

The girl arches herself over the counter to get my face in frame, and the manager wordlessly beckons her behind the counter. Good press is everything, I guess. "I'll take thirty donuts. And can you write 'Marry me?' in frosting across the top?" The clerk nods, and I pass him a one-hundred-dollar bill. "Keep the change—"

Suddenly, the noise of the crowd behind me gives way to one familiar voice.

"Emerson?"

CHAPTER FORTY-SIX

Theo

As soon as we touched down in Dallas, on my hour layover to LA, I booked it to the donut shop I frequented. Dallas was a hub, and if I ever had over an hour, I went here and got a tiny, maple-frosted donut. At first, I thought the crowds were due to this shop being featured on a "best of" list. But I heard Emerson's name being whispered, and when I made my way through the crowd, there she was.

"Theo? What are you doing here?"

"I'm going to LA—to see you!" It's pure chaos around us, but all I can see is her face. To my relief, she's smiling.

"But *I'm* going to *Boston* to see *you*! What about your shoot?"

"Allison's shooting it. I had something much more important to do." I had planned on waiting for a perfect moment, a nice dinner, a day trip, something besides a grimy airport, but once I see her I can't wait another second. I need her to know how much she means to me, because I don't want to spend another moment without her.

Emerson reaches for me, but before she can touch me, I drop to one knee. The people around us part, and everyone goes quiet.

I pull a small box out of my pocket, a box that my mom has been safe keeping for me for ten years, ever since Emerson sighed over the ring in a Provincetown shop window.

I open the box and reveal a small diamond next to a pearl, set on a delicate gold band. I hope she still loves it as much as she did then.

"Emerson, the day I met you was the best day of my entire life. I have been completely in love with you from that day forward and I'd be lying if I said I didn't spend all of high school trying to muster up the courage to ask you to be more than my best friend.

"I'm not perfect, but I will spend every day working to be the best person I can be, so that I have a chance in hell at spending the rest of my life with you. I know we have so much more to learn about each other after all this time, about how to be the best couple we can be together. And I'm so sorry I left, that I let my own feelings get in the way of being there for you in that moment. I want to learn how to be everything you need. No matter what happens, I will be here. Even on the days you can't stand me. Nothing will keep me from being your family. Because this past week I woke up. I realized that I've barely been living these past ten years, and it's because I couldn't be by your side. So please, if you'll have me, let me be by your side for the rest of your life."

I wait with bated breath. Emerson turns to the counter and picks up the box the clerk had placed there. She opens it and my heart soars at the sight of the words in front of me. *Marry me?*

"Theo, I love absolutely every single thing about you. I've loved you since I was fourteen, and through every change in my life I've kept loving you. I want to grow together, wherever that takes us. I'm so sorry I shut you out. I have a hard time trusting people will be there, being vulnerable. I needed a minute to wrap my brain around the last week, but I want you know I want to keep working on becoming the best version of myself, and I want to do it with you by my side. I want us to be a team, forever." She pauses, takes a huge breath. "Theo, will you marry me?"

"Yes," I say, my heart in my throat. "Absolutely yes."

She holds out her hand and I slide the ring on, then take the box of donuts from her. The crowd claps and I sweep her into a kiss, let her sink all the way into me as I hold her up with my free hand. This kiss is a promise. Not a promise that we'll never hurt each other, that we're completely changed people. It's a promise that whatever comes next, we're a team. We're each other's. Together, we're everything.

"Have you had this ring this whole time?" Emerson's eyes are glassy when we break apart, and she can't stop looking at her hand clasped in mine.

"I bought it the day after our first kiss."

"I love you so much." She wraps her arms around my neck, and I squeeze her tightly.

"Turn your AirDrop on." The teenager behind the counter gestures at Emerson's bag. "You'll want this later. But I'm posting it first."

I scowl at the kid, but Emerson gives her a tight hug. I guess there's something going on here that I missed. "Thank you so much," Emerson says. She hands me her phone to get the Air-Drop and turns to the man at the counter and hands over her card. "Mind if I buy out your stock? I want you to give them to all these people." She turns to the line, which is now a massive crowd, phones trained on us. "Thank you all so much!"

The crowd cheers, then surges forward for donuts. Our videographer grabs a few donuts and rushes off, and I pull Emerson away from all of it. We stand in front of the departures board, wrapped around each other tightly. "There's a flight to Hawaii in fifty minutes."

"Or Santorini in an hour."

"Back to Italy in forty."

"Seville in three."

She turns to me, her eyes lit up with excitement. "Boston in twenty. Let's go home."

I take her hand, the ring smooth between my fingers, and we run to the gate.

CHAPTER FORTY-SEVEN

ONE YEAR LATER

Emerson

"I just can't believe it sold out like that." Theo holds me as I lean against him on our porch, watching the sun set on the beach where we had our first kiss. I kept my LA and New York properties, and Theo has maintained his house in Salem, which we spend a lot of time in, but we bought this as our first shared residence. It's the house I had been sure I'd never afford at eighteen. We just flew in from New York, after spending a night celebrating his first show.

"I can. It was a gorgeous show, and I'm not at all biased." I thread my fingers through his, admiring the ring that shines on my finger. I haven't let him buy me anything flashier. This ring means the world to me, and I almost never take it off.

"I do my best work with you." Theo squeezes me tightly. "Thank you."

As much as I appreciate him thanking me, I'm even more taken with his confidence. I was the muse of the show, and he displayed work from when we were in high school, as well as photos he shot over the past year. It's something I would have been too guarded to let go live before, but the way Theo shot it is incredible;

he constantly captures my entire heart in one frame. I know my name draws crowds, but it was his exceptional work that made photos actually sell, and I love hearing him take credit. And I love that even though in the last year he's shot everything from *Vogue* to Harry's album to a Valentino campaign to Georgia's *Forbes* cover, these intimate photos of me are what he wanted for his first gallery show. His first exhibit was from his heart, a labor of his own blood, sweat, and tears, with only his opinions dictating what it became. "I love you. And I loved the show; it was completely amazing."

He pulls me toward him for a languorous kiss, sensual and lingering, until when he finally pulls away, I'm left breathless. "Do you want to read to me?"

"Yes." My smile is impish, filled with unencumbered delight, shining in the way I used to only be able do with him. I grab my computer and begin to read the latest chapter aloud.

After three months with Theo, once we'd gotten into a routine, I decided to do something I'd never done before: take a break. I handed over my social media passwords to Natalie and consciously didn't work for six months. I hoped that at the end of this I'd have a better idea of what I actually cared about and wanted to do, forgetting about maintaining my fame, making more money, all of that. In the meantime, Theo's career was completely taking off, and that left me with more time alone than I'd had since I was a child. And it was completely miserable for the first two months. I was desperate for Theo to come home from shoots, became a daily fixture at yoga, read a book a day, learned to cook, and still had so much time I couldn't help but think about every traumatic experience that ever happened. But then, after I'd made it past the hump of anxiety, I started writing. And I then I signed up to take a writing class at GrubStreet in Boston, even though the thought of taking a class and risking feeling as dumb as I did in high school terrified me.

But I fell in love with writing. For the first time working on something made me feel calm, happy. And it was pretty great to workshop with other people who didn't care about the industry or how much money I made. We each only cared about helping each other with our stories. And then Georgia discovered the file while she was picking a movie on Netflix, and we started working together. We outlined a book together in LA, and since then have gone between writing in person and sending work back and forth in Google Docs. I keep the plot going and she adds the spice, and every night I read my new words to Theo, no matter how rough they are. It's the most vulnerable thing I've ever done. And every night the way he looks at me makes my stomach twist, because he's amazed by what I wrote, not just by how I look, like so many people are, but by all the pieces of me I'm putting onto the page.

Even after the six months, I kept writing. Now, I'm only shooting if I know it will be fun, when Theo's shooting it, or it's for Georgia's line, or I'm in a music video with Harry, or it's a campaign that's exceptionally creative. And it's incredible, because I actually enjoy modeling, maybe for the first time. When I finish reading aloud to him, Theo kisses me deeply. "That was incredible. Stay here, I'll be back in a minute."

He returns with a bottle of champagne and two glasses. "Still celebrating?" I raise an eyebrow and take a glass.

He pops open the bottle and fills both glasses to the brim, bubbles spilling over. "Of course I am. I'm with the love of my life, in a beautiful place, and I just got to be the first to hear the latest chapter of a story you're so passionate about writing. We would be crazy not to be celebrating."

"You know what I meant. It's not an occasion."

Theo hands me the glass and we cheers and take a sip. "We don't need an occasion."

I am so insanely lucky. I feel something that a year ago I didn't even know I was missing. Complete happiness. The joy of living authentically. Of having family. Of being with Theo, who is standing in front of me with the stupidest, widest grin absolutely glued to his face all because he loves me.

I put down the champagne glass and wrap my arms around Theo, hugging him to me so tightly that it feels like we might never be able to separate.

"Theo, I love you relentlessly."

ACKNOWLEDGMENTS

I realized I wanted to be an author when I was working as a fashion videographer. I spent most of my time on photoshoots and snuck in writing sessions between them. And from the first time I sat down and started writing fiction, it was clear to me that writing was what I was meant to be doing. I wanted to publish books. I wanted to be an author. I enjoyed shooting, but I *loved* writing.

It wasn't until over a year later that I had the idea to write a novel set on a photoshoot. In between, I went viral on BookTok and Bookstagram and connected with the most amazing community of readers. I quit my full-time videography job so I could focus on writing. I moved back to my hometown and spent several months reading about craft, taking courses at GrubStreet, acting out books on social media, and traveling. And then I had the idea for this book, a friends-to-lovers novel set on a photoshoot in Cinque Terre. I wrote it and revised it and believed in it and still can't wrap my head around the fact that people are reading it.

So many people came together to help *One Last Shot* go from an idea in my head to the book you're holding in your hands now. First and foremost, I have to thank my mom, Susan Cayouette.

She has supported me tirelessly, regardless of what my dreams are. My mom listened to all of my hopes and fears about *One Last Shot* getting published and always said the right thing. She has supported me throughout my entire life and I would not be the person I am without her guidance. Mom, thank you.

Thank you to my agent, Lauren Spieller, for believing in this book first. Until we met I never felt completely sure the world would meet Emerson and Theo. You are a mastermind, guiding my revisions, the sale, and my career. There is no one else who could have done this better. I am constantly in awe of your work ethic and your great ideas. Thank you for believing in this book, getting me the book deal of my dreams, and changing my life.

A huge thank-you to my incredible editor, Eileen Rothschild. From our first meeting I knew that you were the right editor for *One Last Shot*. Every single moment of this entire process has been an absolute dream. You see my characters and stories the same way I do. You're constantly ten steps ahead and pushing to make this book the best it can be. I firmly believe that you are the best editor this book could have and I feel so lucky to work together. I'm already looking forward to the books to come.

And to all of the amazing people on BookTok, Bookstagram, BookTube . . . I can never thank you enough for watching the past few years. Ever since that third BookTok went viral, my life has been irreversibly changed. I know it has been a long wait for *One Last Shot*, but it's here, and please know that each and every one of you had a part in it. Thank you for being such a kind and supportive community, and for showing me that some people *definitely* do want to read this book.

Thank you also to Lisa Bonvissuto, my associate editor, who convinced me to let Theo and Emerson just kiss already! Your keen eye helped hone *One Last Shot* and make it a tighter, smarter manuscript, for which I am so grateful. And thank you to Brent Taylor, who did a fantastic job on my international deals. I can't wait for people all over the world to read *One Last Shot*.

To my production editor, Michael Clark, and my copy editor, Michael McConnell, thank you for correcting each and every use of the word *toward* and ridding my manuscript of plot holes, grammatical errors, and typos. To Alexis Neuville and Alyssa Gammello from the St. Martin's marketing and publicity teams, thank you for helping *One Last Shot* find all of the right readers. Thank you to the rest of the team at St. Martin's Press for helping to make all of my dreams a reality. And to Olga Grlic, thank you for helping design a cover that looks exactly as I envisioned it (except better!) since the first draft of *One Last Shot*. Marianna Tomaselli, you brought this cover to life! I am in complete awe of how beautiful it is. You made it into a work of art and I am forever grateful.

To Guthrie, the very first reader of *One Last Shot*—thank you so much for telling me it was good. That you thought it would sell like hot cakes, even when it was full of typos and so much less developed. I loved putting moments of our life on the page, preserving our road trips and Devereaux swims, and I'm grateful that you spent the last two years talking about this book with me. Laura, when I left my videography job you were the only one who asked me about my writing, instead of what I was planning on shooting next. Thank you. And thank you to my little sister, Sarah. When I turned to you on the beach that day, thank you for telling me that *obviously* I could write a book.

To my friends, my partner, my aunt, my moms, my sister, my family, and everyone who has believed in me along the way: *Thank you*. Thank you for telling me I could do this. To my writing group, thank you for reading. I can't wait to see your books on the shelves alongside mine. To Stephen McCauley, my first-ever creative writing professor, who helped me believe that maybe one day I could do this, thank you. And to Jess Watterson, who gave amazing early notes, all of the incredible instructors at Grub-Street, and everyone else not mentioned by name . . . thank you.

Thank you for reading.

ABOUT THE AUTHOR

Betty Cayouette is an author, viral video content creator, and cinematographer. She graduated summa cum laude from Brandeis University in only three years and currently lives in Salem, Massachusetts. Betty created @bettysbooklist, the viral TikTok/Instagram/YouTube account that is one of the top book recommendation accounts in the world and is featured in outlets such as *The Boston Globe*, Euronews, Fox News, *The Times* (London), and *Glamour* (UK). *One Last Shot* is her debut novel.